CLAWS AND CROCHET

WOLVES OF PINE FALLS
BOOK 1

LAUREN CONNOLLY

CLAWS AND CROCHET

Lauren Connolly

CLAWS & CROCHET

She's used to hooking yarn, not hooking werewolves...

When Zoey's estranged grandmother passes away, the crafty crocheter volunteers to venture to Pine Falls, Colorado to clean out the woman's cabin. But when a confusing flyer lands Zoey and her balls of yarn in the middle of a motorcycle club's bar, she becomes tangled with the residents of the mysterious small town. One handsome biker in particular seems hell bent on tying her up in knots.

Warner Jameson wants Zoey. She smells like the perfect mate with a side of maple syrup and her laughter is the sweetest sound he's ever heard. When the woman appears in the Dark Moon Riders' bar toting a bag of crafts and showing no fear toward the mass of intimidating bikers, it's all Warner can do to keep from kneeling at her feet. The problem is, not only is Zoey an out-of-towner, she's human. And he's...not.

Unwilling to let his supernatural secret ruin his happiness, Warner decides to show Zoey just how lovable a monster can be. It helps that she needs rescuing a time or two. But what start out as unlucky accidents, soon become clear actions of sabotage against the woman he's falling for. Someone in Pine Falls doesn't want Zoey sticking around...

NEWSLETTER SIGN UP

Get another Folk Haven romance for FREE! Sign up for my newsletter to receive *A Selkie's Secret,* a novella that tells the story of Isla, a selkie, and Finn, the human she refuses to fall in love with...

Visit my website at laurenconnollyromance.com
Cover Designer: MoorBooks Design
Editor: Jovana Shirley, Unforeseen Editing, www.unforeseenediting.com

ISBN-13: 978-1-949794-41-0

CONTENT WARNING

This book deals with emotionally difficult topics, including loss of a loved one, depression, self-harm, attack by a wild animal, fighting, biting, and physical injury. Any readers who believe that such content might upset them or trigger traumatic memories are encouraged to consider their emotional well-being when deciding whether to continue reading this book.

1

ZOEY

THE RABBIT HOLE wouldn't have been my first choice for hosting a crochet club. The building is all old wood with small windows illuminated by neon beer signs. I mean, I knew I was going to a bar. The flyer on the library's bulletin board that shouted *Sip 'N' Stitch* described a gathering of people interested in crocheting, knitting, sewing, and drinking.

Sounded like a group I could get along with.

To fulfill the *sip* half of Sip 'N' Stitch, a bar makes sense.

But I imagine this place sits on the darker end of the watering-hole spectrum.

Maybe it's a hipster bar, I reason.

Back home in Denver, I visited some beat-up-looking places, only to find them filled with people wearing designer jeans, hundred-dollar flannel shirts, and glasses with rims so thick that you'd think half the grad-student population was dealing with glaucoma.

The Rabbit Hole could be one of those. Once I open this battered door, I might find myself in a speakeasy with artisan cocktails.

In that case ...

My hands brush over my sweater and jeans, then finger-comb my hair. Only one stray twig falls loose, which I count as a victory after walking a mile and a half through Colorado country. Part of that on a dirt road with trees crowding in on every side.

At least I had the fading afternoon light on my way here. The return trip is going to be trickier.

But I push that thought to the side as I finally pull open the door.

Okay. Definitely not a hipster bar.

The Rabbit Hole is just as rough-looking on the inside as it is on the outside. Which only makes me more curious about the members of Sip 'N' Stitch.

I scan the large room, taking in the heavy wooden bar against the back wall, various furniture that I'd label steampunk meets Wild West, a pool table with two leather-clad ZZ Top–looking older dudes playing a round, and a general feel that says, *We happily serve criminals of all kinds.*

Interesting.

Other than the pool players, the only person in the place is a tatted-up guy behind the bar. A quick glance at my watch reveals that despite my hike to get here, I'm still fifteen minutes early.

"Okay. That's fine. Early is better than late," I mutter to myself, making my way toward the booze.

The guys playing pool ignore me, but the bartender tracks every one of my steps, thick brows lowered, as if my approach confuses him.

Maybe the Sip 'N' Stitch ladies have a particular table they usually claim. Still, it seems better to wait at the bar for them to arrive.

"Hello." I try a winning smile.

The guy grunts, his eyes tracing over my form. The gesture doesn't seem sexual, more like a cataloging of information.

I climb up onto a stool, settling my bag of supplies in my lap. "Could I have a bourbon on the rocks?" Bourbon always makes me friendly, and if I only get one drink tonight, I'm ordering a good one.

"Something local, from Colorado, if you've got it." Crap, now, *I* sound like a hipster. "But really, any bourbon is fine."

Another grunt, and then he turns away. A moment later, I have some liquid courage in a short glass. He didn't give me the name of the brew. But he hasn't said any actual words to me, so maybe that was expecting too much.

I try not to look pretentious as I sniff the amber liquid before taking a sip.

Whatever he gave me is good. Under the burn of the alcohol, there's a soft hint of caramel, teased with vanilla.

As I enjoy the play of flavors over my tongue, I angle my chair toward the front door.

Soon, I catch a hint of female laughter carrying from outside. I smile in anticipation, but lose some of my enthusiasm when the door opens. A group of women saunter in, but I doubt they're at The Rabbit Hole for fiber crafts.

They're dressed for a night out. Of course, it's night, and I'm out. But I'm not out like they're out. Specifically, I dressed to combat the growing chill in the air. These three women are dressed as if they're ready to tell the cold to go fuck itself.

Their Daisy Dukes and midriff-revealing tops make me wistful for hot summer days. Ones I've sadly waved goodbye to for the year. Ones these women cling to in an admirable manner.

Now, it's completely possible the members of Sip 'N' Stitch treat the gathering like a tailgate party. But the bar's newest arrivals also have no kinds of supplies. Not even a purse between them.

Not the group I'm waiting for, but I still offer a friendly smile when their sharp eyes settle on me.

One smiles back with a wink, and the other two dismiss me in favor of leaning on the bar to call out drink orders to Grunt. He has no name tag, so that's what I've named him. A small twinge of worry in my chest disappears when he doesn't talk to these women either. At least I'm not the only one unworthy of verbal acknowledgment.

I go back to door-gazing.

The girls get their drinks and claim a table, their laughter bringing brightness to the dingy bar.

Five minutes pass. I sip my drink.

Ten minutes go. I realize I'm halfway through my glass and tell myself to slow down.

Another five.

Shouldn't someone have shown up by now?

Could they have canceled this week's get-together?

The flyer said Sip 'N' Stitch meets at The Rabbit Hole every Wednesday night at seven p.m. No mention of blackout dates, and today is not any holiday that I know of.

I'm about to check if my phone gets service here so maybe I can look up announcements on the library's website when a soft roaring rumbles from outside the bar.

The girls' chatter pauses briefly, then starts up again with renewed vigor. I take another precious sip of my bourbon as the familiar sound grows louder, giving me an unexpected taste of home.

Away for less than a week, but I guess I've been missing it.

Soon, there's an almost-orchestra-level of roaring engines, the chorus practically surrounding the bar.

That's when I realize they *are* surrounding the bar.

Apparently, in small towns, holding a crocheting club at a biker bar is no big deal.

The bikes begin to cut off their roaring engines, and I can envision a crowd of them lining up on the blacktop I crossed—I glance at my watch—a half hour ago.

Fifteen minutes late? Time for me to call it.

Looks like my attempt at subverting my introverted tendencies has failed. I glance at the girls, wondering if I should go over and introduce myself. Try to make some friends anyway.

But their smoky eyes continue to skitter toward the entrance, and I sense that I'd just be an obstruction to their evening entertainment.

Instead, I face the bar and focus on the last of my bourbon, satisfied that I at least left the cabin and found myself a decent drink.

Without anyone's prompting, Grunt puts two pitchers under the taps, filling them to the brim.

Seems the regulars have arrived.

Some bikes are still settling down when the front door's hinges squeak and deep voices fill the room. The once-quiet bar is now overwhelmed with the noise of rowdy men. Or maybe I'm just the one feeling overwhelmed. The shouts and ribbing and grumbles and laughter shouldn't be unpleasant.

Only it's like taking a week vacation from work, then finding out your boss booked a stay in the same hotel.

I came to this town to get *away* from rambunctious men.

Picking up my drink, I swirl the remaining liquid, considering finishing it off in one large swallow.

But that's wasteful, and it's not as if the bikers are doing anything to me.

In my peripheral vision, I watch the group claim a handful of tables. I can practically smell the leather—there's so much if it. Black jackets and vests, each with a huge patch on the back. Probably the name of their club. I'd have to turn and stare at one of them to find out, but that might result in unintentional eye contact. I try only to meet someone's eyes if I want to make conversation with them, and while I considered making friends with the small group of women, this massive crowd of bikers is not my speed.

Give me a handful of friends, and I'm good. A crowd? Hello, Irish goodbye.

But the tiny group is lost to me, having thoroughly enmeshed themselves in with the larger. They aren't the only women in the bar. The sight of some ladies in leather makes me smile against my glass. Good to know I'm not surrounded by a bunch of misogynists that don't allow women in their club.

I mean, they still might be misogynists. It just seems slightly less likely.

A flash catches my eye, tempting me to turn enough to seek out the errant sparkle. That's when I realize one of the Daisy Dukes girls has on a set of cowboy boots covered in crystals.

Bedazzled boots. *Now, there's a project.* I file it in the back of my brain for future consideration.

Tearing my gaze away, I accidentally snag it on something even more distracting.

A set of eyes.

Oh no. Unintentional eye contact.

Abort! Abort!

But I can't. Not right away. Not when I'm staring at a set of irises the same beautiful gold as the liquid in my glass.

Caught as I am in the bourbon stare, for the first time tonight, I start to feel tipsy.

2

WARNER

THE BAR SMELLS DIFFERENT.

There's the normal mixture of beer, leather, old wood, motor oil, and the scents of all my pack mates. Courtney and her sparkly boots brought some friends, and one was liberal with her grapefruit perfume. But she's hung around The Rabbit Hole before, so I'm used to the smell.

The hint that lurks underneath all those is what catches my attention.

Something sweet and earthy. Like maple syrup tapped directly from the tree.

Doesn't take long to realize what's different about my normal haunt.

She's sitting at the bar.

A few of the other guys notice too. Every one of them has as good of a nose as I do. As we settle in, multiple heads turn toward the stranger.

She keeps her face angled away from us, as if fully focused on her drink. The opposite reaction of Courtney and her two friends. We've barely got our butts in chairs before they're mixing in with us.

The smallest of the group, one with red hair and big blue eyes, focuses on me. Not perfume girl. This one is new, although I've seen her around town.

Not like the woman at the bar.

The redhead's interest is flattering, and another night, I might have folded myself into the larger group and flirted with her. But tonight, I want to solve the mystery of the newcomer with the tantalizing scent.

I sidle over to my older brother. Roderick leans against a wall, performing what I am convinced is his favorite activity—emulating the unmoving intimidation of a stone gargoyle.

But even as he holds himself still, I can sense the energy thrumming off him. We're all a little high after our ride. Soaring down the open road on our bikes is almost as good as a full-moon run.

Still, as our leader, Roderick would never let his baser nature make him look like anything other than an unwavering hard-ass.

"Who's that?" I settle on the wall next to him, a little too close on purpose, my shoulder knocking into his.

He doesn't even wobble.

I'll have to try some other way to set him off-balance.

He glances toward the woman at the bar, then shrugs. "Outsider."

"Really? That's your *best* guess?"

"She's not from here." My brother points out with a judgmental note in his voice. Anyone who isn't a local automatically lands on his shit list.

"Wow. You are a fount of information. Seriously, you should charge money for that kind of insider knowledge."

Roderick growls at me, and I smirk at him before retreating. Normally, his grumpiness wouldn't faze me, but if I piss him off too much, he might decide to kick the stranger out.

Moose owns the bar, but everyone knows who's really in charge.

"Hey, Warner. Why don't you come sit with us?" Courtney has made her way over to me, grinning like she's about to do me a huge favor. "My friend Missy"—she tilts her chin toward the redhead— "wants to meet you."

"Of course she does. I'm a charming guy." I offer my cheekiest grin, not making any promises.

Courtney and I have been friends since we were in diapers, and at some point, she made it her personal mission to act as my wing-woman. Probably because it exasperates me, which she finds hilarious.

"Nice boots, by the way. I've always dreamed of wearing a disco ball on my feet."

She returns my smile with a saucy one of her own. "You like? If you ask nicely, maybe I'll make you a pair."

She stretches out her toned, tanned leg, letting the little jewels on her boot catch the light. Something in her movement snags the attention of the mystery woman. Her head turns, stare seeking out Courtney's boots.

She's cute.

If there was a battle for the descriptor of hot, Courtney would win.

But the woman still holds my focus with her dramatically curved Cupid's bow lips. Probably aware of just how interesting that lip is, she went so far as to pierce it. A tiny golden stud, like a beauty mark, makes it hard to convince myself to leave off staring at her mouth.

Everything about her is brown and gold.

Brown eyes. Golden lashes. Brown and golden brows, bright against her pale skin.

She's maple syrup poured over a perfectly cooked waffle.

Then, she meets my eyes.

Finding me staring at her, she jerks back slightly.

I expect her to blush, maybe duck her head. Or if she's looking for a good time, give me an inviting smile.

Mystery Woman chooses none of the above.

Instead, she stares back, just for a moment, before tightening her mouth into a polite smile. Then, after a shallow nod that seems to say,

I saw you staring, but we're done with that now, she turns back to her drink.

"Ooh. Denied." Courtney chuckles, having watched the barely existent exchange.

About to retort, I'm distracted when Mystery Woman reaches into the bag on her lap and pulls out what appears to be a mess of string. She fiddles with it for a moment, finally dislodging a metal implement. Her fingers manipulate the item until I realize she's making something. Like she's knitting.

In a bar.

A biker bar.

I ... can't.

I *cannot* see any reality where I end this night without speaking to a woman who brings crafts to one of the most dangerous places in town.

"I don't give up easily," I murmur, maneuvering around Courtney.

Unfortunately, on my way to meet Mystery Woman, the redhead named Missy acts as a roadblock, stepping into my path. I consider dodging around her too. But I've never been the type to blow people off. She deserves respect, even if I don't want to date her.

Every woman is interesting in her own way, but none have ever *knitted* while they flirted. Maybe that's why my hookups have dwindled over the past years.

"Hi, Warner, right? Courtney told me about you." Missy blinks at me, hopeful.

"Don't listen to anything she said. She's a notorious liar."

I smile so the girl knows I'm joking. And *girl* is the right word to describe her. This close, I'm able to see every detail of her sweet, round face, and I'd put money down that she's only been able to legally get into a bar for a handful of months.

I might even guess younger, but everyone in this town knows it's a colossally bad idea to try a fake ID at The Rabbit Hole.

"Oh, I don't think so. I can already see she was telling the truth about some things."

Her gaze trails up and down my body, and I try not to sigh in frustration.

Mystery Woman sips her drink. Her glass is almost empty.

When she finishes, will she leave? When she leaves, will she disappear?

"Jim!" I reach out to grab the arm of the newest member of the club.

He's a nice guy. Nervous but nice. His eyes immediately land on Missy's low neckline, but then quickly jump up to her face.

"Jim, this is Missy. Missy, this is Jim. Did you know that Jim got into a fight with a bear?"

I'm not even lying. It's a badass story.

Her perfectly shaped eyebrows curve up. "Really?"

Jim reaches back to scratch his neck, self-conscious, but he grins at the girl. "Yeah ..."

"I'll let you tell it." I give him an encouraging push, relieving myself of any guilt about abandoning the guerrilla-warfare dating setup.

The Rabbit Hole has never seemed so crowded before. It's like every member in the club wants to call out my name or stand in my path.

By the time I reach the bar, it's all I can do not to collapse into the stool beside Mystery Woman. Pulling myself together, I sit down and lean my elbows on the bar. Like I'm more interested in getting Moose's attention than catching her eye.

My act crumbles the second she turns her head to look at me. I'm not about to play hard to get when all I want is to hear her voice.

Will it sound as good as she smells?

She's fucking intoxicating. And she's also silent, which means my mouth takes the lead.

"You looking to join the club? Because I gotta tell you, it's a rigorous initiation process, and I'm not convinced you're up for it."

Her maple-brown eyes widen as she stares at me. "Which club?"

"The Dark Moon Riders." I turn my back to her briefly, showing off the patch on my vest, then lean in close, doing my best to be subtle about the fact that I'm breathing in more of her scent. This close, I could easily drown in it and die happy. "You're in our bar, you know?"

Some other guys here would add an edge to their voice. A warning.

But I keep my words light. She's the last person I want to scare.

And why is that?

She glances behind me at the group that's getting rowdier with every pitcher of beer, then scans the entire bar. There's only a shadow of curiosity on her face. Not a single bit of fear.

Not that I want her to be afraid. But sometimes, fear is the smartest reaction to have.

"Is this a bar you all happen to drink at, or is it *your* bar?" She watches me, her fingers still moving, looping and hooking the yarn, as if all she needs is touch to create whatever she's making.

"It's mine. It's ours. The Rabbit Hole is Dark Moon territory."

I can't take my eyes off her hands. The motion is hypnotizing.

I imagine her fiddling with her project in front of a warm fireplace, curled up in an overstuffed chair, the flickering light playing with the gold in her hair. And when the night grows cold and the fire isn't warm enough to keep her from getting chilled, she'll look around for a blanket. But I'll have the only one, and she'll have to crawl under it with me. So I can keep her warm.

"Territory? That sounds a little possessive. But I guess you're not too restrictive on who you let in, right? Since the crochet club meets here?"

This stops my mind on its imaginary trip. I examine her face, trying to decipher if she's joking. But there's no playful smile or silly wink. She just watches me, waiting for a response.

"Crochet club?"

She nods. "I saw the flyer at the library. Sip 'N' Stitch at The Rabbit Hole every Wednesday evening." She holds up her yarn. "But I guess they canceled tonight's meeting. Unless you all ..." Her busy fingers take a break as she waves to indicate the group of bikers behind me.

I bite my lip until I have my grin under control. "Unless we all ..."

"Do any of you crochet? Or knit?"

The hopeful rise of her brows sets off an excited buzz in my chest. I shake my head.

"Needlepoint?"

"Sorry. I think you've got the wrong place."

Her face drops, a frown twisting her lips. "But the flyer ... here, can you hold this?"

The craft she's been working on gets shoved into my hands before she dives into her bag.

I sit patiently, grinning all the while.

She is blatantly uncaring that she's not only making some kind of scarf in the middle of a biker bar, but that she also just asked one of said bikers to hold her project while she hunts through her purse.

Who is this woman?

"Ha! Got it." She pulls out a phone and swipes her thumb across the screen. "I took a picture of the flyer. Look."

Tilting the device so I can see, she zooms in on a neon-blue flyer.

"See? Sip 'N' Stitch. Every Wednesday. Seven p.m. at the ..."

When she pauses, I finish for her, "Wild Rabbit."

"Damn," she whispers, glaring at her phone. "Double damn."

The curses are sweet on her lips. They make me want to hear more dirty words from her mouth.

After a weary sigh, she downs the last of her bourbon and retrieves her yarn creation from me, only to stow it into her bag.

"Are you leaving?" I can't stifle the tinge of disappointment in my voice.

"Two rabbit bars? In the same town? Is there some theme I don't know about?" she mutters to herself, ignoring my question and laying cash down beside her empty glass before typing something on her phone.

"That might help with tourism. Make everything in town revolve around rabbits. We could have a whole festival. Maybe a running of the rabbits. Fill the streets with them." My jokes come out fast and desperate.

Because she's leaving. I want to get her to laugh. Get her to stay.

She pauses, raising her eyes from her phone, awarding me with her full attention and a brief smile.

Only the expression seems sad. Which might as well be an energy drink for my curiosity.

"Thanks for ... sitting in my vicinity, I guess. Have a good night, Biker Boy."

Biker Boy?

She doesn't know my name.

I never told her my name.

And she hasn't given me hers.

This is not how this ends.

As she heads toward the exit, my instincts demand I do something. Anything.

Because the second her sweet scent teased my nose, filled my lungs, my wolf took notice.

3

ZOEY

THE WILD RABBIT is on the other side of Pine Falls. At least a three-mile walk.

I frown at the map on my phone, its little lines telling me that there's no way I'll make it to this week's Sip 'N' Stitch.

The bar door creaks open, spilling light out into the quickly darkening parking lot.

"Mystery Girl! Wait up!"

The amber-eyed biker with a handsome smile jogs toward me.

"You walked away before I could ask your name."

The gravel grinds together under his heavy black boots. Staring up into his face, I decide he's just a little bit too pretty to be an intimidating biker. His chocolate-brown hair curls softly around his ears and brushes cheekbones that must have been sculpted from pearly marble.

He needs something to grunge him up. Maybe a coat of scruff to hide the charming dimple in his chin. Shaving the shampoo commercial–worthy curls would do it, but anyone who'd suggest such a thing would be doing the world a disservice.

"So, can I have it?" He's grinning down at me, and I realize I've forgotten what he was asking.

"Have what?"

His lips stretch wider. And there, on the side of one canine tooth, sits a slight chip. The little imperfection is strangely endearing.

"Your name," he says.

"Oh. Sure. I'm Zoey Gunner." I offer my hand, and he wraps his fingers around mine.

His palm is warm in the cool night air, and I'm not sure I've ever had a more comforting handshake.

"Warner Jameson." He hangs on to me slightly longer than is socially acceptable, but I don't mind. My fingers get cold easily, and he's a friendly furnace.

Eventually though, he lets me go.

"You heading over to The Wild Rabbit?"

I shake my head, trying not to frown too hard. Sip 'N' Stitch was the perfect excuse to get me out of the house. And I screwed it up.

"I won't make it in time."

Warner waves that off. "They're maybe ten minutes down the road. That flyer said it went till nine."

"Ten minutes if I was driving," I mutter, doing the math in my head.

It's already seven thirty. If I hustle, I can probably walk three miles in an hour. Still enough time to introduce myself around and crochet a few rows.

Might be worth it.

"Did you walk here, Zoey?"

"Yes."

I don't pay Warner much attention as I stare down the dark road toward town. Time isn't the biggest problem. I'm not contemplating walking miles through a bustling metropolis. Pine Falls is a small town with nature pushing in on all sides.

"Do you all have issues with wild animals?" I turn back to Warner, glad to have a local on hand.

He stares at me, his expression seeming to war between confusion and fascination. "We're in the Rocky Mountains. So, yeah, there are wild animals."

Well, that makes things trickier.

My hand dives into my bag, pushing through the assorted items that have congregated in the bottom, eventually grasping hold of what I'm searching for. The flashlight I brandish is small but powerful as I flick it on.

"Do you think this would scare them off?" Personally, I find the beam of light impressive.

His headshake is slow, his smile amused. "Maybe a skunk, but a mountain lion wouldn't give two shits. And there are larger predators than that in these woods."

Shoot. I sigh and point the beam in the opposite direction, toward my grandma's cabin. A shorter, safer distance away.

"Are you going home?"

His question has me turning, and that's when I realize I was about to march off without another word to Warner, the biker guy.

"Yeah. I'm staying just over a mile down the road. Had to walk here since my truck wouldn't start."

Maybe I shouldn't have shared that. Too late now.

"You know"—he steps forward, situating himself in my path—"I could drive you."

"You could what?"

"I could drive you," Warner repeats. "To The Wild Rabbit."

He's close. The warmth of his body presses against my exposed skin, warding away the growing chill in the night air. It's intoxicating. But just because something starts out feeling good doesn't mean it'll stay that way.

My father is part of a motorcycle club in Denver. The sight of Harleys and leathers is normal for me. I've been to plenty of their barbecues and even ridden on the back of my dad's bike a few times when I was a kid. Seeing so much chrome was a taste of home.

I'm not wary of Warner because he rides. What I'm trying to remind myself of, even as my body is tempted to lean into his radius of warmth, is that he's a stranger.

Stranger danger.

Maybe if I were a badass black belt, I'd climb onto the back of his bike, no problem. But if he tries something, I'm more of a flight than a fight. And flight doesn't work as well if he's driven me to an unfamiliar part of town.

"What if I say no?"

He looks confused. "Um ... then I don't drive you?"

"And you'd go inside and leave me alone?"

Warner tips back on his heels, and even with the dim lighting, I think I make out a blush on his cheeks. "I'm sorry. I'm crowding you, aren't I?"

I shrug. "That depends."

"On what?"

"If you stop when I say stop."

"Do you want me to go?" He tilts his head toward the bar, and I realize that he would. He'd walk away.

And he doesn't seem annoyed with me or like he's planning on calling me a bitch for not accepting his offer of help.

Seems I might have stumbled onto a decent guy.

"Not sure yet. Can I see your license?"

With his eyebrows sitting high on his head, he fishes around in a back pocket before coming out with a wallet. When he passes over his license, the card is warm in my hand. I shine my flashlight so I can read the small print.

Warner Jameson. Just like he said.

His picture doesn't do him justice. This man was meant to be seen in 3D. I find the annotation proclaiming him qualified to drive a motorcycle.

"Everything check out?"

"Looks like it. Here, hold this." I offer the flashlight to him. Even with a bewildered expression, he accepts it. "A bit higher. There, that's good." As Warner keeps the light turned on his ID, I take out my phone, snap a picture, and text it to my dad.

"And you did that because ..."

I return his license and accept my flashlight. "Preemptive murder protection."

Warner stares at me, the neon lights from the bar's beer signs giving his skin a colorful cast. "That's ... really smart." He hands me back the flashlight. "Damn, Zoey Gunner. You're kinda intimidating."

"Only kinda?" I smile, then approach the line of bikes, admiring the variety of beautifully crafted machines. "Which one is yours?"

"You'll let me drive you?" Warner's eagerness bleeds into his voice and his grin. Happy Biker Guy is almost too handsome for me to deal with.

"I don't know why you want to, but sure." I follow my new acquaintance to a pitch-black Harley, whose seat he pats with affection.

Just then my phone buzzes with a text from Dad.

Got it. Have fun. Don't get murdered. Text me by tomorrow morning if you don't want me to call the cops. Or your brothers.

There's no better threat he could've issued.

4

WARNER

"Helmet, please." Zoey holds her hand out.

"You're not worried about messing up your hair?" I unsnap a saddlebag and pull out the half helmet I barely ever bother with.

Her lips twist to the side in a grimace. "I'm betting a skull fracture would do a hell of a lot more to mess with my side part."

Before she can take the head protection from me, I'm already settling it in place, enjoying the silky brush of her hair against my fingertips as I go to snap the buckle. After tightening the chinstrap, I slide a finger in between the strap and her chin, noticing the flutter of her pulse.

I can't pass up any opportunity to touch her. Still, I don't linger. If I come on as strong as my instincts clamor to, I might scare her away.

Slow and steady. Let her come to me.

I step to my bike, about to throw a leg over, when Zoey's hand on my arm stops me.

"Where's yours?"

"My what?"

She gives me an *are you trying to be dense* look. "Your helmet."

"I'm good." I flash her my most confident smile. My lady-catching smile, as my sister dubbed it.

Must be losing my touch because Zoey crosses her arms and glares at me.

"No. Anyone riding a motorcycle should be wearing a helmet."

Sure. Any human *should wear one*, I want to say.

But I keep that distinction to myself.

"Really, it's okay. I ride without one all the time."

If I thought she was glaring before, it's nothing compared to the intense smolder that furrows her brows. Zoey steps forward, placing a hand flat on my chest, almost in a caress. Then, she fists my shirt and drags me close.

"Put on a helmet. Now." Her growl is impressive for a human.

"Zoey—"

"Warner, I swear to whatever biker gods you pray to, if you do not wear a helmet, I will find a way to superglue one to your head." She gives another tug, rising on her tiptoes to get in my face, voice dropping low with menace. "And trust me when I say, however much superglue you think I have"—her fierce eyes scorch—"you are underestimating."

That last threat sounded like she was spelling out how she planned on murdering me.

In my entire life, I've never wanted to kiss a woman as badly as I do Zoey Gunner in this moment.

As I stare down at a scowling Zoey, my mind fixates on the idea of kissing her.

Would she taste as sweet as honey straight from the comb?

Better not risk it. She might superglue my mouth shut too.

Instead of sliding my arms around her waist and nipping at her tempting lips, I step back, forcing her to release her grip. I raise my hands in defeat.

"All right. Holster your glue guns. I'll find another helmet."

As I make my way down the line of bikes, she calls out to me, "A spare one! I don't want anyone else riding without one."

Damn it. She's making it really hard not to turn around, scoop her up, and kiss her senseless. There aren't many people in this town who would talk back to a member of The Dark Moon Riders, much less lecture them about motorcycle safety and threaten them with crafting tools.

If I thought talking to Zoey would make me less curious, I was naive.

Roderick often carries extra supplies. When I check his pack, I sigh in relief, spotting two helmets. After holding them both up for Zoey to see, I tuck one back in his bag.

Returning to my bike, I strap on the head gear and throw a leg over my pride and joy. This bike was basically scrap when I first got my hands on it, but now, it gleams in the parking lot spotlight, and the engine runs smoother than any other one here.

"You good to go now?"

Zoey nods, hands resting on my shoulders while she climbs on. I rev the bike to life. The engine purrs, vibrating through my limbs, more soothing than a massage chair.

For the first time in a long while, a warm body presses into my back.

Did it always feel this good to have a woman riding with me?

Wouldn't I have offered more rides if it had?

Maybe it's just Zoey. Knowing that the chest cushioned against my shoulder blades is hers, same with the arms twining around my middle. And, hell, those perfectly shaped thighs are the ones cupping my own legs. Plus, that extra bit of heat soaking into my lower back is from her—

I shake my head, trying to focus on guiding my bike out onto the dark road toward town. If I let thoughts of Zoey's body wrapped around mine take up too much of my concentration, we might end up careening into a ditch on the side of the road.

At least, if that happens, we're both wearing helmets.

5

ZOEY

THE WILD RABBIT sits on a corner of Main Street, alight with a warm glow and inviting laughter that spills out the front door as a couple exits, hand in hand. Above the door hangs a sign with the name and a hand-painted bunny, balancing a serving tray with a frothy mug of beer.

This atmosphere makes sense for a crochet group. Still, I can't help but wonder how the dynamic would be different if a group of women claimed half of The Rabbit Hole every Wednesday night to drink and stitch and gossip.

Would the atmosphere be tense? Or would the night end with the crocheters handing the bikers their asses at the pool tables?

I guess we'll never know.

The bike rocks as Warner parks it along the curb and pushes out the kickstand.

The man is a good driver. After the helmet issue, I was worried. But he kept to the speed limit, used his signals, and made it an all-around smooth ride. That, combined with the vibration of the bike between my legs and the comforting heat radiating off his back, had my lady parts taking all sorts of notice.

Which is ridiculous. I've known the guy for maybe thirty minutes.

"You want to head inside? If not, we can go for a longer ride." The biker smiles at me over his shoulder.

At his suggestion, I realize I've been silently admiring Warner's driving skills while we sit on a now-dormant motorcycle.

"Another time," I say as I dismount, even though I should be declining the invite with a firm but friendly refusal.

I'm attending Sip 'N' Stitch to avoid my hermit tendencies. That does not mean I need to start flirting with a sexy man.

Maybe if I was a sex-'em-up-and-wave-goodbye kind of girl. A lot of times I wish I could be. Or my vagina wishes I could be. I'm certain I've heard her crying out a time or two ...

Get some dick! Any dick will do!

But that's a lie, and I know it. If I let anyone close, I'm bound to love them. That's just the way it goes. I don't seek people out because I'm fine on my own. But those who figure out a way into my life earn my love almost in spite of myself.

And Warner's helpful ways and charming smile are strong indicators I could like him. Which means I could love him.

I did not come to Pine Falls to find love. I came here to figure out if I could survive without it.

This trip is for me and me alone.

Firmly resolved not to fall for the helpful biker, I turn to wave him good night, only to find him a step behind me.

"What are you doing?" The question comes out more abrupt than I meant it to. But abrupt is my default setting.

Warner doesn't seem to mind as he gifts me with a cheeky grin. "You're so determined to get to this Sip and Sew thing; no way can I leave without checking it out."

"Sip 'N' Stitch," I correct. Then wait, staring at him.

"Sip 'N' Stitch," he amends, giving what I expect is supposed to be a humble nod. The affect is ruined by his twitching lips.

It would be easier to be annoyed with him if he wasn't the perfect combination of sexy and adorable.

"All right. You can come in. But don't embarrass me, Biker Boy. This is my only shot to make a first impression, and I'm already late."

"Sure thing, Mystery Girl."

Warner steps forward, placing his hand on my lower back as if he plans on guiding me into the bar. But the position strikes me as too much like the couple that I just saw leave, and I don't need to give anyone, including myself, ideas. I speed my steps up until his hand falls away.

"How am I Mystery Girl if you know my name?" I pass through the door, holding it open long enough for him to catch the edge.

"A name is barely anything. There's a lot more I plan on learning."

"Well, I'm not holding lessons."

"I'll learn on the job."

"Glad to know you think spending time with me is work."

That gets him. He booms out a laugh that luckily fits in with this vibrant, crowded restaurant. The cheerful sound makes me want to join in, but I shove away the urge. For some reason, I get the sense that Warner is the one used to making people laugh, and I've somehow accomplished something by charming the comedian.

I make my way to the bar, leaning on it to get a bartender's attention as I take in the many framed rabbit pictures hanging haphazardly between bottles of alcohol. There's even a chalkboard with a list of Cottontail Cocktails.

Yeah, this place is *very* different from The Rabbit Hole.

A second away from ordering an Easter Bunny Bourbon, I stop myself.

Your limit is one.

Instead, I ask for a soda water with lime. As my drink is poured, Warner settles at my side.

"I think we've found your group."

At his subtle nod, I glance toward the back corner.

Bingo.

A gathering of about eight women sits, chatting and drinking, around a table situated under a portrait of *The Velveteen Rabbit*. Each one holds a fabric craft. Their ages look to range from twenties to fifties, which also makes me giddy. A lot of times these types of groups are made up of only women my mom's age, and I feel like the inexperienced baby of the club.

"Good eye. Thanks for the ride, Warner." I slide cash to the barman as he sets down my glass. "His drink is on me."

The biker raises his eyebrows as I toast him before navigating the crowd to the group I've been struggling to find all night. A couple of the women notice my approach and offer curious smiles.

Please don't be annoyed that I'm late.

Once I'm on the perimeter, their conversations trickle off as each one studies me.

"Hello. I'm so sorry I'm late. I'm new to town, and I misread the flyer and ended up at the wrong place. Is it a problem if I join you all?" To prove my legitimacy, I reach into my bag, pulling out my half-finished hat.

I get a few more smiles, and one woman leans forward. "Of course you can join us. May I ask your name?"

"I'm Zoey. Zoey Gunner."

There's some murmuring from the group as eyes trace over my face.

"I'm Amy Spencer," the woman offers with a warm smile that creases her tan cheeks. "You wouldn't be related to Minnie Gunner, would you?"

"She was my grandmother."

"I'm so sorry for your loss," Amy says. "You look so much like your mother. Is Selena in town with you?"

I shake my head. "Just me. I'm cleaning out Minnie's cabin so we can put it up for sale."

Amy nods with another sad smile. The other women start offering their names. They're about halfway around the circle when I notice the welcoming smiles dropping from some of the faces. By the time we reach the last in the group, I'd say a third have changed their attitudes toward me.

I can't fathom why until—

"And I'm Warner!"

At the sound of his jolly proclamation, I realize the biker didn't stay back at the bar. He's standing directly behind me.

Warner followed me to my crafters meeting.

The ladies' disquiet begins to make sense. My bet is, this group of crafters is not used to having guys from the local motorcycle club approaching them while they're gathered here.

I've brought an interloper.

"Yes, Warner," Amy says, "we know who you are. You've decided to join us for Sip 'N' Stitch?" While some of the women look uncomfortable or downright hostile, Amy gives Warner an almost-maternal smile as she questions him. "May I ask what project you brought to work on?"

"Got my project right here." His shoulder bumps mine, and I glance back at him with surprise.

Caught off guard, I find myself stammering, "I-I didn't bring anything for you to work on." I scowl at him. "I didn't even know you until a half hour ago."

Warner's cheeky grin makes another appearance. "You're my project. Goal is to be your best friend by the end of the night."

The women in the group titter. That's right. They titter, like a cluster of ladies in a Regency ballroom.

I sigh. Warner is a puppy. He's just too enthusiastic and cute to deny.

"Fine." I face the Sip 'N' Stitch gals again. "If we're quiet, would it be all right if we both joined you?"

"I don't—" A particularly pinch-mouthed woman starts, but Amy cuts her off.

"Of course. This group is open to any who would like to join. Our only rules are to be respectful"—Amy's eyes flit over to the woman who began what I think must have been a protest—"and to have fun. Please, pull up some chairs."

Before I can search the surrounding tables, Warner is already sliding a seat against the back of my knees. I plop down on the cushion, and the women on either side of me shift their chairs until my new biker buddy has space to add his to the mix.

For a moment, awkward silence hangs over the group. Then, one woman asks another about a book she recently read, and the conversations all start up again, slowly at first, but gaining momentum.

The lady next to me, Cathy, compliments my crocheting, and I show her the progress I've made on my hat. Well, not *my* hat. I plan on giving it to one of my brothers. Probably Donovan, with his close-cropped hair. She shows me her cross-stitch, a beautiful cluster of colorful flowers, and I have no trouble complimenting her skillful needlework.

The exchange is polite but pleasant, and I feel like I'm making a successful effort to step out of my hermit cave.

Taking a sip of my drink requires juggling, and I find myself adjusting my legs again and again to keep my yarn in my lap. The setup isn't optimal, making it hard to enjoy the sip aspect of this gathering.

Glancing to my left, where Warner sits, quiet and well-behaved, I can't help the envy that spikes through me at the sight of his spacious lap. Under his jeans is a lovely set of muscular thighs. He's basically got a sturdy shelf automatically built in.

If he wants to be my friend, then that means helping me out. Right?

I lean over to whisper in his ear, "Can you hold my balls?"

Warner chokes, doubling over to cough out some beer he breathed in. I slap his back a few times, wondering if this aggressive aid has ever really helped. Once his throat clears and he's done wiping tears from his eyes, Warner gives me his full attention.

"Could you repeat that?"

"My balls keep rolling everywhere." I indicate the yarn in my lap that even now teeters, just a second away from falling onto the floor. "Do you mind holding them? In your lap?"

The biker doesn't hesitate. He plucks the yarn from me and settles it into the dip where his legs meet. As if he doesn't care that he's not only the lone man in our group, I've now asked him to be my yarn assistant.

Warner takes another swig of his beer and grins at me.

Damn. This man is dangerous.

6

WARNER

"THIS IS Minnie's old place, isn't it?" I ask once we pull up to the cabin and I cut off the engine on my bike.

"You knew her?"

"Only in passing. She didn't come into town much."

Minnie Gunner was a woman more prone to glares than smiles. The few times our paths crossed, she had a much different reaction to my jokes than her granddaughter.

"Yeah, she wasn't a fan of people. At least, that's what I've been told."

"You weren't close?" That would explain why I've never met Zoey despite having spent my entire life in Pine Falls.

"Nope. This is my first time coming here, and she never bothered driving to Denver. Not to visit me or my brothers or my mom. I basically just know that she was my grandmother."

The cabin has a spooky air with its dark windows and the shadowy forest looming behind it.

"Are you staying here by yourself?"

"No." Zoey dismounts from the bike, taking her teasing warmth with her. "I've got Bruce with me."

"Oh." I manage to keep the word from sounding tense. Still, my hands clench into fists on my thighs.

Of course a woman as quirky and beautiful and delicious-smelling as Zoey would have a man following after her. Who wouldn't fight for a chance to win her affections?

I'm debating asking how serious things are with this Bruce guy when a loud, intimidating barking fills the quiet night air.

"That's him. Are you scared of dogs?" Zoey throws the question over her shoulder as she mounts the front porch.

Could she mean ...

There's another commanding bark as she opens the screen door.

"Speak now or else you're about to come face-to-face with Bruce Banner. Or maybe the Hulk. Depends what mood he's in."

The shadowy night obscures Zoey's features, but I'm pretty sure she's grinning at me as she slides her key into the lock.

"I love dogs," I call out just before the wooden front door is pulled wide and a massive form barrels toward me.

The lumbering creature is easily two hundred pounds. I hurry to stand up off my bike, worried the dog might topple me and the machine over with one swipe of his huge paws.

When he's only a handful of feet away from me, Bruce slows to a stop, sniffing the air.

I can guess what's throwing him off. I might look like a man, but that doesn't mean I smell like one. In this way, dogs are more perceptive than humans.

Something I'd have to spell out for Zoey, Bruce has discovered with a few deep breaths.

I'm a werewolf.

To put him at ease, I crouch down so our heads are level. We meet eyes, and I enjoy the curious confusion in his liquid brown gaze. As I extend my hand, I hum a nonsensical noise in the back of my throat, knowing that the dog will find it soothing. After a moment, there's a wet nose snuffling my palm.

"Pushover. My brothers wouldn't be happy to know that this is how you act as a guard dog."

I grin up at Zoey as I scratch the mastiff's ears. "Sorry. Dogs love me."

She snorts, her attention drifting away, and I realize she's staring over at an ancient truck.

The reason she was walking alone. At night. Into a biker bar.

"You said it wouldn't start?"

Zoey's eyes snap back to me when she realizes I noted the direction of her gaze. She nods with a sigh.

"I'll deal with it tomorrow. Probably have to get a tow truck out here. Hopefully, it isn't forever dead. Still, it was my mom's truck, so I guess it would be poetic for it to meet its end at her childhood home."

"You mind if I take a look?"

I'm already moving toward the vehicle, wanting to discover what might be wrong with it. Zoey steps down from the front porch to follow me.

"Do you know your way around cars? I've always meant to learn."

The idea of Zoey bent over an engine is sexy as fuck.

"I help out the local mechanic, so I know enough. What happens when you try to start it?"

"Nothing. Literally. No lights turn on. It doesn't try to sputter to life. It's just ... dead."

Interesting.

I pop the hood, but even with my advanced eyesight, I can't see much.

"Got a light?"

"Sure. About the only thing my phone is good for out here." Zoey turns on the flashlight capability, apparently preferring to use that than dig around for the actual flashlight in her bag.

"No service?" I ask while examining the wiring.

"Nope. Not unless I want to climb up in the old tree house out back. Up there, I get one, maybe two bars if I'm lucky."

She steps closer, watching my movements over my shoulder. A light breeze has her maple fragrance swirling around me. I have a theory about her scent's effect on me, but I'm not jumping to any conclusions until I talk to my brother. Still, I want her to press up against me, let me bury my nose in the juncture of her collar and neck so I can get lost in that delicious smell.

Instead, I concentrate on the engine. That's when I spot the obvious problem.

"Here. Found the issue." There's a wire that's dangling loose, clearly missing its home. "Without this attached, the battery won't work. Do you have a wrench? I'm going to need to tighten the bolt to keep it in place."

"I know I saw a toolbox. I think it's in the front closet." Zoey strides back to the house, taking the light with her.

In its retreating glow, I watch the way her shapely body moves. That pair of jeans is hugging her ass as if the material finds her as attractive as I do.

I should look away.

A decent guy wouldn't be gawking at her.

But she's just so ... gawk-able.

All those soft curves have my fingers curling. I want to feel her, grip her, but not too hard. I want to sink into her.

Fuck. Now, I'm getting hard.

Trying to distract myself, I turn back to the engine. Without the light, I can't see all the nuances, but now that I know where the problem is, I reach out to finger the loose wire.

I'm simultaneously grateful for this malfunction and annoyed. Because her truck wasn't working, I was able to convince her to get on the back of my bike. But I don't like the idea of her vehicle failing on her. It's not unheard of for a battery wire to come loose, but only if whoever last worked on Zoey's truck didn't do their job right.

What else might they have messed up?

"This is all I've got. Well, as far as I know. I'm not even a quarter of the way through her stuff." Zoey hobbles back, lugging a large metal box. She drops it next to me and holds up her light so I can see.

The tools inside are jumbled together, but I'm able to find a wrench.

"What all is in here?" Zoey crouches at my side, still holding the light, but also reaching in to sift through the tools.

"Well, that's a hammer. And there's a screwdriver—"

"Warner," she cuts me off, "if you try to mansplain tools to me, I'm going to convince Bruce to piss on your bike." Zoey's dry comment has me choking on a laugh. "I just wanted to know what Minnie had in case I need to use it." She rifles through the items.

I stare at her, not even trying to pretend I don't find her fascinating.

"Not much. Just the basics," she mutters. "Is there a good hardware store in town?"

"Yeah." The question has my pulse thrumming. I know exactly where to send her. "Sawdust and Supplies."

I catch a curl at the edge of her mouth.

Good. She likes the name. Just a matter of time before she shows up at the place.

Assured that tonight isn't the only night I'll run into Zoey Gunner, I'm able to return to the task at hand with enthusiasm. It's not long before the wire is sitting back in place.

Still, a thought has snagged in the back of my head, and I can't shake it loose.

"Zoey?"

"Hmm?"

She's so close that my mind gets muddled as I soak in her scent. I shake my head and breathe through my mouth. It barely helps.

Still, her answer is important.

"Do you remember the Check Engine light coming on the last time you drove the truck?"

She's quiet for a minute, and when I glance her way, I see a thoughtful expression on her face as she chews her lip. When she releases the poor, abused lip, I want to lean in and soothe it with my tongue.

Not yet. Go slow with her.

"I don't *think* so, but honestly, I can't remember. Was it supposed to turn on?"

"If the wire came loose while you were driving, then yeah."

I don't say the rest out loud, but I can't help thinking it.

If the light didn't turn on, that means the wire came loose after the truck was shut off.

And the only way I can see that happening is if someone popped the hood and took a wrench to the battery.

"I guess it did then. I'm still getting used to Minnie's driveway. My eyes are usually more focused on the road than my dashboard." Zoey shrugs, the light moving with the motion.

She's probably right.

Yet, for some reason, the idea of someone messing with Zoey's truck won't leave my mind as I climb back onto my bike and rev it to life.

Keep her safe. Protect her.

The thoughts come through clear and in a distinctly growling tone.

My wolf is more present than I've ever felt before.

I wonder if that's something I should be worried about.

7

ZOEY

"Hello!" I call out, bending at a strange angle to stick my head into the hardware shop while leaving the rest of my body outside.

"Hello?" A middle-aged white woman with thick, dark hair, pulled back from a beautifully angular face, steps out from behind the register, approaching me with a tilt to her brow.

The expression looks familiar, but I don't remember ever meeting her before. She's not one of the Sip 'N' Stitch gals, but maybe she was in The Wild Rabbit last night.

"Hi there. I would love to come in your store and spend more money than I probably should, but I need to ask you a question."

That smirking curve to her lips also tickles at my memory. "And what's that?"

I shift to the side so she can see who's lingering behind me. Bruce sits on the sidewalk, looking like the well-behaved mammoth he is. "Does your store allow dogs inside?"

The woman grins wide. "Seeing as how I'm the owner and I make all the rules, I say yes. We have dogs in here all the time. As long as he doesn't chew on anything important, we'll get along just fine."

What a relief. Bruce does *not* do well with being left alone in the car. Alone in the house? Perfectly fine. Someone in the car with him? No problem. But the minute I shut the driver's door and walk away, he sets to howling.

I'm not sure I've heard a more pathetic sound. Passersby always think he's wounded or one step away from dying.

But no. He's just dramatic.

"Thank you." I smile at the woman as I open the door wider and pull my overgrown puppy in after me.

He trundles into the store, sniffing the tiles with mild curiosity.

If I had planned on visiting the hardware store today, I would've left Bruce at home. This was just supposed to be a get-out-of-the-house outing, where we could wander around the town and see what there was to see. Map out places where I could utilize Wi-Fi and get back to work for my website design clients.

But then I saw the sign for Sawdust and Supplies, and I couldn't resist its siren call.

"That's a big boy you have there." The store owner hooks her thumbs in her pockets, grinning at the two of us. "I'm sure I would've remembered seeing him around town. You two new?"

I nod. "We've been here just over a week." I pat Bruce's head, which is conveniently as high as my waist.

Then, I rummage in my bag for the list of supplies I wrote up a couple of days ago. I'm not done cleaning out all the odds and ends in the cabin, but I've already got ideas for refurbishing some of the furniture.

"I'm looking for a few things, if you wouldn't mind helping me out?"

"Of course." She accepts the list, her eyes scanning the items. "So, where are you all staying? Bought a place?"

"We're in a cabin about twenty minutes north of town. Off Birch Road."

"Birch Road? You mean the Gunner place?" Up until this moment, the woman's questions all had a tone of mild curiosity, but these carry a sharp note of interest.

Is Grandma Minnie's cabin really that fascinating?

"That's the one."

The woman's golden gaze traces over me rather than my list. "You renting?"

"No. My family owns it. I'm Zoey Gunner. The woman who lived there was my grandmother."

The shop owner's eyes go wide, and I get the feeling I'm missing something.

"Selena's your mother?"

Ah, sometimes, I forget that despite never visiting Pine Falls before, these people still have a shared history with my family.

"She is. Do you know her?"

"Knew her." The woman's mouth goes tight at the corners. "Lost touch after she left."

Well, isn't that great? Apparently, Mom left some people behind when she moved to Denver and never looked back.

My mother is a vibrant personality. She can make someone fall in love with her in a minute. Losing that love probably doesn't feel too good.

"I'd be happy to tell her I ran into you the next time I get her on the phone. Just ... I'm sorry. I don't know your name."

She gives me a small smile as the tension in her body fades away. "I'm Rebecca Jameson. But don't worry about it. We weren't that close. Let's go find you these bits." She turns and heads down the nearest aisle.

I try not to look surprised at the discovery of her last name. *Jameson.* No doubt related to Warner Jameson. Maybe his mother. Or aunt. Or older sister.

And not completely out of the realm of possibility: his wife. I gauged Warner at late twenties, but it wouldn't be the first time an older woman and younger man got together.

My bet would still be on blood relation, but because I have no idea, I decide to keep my mouth shut. Sawdust and Supplies is the only hardware store in Pine Falls, and I do not want to piss off the owner by unknowingly revealing I rode on the back of her husband's bike.

And also ... just possibly ... flirted with him.

Best to keep my mouth shut.

Fifteen minutes later, I'm at the register, racking up a hefty bill on my credit card.

But there were just so many lovely tools! I reach out a finger to stroke an electric dremel that I can't wait to use on a certain rocking chair.

"Zoey?"

The familiar voice elicits goose bumps down the back of my neck.

Warner Jameson.

I guess I shouldn't be surprised that I've run into Warner here now that I know he's somehow connected to the owner of the shop.

When I turn, he stands framed by the doorway, midday light making his edges glow.

"Hi, Warner."

"You two know each other?" Rebecca's eyes flick between us.

Please don't be his wife. Please don't be his wife.

"Hey, Mom."

Oh, thank the universe.

"Yeah, we met at Sip 'N' Sew."

"Sip 'N' *Stitch*," I correct.

"Of course. My bad."

Warner saunters into the store, and I can't help noticing the difference in his appearance. At the biker bar, he was in a black T-shirt, jeans, and his leathers. Today, he has on jeans again, but he's paired them with a torn tank top that shows off his arms and a neon safety vest. The bright color should look garish, but it only helps to enhance the tan shade of his skin. His hair is slicked back from his face, sitting flat against his head in a funny way. My guess is, it's the result of wearing a hard hat.

"Do you work on a construction crew?" I ask.

Warner grins down at his vest and ruffles a hand in his hair. "What gave me away?"

"Why were you at Sip 'N' Stitch?" Rebecca is clearly still stuck on how her son met the new girl in town.

"For Zoey, of course." He aims a charming grin at his mother, which she answers with a grimace.

"You're sassing me."

"Never," he responds, still smiling before turning back to me. "What did you buy? Please tell me power tools. There is nothing sexier than a woman wielding power tools."

He's teasing me, a wicked glimmer in his eyes, and I get the urge to give it back to him.

"That's good to know. I would hate to have spent so much money on props for my porno, only to find out power tools *aren't* sexy." I keep a straight face through the delivery.

Warner's mouth drops open, then morphs into a delighted grin.

"You're not helping. He's already hell to deal with on a normal day," Rebecca mutters as she sets my bags on the counter.

"Apologies."

Damn, I was so focused on flirting with Warner that I forgot I was standing in front of his mother. Besides, I shouldn't be flirting. He might think I'm interested in something more than friendship. Which I am definitely *not*.

"Ruining my fun, Mom," Warner murmurs, still wearing a happy smile. "So, how does our small-town hardware store compare to the retail giants in Denver?"

"This place has everything I need—and more than I can afford." I glance back at the aisles, trying to stifle my longing. "I might be back for that table saw after I sell a few organs."

Rebecca smirks as she prints my receipt.

"The MacGyver? You can borrow mine." Warner moves closer, his gaze tracing over me, leaving a disconcerting tingle in its wake. "I might have a few more tools you can use if you want."

Was that supposed to have a double meaning?

Either way, now, my mind is focused on one particular tool Warner carries with him at all times. And all the ways I could use it.

"You trying to take my business from me?" Rebecca scowls at her son, but there's a smile in her eyes.

"Of course not. Just being neighborly." He walks around the counter to press a kiss to her cheek before hefting one of my bags off the counter. "I'm on my lunch break. Wanna grab a sandwich, Mystery Woman?" He circles back around to crouch down in front of Bruce, scratching behind his floppy ears. "Or should I ask your man for permission?"

I snort, loading my arms up with the rest of my new materials. "Bruce knows I'm done with domineering men. He's happy to follow my lead as long as I'm handing out treats along the way."

When I tilt under the weight of one of my bags, Warner stands and goes to grab it. I turn, holding the bag just out of his reach.

"How am I going to get strong enough to carry it if you take it from me?"

Warner pauses, staring down at me as if fascinated with what he sees. Then, his grin comes back, wide and welcoming and too handsome for any man. "You're right. Sorry 'bout that."

His reaction is as refreshing as my dad's homemade lemonade. Nothing like what my brothers would've done.

Abram would have told me to stop being stupid and used his longer arms to reach around me and grab the bag.

Byron would have given me puppy-dog eyes and waxed on about how he just wanted to help me out, and how he never saw me anymore, and how he felt so useless sometimes, until I was guilted into giving up my burden.

Carver would have made a joke about my spaghetti arms, then tickled me until I physically couldn't hold the bag anymore.

Donovan wouldn't have said anything. He's all about the sneak attack. The second I let my guard down, he'd have crept up behind me and snatched the bag from my hand.

But Warner doesn't do any of that. Instead, he listens to me.

And for some reason, that seems dangerous. Mainly because I like it so much.

8

WARNER

"It seems you're a fan of large dogs," a snide voice comes from just ahead of us on the sidewalk, forcing me to take my eyes off of Zoey's smiling face.

"Hello, Mrs. Applewood." I keep my voice cordial, even as the sneering woman makes that hard to do.

Her animosity toward me is only slightly understandable.

I'm a wolf. She hates wolves.

Mainly because her daughter is dating one of the pack members.

As Zoey adjusts Bruce's leash in her hands, she glances between the two of us, clearly picking up on the tension, but having no idea where it's coming from. And it's not like I can explain.

As much as I'd like to.

I'm a werewolf. But a friendly one. Can I please bury my face in your neck to smell more of your delicious, earthy scent that I pick up with my supernatural nose? And after that, can I carry you back to my place and show you just how friendly I can be?

But I don't say any of that. Yet.

After a conversation with Roderick, I have a good idea what Zoey's alluring scent means for me.

"Zoey, you met Mrs. Applewood at Sip 'N' Stitch."

Recognition dawns in my companion's eyes, and she turns back to the frowning woman with a genuine smile. "Yes, I did. You were making quilting squares, weren't you? I haven't tried quilting yet, but I want to. Do you have any tips? Is there a good fabric store in town?"

With her curious questions, Zoey takes a step toward Mrs. Applewood, who looks stunned at the enthusiastic greeting. She opens her mouth, then glances down to see Bruce sniffing her immaculate heels. The stodgy woman shuffles back a step with a huff, glaring at the both of us.

"I don't associate with *dogs*."

Zoey's smile fades, and the loss of it chips away at my normally unshakable good humor. The bigots in this town can insult me all they want, but Zoey doesn't deserve any of their animosity.

"He's friendly," Zoey offers, her fingers fiddling with one of Bruce's ears.

The woman sniffs, her scowl focusing on me. "Oh, I'm sure they *seem* that way." Finally done with her not-so-subtle barbs, Mrs. Applewood clutches her purse tight to her shoulder and crosses the street before continuing on her way.

"Wow." Zoey's lips slowly circle the word, and I'm torn between my simmering fury and my fascination with watching her mouth move. Her chin tilts up, brown eyes catching mine. "Do you think she needs medical help with removing that stick from her ass?"

For a moment, I can do nothing but stare. Then, laughter explodes through me, and I lean back against the nearest building to keep my balance as I lose it. Zoey offers an almost-secretive smile. She crouches beside Bruce, muttering nonsense baby talk and giving his chest a scratch while he pants, his massive tongue lolling and his tail wagging.

I suck in air through my nose, trying to stifle my unrelenting chuckles. But the deep breaths only pull in more of her maple scent, and saliva collects in my mouth.

This woman is making me both horny and hungry.

As if reading my mind, Zoey straightens and waves for me to continue walking. "We're wasting your lunch break."

I shrug, but can't get rid of my grin. "Any time I spend with you can't be considered a waste."

A lot of girls blush and giggle when I flirt with them. It's a fun reaction. I love to hear people laugh.

But Zoey doesn't get embarrassed. Instead, she offers me a solemn nod. "That's true."

Damn. She's perfect. Getting her to crack will be all the sweeter because she doesn't give her laughter away for free. She's making me work.

I accept the challenge.

"Sandwiches?" I shove off the wall and take a chance by reaching down to twine our fingers together.

"Sandwiches," she agrees.

She glances at our clasped palms, but doesn't pull away.

I have to give her hand up when we reach the café and go inside to place our lunch orders. Once we're sitting down at an outside table, I lose interest in my food. There's maybe thirty minutes before I need to get back to the build site, and I want to spend them all getting to know the woman across from me.

"So, you're in your grandma's old cabin, and you're buying up a shop's worth of power tools. Is there a remodel on the docket?"

Zoey offers Bruce a potato chip while answering, "I wouldn't say a remodel exactly. More like a revamp. And a clean-out. I'm just here to sort through Minnie's stuff and make the cabin prettier for sale."

"I don't want this to come out the wrong way, but didn't your grandmother pass close to a year back?" Not my real questions. More like ...

Why did you stay away for so long? Why haven't you been here my whole life?

"She did. Someone should have come down here sooner. But my mom is really busy. She has a popular morning show on the radio up in Denver. Kinda hard to take a vacation. Still"—Zoey hesitates, fiddling with the pickle on her plate—"from the little she's said about it, I think living here was a not-so-great childhood. I guess Minnie was kind of reclusive."

She meets my eyes after that last bit, her honeyed eyebrows rising.

I nod. "Didn't see her around town much."

Zoey sighs as she scratches Bruce's giant block head. "When I realized Mom might never come here, I decided to volunteer."

"Really? Just like that?"

Zoey grimaces. "To be honest, I was also looking for a reason to get away from Denver. After the incident."

"The incident?" I force myself not to lean forward, instead picking up my sandwich. One huge bite keeps my mouth full and too busy to pester for more details.

Zoey chomps down on a chip and stares off into space. I wonder if I've lost her attention or if she didn't mean to let that slip. Still, I want to push her. I want to know all there is to learn about Zoey Gunner.

To distract myself, I reach under the table to slip Bruce a piece of roast beef from my sandwich. A fed dog is a good ally.

"Okay"—Zoey returns her attention to me—"I've decided. The embarrassment has dimmed enough that I'm willing to tell you what happened."

Anything called *the incident* is bound to be a good story, and Zoey just agreed to share it with me.

Stifling my cheer, I recline back in my chair and give her a nod to continue.

"I have four brothers," she starts. "They're all big brutes, but they love me, and I love them."

Sibling love is something I can relate to.

"I'm the youngest. The baby of the family, they say. *I* say they need to get their heads out of the Regency era. Just because I'm younger and a girl doesn't mean I need four bodyguards poking their noses into every aspect of my life." Zoey huffs, emotion coloring her cheeks.

"Makes sense," I offer.

"Right?" She munches on another chip before continuing, "Anyway, I thought I was used to their overbearing version of love. My whole life, they've done their best to be good brothers. But I feel like the fact that there're so many of them tips their helpful acts into bonkers town."

My body shifts forward in anticipation.

"Like, there was one day, before school, I realized I was out of tampons. And I needed them, obviously. But my parents were already at work. Plus, I was thirteen. So, I couldn't drive myself to the store."

The noises of Main Street fade away as Zoey's voice pulls me into the story of her past.

"Abram is the most responsible. I feel like he was born to be a dad. Or a drill sergeant. Maybe both. Anyway, I figured at eighteen, he'd be the one least likely to laugh." She shrugs and eats another chip, drawing out the drama of the tale. "I was right. He told me to finish my breakfast and that he'd take care of it. But next thing I know, I'm alone in the house." She waves her hands as if we were sitting in her kitchen, empty, silent house around us. "All four of my brothers disappeared. The bus was going to show up in, like, ten minutes, and I was sure I'd have to stay home sick."

My lips pinch in a grimace, as I don't find the story amusing anymore. Did all of Zoey's brothers really abandon her just because they were squeamish about buying feminine products?

"Then, I hear the screech of tires on the driveway, and when I look out the window, I spot all four of the Gunner boys climbing out of Abram's car, each one weighed down with shopping bags."

Humor returns fast.

"Now, I know guys can be clueless about menstruation. If Abram had come back with a few extra boxes or the wrong brand, no big deal. But no. He recruited the rest of my brothers, and they drove to the closest drugstore and bought as many products as they could carry."

"They didn't," I whisper in horrified wonder.

"They did. An *entire* aisle. You would've thought I was hemorrhaging. Good thing tampons don't expire." Zoey shakes her head, but I catch the hint of a smile at the corner of her mouth.

That's the way it tends to be with loving families. In the moment, you want to murder them, but later, everything just becomes a funny memory.

"And that happens a lot with them?"

"Taking things way too far? Oh, yeah. My parents and I refer to them as Occurrences with a capital *O*. I've had many Gunner brother Occurrences. There was the time in high school when they convinced the front office to let them all sing me 'Happy Birthday' over the intercom system. Don't get me wrong; they're fantastic singers. But my anxiety went through the roof when everyone in the school stared at me for the rest of the day. And, hell, don't even get me started on prom."

I want to get her started and never have her stop.

"Please. I *need* to know."

Zoey smirks. "You'd think three college guys and a guy working on his MBA would have something better to do on a Saturday night than chauffeur their sister and her date to a school dance. Timmy was terrified to hold my hand after that car ride."

It's all I can do to shove the laughter down.

"Not that they threatened him." She gives me a placating gesture, though I have to wonder if maybe Zoey doesn't know the whole story of that evening. "I don't even know if that was the point of them driving us. Sometimes, I think they just want to make sure all five of us are experiencing important life moments together. And that's the thing about Occurrences. Each one was kind of embarrassing, but it was hard to get mad at them because they're my brothers and they're trying. After a day or maybe a week, I forgive them, and we move on."

"But something happened?" I guess.

Sun shines off the streaks of gold in Zoey's hair as she tucks the mass of it behind her fingers. I want to reach out and run my fingers through the strands to learn the texture.

She huffs out a breath and crumples her empty chip bag.

"The incident happened."

9

ZOEY

"I was dating someone."

Something about Warner's attention shifts. Not that it increases or decreases. It just changes.

"It had been close to a year. We were getting serious. At least, *I* thought we were."

Warner's sandwich lays forgotten, and I reach across the table to nudge it toward him. This story is easier to tell if I don't have someone's undivided attention. His lips twitch before he raises the food to his mouth.

"Apparently, he and I had different ideas of commitment. Mainly monogamy."

"He cheated on you?"

I don't know if I should be flattered by the disbelief in Warner's voice. I decide to have no opinion about his tone at all and simply nod.

"Made the mistake of taking the girl to a restaurant where my friend works. She let me know, and when I confronted him, he confessed and asked me to forgive him. I didn't. I broke up with him. Sounds like the end to the story, right?"

Warner continues to watch me as he wears a deep frown. He's still handsome, but the expression does not suit his face. Warner is meant to grin and laugh. Maybe he'll find the next part of the story funny, even if I still can't.

"What happened?"

A sigh from my soul leaks out, heavy and resigned. "I made the mistake of telling my brothers exactly why we broke up. They had a more intense reaction than I'd expected."

"Why wouldn't they? I'd be furious if someone cheated on one of my siblings."

Taking a moment, I bite my own sandwich, only answering after I swallow. "Being angry is fine. Taking revenge when it wasn't their problem to deal with was not."

Even now, I wonder if there was a way I could've stopped them.

"Did they beat the guy up?" Warner asks.

"No. Thank the universe. That would've been a different level of horribleness. I hope I never have to bail any of them out of jail, let alone all four at one time." I take a fortifying sip of my iced tea.

"What did they do then?"

Instead of answering right away, I stare at his sandwich until he gets the hint and takes an obliging bite.

"They rented a billboard."

"A billboard? Why ... oh no."

"Oh, yes. My brothers decided that the best way to get back at the guy was to rent a billboard across from his apartment building and to have a massive sign put up, proclaiming, *Billy Arnold is a lying cheater who*"—and I feel the mortified blush creep over my cheeks—"*lost the best thing he ever had.*"

"Well, at least it was accurate," Warner offers.

"It was *humiliating*," I moan, choosing to ignore the flutters his words set off in my stomach. "The whole thing was over. I'd broken it off with him, and that should've been the end of it. No one needed to know that he'd screwed me over. That I had been stupid enough to date a guy who cheated on me."

"Whoa, Zoey, no. No way. That does not make you stupid."

I finish my sandwich, staring off into the distance. "I know, logically, that it's not my fault. But still." I can't help another sigh, all long and lonely. "It was so disheartening."

"You loved him?"

My food is gone, and needing something to do with my hands, I reach into my bag to pull out my almost-finished hat.

"I was going to."

"Going to? What does that mean?" Warner stares at me, eyes intense with an emotion I can't interpret. Probably curiosity.

I know, sometimes, I can be odd and that people might find my reasoning weird.

I rack my brain, trying to figure out a way to explain. "I don't seek people out. I tend to keep to myself. When I do make a friend or start dating someone, it's inevitable that they mean a lot to me. Casual relationships aren't really my bag. It's all or nothing. So, if he hadn't betrayed me, I definitely would've loved him. Just a matter of time."

"Are you saying that if I keep showing up in your life, you'll love me?" Warner smiles in a way that makes my heart clench and my lungs struggle for breath.

Yes. That's the answer. No question. I might already be halfway there.

"I'm not looking to add to my love roster," I warn him instead.

He doesn't respond, but I get a sense he was hoping for another answer. Warner chews another bite of his sandwich, and I admire the way his jaw muscles tense with each movement. My fingers stay busy, hooking yarn, but I don't need to watch my hands, which gives me continued permission to stare.

After a swallow of his drink, he speaks again. "The billboard drove you out of Denver?"

I grimace. "That, and the singing telegram they sent to his office."

Warner chokes on something, and I feel bad that I keep almost killing him with my poorly timed comments.

As he coughs, I continue the humiliating story.

"My brothers are pretty talented when it comes to music. They play in a band together and everything. They composed an entire song about how Billy was a piece-of-shit cheater. Then, they paid a barbershop quartet to visit his office and serenade it to him."

"That's masterfully brutal."

"Yeah. Objectively, it's a good song. And the internet agreed. Someone in his office recorded it and posted it online. It went viral. Honestly, it wouldn't surprise me if you'd seen it." Now, I'm descending into petulant muttering, and I don't like being in this frame of mind, especially when thinking about my brothers. Normally, I love them to distraction. But, hell, they screwed up this time.

"I agree."

"That you should've seen it?"

"No. Although I'm tempted to look it up."

I grimace. "You can. I won't hold it against you. The whole world has seen it at this point. What's one more person?"

Warner watches me, his head tilted in a way that almost reminds me of Bruce.

"So, what do you agree with?" I push.

"That does sound like an incident."

Silence falls between us. Then, I let out a reluctant chuckle. I guess I can admit the incident is funny as long as my brothers aren't around to hear.

Warner props his elbows on the table, giving me every ounce of his amber-eyed stare. "I like it when you laugh."

Oh no.

That's it. Time to go.

I stand up from my chair, wrapping Bruce's leash around my hand. Luckily, we already dropped my bags off in my truck, so I'm free and clear to make an escape.

"Thank you for having lunch with me. This was not a date. I am not going to fall in love with you, Warner Jameson. Have a good day at work."

Bruce and I are halfway down the block when I give in to the urge to glance back. Warner watches us and offers a wave when our eyes meet. My only response is a nod before I refocus on the sidewalk in front of me.

And I decide that I'll be better off if I avoid him from now on.

10

ZOEY

GRANDMA MINNIE'S closet is an organized mess. At first glance, everything seems orderly. Arranged in neat boxes and tucked onto shelves. But then, once my eyes finish enjoying the beauty of a well-put-together space, I'm overwhelmed by the massive amount of *stuff*.

When I start taking out boxes, I realize, at one point, this was a walk-in closet.

Now, it's a storage locker of random things Minnie felt the need to hold on to.

Hopefully, I'm not about to find thirty-year-old newspapers in these shoeboxes. Although that would make the decision about whether to throw it out or keep it easy.

The size of this task intimidates me. So much so that I feel the need to sit on the bed and stare at the closet and mentally prepare myself.

Other people might think my ideas for the furniture refurbishment are daunting ones. All that sanding and staining and reupholstering. And, sure, those projects will take up a good chunk of time.

But time isn't what scares me. Time is the whole reason I came to Grandma Minnie's cabin.

This closet has me pausing because of the emotional strength I'm worried I might need to get through this.

Dragging out all these items seems akin to poking at a woman's inner self. This closet is all that's left of Minnie's treasured possessions. Like a fragment of her soul she left behind.

Am I the right person to sort these things? To make decisions about them?

Is this closet the reason months went by without Mom making any mention of coming here to deal with the house?

"Sitting on the bed isn't getting anything done," I scold myself.

Too much sentimentality. Minnie is gone, and this closet is just stuff.

With a fortifying breath, I shove up from the old, squeaky mattress and zero in on the first box.

Opening it seems almost anticlimactic. Boots.

The box reads *Hellmen's Shoes*—a shop I drove by on Main Street the other day. No surprise that Minnie shopped local. The boots are nice, barely worn. On a whim, I slip one on. Pretty good fit, which is surprising, seeing as how Minnie was a half a foot taller than me, if Mom told it right.

Guess I have big feet.

I set the box to the side of the room I designate as the Keep side. The next box in the stack is bigger and contains some worn flannel shirts and thick knit cardigans. Weirdly, my grandmother's frumpy mountain woman clothes are exactly what's in style. Despite them being a few sizes larger than my normal, I place the box next to the boots.

Last box in the first stack has ratty, old sheets, which make for good drop cloths.

I keep them too.

"Maybe I'm not so good at this clear-out-the-house business," I mutter to myself while reaching for the next container.

This one is different, a wooden box about the size of a toaster oven. It sits on the top of a middle stack, easily accessible.

Curiosity piqued and worries set at ease after dealing with relatively impersonal materials so far, I place the wooden box on the floor and plop down in front of it. There's a brass latch, but no lock, so I don't expect any kind of valuables when I open the lid.

Still, the contents surprise me.

Cassette tapes. Neatly arranged in rows, as if this box was built for the exact purpose of housing them. I count them, coming up with just over forty.

Carefully, I slide one from the box and pop open its little plastic case. The old tech makes me smile. I'm just the right age to have used cassette tapes for a handful of years before CDs took over. The Walkman I used to have was one of my first prized possessions. I played my *NSYNC tape so often that the ribbon broke.

The curious thing about Minnie's collection is that every tape is blank. Not blank of recording. They probably have some type of audio on them. What they're all missing is labeling. The spines of the containers have blank white space, where someone could make a note of the contents of the tapes. But every one is void of any title or description.

I should put the box to the side and return to the closet. But I'm a cat, ready to die for the sake of curiosity.

I go on a hunt.

What I'm looking for isn't in the bedroom, so I move to the main living area. Finally, after opening almost every closet and cupboard, I spot it sitting on top of the refrigerator.

A boom box.

The thing might be in easy reach for a woman approaching six feet tall, but I have to pull out the step stool.

I return to the bedroom with the boom box clutched to my chest.

My grandparents invested in wiring the cabin for electricity, but they didn't opt for many outlets. I have to push the bedside table out of the way and unplug a lamp to set everything up. Any worries about the music player not working disappear when the analog numbers flash to life. I settle with the box of tapes in my lap and select the one from the top-left corner.

Nostalgia gives me a warm phantom hug at the practice of inserting the tape. After turning up the volume, I wait, knowing the tape is playing from the crackle the speakers emit.

Then ...

"Helloooo, Denver! Are you ready to rock and roll? You'd better be because you're listening to me—"

Holy shit. Is that—

"Silly Selena! The hottest DJ in the biz. And I've got all the grooviest tunes on the radio."

Oh no. This is too much.

"Right now, I want to play one for anyone who's ever had a crush! Sing along if you know it!"

Behind the last few words, a song begins to play, and suddenly, I'm listening to Rick Springfield's "Jessie's Girl." Brought to me by my adolescent mother's first attempts at acting the DJ.

As the song goes on, I lie back on the bedroom floor, clutching my stomach as my uncontrollable laughter threatens to give me a hernia. Tears leak out of the corners of my eyes, but I'm too lost in my hysterics to bother wiping them away.

When the song comes to an end, Mom's young voice pipes up with more enthusiastic radio-host clichés, and my giggles ramp up all over again.

Halfway through the tape, I finally exhaust myself to the point where I simply lie on the floor, panting and grinning.

Some of the joy at finding this jewel from my mother's childhood trickles away when I turn my head enough to examine the boom box.

Despite the fact that it can play cassette tapes, it's not some ancient machine. My guess is, it's at least ten years old. Which means Minnie bought it long after my mom moved out.

A picture forms in my mind—of my stern grandmother in her kitchen, messing around with some of her mason jars. And at her elbow is this boom box, playing the voice of the daughter who left and never looked back.

How lonely must she have been?

And I wonder if it was anything like when I lived on my own for the first time.

My first semester of college.

The memories don't come to me as individual days. They all flow together.

When I first left for my East Coast college, I was excited to strike out on my own. To show that I could do just fine without my family.

The first few weeks were okay, but at some point, everything shifted.

Living started to feel like a long, cold stream that dragged me along, keeping me on the edge of drowning. Floating always in the middle, where I couldn't grasp anything to stop a forward progression to nowhere.

In the beginning, I made it out of my room, attended classes, wrote words that resembled notes.

But near the end, I couldn't leave my bed.

And I couldn't figure out why.

In my mind, I would tell myself to get up, to function. But my limbs were heavy. Waterlogged with depression.

I didn't have that word then.

The only word I had was drowning.

Someone had to jump in after me. Someones. My brothers drove hundreds of miles when I stopped returning their calls. They found me in the cold river of my misery, dragged me out, bundled me up, and brought me home.

I didn't save myself.

That's something I'm working on.

Can I survive here? Can I survive anywhere that's not right next to my lifeline?

Or will my head slip under the surface again?

I glance over at the bottle of pills on the nightstand. They help. I can take my medication without my brothers. I can talk to my therapist without my brothers.

But can I build a life? Make friends? Fall in love?

Terror that the current will drag me under again has me wanting to get in my truck and drive back to Denver. This experiment could be cataclysmic.

And that's all this is. A test.

Anything I build here, I need to be ready to leave behind. Like a temporary structure in a flood zone.

11

WARNER

THE RUSTED BOLT comes loose easily for me.

"You keep helping me out like this, I'm gonna have to put you on payroll." Harvey, owner of the mechanics shop where I'm working, glares at me. But that's normal for the man, so I'm not concerned. Plus, he's spent the last twenty minutes cursing at this bolt, trying to get it off without damaging anything.

"Don't worry about it. You let me work on my bikes here. We're square."

The gray-haired human huffs and holds out his hand. I drop the lug nut into his palm and move on to the next one on the wheel.

"I got the rest," he grumbles, but I wave him off.

"I'm almost done. Least I can do."

He stalks off, toward the set of new tires, muttering under his breath about overly helpful werewolves.

His complaining always makes me grin.

When I'm not on one of Uncle Mason's build sites, I'm usually working on a bike-refurbishing project. Since I live in an apartment, I needed a workspace. Harvey agreed to let me house my projects in his garage and use his tools for a completely reasonable rent, plus lending a hand every so often. But that's hard to do when the man loathes asking for help. Normally, I have to force my help on him or take a sneak-attack approach.

Kind of reminds me of Zoey.

Of course, she's much more enjoyable to be around than the gray-haired mechanic, but she also seems hell-bent on doing everything herself if she can. The few times I've been able to help are little victories.

Thoughts of Pine Falls' newest arrival threaten to distract me as I finish the tires on Mrs. Applewood's BMW, and I'm still thinking about Zoey Gunner when I'm perched on the low box I use as a seat next to my current refurb project.

A 1980 Ducati Pantah 500 SL.

A few weeks in, and the machine is starting to look presentable.

When it's done, the thing'll be beautiful. Lighter and sleeker than what I prefer to ride, but it'll make me a nice chunk of change when I resell it.

Or I could give it as a gift.

Tanya and Isaac's eighteenth birthday is coming up in a few months. Tanya loves vintage things, and I could see my little sister riding this.

Well, if she gets her license back soon.

Maybe I should avoid gifts with motors. Plus, I'd have to figure out a present just as huge for Isaac. I know he wants a bike, but he's been working at a local farm to earn enough to buy his own. I wouldn't want to take away the excitement and pride of that first big purchase from him.

Selling the Ducati it is.

While I work on replacing the worn brake pads, an image drifts into my mind of another woman driving the bike.

Zoey would look gorgeous straddling this classic ride, honey-brown hair streaming out behind her—from underneath her helmet, of course—cruising down an empty two-lane beside me.

Only problem is, I'd have to forgo the glory that is having her on the back of my own bike.

Still, it's something to think about.

Whoa. Slow down. You can't show up at her place with a bike. She'll get spooked.

But, damn, the urge to claim her is a steady thrum in the back of my brain, like a constant growl from my wolf.

She has the mating scent.

I talked to Roderick about the lore, figuring our Alpha would know best. He confirmed multiple pack members had experienced the phenomenon.

All werewolves know, in a theoretical sense, about the mating scent. The idea that optimal partners will smell particularly appealing to our wolves. But there's nothing binding about the special pheromone. The fragrance is different for all of us, and a wolf can have more than one person with mating potential. We can also take a mate without the alluring scent.

And someone who smells like the perfect mate is plenty capable of rejecting us.

I clench my jaw and try to shrug off the discomfort from the idea that Zoey might not be okay with mating a small-town werewolf.

Already, I'm doubting my chances after breaking down and watching the video of her ex getting mocked by a barbershop quartet. Wasn't hard to find online, and I spent a good five minutes dying of laughter at the horrified expression on the dick's face.

But then I took a closer look at the asshole.

The guy's hair was styled with gel, his button-up shirt free of wrinkles and neatly tucked into slacks. There was a sparkle of a thick watch on his wrist, and the humiliating serenade took place inside of an office with huge windows overlooking Denver.

I glance down at my grease-smeared jeans and T-shirt. My work boots are scuffed, and I've never done more than comb my hair after I get out of a shower.

Zoey's ex is on the opposite end of the spectrum from me, and I can't help comparing myself to him.

Is that what she goes for? The well-dressed corporate type?

I barely stop myself from swiping a grimy hand across my forehead, grimacing at the black marks on my fingers I've never noticed before.

I'll never be like that. Not in a million years.

But I can at least make sure to clean myself up before I track her down again. Maybe swing by the store to get some more shirts without holes in them. Anything to get her to give me a chance as a man. After that, we can deal with the wolf.

"This was not a date. I am not going to fall in love with you, Warner Jameson."

She didn't tell me to stay away from her. She didn't say she didn't want to know me. In fact, her statements almost seemed like she was trying to convince herself of them, not me.

Zoey Gunner is a challenge. She's long-term.

She's already crawling under my skin, melding herself into my thoughts of the future.

What would it be like to have Zoey as my mate?

A partner. My own person, who I can rely on and take care of and laugh with and hold.

I'm suddenly tipsy from wanting.

The idea brings into stark relief the emptiness in my chest I try to ignore. But with Zoey in my mind, I can't help thinking about how much I long to be needed.

All my life, I've been the extra.

When my dad died, Mom stood on her own, never looking for comfort from her children, only trying to be a constant rock for us. Where the fatherly duties were left open, Uncle Mason stepped in. There was no space for me there. In other families, it might have fallen to me to care for the younger siblings, but Roderick took the reins on that, along with the needs of the entire pack. Plus, Tanya and Isaac have always had each other.

People around town like me. They think I'm charming and good for a laugh or a friendly favor.

But no one has ever *needed* me.

Could Zoey?

12

ZOEY

THE PINE FALLS PUBLIC LIBRARY has officially made it into my list of top five places to work remotely. I'm not sure anything will beat McConnell's Pub in Denver, where they make sure to give me a table in the corner, near an outlet, and they always have a new beer on tap for me to sample.

At least, they did until I realized how drinking affected my medication. Now, the staff is just as quick with a Dr. Pepper and a basket of cheese fries.

Maybe a library is a better choice than a pub.

Plus, there's a cute coffee shop just down the block that makes those frothy drinks with delicious syrups added. The only way I can consume coffee is if it's halfway to becoming a milkshake. One more way I'm the black sheep in my family. Or more like they're a herd of black sheep drinking black coffee, and I'm the super-fluffy white sheep that insists on wearing a pink bow while it sips on a foamy Almond Joy latte.

I finish off my delicious drink as I put the final touches on a style sheet for my new client. After saving and sending it to the Denver brewery that hired me to design their website, I lean back in my chair, enjoying the sun on my face.

This small-town library has a patio that overlooks a river. The water meanders by at a leisurely pace, splashing against rocks to create the perfect background white noise. My bet is that the crashing of waves was louder during the summer when the banks were swollen with snow melt. But as the temperature drops, so does the water level.

Satisfied with my work for the day, I take one last wistful look at the full Wi-Fi signal before shutting my laptop and sliding it into my bag.

Time to head back to the cellular service wasteland that is my grandmother's cabin.

At least there's electricity and a water heater. Have to be thankful for the small things.

Before I leave, I take the opportunity to pick out some reading material for the evening. Normally, I gravitate toward historical romance, loving the brief trip I get to take into ornate ballrooms from centuries ago. But a particular style of font on one book spine captures my attention.

Similar to what I've seen stitched on the back of a leather jacket.

Minutes later, I'm heading to the checkout with a motorcycle-club romance novel and trying hard not to think about my motivations.

"I've read this one. It's really good." The white woman with vibrant red hair who scans the barcode gives me an approving nod.

"Good to know. I've never read her work before." I hand over my temporary library card. Luckily, I was able to get a card, even as an out-of-towner. Five bucks and unlimited books? I didn't hesitate.

Still, I miss using my nice, sturdy Denver public library card. Plastic is so much more official.

"You new to town?" she asks, fingering the flimsy card stock before waving it under the scanner.

"Kind of. I'm just here to clean out my grandmother's house. She passed away in March."

"I'm sorry to hear that."

"I didn't know her that well." I didn't know her at all. Guilt pricks at my gut to accompany the thought. "Maybe you did? Her name was Minnie Gunner."

The librarian shakes her head. "I just moved here at the beginning of the summer, so our paths wouldn't have crossed."

You moved here? Why?

The questions flash through my brain, but I'm able to cut them off before they tumble out of my mouth.

"I'm Juliet." The woman offers her name as she hands my book back to me.

"I'm Zoey."

"Well, Zoey, I hope you enjoy your book. I read it years ago but devoured it in one night. Couldn't put it down. Something about a man on a bike ..." Juliet trails off, her face turning as red as her hair. "Never mind. I did *not* mean to say that."

Glancing down at the cover of the book, where we see a muscular guy dressed in a leather vest, I can't help but grin. Plus, I get the sudden urge to put the librarian at ease. No judgment here.

"I met a member of The Dark Moon Riders the other day. So, I might be in a biker kind of mood. Do you know anyone in the club?"

Juliet shrugs, but her flush starts to fade, her mouth tilting into a frown. "Seen them around town. Maybe said a few words to one or two."

The tight tone she uses has my interest bells ringing.

"Is there something wrong with them?"

"Not exactly. It's just ..." The librarian glances around the empty lobby. "From what I can tell, there's no real consensus on the club."

"What do you mean?" I lean on the counter, sensing that Juliet would rather keep her voice low.

"Some people seem to think they're separate from the town. Like they shouldn't have to follow the same laws we do. And there are others who basically ignore them. But I get the feeling a lot of people are scared of them."

"Scared of them? Why?"

She raises a crimson brow at me. "Loud bikes. Mean faces.

Dressed head to toe in leather. Bikers aren't really the happy, cuddly type."

I wonder if Juliet has ever met Warner. No way would I ever call his face mean. And he might not be so bad to cuddle with. He certainly was warm when I had my arms wrapped around him on his bike.

I push the teasing thoughts away and focus on the conversation.

"My dad is in a biker club. Up in Denver. They go riding on weekends, and they hold fundraisers for veterans suffering from PTSD." My shoulders shrug. "I guess bikers don't really scare me."

Juliet sits back in her chair, eyes running over me as if I were something to be studied. She sighs, almost sounding relieved. "Me neither." Then, she smiles with a soft curve of her lip.

In that moment, I can't help noticing how beautiful she is. Not in a walk-down-the-runway kind of way. Juliet has the type of face that tricks you into thinking it's ordinary. That every bit of it is just fine and nothing more. But the moment she smiles, it's as if the light takes notice, chiding itself for not giving her the proper attention moments ago. She's all red and gold, like a phoenix. My mind starts cycling through color palettes that would pair well with her complexion.

I want to crochet her a forest-green scarf and hat set. With matching mittens.

I want to invite my brothers out here, herd them into the library, point to Juliet, and demand one of them woo her so she can be a member of our family. That way, I can enjoy her smile for the rest of our days.

But knowing the Gunner boys, they'd never leave, and then I'd be stuck in the same mess I just escaped from.

Still, I realize something very important.

Juliet is going to be one of my few cherished friends.

Now, I just need to figure out the best course of action to make that happen. If I tell her outright, I might scare her off.

"Would you like to be friends?" My abrupt mouth spits in caution's face. At least I framed it as a question rather than a demand.

Her smile flickers, and I'm worried it might go out. But then a grin flashes wide, and her gorgeous face threatens to burn my retinas. Reflexively, I reach for my sunglasses, but just keep myself from putting them on.

"Yes."

"Fantastic." I smooth my hands over the front of my T-shirt. "When are you free for our first friend date?"

The fact that Juliet laughs rather than cringes from me is the last bit of proof I need.

She's my kind of person.

13

ZOEY

THERE'S no harm in using a man for his tool.

His electric jigsaw, that is.

Some pieces of furniture I'm refurbishing require more than a simple sand and stain. I need to make precise cuts, which means I need a jigsaw. Briefly, I considered buying one. But I already have one back in Denver, and I simply forgot to pack it.

Way too much of my truck space was allotted to crafting supplies. *Why did I think I needed a gallon of glitter?*

To keep my wallet happy, I opt for borrowing from Warner.

And that's the *only* reason I called Sawdust and Supplies, asking after him.

My visit to his place is definitely not inspired by the steamy sex scenes in the romance novel I checked out earlier this week.

Not at all.

A man by the name of Mason answered the phone when I called last evening. A minute later, he passed the receiver off to Warner, who immediately agreed to help me out.

I park in front of the hardware store. Turns out, Warner lives in the apartment above his family's shop.

Small-town life. It's kind of sweet.

Walking around to the side alley, I spot the door he told me to knock on.

Just as I'm raising my fist, a voice sounds from behind me. "Who are you?"

I turn, meeting the amber eyes of a beautiful young woman. She's wearing torn jeans and a general air that asks, *Why should I give a fuck about you?* Her tangle of dark hair frames a pale face that could belong to a sixteen-year-old or just as easily a twenty-six-year-old.

"I'm Zoey Gunner." I hold out my hand. "And you?"

The girl glances from my hand to my face and back to my hand before finally accepting it in a surprisingly firm grip. "Tanya." Then, she steps in closer, her nostrils flaring slightly as her head cocks. "You're not from around here."

Not a question, but I answer anyway. "My grandmother was Minnie Gunner. I'm fixing up her cabin to sell."

Tanya finally lets go of my hand, but continues to watch me with a certain amount of intensity. "No one was invited to your grandma's funeral."

"There wasn't one."

The woman was cremated, and Dad drove down to collect the ashes. I have zero knowledge of what my mom did with them.

"Did you want to be invited?" The little I know of my grandmother indicated she didn't have many friends.

The girl shoves her hands in her pockets. "Nope. Didn't know her. But the gossips could not get enough of being affronted about the lack of an invite."

"Why? No one was invited. There wasn't even something to *be* invited to."

Tanya rolls her eyes and steps around me, reaching for the doorknob. "That's just as bad. You denied them the chance to gossip about old lady Gunner. Plus, they've been dying for a peek at your mom after all these years. You here to see Warner?"

"Yes," I murmur, following her up a set of stairs, my thoughts on her words.

Is my family really that interesting to these people?

I kinda thought my mom would've been forgotten after being gone for over three decades and my grandmother acting the hermit.

But maybe that just made the mystery grow.

I refocus on the young woman in front of me, finding my own curiosity piqued.

"Are you Warner's girlfriend?"

"Are you kidding me?" She glares over her shoulder. "Gross! Give me a second while I locate the nearest bucket to puke in."

"So, no?"

"Hell no. I'm his sister. His favorite sister."

"You're my only sister." The man in question appears at the top of the steps, smiling down at us. "Which means you're my least favorite too. Hi, Zoey."

"Hi—"

Tanya juts her hip to the side, blocking me from view. "Yeah, well, I have three brothers to choose from, so you'd better be nicer to me, or you'll make the bottom of *my* list."

I continue up the stairs until I can see him over her shoulder.

Warner clutches his chest, as if wounded. "Words hurt, baby sis. Now, move your ass. You're blocking Zoey."

"You know what? Maybe I *should* be blocking Zoey. I think she might be my new best friend, which means I need to guard her from cruel men."

My arm is snagged in an unforgivingly friendly embrace.

The exchange is fascinating. Like Tanya, I'm also the only girl in my family. I wonder if this is how dramatic I sound when bickering with my brothers.

I offer her a placating smile. "No guarding needed. I'm just here for his tool."

The girl's face goes slack, and then she mimes gagging. "TMI!"

"Power tool!" I hurry to clarify. Only, now, I'm thinking about his other tool. Wondering about the size of it. The feel of it. Imagining all the things I'd tell him to do with it ...

"I don't need to know what you call it!" Tanya covers her ears and sprints up the steps, leaving me with Warner, who seems to be strangling on suppressed laughter as his eyes glitter with amusement.

"Did I just scar your sister?"

The guy leans back against the wall, letting loud guffaws spill out. A reluctant grin plucks at my mouth as I finish climbing the steps.

Chuckles trailing off, Warner leads me through another door into an apartment that could be cozy if it had a little more personality. A coat rack holds both a leather vest and leather jacket with The Dark Moon Riders patch stitched on the back of both. The only wall decoration is a large, mounted TV. Two mismatched couches face the screen, and one holds a young man that looks strikingly similar to Tanya, who now leans on a kitchen island, eyes focused on her phone.

"This is my younger brother, Isaac." Warner gestures to the guy, who nods silently before his eyes flick back to whatever game is playing on the TV.

"Nice to meet you both," I announce.

Tanya waves a distracted hand at me.

"This way." Warner gestures I should follow him into another room, where I find myself in a small workshop.

"Wow. Not the normal setup you'd expect in an apartment." I run my fingers along the high top of his workbench and admire the wide array of tools hanging in organized patterns on the walls.

Warner shrugs. "Some people need an office. I wanted a workshop. Besides, it's not like I have downstairs neighbors who'd be bothered by the sound of a power saw."

"Do you make things?"

He nods. "Sometimes. More often, I'm repairing things. Broken chair leg here, cracked floorboard there."

"That's your job?"

His grin is rueful as he scratches the back of his neck. "Nah. I earn a paycheck at my uncle's construction company. This is like a hobby. People bring me their small projects."

"That's sweet. Are you sure you're part of a badass motorcycle gang?"

Warner seems more like the guy to help an old woman cross the street rather than roar down it on his insanely loud hog.

He grimaces. "It's not that kind of gang. We're not running drugs or anything."

"So, everyone in town loves The Dark Moon Riders?" I ask, thinking back on Juliet's words.

A few different emotions flick across his face until he pulls a casual give-nothing-away mask into place. "Feelings are mixed."

I'm tempted to ask more, but I don't want to keep Warner from what looks like a family gathering.

"Well, so far, I have nothing bad to say about you all. Especially since you're helping me out with this jigsaw."

That earns me a genuine smile, and he pulls open a metal cabinet drawer, only to come out holding the beautiful, versatile saw. The fact that it's a lime-green color only delights me more.

"You're a lifesaver. I owe you."

"Really? What exactly do you owe me? What's this saw worth to you?" Warner holds the tool just out of reach, tempting me to step closer to him.

This is flirting. I know it is. And I should run in the other direction. But I can't help moving in closer.

"You're doing me a favor, so I owe you a favor. What that entails is up to you." I hold my hands out, and he relinquishes the saw. "But honestly, I think me holding this in your presence should be payment enough. What with women and power tools being the sexiest thing you can imagine."

His eyes get darker while I taunt him with his previous claims.

"I—" he starts, but I don't get to hear the end of his thought.

"We're out of here," Tanya yells.

Warner frowns and strides out of the room. I follow.

"What do you mean, *we*?"

Tanya tucks her phone in her back pocket and tosses a jacket at the younger man. "Isaac and I are heading out."

"Where are you taking him?" Warner glares. "We were going to watch football."

"Too bad. Mom said she'd lend Isaac the car, and he promised to drive me to Cheyenne's party."

"Why would you promise that?" Warner faces his brother. "You hate parties."

Isaac shrugs, but his sister answers for him.

"Because there's a girl," Tanya explains.

"A girl?"

"Shut up," Isaac mutters.

"That's right. Shut up and get your own twin." Tanya reaches up to pat her older brother on the head before strolling out the door. "Nice to meet you, Zoey!" she calls once she's out of sight.

"You too," I call out, then turn to Isaac. "And you."

The guy gives me a half smile and nod, then turns to Warner. "Sorry, but I did promise. Just forgot what night it was. Rain check?"

"Yeah, fine. Go keep her out of trouble."

Without the two younger siblings, his apartment suddenly seems very quiet. I stand awkwardly, cradling the saw against my chest.

And for the first time, Warner's smile appears forced.

"Well"—he clears his throat—"I guess you've got places to be."

That's it. No way can I leave this man to watch football alone, abandoned by his brother.

"Are the Broncos playing?"

Something sparks in his eyes.

"Yeah. Are you a fan?"

I shrug. "Hard to live in Denver and not be. But the cabin doesn't have cable, so I can't really keep up. Mind if I stay to watch?"

Warner's mouth bobs open, and then he practically carries me to the couch, ushering with his long arms that I should take a seat.

"Do you want something to eat? I've got snacks." He offers a bowl of pretzels.

After setting the saw down, I scoop up a handful.

"Do you want a beer?" He's already in front of the fridge, as if I'll leave if he doesn't give me libations fast enough.

Alcohol is a special-occasion thing for me. It doesn't always react well with my medication.

"Do you have soda or something?"

"Dr. Pepper okay?" Warner holds up one of the red cans, and I reach over the back of the couch to accept it.

"Look at you, Biker Boy. How'd you know that's my favorite?"

Amber eyes flick between me and the can in his hand, and a satisfied smile pulls at the corners of his mouth as he passes the drink over.

"Not sure, Mystery Woman. Maybe it's fate."

I snort, getting comfy on the surprisingly soft couch. "Soda is not fate."

The refreshing crack and sigh of me popping open the can almost drown out his next words. At least, I tell myself it does because I'm not sure I want to acknowledge what I just heard.

Something that sounded an awful lot like, *We might be.*

14

WARNER

RODERICK HAS a bloody rabbit in his mouth.

"*Show-off,*" I think at him.

He huffs out a laugh around his catch, lying down in the damp leaves to feast.

My brother can't actually read my mind in wolf form. At least, that's what he claims. But as pack leader, one of the extra enhancements is to get *impressions* from pack members. He might not hear exact words, but he can pick up intent.

While he eats, I take another few minutes to sprint through the underbrush, stretching muscles that will shift into different shapes when I change back.

Tonight, despite it still being weeks from the full moon, I'm overflowing with energy.

Likely leftover from the afternoon spent watching football with Zoey. Days might have passed since she lounged on my couch, cheering for touchdowns and chugging Dr. Peppers, but I can still smell hints of her in my apartment.

That's made for some erotic dreams.

My wolf impulses keep pushing me to make a move, but my human brain knows I can't just walk up to her and say, *Be mine.*

I need to woo her.

And in order to do that without appearing obsessed, I need to work off my excessive energy and lust.

Luckily, Roderick was available and willing to go on a run with me tonight. When I circle back to him, we head for our bikes.

Pulling on the thread in my mind that ties me to my human self, shadows shift around me as my bones flex and reform. Joints crack, muscles stretch, and I shake off the small aches and pains of the change.

When I stand as a man again, I feel more centered. My thoughts are clearer, and I'm able to plot how to approach my crocheting temptress as I pull my clothes on.

Heading back to town, Roderick and I rev our engines and let our choppers devour the blacktop. My mind is so focused on how to pursue Zoey that I almost miss the familiar truck parked in a gravel lot on the side of the highway. If it had been any darker, I might have ridden straight past without giving it a second thought. But the faded rust color and particular-shaped dent in the bumper catch my attention.

Zoey is out in the middle of nowhere, and the sun is about to set.

Roderick is ahead of me, taking point, like he always does. Doesn't matter if it's the whole club riding or just the two of us, like tonight. We haven't gotten to ride together, just us brothers, for a while. I hate to cut it short. Still, there's no way I can head back to town with this rising curiosity threatening to drown out all other thoughts.

I accelerate, coming level with my brother and catching his eye. Using hand signals, I let him know what I intend to do before slowing to pull a U-turn and heading back to the truck. A lot of people would probably be surprised to discover a biker gang where every member has a basic knowledge of American Sign Language. But that's just another one of Roderick's protective instincts showing. Or his paranoia. He doesn't want to rely on radios while we're riding, and so he insisted everyone learn.

Worked out in our favor though, seeing as how we were able to add a werewolf to our pack who had struggled in other places because he'd lost his hearing before aging into his powers. We're deaf-friendly, and it got us a tech genius.

When I shut my engine off, Roderick is just pulling in beside me. I wait for him to cut his too. The silence of the night is shocking without the roar of our bikes. It's only after the ringing in my ears fades that the chorus of the forest filters in and the surroundings don't seem so quiet.

"You can keep going. That's Zoey Gunner's truck. I want to see why she's out here."

Roderick has his stoic-statue face on. "Why?"

I climb off my bike. "She's a city girl. Want to make sure she hasn't gotten lost in the woods."

Plus, I've been craving the sight of her since the moment she left my apartment. I didn't know who to thank for my luck when she asked to stay and watch the game with me. During commercial breaks, I got her talking, picking up small facts about her life. Now, I know she works remotely as a website designer, which means she can stick around Pine Falls as long as she has internet access. I paid close attention to every fact she let drop about her brothers. When I meet her family, I want them to like me, so the more I know, the better.

Yeah, that's presumptuous. But my wolf and I are in full agreement. Zoey Gunner is something special, and missing out on a chance with her would haunt me.

Unfortunately, she only stayed until the end of the game. The past couple of days have been longer than usual at work, meaning I couldn't figure out a way to casually run into her around town.

But this? It's more than just trying to set up an accidental meeting. I'm legitimately worried about Zoey getting turned around in the unfamiliar area.

Pine Falls is different from Denver. Wilder.

I would know. I'm one of the monsters that lurks in these woods.

Roderick continues to study me, and I let him. Suddenly, his head tilts, his nose to the wind, and he breathes in deep. I follow his lead, scenting the air. Almost immediately, I catch the familiar hint of sweet earthiness.

But there's another scent. Another person. Someone who smells like paper and lemons.

Could she be out here with a man?

The thought has my wolf growling, but I stifle the urge before it reaches my throat.

"Juliet is here," Roderick says, climbing off of his bike.

"Juliet?" The name sounds kind of familiar, but it takes me a second of going through my mental tally of Pine Falls residents to remember. "The librarian?"

A silent nod from Roderick as he stares at the woods.

Interesting.

My first instinct is to tease Roderick about his first-name-basis situation with the cute woman who is also a recent transplant to our small town. But I keep my big mouth shut with some effort, wary of him ordering me to get back on my bike and continue on to Pine Falls.

Being pack leader is more than a title. There's magic in the designation. I'd have a hard time circumventing his direct order.

Instead, I track the maple trail into the woods and stifle a smile at the sound of my brother following me. He wants to come, but doesn't want to take point?

Even more interesting.

The trail would be hard for a human to see, but my eyes easily pick out the slim dirt path that winds through the trees. I really hope Zoey came this way during daylight. There are a lot of roots looking to twist unaware ankles.

Having grown up in Pine Falls and having spent at least one night a month running wild in these woods, I know exactly where this trail leads. Yellow Pine Lake.

Soon, the humid scent of water intertwines with Zoey's trail.

When I break through the trees, my feet crunch on the rocky

shore. There's a calming slap of waves against stone and the squeak of bats feasting on nighttime bugs. Down the way, I spot the glow of a fire. Feminine laughter drifts toward us, traveling easily over the calm water.

"Guess they're not in trouble," I say, glancing over my shoulder, expecting Roderick to be just a few feet away.

He's not. But he hasn't left either. Instead, I make out his shadowy form, back in the woods. He stands still, looming like a ghostly presence.

"You're being fucking weird."

He doesn't respond, which only proves my point.

I choose to ignore him, making my way down along the beach toward the sound of laughter. When I'm maybe twenty feet away, a warning bark cuts off whatever conversation was happening. Then, a massive body trots toward me.

"Hey, buddy. Just me," I murmur, holding out my hand for Bruce to sniff. He does, offering a brief tail wag, then lumbers back to the warm glow of the fire, where two women stand, clutching beers and squinting into the darkness.

"Who's there? Show your face!" Zoey shoves up from her seat and steps away from the campfire, approaching the edge of the light. As if I'm enticing her into the darkness.

Not liking that thought, I move forward instead. "Just Warner Jameson. Your friendly neighborhood biker." I put on my most charming smile as I step into the glow of their fire.

Neither woman seems particularly bothered by my sudden appearance. That might have some relation to the unmistakable scent of alcohol.

The redheaded woman, Juliet, lets out a snort at my description. "Friendly. Sure."

"I mean, he's kinda friendly," Zoey offers, facing her companion. There's a thickness to her words, the hint of a slur, that makes me think these two women have been drinking for a little while.

And I'm suddenly fascinated to discover exactly what a drunk Zoey means.

"Oh, really?" Juliet leans back in her camping chair, giving me a thorough once-over. "How's he been friendly?"

Zoey holds up her hand, ticking favors off on fingers. "He gave me a ride. Fixed my car. Helped carry some shopping bags. Invited me to lunch. Lent me a saw." She wiggles her five digits.

"Is he trying to get in your pants?" Juliet's words come out clearer than Zoey's. She throws her can into a paper bag that clanks with the sound of multiple empties before diving into a large cooler and coming out with another.

Either the librarian holds her booze better than Zoey or she's just a more articulate drunk.

"Can you come here?" Zoey waves her hand in an overly vigorous motion, enticing me forward.

The closer I get, the more of her beautiful, flushed cheeks I see. Her eyes shine in the firelight as they trace over my face, seemingly unable to stay still.

"Are you trying to get in my pants?"

Zoey is wearing a pair of jeans and hiking boots with a large fleece that falls halfway down her thighs. A crocheted hat covers her head, and she grips her beer with gloved hands. She's dressed for warmth, and I'm tempted to tell her just how I could heat her up.

Hell yeah, I want to get in her pants.

But not in the way Juliet is implying. Not some quick, impersonal bang.

And right now, with Juliet and my brother nearby, I can honestly say, "Not at this moment."

"Nonanswer!" Juliet proclaims.

Before the librarian can call me out again, I change the subject. "You two having a party?"

"We're celebrating our new friendship. With beer!" Zoey goes to take a sip from her can, but comes away frowning, apparently finding it empty.

"Aren't you worried about animals?"

Yellow Pine Lake is a common campsite, but it's still wild.

Zoey juts her jaw out, as if she's trying to make her face look heavier, like a Neanderthal. The effect is emphasized and made all the more hilarious when she speaks in a deep voice. "Women make fire." She waves at said fire. "Fire scare animals."

"Plus, we've got this big guy." Juliet heaves out of her chair to crouch beside Bruce, patting the giant dog on his belly.

"And Juliet gave me bear mace!" Zoey shouts like it's the best gift she's ever received.

Probably not an item I'd offer up to someone when they're drunk.

"How late were you three planning on celebrating?" Damn, I sound like an overprotective parent.

The women seem to agree, sharing a look between them before breaking into laughter. The sound has me grinning. Zoey looks so carefree, clutching her stomach as she leans back, letting her chuckles drift up into the starry night sky.

When she catches her breath, I'm treated to a beautiful grin. "We're camping! Look." She points past the edge of the firelight, and I spot a small tent. "Juliet is teaching me some outdoorsy stuff."

"We are strong, independent women!" the librarian declares before taking a deep swallow of her beer.

"Damn right we are!" Zoey faces the lake as she shouts her words. As they tumble into the night, she lets out a happy sigh.

"Why are you lurking, Roderick?" Juliet calls to the shadows behind me. "You're being creepy!"

She doesn't get an answer, but Zoey whirls around, clearly searching for Roderick in the darkness. Roots creep over the beach, and she loses her footing. My arms are out to catch her a second before she regains her balance on her own.

"Nailed it!" she crows before glancing back at me and noticing my reach, still there if she becomes unsteady again.

A delighted smile cracks across Zoey's face.

"Trust fall!" And then she's toppling over once more, this time on purpose, and I lunge forward to make sure she ends up in my arms rather than sprawled on the ground. She lands with a gasp, then chuckles. "Guess I have to trust you now, Biker Boy."

She's soft against me and smells like every delicious dessert I've ever consumed. I want to curl my arms around her. Hold her to my chest.

Instead, I make a joke.

"Can't I at least be Biker *Man*?"

"Aww." She reaches up to pat my cheek. "Not when you're so cute."

"Careful, Zoey." Juliet takes another swig from her can before continuing in a mock whisper. "All that cutesy talk might scare these big, tough Dark Moon Riders. Roderick won't even come out of the woods!" She snorts out a giggle.

Zoey trains her curious gaze on me. "Who's Roderick?"

I affect a rueful grimace. "My older brother. He's a little antisocial."

"That's okay. I am too." Zoey gives me a sweet smile. Then, she boops me on my nose with her forefinger.

"Not tonight!" Juliet climbs up on top of a large rock, holding her beer up to the sky, as if toasting the world. "Tonight, we christen our friendship! Two outsiders, taking over Pine Falls. To hell with the bikers! This town will be run by women!"

"You're right!" In the way that drunk people do, Zoey's response to me flips on a switch. She springs from my arms, shoving at my chest. "This is a friend date! No boys allowed! No boys allowed!"

Juliet joins in the chant, and soon, the trees are ringing with the sound, each exclamation point emphasized with another push.

Another guy might be annoyed by the manhandling, but I'm having trouble stifling my laughter. She's so fucking adorable with her cheeks ruddy from the alcohol. The heat spills down to her neck and supercharges her scent.

I wish I could bury my nose there, breathe in the sweet earthiness. Then lick her.

Instead, I stumble backward as if I don't have the strength to battle her assault.

"All right! No boys allowed. I'll leave you to your camping. And your conquering."

"To conquering!" Zoey climbs up on her own rock, arms held high.

"To conquering!" Juliet thrusts her beer up, then chugs the whole of it down in an impressive display.

I let the shadows of the trees envelop me, shaking my head and chuckling all the while.

"They're ridiculous." It's the first thing Roderick says since we followed the women's trail.

"They're drunk." I shrug.

"It's not safe," he mutters.

"Well, yeah. That's why I'm not actually leaving."

Roderick raises one eyebrow at me, but then lets me lead the way again. I move deeper into the woods. When the sound of the girls' laughter has almost faded, I pause by a tree with low, thick limbs. There, I strip off my clothes, folding them neatly before setting them up in the tree. I hope no curious critters decide to claim them. I'd have a hard time explaining to highway patrol why I'm riding my bike home naked.

Make for a good story though.

Once I'm completely bare, I coax my wolf forward, letting the form envelop my body. The change is slower. If my wolf sensed danger or responded to the call of the full moon, then I'd be able to switch to four legs in a matter of seconds. But pulling the change out without the aid of adrenaline or lunar magic means I'm struggling for a minute or two, grimacing at the pain of my bones snapping and reshaping.

Eventually, I'm in my wolf form, panting and shaking off the last lingering bit of discomfort. When I turn back toward the campsite, I see Roderick's wolf sitting calmly, waiting for me.

Another perk of being the pack leader: more magic means a faster change.

I huff at him as I pass by.

Soon, I'm staring out at the crackling fire and cackling women, my gray coat camouflaging me. Roderick settles at my side, his black coat just as good for spying.

Protecting, I correct myself.

"I think it's time," Zoey announces.

Time for what? I wonder.

"I knew it. That fourth beer was the turning point, huh?" Juliet says.

Roderick shifts beside me, probably also wondering what this is a preamble to.

"It was. Okay. I'm ready. This is happening." Zoey strolls toward the woods, and my protective nature stirs.

"Good luck," the librarian offers.

Zoey raises a fist in the air before declaring, "I'm going to pee outside! This is a special event!"

"Yeah, I'll mark it down in the history books," Juliet calls after her, chuckling as she sinks back into her camping chair.

Zoey passes by our hiding spot, not even ten feet separating us. But we're hunters. We know how to hide well.

"I'm going to pee. Pee on a tree," Zoey sings to herself.

Even in wolf form, Roderick knows how to roll his eyes, which he does now as I stand to trot after her. I, on the other hand, have my jaws open in a wolfish grin.

Zoey keeps up her funny chant until she's a decent distance from her little campsite. Coming to a stop, she turns in a circle, her movements hinting at a lack of balance.

"Now, which one of you naughty boys is looking for a golden shower?"

If I were in human form, there's no way I'd be able to stifle my laughter. But I keep my jaws clenched shut and turn my back to give her privacy.

And I start making plans for how to convince this odd woman to be mine.

15

ZOEY

WHEN MY PANTS are around my ankles, I get the sense I'm being watched.

Super convenient.

I've got my back pressed against a tree, my thigh muscles put to use as I brace myself in a sitting position. Up until the feeling I have an audience, I was proud of myself for figuring out this whole pee-in-the-woods thing.

Whenever someone hears I'm from Denver, they automatically assume I spend my weekends climbing mountains and hiking mile-long trails in the wilderness.

Yeah, no. I love looking at the gorgeous mountain landscape, maybe taking a drive on the twisty mountain roads. But get out and explore them? I've never really been brave enough.

But here I am, camping with my new friend, using nature as my toilet, and I'm pretty sure there's something lurking in the nearby shadows.

This is why people pee surrounded by four walls. Such a vulnerable time requires shelter.

"Juliet? Did you follow me?" I call out.

That's one way to get close to someone fast. Kind of like going to the restroom together at a club. Would've preferred we discussed it first, but, hey, I'll take a surprise Juliet over a surprise bear.

There's no answer.

Warner's comment about wild animals has me paranoid.

Then, a twig snaps, and I'm scrambling to pull up my jeans.

"Shit! Shit, shit, shit." I don't bother zipping before lunging toward my flashlight. When I have it in my hand, I shine the beam in a broad circle, needing to know what kind of creature I'm about to face.

It lumbers out of the trees, huge head focused on me.

"Fucking hell." I collapse back against a non-pee tree, clutching my chest. "Goddamn it, Bruce! I almost peed all over myself!"

My dog seems thoroughly unconcerned, sniffing the air as he wanders around.

"You're lucky I was done," I mutter, taking a moment to zip my fly and calm my clamoring heart. "Come on, you big oaf. I need another beer. You scared me sober."

And I'm missing my happy buzz. Part of it caused by the alcohol, but the other bit by a certain biker who made a unplanned appearance. Despite this being the first foray into bonding with my new librarian friend, I have to admit I was slightly bummed to send Warner away. He's just so … nice.

To be around.

He gives me a warm, giggly feeling that I haven't had in a while. Maybe ever.

And when I have beer running through my veins, I don't have to think about how I'm not planning on staying in Pine Falls. I can enjoy the sensation of having a crush. I can laugh at his jokes. Fall into his arms. Pretend that I have an idea of where my life is headed and maybe it's not impossible to pursue a small-town biker.

"She's back!" Juliet cheers me as I approach the campfire. She moved to stand near the edge of the lake. "How'd you do?"

"This big dope scared me half to death, but I survived." I throw a thumb at Bruce, who reclaims his spot on a worn blanket. "And my bladder is empty, so mission accomplished."

"Success!" Juliet grins, then turns back to the water and launches a rock out of her hand. The pebble skips until it's swallowed by darkness.

After grabbing myself another beer, I join her by the water's edge. The whole afternoon, we talked about lighthearted things, like our favorite books and foods and hobbies. I now know that Juliet isn't only good at camping, but she's also a rock climber. She makes sense in a Colorado town more than I do.

Still, Pine Falls is kind of removed. I'm curious how she ended up here, and my tongue is just loose enough that I'm ready to ask.

"Do you have family in town?"

"Nope." She skips another rock that goes even farther than the first.

"How'd you hear about Pine Falls then?"

"The job posting was online, and I was looking ..." She hesitates, and my curiosity is thoroughly piqued. "I wanted to get away."

"And Pine Falls fit the bill?" This is prying, isn't it? I'm being pushy.

"Better than most." This comes out softer, lacking her enthusiasm from a moment ago.

I glance at the side of her head for a moment, but Juliet stares fixedly out at the water. Eventually, I turn to stare into the darkness with her.

"We're friends, right?" I ask.

Juliet visibly tenses. "Yeah ..."

The word doesn't come out solid. It's as if she's only loaning it to me and is bracing to take it back at any moment.

"Then, I want to establish a very important rule of our friendship."

"What's that?" Wariness fills her tone.

Juliet probably expects me to say something like we have to be one hundred percent honest with each other or that she's required to divulge all her deepest, darkest secrets to me.

But building a friendship isn't the same as making a deal with the devil.

"Rule number one: feel free to tell me to shut up whenever you feel it's necessary."

Silence stretches between us, and I look over again to find Juliet now staring at me, a glimmer of hope in her sweet, dark eyes.

"Zoey?"

"Yeah?"

"Would you mind shutting up?"

"Not in the slightest."

We spend the next half hour drinking beer and throwing rocks. The only sounds are the tiny splashes in the water, crickets chirping, branches rustling in the wind, and my big, lazy dog snoring.

And I ignore the sensation of eyes watching me.

16

ZOEY

Around noon, I finally stop sobbing.

There wasn't just one thing that set me off. A bunch of little things did.

Stubbing my toe on a rock. Missing my family. Thoughts of Minnie. Dropping Juliet off because our friend date was done.

But the real culprit was beer.

I knew, even as I was cracking open my fifth can of Coors, that I was making an unhealthy choice. When I'd first started on my antidepressants, I was lucky enough to discover that one drink had no noticeable effect on my mental health. But there's a threshold, and when I pass it, I roll dice with misery.

Now, after spending a night getting to know Juliet, I know she wouldn't have judged me or made me feel bad about needing to stay sober. But at the start of our little camping trip, she'd shown up with a cooler full of beer, proudly declaring we were going to get wasted in the wilderness.

The idea sounded *so fun*. I convinced myself the repercussions weren't as bad as I remembered.

Mistake.

I barely made it halfway home when the wretchedness crashed over me. Not the *true* darkness that arrives slowly and drags me under the surface. This is a malfunction with my meds and hopefully short-lived.

I parked on the side of the road as the tears fell in rivers. Eventually, I calmed long enough to drive again, but only made it as far as the front porch before I collapsed on a rocking chair and wallowed in my unexplainable sadness.

Well, there is an explanation, just not a satisfying one. My brain sometimes decides to be unhappy without cause.

When the misery subsides, I'm left with itchy eyes, a sore throat, and an aching head. All of these lend a sharp edge to my voice as I search for my dog.

"Bruce!" The screen door opens with a creak as I move to the back porch, calling out for the furry brute. "Bruce! Dinnertime!"

The sun hasn't set, but the day seems almost done as charcoal clouds gather in the sky. A rumble of thunder warns of a coming storm.

If I had Wi-Fi at this goddamn cabin, then I would've been able to check the weather. And if I had checked the weather, I never would have let Bruce out to wander freely when there's about to be rain. Trying to dry off a dog that weighs almost twice as much as I do is not a tango I want to dance today.

Only solution: get him back inside before the rain comes.

"Bruce! Don't make me come looking for you!"

I let him out when I stumbled inside a while back, still in the midst of my sobbing haze. Honestly, I'm surprised he didn't scratch at the door hours ago. As another minute or so passes with no sign of the mastiff, I accept that I can't just linger on the porch.

Grumbling about poorly trained dogs that don't listen to commands, I pull on my sneakers and grab his leash. I start my search by circling the yard, looking to see if he just fell asleep and was too passed out to hear me calling.

No sign of a giant tan mound of fur—and Bruce is not an easy target to hide.

Apparently, he decided to go on an adventure in the woods.

The woods mean dirt and twigs and leaves. So many random things I'll have to scrub him clean of if he gets wet on his jaunt. There's still time, a slim chance I can find him before the downpour.

Problem is, the forest stretches out in all directions, and I'm not sure what way he went.

I circle around to the backyard again, calling his name as I go, just in case. As I scan the line of trees, I notice a break in the branches. Not a trail exactly, but the grass seems to have been flattened, as if it was stepped on.

While I waffle between trying the not-trail or staying at the cabin, another crack of thunder sounds out like a warning. Or the start of a countdown timer.

"Fifteen minutes. Straight in and straight out," I mutter to myself.

If I don't find him, then I'll just pile an arsenal of towels by the back door.

The scent of pine and damp air surrounds me the moment I step into the forest. I focus on my annoyance because the minute I let it go, worry will set in. Bruce might seem like an unbreakable mammoth, but he's not immortal.

What if he got lost?

What if he hurt himself?

No. Stop it. He's just being an ass.

As I push through the undergrowth and duck under low-hanging branches, the not-trail becomes a no-way-in-hell- anyone-could-call-this-a-trail.

"Bruce!"

The air takes on a humid, sticky texture, and the sky grows ominously dark above the canopy.

Rain is coming, and I don't think it's going to be a little sprinkle.

"Bruce!"

A root trips me up, and I stumble, barely catching myself before I face-plant. A snarl of frustration seeps from my chest.

"If you don't show up in the next five seconds, then you do not get to lick my ice cream bowl tonight. Do you hear me? No dessert!"

The woods are silent, all the chirping birds and chattering squirrels having gone to ground in anticipation of the coming storm. They're probably watching me from their nice, warm nests, laughing at the silly human wandering aimlessly through the trees.

"You have five seconds, Bruce! Five!" The thick air muffles my shout.

No dog.

"Four!" I call out, a growl in my voice.

No dog.

"Three!" More growling.

Only, this time, it's not mine.

Immediately, my frustration vanishes, no room for it left in my body. Every inch of me has gone still, frozen in place by wary fear.

The forest is quiet.

I thought ... I was sure ...

But maybe it was thunder.

Or maybe it was ...

"Bruce?" This time, I don't shout, keeping my voice just above a whisper.

Silence.

No dog and no growling.

I take another step, my movements noisy with the crack of twigs and the crumbling of dead leaves.

And then, even over my self-made racket, I catch the sound again.

A low, threatening growl.

There's an animal nearby, and it's not my easygoing mastiff.

"Shit. Shit, shit, shit." Chanting the curses aloud, I slowly turn in place, searching for the owner of the noise.

But the storm clouds have blocked out the sun, and the woods now sit in a perpetual twilight. I'm surrounded by looming trees and thick, shadowy brush. Plenty of places for an animal to hide. Anything could be stalking me, and I won't know what it is until their teeth tear into my throat.

A wolf? Maybe.

Or a bear? Do bears growl?

Whatever it is, I'm screwed.

What weapons do I have?

A leash.

Yeah, great, I'll just hook it to the wolf-bear's collar and take it for a soothing walk. That'll definitely circumvent any possible death by mauling.

"Stop being sarcastic and think," I mutter to myself, trying my best to push away the rising tide of panic.

People go hiking in Colorado all the time. This isn't the first instance of someone stumbling across a wild animal. There are ways to survive.

I just need my brain to focus enough to remember them.

With frantic thoughts, I try to scroll through my mental Rolodex and come up with what little wilderness knowledge I have. Bears are supposed to leave people alone in the fetal position. So, my best bet is to curl into a ball on the ground and hope it does nothing more than sniff me.

That is, if the animal is a bear.

What if it's a wolf?

Lying on the ground will make it easier to tear me to shreds. I should climb a tree to get away from a wolf.

But bears can climb trees.

Another growl is overwhelmed by a thunderclap, and for a moment, I think my heart gives up in fear. When it restarts, the pounding has adrenaline coursing through my veins, demanding I make a decision.

I choose the only logical solution I can fathom in the heat of my fear.

I need to climb a tree, and once I'm up high enough, I'll get in the fetal position.

Is that even possible?

Will it work?

Time to find out.

This time, when I scan the shadowy forest around me, I look for a tree that will serve my purpose. The wind picks up just as I choose one. I grasp the rough bark of a low branch, pressing the soles of my sneakers against the trunk as I heave myself upward. Hooking my heel on the limb, I'm able to mount the thing with the grace of a hippopotamus using a balance beam.

But I'm up.

Time to get up farther. Pulling myself branch by branch, I'm about halfway to a height I figure is safe from wolves when the clouds dump their load. As my fingers slip, trying to find a grip, I pray to the universe that Bruce is far away from here and that the creature growling at me doesn't like getting wet.

When I judge myself a good fifteen feet off the ground, I perch on the thick branch, hugging the tree trunk and trying my best to curl into a ball. The rain pounds down, soaking my sweatshirt and yoga pants. The steady thrumming of it against every surface drowns out all other sounds. I have no way of knowing if the creature has left or if it's at the foot of the tree, circling me even now.

Lightning cracks across the sky, illuminating the twisting branches in an eerie, disjointed display.

As I shiver in my soggy clothing, I try to think of a way out of this mess.

Staying here is no good. While Colorado fall days are pleasantly crisp, the nights drop close to freezing. Pair that with my wet clothing, and I'm rolling the dice with pneumonia.

But if I leave my perch, I'll probably be met with a pair of hungry jaws.

If I can't stay here but I can't climb down, what other solution is there?

The sky splits with another angry flash, and I flinch at the noise.

With the spotlight-like flash illuminating my surroundings, I realize just how close the neighboring trees are. Their branches overlap, beckoning me like a flimsy rope bridge over a deep crevasse.

The limbs sway in the wind, but I can't help considering their escape. If I'm careful, take my time, lay my feet right, and grab what I need to grab, I could theoretically traverse the tree tops all the way back to Grandma Minnie's yard. The whole time, I would be out of reach of wolves, and even if a bear climbs this tree to follow me, would they try hopping from branch to branch? Surely, they weigh too much to pull off the same maneuver I'm planning.

Sheets of rain crash down harder, causing shivers to rack my body. The cold, wet weather isn't going to help with my grip, but if I don't leave this tree soon, I'm not sure I'll be able to move my quickly cramping fingers.

Slowly, I release my death grip on the tree trunk, moving my grasp to an overhead limb. Then, I inch forward. The wood creaks under my weight, but I can already brush the smallest twigs on the neighboring tree.

I've just about worked up the courage to make a grab for the first step in a long journey when I hear a noise over the torrential downpour.

17

ZOEY

"Zoey! Where the hell are you?"

I don't know if I'm more elated at the sound of another human being looking for me or terrified that they might come face-to-face with the very creature I'm hiding from.

"Here!" My shout comes out desperate and high-pitched, turning it into more of a screech.

"Zoey?" A few seconds later, Warner crashes through the bushes. He's so determined in his searching that he's about to pass right under my hiding spot.

"Wait! I'm up here!"

He whirls around, blinking rain out of his eyes as he gazes up at me. "Thank fuck."

I couldn't convince myself to climb down before when it was only my safety at risk, but for Warner, I accept the danger.

My descent is just as ungainly as the initial climb, plus a few uncoordinated slips because of the wet surfaces. Finally, I'm standing on solid ground, but that lasts only a second before I'm swept up into a pair of strong arms.

"What the hell, Zoey? Do you always climb trees in thunderstorms?"

"N-n-n-o." My answer quivers out through chattering teeth.

"Damn it. You're soaked."

His one arm goes tighter around my waist as the other hand lifts to push wet strands of hair off my face. The warmth of his body seeps through my drenched clothes, and I'm powerless against a happy groan. Hugging Warner after sitting cold and wet in a tree is equivalent to slipping into a sulfurous hot spring.

"You can't make those kinds of noises around me," he grumbles, even as his lips threaten a smile. But it drops away again. "What were you doing?"

"Tr-trying to stay safe." The chattering of my teeth begins to slow as more of Warner's body heat soaks into my chilly limbs. I worry that I'm stealing it all, but my concern isn't enough to detach from him. "I w-was being stalked b-by a wolf-bear."

"What's a wolf-bear?"

"A demonstration of m-my inability to d-distinguish animal noises."

"Zoey." At the tone of his voice, I glance up at Warner, noting that he seems to be battling amusement and frustration. "Normally, I would find your roundabout answers adorable. But right now, you need to be *very* clear. Why were you up in that tree?"

"That's as clear as I can b-be! I heard something growling. It m-might have been a bear. It might have been a w-wolf. I didn't want to hang around to find out. So, I climbed the t-tree."

"You think it could've been a wolf? Did you see any of it? Do you know what color it was?"

Color?

"If I s-saw it, I wouldn't be referring to it as a wolf-bear, would I?"

He nods, but his attention isn't focused on me like it was a moment ago. Right now, he's more concerned with scanning the trees, as if my animal stalker might still be lurking in the shadows, even now.

I really hope not.

Despite the warmth of him, another shiver quakes through my body, approaching a ten on the Richter scale. The rattling is enough to regain Warner's attention.

"Let's get you home and warm."

No argument here.

He shelters me under his arm, and we dive back into the underbrush.

Time drags on longer with rain pouring down, every footstep a squelching mess. The cold numbs all the edges of me. My fingers, the tip of my nose, the tops of my cheeks, and my toes.

Hell in a handbasket, my *toes*. They ache terribly before all sensation disappears.

This is how trench foot starts.

When we break through another cluster of trees, Grandma Minnie's cabin finally comes into view. A few tears might leak out at the sight, but there's no way Warner will notice with my face already drenched with rain.

Once we're on the porch, the overhang blocks most of the rain.

"Do you see B-Bruce?"

My big, dopey dog isn't waiting by the back door like I hoped, and as I stare out into the yard, I can barely make out anything as sheets of rain tear down.

"Is that why you were out there?" Warner's arms come back around my shoulders, guiding me toward the door.

"Y-you don't think the w-wolf-bear g-got him? D-do you?" My chattering teeth are back and won't let me get out a full sentence without stumbling over my words. But I don't care.

No matter how cold I am, Bruce will be equally bad, still stuck in the storm. I pull away from Warner's arms, needing to make another round of the yard.

Did I check under the car?

"Damn it, Zoey. Bruce is inside the house." Warner wraps his warm hands around my chilled ones.

How is he not morphing into an icicle like me? His clothes are just as soaked as mine.

"W-what?"

"Come inside. Bruce is inside."

Despite not fully believing him, I still allow myself to be led out of the cold, wet evening into the warm cabin. But even as the door shuts behind us, I don't see my dog.

"H-he's not—"

"He is. Come on." Warner heads to the guest bedroom, and I follow, stumbling on my numb feet.

Still no Bruce. That is, until Warner gestures I should circle to the other side of the bed.

There, sticking out from under the frame, is a big, beautiful dog butt.

I fall to my soggy knees to peer under the bed, and as I do, I hear a comically loud snore.

"You f-fucking asshole. I almost got eaten for you." The words should come out angry, but I'm too relieved that he's here and safe to be mad.

At the sound of my voice, Bruce snorts himself awake. He does a funny roll-shimmy to get out from under the bed before sniffing at my drenched clothes. Shivers still hit me in random bursts as I scratch behind his ears.

"You went searching for him?" Warner asks as he leans on the doorframe, dripping on the hardwood.

"I guess I forgot I let him back in. And when he didn't come when I called ..." I shrug and push myself up from the floor. My shoes squelch with every movement, and my waterlogged clothes cling to my chilled skin. I imagine Warner feels the same discomfort I do. "I'm going to change."

He nods and makes to move back.

"Do you want to stay? I mean, you should. It can't be safe to drive in that."

Rain assaults the windows, and more thunder rumbles.

"I would ..." Warner gives me a rueful smile before glancing down at his own soggy state.

I grimace. "Sorry. I don't think Minnie has anything that'll fit you." I bite my lip as I brainstorm, coming up with a solution that I might like a little too much. "If you want, I can stick your clothes in the dryer. You can work some toga magic with a couple of towels till then." Maneuvering past him, I open the hallway linen closet to pull out an armful of towels.

"Are you trying to get me to strip, Zoey Gunner?"

I hide my smile by pushing him toward the bathroom. "Technically? Yes. But with fully innocent intentions."

Liar.

Warner chuckles and goes where he's directed. When the door closes, I head to the master bedroom to peel off my damp layers. Painful pricks jab into the soles of my feet and pads of my fingers as I regain feeling. I towel off the cold droplets still clinging to my skin before pulling on a set of flannel pajamas. I'm hugging the soft material close, loving the warm feel of it fighting off the chill, when I hear the bathroom door creak open.

The second before I turn around, I realize I've chosen some of the most shapeless, least sexy garments I own. Then, I do turn, and the regret of my choice doubles.

Triples.

Multiplies by a million.

Because I get a gorgeous view of Warner—damp hair, chest bare, towel hanging low on trim hips, grinning wickedly at me.

And I am not dressed for seduction.

It's hard to remind myself that I decided against getting flirty with this biker when he's one tug of a towel away from being naked.

So. Deliciously. Naked.

And oh, the things I could do with a naked Warner. Like spread him on my bed and lick his—

"See something you like?" he asks with sin in his voice.

I shove my lust away, the task akin to Sisyphus struggling with his boulder.

"Yes," I mutter, ignoring how Warner's grin grows wider. "Grandma Minnie has very nice towels."

18

WARNER

Zoey slips around me, heads into the bathroom, and shuts the door.

While she takes a moment to herself, I move to the main room, pulling back a curtain to check on the storm.

Still raging away. Fine by me. I'll take any excuse to hole up in a cabin with Zoey. Maybe the rain will go on all night, and she'll invite me for a sleepover.

A guy can dream.

Even with my hair wet and my body only covered by a towel, I'm not uncomfortable. But I noticed the thick flannel Zoey cloaked herself in.

I head to the fireplace and spend the next few minutes arranging wood and working to get my lit match to catch the tinder. By the time I hear the bathroom door open, there's a decent blaze going.

"Oh. Fire. That's a good idea." Zoey walks up beside me, holding her hands out to the flames, humming happily as the heat plays over her skin.

She's beautiful, standing above me, firelight bringing out the gold in her chestnut hair.

"I'm going to feed Bruce. Are you hungry?"

I'm on the verge of making a joke about werewolves and dog food when I catch myself, choking on the words and coughing as I do.

Can't believe I almost let my secret slip. Just because I'm comfortable around Zoey does not mean she's ready for that. For all of me.

As I clear my throat, she pats my back, firmly at first, all business, but then she slows. Her hand lingers on the bare skin between my shoulder blades. As if she likes how I feel. I stifle a groan and stop myself from leaning over to bury my face in her stomach. Her scent, which only teases my nose at the moment, would be strong there. One of her warm spots.

Zoey snatches her hand away and retreats to the kitchen. A second later, the clatter of kibble hitting a metal bowl sounds, followed quickly by the heavy padding of Bruce's feet on the hardwood.

"I'm going to make myself a grilled cheese. Do you want one?" she asks.

I straighten from my crouch, making sure to clutch my towel as I do. "Yes, please."

My heart pounds faster, but I command it to calm down. It's just a grilled cheese. She has no idea what other meanings I might find in her offer.

Zoey wields a large cast iron skillet, arranging it on the stovetop. "What is your preferred cheese?"

My brain stutters over the question. "My preferred cheese?"

"Yes. Your preferred cheese. The cheese that you prefer." She opens the fridge, bending at the waist in a distracting display of her round bottom.

"I don't know. You mean, like my favorite cheese?"

"If you want to play around with synonyms, sure. What's your favorite cheese?"

Shit, I don't think I have a favorite cheese either.

Then, she stands, turning to stare at me like this question means something.

I panic. "Um ... yellow?"

Zoey's eyebrows pull down, disbelief staining her face. "Yellow?" Her bare feet are silent on the wood floor as she steps toward me. "Did you just tell me your favorite cheese is *yellow* cheese?"

"Yes?" I offer my most hopeful smile and pray that she moves on to a topic I'm more familiar with.

Want to know my favorite meat? Pulled pork. Favorite beer? Dogfish Head 60 Minute IPA. Favorite dessert? Roderick's rhubarb pie. Favorite smell? Wet Zoey.

Mmmm ... wet Zoey.

As my mind threatens to go to dirty places, the sexy human can't get past my mental block on dairy products.

"Warner, can you name five different types of cheeses?"

"Sure." I'm a liar who likes to dig himself into deep holes to impress a woman.

"Okay. Go." Said woman waits, arms crossed over her chest, her delicious, sweet scent amplified by her damp hair.

"Right now?"

"Yes."

I'm screwed.

"Okay. Well, there's the obvious"—I speak with false confidence—"yellow cheese."

She pinches her bottom lip, as if in deep thought. "Of course."

"And, you know ... white cheese."

"Sure," she responds, deadpan.

"Plus"—I flounder—"nacho cheese."

Zoey presses her fingers to her mouth, as if concerned. "Uh-huh."

"And can't forget"—I talk slowly as my brain scrambles to fill in the blanks—"string."

"Who would forget that?" Her voice is tight with some kind of emotion.

"Not me. And there you go. Five cheeses." My relief is short-lived because she shakes her head.

"Nope. That was four. Yellow cheese, white cheese, nacho cheese, and string cheese." Her slim fingers count each off. "What's one more type of cheese, Warner? Any type. Any at all."

My eyes search the room, as if Zoey had put up a poster, listing all the different kinds of cheeses she expects me to know. I have to know the name of some kind of cheese, right? But my mind is a mess, and finally, I mumble the only other cheese-related thing I'm able to pull out of my panicked ass.

"Sorry, what was that? I didn't catch it." Zoey leans forward, her eyes sparkling.

I clear my throat and commit to my answer. "Goldfish crackers."

Silence descends over the cabin, and I try to look confident, even as I worry that I failed a test.

After long seconds tick by, Zoey crosses the few feet separating us, and suddenly, her arms are around my waist, her forehead pressed into my bare chest. And she's shaking. While I want to bask in the touch of her against my skin, the shaking worries me.

Is she cold again?

"Goldfish—" She chokes on the word, finally tilting her head up to look at me, tears streaming down her cheeks, her mouth hanging open in a disbelieving grin. "Crackers?"

She's laughing. I don't care that it's at my expense. Because Zoey's laughter has recently become my favorite sound in the world.

I affect my most earnest expression. "Aren't they made of cheese?"

Zoey gasps in delight, then hugs me tight as the hilarity rolls through her. She doesn't bother to stifle it, and I love that. The wild abandon. She's glorious and adorable.

Eventually, she pulls away, using a flat hand on my chest to push me toward the couch.

I like where this is going.

But then she backs away.

"Stop looking at me like that," Zoey scolds, even as her lips fight a smile.

"Like what?" Now, I'm grinning.

"Like *that*." Zoey waves at me, all of me, like my entire body is taking part in the expression she claims she wants me to stop.

I *am* shirtless, so maybe she's not wrong.

"All right." I move my hands, bringing them up to cover my exposed nipples. "Better?"

"No!" But she's giggling again. "You're terrible."

"Sorry. Do you want to punish me?" My voice goes low, a touch suggestive.

Flirting with Zoey is as easy as breathing.

"Yes," she says. The conviction in her voice has my cock twitching, and I consider if I need to move my hands lower. "Your punishment is that you have to eat whatever I make you, even if you don't know what it is." She turns back to the stove, as if that'll keep me from hearing her chuckles.

My stomach has no objections. As she preps the mystery food, I return to the fire.

After a few minutes of comfortable silence, during which delicious smells begin to waft from the kitchen, Zoey asks another question.

"How do you keep finding me in the middle of the woods?"

I pause while shifting a log on the fire, considering how best to answer. My guess, she won't appreciate it if I say I followed her smell. Human women would rather you didn't mention you can sniff them out. Plus, I doubt she'd believe me unless I revealed my little hairy secret.

Still, I stick as close to the truth as I can. The idea of lying to Zoey makes my gut twist uncomfortably.

"When you were camping, I recognized your truck. I was worried about you out in the woods at night. So, I followed the trail to the lake and saw your campsite." Only the trail I followed wasn't one humans could pick up.

When I glance over, Zoey is focused on her cooking, but she nods in acknowledgment.

"And today, I came by to say hi. To apologize for crashing your friend date." And to discover if this attraction is mutual. My wolf has locked on to her mating scent, and I can't seem to stop pining after her. "I saw you ducking into the woods when I was parking. Wasn't sure where you were headed, but figured you didn't plan to go far."

I settled on the steps of the back porch, looking forward to surprising her. But Zoey never came back.

"When you were gone for a half hour, I worried." More like panicked. At the first few drops of rain, I knew it wouldn't be long before her trail was gone, and I'd have no way of finding her. "I went the direction you did, hoping I'd stumble onto you."

By the end of my rescue mission, that was exactly how it was. Once the rain came, all traces of Zoey were washed away. I couldn't find her.

A shadow of that panic reemerges now with the memory of her soaked through, clutching that tree as if it might somehow keep her alive.

But I'm pulled out of the fear of what could have been by the approach of her, safe and whole and carrying two plates with steaming sandwiches.

"Well, I don't want to condone stalking. But I'm glad you showed up. Not that you're any more equipped to fight a wolf-bear than I am."

Little does she know.

"What if it had been a mountain lion?" I ask.

Zoey scowls, setting the plates down on the coffee table in front of the fire and pushing Bruce's head away when he goes to sniff at them. "That is ridiculous. Seriously. It's unacceptable. How are there that many large predators in one place?" She collapses on the couch with a disgruntled huff. "Nature should set clear boundaries."

I chuckle, settling next to her. Close, but not touching.

"I'm sure nature will take your complaint into consideration." The plate is warm as I rest it in my lap.

This whole situation feels practically domestic. And I crave more of it.

"Stop stalling." Zoey pokes my shoulder, playfulness in her smirk. "Take your punishment."

"Yes, ma'am." Not that I need any convincing to eat the mouthwatering creation. The smell alone has my stomach demanding its fair share.

One bite, and I'm drowning in savory, melted goodness.

"Fucking hell," I mumble around a mouthful. After I swallow, I gaze at Zoey, sure my obsession with her is shining from my eyes. "What kind of grilled cheese is this?"

"The kind made with my preferred cheese," she teases before taking her own bite and humming in appreciation at her work.

Unfortunately, my sandwich only lasts three more bites. I could eat half a dozen and still want more.

After collecting our dishes and washing them, I return to the couch in front of the fire, thankful for the continuous, loud pounding of the rain outside. Perfect excuse to stick around longer.

"Your clothes should be dry soon." Zoey sits on her side of the couch, legs pulled into her chest, chin resting on her knees as she watches me move around.

"Don't worry about me. I'm perfectly comfortable." Showing off just a bit, I stretch my arms along the back of the couch, lounging in my terry-cloth skirt.

"I don't know how. Even in this flannel tent, I'm still chilly." She clutches the collar of her pajama top closed, and I notice the occasional quiver run through her body. Shiver aftershocks.

There's a blanket folded over the back of the couch. Leaning forward, I pull it off and drape the quilt over her shoulders. But as I begin to move back to my spot, I notice how Zoey sways toward me.

Like she wants to follow where I lead.

"Can I help warm you up?" My voice comes out deeper, with more suggestiveness than I meant. The offer should be selfless, and part of my brain is full of concern for Zoey. But there's still the animalistic section that can think of nothing other than touching her again.

"How do you plan on doing that?" Her eyes trace over me in the way I wish her fingers would.

I clear my throat and try to keep my tone lighthearted. "We could cuddle. I'm an expert cuddler."

Zoey purses her lips, but there's something in her gaze, a mixture of heat and humor, that gives me hope.

"I do love a good cuddle," she admits.

"Then, by all means, use me as your body pillow." I recline on the couch's armrest, determined that if there's any more contact between us this evening, it'll be because Zoey wants it.

Zoey only hesitates for a second before crawling toward me.

I try not to smirk in triumph.

"You're too muscly to be considered a pillow." Zoey crosses her arms on my pecs and rests her chin on them, maintaining eye contact. "Ever considered developing a bit of a belly?"

We're pressed together now, and I've never been more comfortable.

"That's the next part of the plan. First, I use my sexy, muscly body to draw you in, and then I eat as many grilled cheeses as you're willing to make me until I get to your desired level of cushiness."

"So, it's *my* job to turn you into a pillow?" She raises one eyebrow.

I nod solemnly. "I'm here for your pleasure. Do whatever makes you happy."

Zoey's face shifts from humor to curiosity, her attention dropping to my lips. I keep still, holding on to my decision to let her make all the first moves.

But I should've known that Zoey doesn't move without asking questions first.

"Are you this flirty with everyone?"

"No." I shrug. "I'm *friendly* with everyone." Breaking my rule, I reach out to finger a lock of her damp hair, twining the strands around my finger. "I only flirt with you, Zoey Gunner."

Will admitting that I'm flirting scare her off?

She's not running even though I've followed her into the woods multiple times. She's got to know that I'm obsessed.

"Do you want to have sex with me?"

I jerk, her words electric. My wolf shifts, restless for me to take this woman as mine. To claim her.

She continues to stare at me, giving nothing away, while my body heats up, blood pumping thick and fast and south.

"That depends." My voice rasps like sandpaper on rough wood.

"On what?"

"If you want to sleep with me."

"How is that a determining factor?"

I shift, keeping my hardness away from her and attempting a light tone. "Because I don't make a practice of sleeping with women who don't want to sleep with me."

"Good point." Zoey levers her torso up, moving forward so she can loom over me. The flannel of her pajamas drags against my overly sensitive skin. "Okay then. My answer is, I haven't decided."

Hope roars through my chest. I have a chance.

"Tell me what I need to do." The words are hoarse, aching with need.

"Well, now, that sounds like a man whose mind is made up." Zoey smirks, and I grin in response. Once more, her gaze trips down to my mouth. "Can I kiss you, Warner Jameson?"

For a moment, my body freezes, but then the raging heat is back, and my inner beast is howling. I nod, head bobbing more times than needed and with more vigor than normal.

Zoey reaches up, brushing away a curl that teases my forehead. "Just kissing, okay?"

"Just kissing," I agree, willing her to cross the last few inches separating us.

Maybe she sees the desperation in my eyes because she finally dips her head, bringing a wave of her sugary and earthy scent with her.

Zoey approaches kissing as if she's researching. Each brush of her mouth against mine is a question. An exploration.

She teases her lips over mine slowly, learning the shape, turning my brain to mush.

I don't detect hesitation in her movements. The sedate pace isn't because she's unsure. This approach speaks of a certain type of skill. Zoey knows not every kiss is the same, and she's determined to discover the right way to fit our mouths together.

I, the animal that I am, fight the urge to plunder and suck and bite. Instead, I mirror her gentle movements. Showing I can follow her lead.

My restraint is rewarded when she resettles her chest on mine and pushes her fingers into my hair. She nips at my lower lip before licking the spot with her tongue, as if I might need to be soothed after any rough treatment.

A groan spills out of my throat.

Zoey captures it with a naughty kiss, delving her tongue into my mouth.

We twine together in multiple ways. I find my way past her lush lips, seeking out the cool metal of her piercing. The jewelry has been tormenting me since the first moment I saw Zoey. The glint of gold making it impossible to look anywhere other than her sexy mouth.

The attention I pay to it is a tribute. Letting Zoey know I worship every bit of her.

She gasps, tightening her fingers until I feel the scrape of nails against my scalp.

My hands want to participate too. They beg to cup and fondle and undo buttons.

"Just kissing," whispers through my head.

I would never break my promise to her. Never do anything to make Zoey feel unsafe.

So, I simply wrap my arms around her lower back, hugging her. Clutching her close.

At some point, we roll to the side, Zoey's back to the fire, her head resting on a throw pillow. The questioning quality fades from her caresses. Now, there's a relaxed element, a playful one as she sneaks in an occasional teasing bite, snickering at the way I groan whenever she does.

Time doesn't mean much when I'm kissing Zoey. The most attention I give to anything outside our little cocoon of happiness is to appreciate the steady pounding of rain that hasn't let up.

At some point, in a natural progression, my lips wander away from hers, pressing against the curve of her cheekbone, then trailing up to her forehead, where I bury my nose in her loose, damp hair. Breathing her in relaxes me more than any drug ever could.

This is more than attraction.

Which is why I had to fight off a wave of angry fear when I found her hiding in that tree.

When Zoey said the growling might have come from a wolf, I was instantly alert. There aren't any wolf packs near Pine Falls. The pure wolves scent us. They know this is our territory.

Which means the only wolf that could have been nipping at her heels was a werewolf.

And I don't know what that means. The mystery agitates my inner beast.

There's no reason for any of our pack to harass a human. Sure, we maintain an air of intimidation in town. But we don't come after people in our animal forms. That's just begging for wary acceptance to morph into a mortal versus supernatural civil war.

Roderick would be furious.

I remind myself it might not have been a wolf. Zoey said the animal could've been a bear, and there are plenty of those in the woods around here. Wolves and bears don't really discuss property lines.

Normally, I'd be able to figure out the culprit with little effort. That's the beauty of heightened senses. But the rain washed away any scent trail or tracks, and I couldn't even hear Zoey's panicked panting when I found her hiding up in that tree. I almost missed her completely.

What would have happened if I hadn't come along?

She's strong and resourceful, but that doesn't mean she can fight off a bear.

Zoey settles deeper into my arms, and I realize she's dozed off. She buries her face into my neck as if she's seeking warmth from me. I'll give it to her. Every ounce that she needs. The memory of her lips, trembling and turning blue with cold, has my heart pounding heavy and panicked. I tighten my hold and adjust the blanket thrown over us so it sits just beneath her chin.

And I take comfort in the fact that her lips are flushed red now. Warmed to life by lazy kisses.

19

ZOEY

I SLIP one of the cassette tapes into the stereo, hit play, and gaze around the cabin as my mom's voice fills the room. The glimpse into her past along with her superior music taste, makes each new tape an enjoyable surprise. I savor them, only putting one on when I'm doing something productive.

Now, I just need to figure out exactly what my productive activity will be.

The rocking chairs I've been working on are out in the front yard, their new coat of stain needing some time to dry. Minnie's closet is only half cleared, so there's that option.

But that task sets off an ache in my chest, and I shy away from the potential emotions paired with touching her personal items. When I decided to come to Pine Falls, I thought cleaning out the cabin would be a mind-numbing task. I figured as my hands kept busy, I could ponder my relationship with my family and what future I saw for myself.

Hoping I could discover the balance between what I wanted, what I needed, and what I was capable of.

But Minnie's presence is everywhere, and I'm having trouble separating myself from thoughts of her.

After yesterday's interaction with Warner, I'm hoping for less emotion, not more.

After we stopped kissing, I drifted off to sleep. He might have, too, but by the time I woke back up, Warner was staring down at me with a secret smile.

Also, the rain had stopped.

In the moment, I had multiple routes. I could have drawn his face down to mine and started up another round of making out. Or I could have taken advantage of his almost-naked state to move the interaction to the next level. Instead, I declared that his clothes were probably dry and asked if he wanted me to get them.

Warner smirked down at me and said, "Whether I want them or not, it's probably better if I put them on."

When he was dressed, we stood quietly in the kitchen for some time. He watched me, and I tried to think straight with his entire focus trained my way.

"Are you looking for a hookup?" Maybe I could be the type of woman who allowed herself pleasure without diving into deep emotions.

His eyes widened.

"If you are, I'm not judging you," I said. "I might be open to it."

"You *might* be?"

"Well, I'm not about to stroke your ego by begging you for it."

Warner's lips pinched together, but a snort still escaped.

Annoyance spiked through my chest. "Are you laughing at the idea of hooking up with me?"

"No, Zoey. I'm laughing at the idea that you'd have to beg me for anything when I've been following you around like a lovesick puppy."

The statement caused a strange tangle of emotions. I wanted to laugh at the image while I also fought the urge to cringe away at any mention of the word *love*.

It was just a joke, I remind myself.

Warner moved to stand in front of me.

"Let's start off simple. Did you like kissing me?" he asked, his voice a low rumble.

I nodded.

"Do you want to do it again in the future?"

"I would."

A grin split his face. "Then, we're on the same page."

He kissed me, another slow, sweet press of his lips against mine. Then, he snagged my phone, typed his number into it, and left.

And here I am, a day later, wondering if we actually are on the same page. Probably not. That would require me to know exactly what page I'm on. I'm not even sure I know what book I'm in.

I tick off facts as they stand.

I like Warner.

Warner lives in Pine Falls.

Pine Falls is temporary for me.

When I leave, I have no idea where I'm going.

I don't even know when I'm leaving.

These are all facts purely based on me. Warner has his own list, and it might include things like ...

He's not looking for anything serious.

He's looking for something super serious.

He wouldn't mind leaving Pine Falls.

He's set down roots, and he wants to stay here forever.

And on and on the mysterious knowledge goes. If I felt in the right headspace, I'd have no trouble asking him to figure out the answers. Questions are my comfort space.

But I tend to stick to ones I want the answers to, and I haven't figured out what I want Warner to feel toward me.

I like him.

That's fine, I decide. It's perfectly fine to like someone.

The problems pile on when heavier feelings come into play.

"I won't fall in love with him," I say this to Bruce, as if my dog will hold me accountable.

He raises his giant head from his plush bed for a moment before settling down again with a sigh.

Huge help.

Thinking about Warner isn't productive. Time to get back to work.

The only task I can come up with that will keep me busy while avoiding deeper, potentially dark emotions involves cleaning out Grandma Minnie's pantry.

A tower of preserves awaits me.

The glass jars are cool in my hands as I begin to pull them out.

I focus on that feeling, using the chill to drive away the memories of warm, soft skin under my palms. There's even the temptation to press their cold surface to my lips in an attempt to make me forget the heat of his kiss.

Only I'm not sure I'm strong enough to give that memory up.

20

WARNER

"Are you preparing for the apocalypse?"

Zoey doesn't give me the I-have-my-own-bunker-in-the-basement vibe, but I'm looking at a lot of jars of food on her kitchen table. I drove over here after showering off the grime from my workday, wondering what Zoey had gotten into since I'd left her the night before.

Apparently, it's got something to do with jars.

"Not me. I wouldn't put it past Grandma Minnie though. She didn't really trust people. That could easily include the human population as a whole." Zoey clutches a stack of sticky notes with a pen poised above them as she leans in close to examine one of the jars. She writes something, sticks it to the top, and moves on to the next.

I step in closer to read the blue Post-it.

Fruit?

"What's with the question mark?"

Zoey picks up a jar, staring at the contents with a frown. "Minnie didn't label any of these. I guess she knew just by looking. I'm trying to figure out what each one is."

"Why don't you just open them?"

She wrinkles her nose, still glaring at the container in her hand. "People jar meat sometimes, don't they? If I'm going to open a jar of raw meat, I need to brace myself."

"Because you're worried it'll have spoiled?"

"Oh gosh." Her eyes flick to my face, wide in horror. "I didn't even consider that. I will vomit if that happens. Seriously. I will spew." Zoey sighs, her shoulders drooping as she sets down her jar and sticks it with a note that simply has one big question mark. "Of course, I'll probably puke even if it hasn't spoiled."

"You hate raw meat that much?"

"I'm a vegetarian, so yeah." She reaches for the next mason jar.

"A vegetarian?" The wolf in me lets out a silent, disbelieving huff. "How can you be a vegetarian?"

"Well"—Zoey talks as she holds another jar up to the lamp—"I wake up in the morning, and I don't eat meat. Then, I go through the day, and I don't eat meat. And I get ready for bed, and I don't eat meat. Then, I find another day has gone by, and I'm still a vegetarian."

"Smart-ass," I mutter, even as I grin.

She smirks over at me, then offers up the jar. "Any guesses?"

Little does she know, I don't have to guess. With my supernatural nose, I can catch traces, even through the unopened lid. I take it from her and breathe deep.

"Apples and spices. Probably pie filling."

"Seriously? You can tell that?"

I shrug, pretending it's no big deal. "People jar stuff around here. Guess I just know my preserves."

"What about this one?"

She hands me another, and soon, I'm the one picking up each jar, making as if I'm examining the contents with my eyes when, really, I'm using my nose. Zoey follows behind with her pen poised to write down whatever I say.

By the end, every jar is labeled, and I'm hungry.

"I'm assuming by your previous shocked reaction that you are not a vegetarian." Zoey doesn't look at me as she organizes the jars, so she misses my grimace.

A life without meat? My wolf would stage a revolt.

"Pure carnivore. Or omnivore, I guess. Hope we can still be friends." The answer starts off as a joke, but then a tinge of panic pricks at the back of my brain.

What if Zoey is looking for a partner who shares her eating habits?

My wolf shifts restlessly under my skin.

Zoey doesn't seem to notice my unease as she gathers about ten jars together and pushes them toward me.

"On the contrary. An omnivore is exactly what I need. Please accept these jars of meat as a token of my affection." Zoey grins up at me.

She has no idea what she just did.

"You're ... gifting me food?"

"Well, I'm not about to eat it. And I don't like the idea of an animal having died and me just throwing them away. You should take them and eat them. Here, I'll get you a bag." Zoey leaves the room, which gives me a minute to compose myself.

She doesn't know, I remind myself and my wolf.

Zoey has no idea that the offering of food is one of the main parts of a mating ritual. That it's the go-to method for wooing a werewolf.

Doesn't change the fact that my wolf preens under the offering of an edible gift, meanwhile begging me to take her. Make her my mate. Werewolves aren't known for subtlety in the world of romance. Once we figure out what we want, we go for it. I'm trying to strike a balance that won't push her away.

Zoey returns to the kitchen area with a cloth bag and carefully places the jars into the sack, pausing halfway through. "Can you carry this while riding your bike?"

The image pops into my head. Me cruising through town, a shopping bag over my shoulder. If any of my pack mates spot me, I'll be teased for years.

Still, I shrug. Who gives a damn? It's a gift from Zoey. If she wants to shove the food into a hot-pink purse, I'll deal.

"I don't want you to drop them. Let's go put them in your saddlebags."

She finishes packing them and heads for the front door. Bruce follows on her heel, thick tail wagging in anticipation. I mimic the animal, trailing after the beautiful woman.

Zoey is kind of a mess today, wearing loose overalls, paired with a raggedy T-shirt. There are brown splotches all over her outfit, which my nose tells me are wood stains. She's piled her honey-brown hair on top of her head, but random strands tumble free. There's a subtle hint of dustiness to her scent, probably from pulling out all these long-stored preserve jars.

Seeing her like this makes me want her more. She's so ... relaxed. In her element. Zoey never puts on a mask or a show, and every different version of her is just another glimpse of the woman I know I'm falling for.

The sun dips below the trees, signaling the quickly approaching night. Normally, I like working at my uncle's construction site, but today felt like I was counting minutes until I could ride back out here. Until I could talk to Zoey again.

"Hold your helmet."

She's beside my bike, having opened one of the saddlebags and pulled out the head protection I wear every time I ride now. When I accept it from her, our fingers graze, and her eyes flick to mine before she returns to her task. It's not long before the two leather bags are bulging with the glass jars.

"There. Good to go." Zoey smiles up at me, and I'm done holding back.

My arms snake around her waist, pulling her close.

"I've decided how you can repay me for the jigsaw."

Gently, I trace my lips over the lines of her face. I taste her skin, loving the bit of salt mixed with the heat of a rising blush.

"Oh, really?" Her voice sounds light, breathless.

"How would you feel about taking a break tomorrow?"

"Taking a break?" Zoey asks, as if the idea never occurred to her.

"Yes. As in give yourself a day off from the cabin and website designing. Let me take you out."

She tilts her head up to meet my eyes. "Like, on a date? For dinner?"

"More than just dinner. I'm requesting a full day. You and me, going on an adventure. And, yes, a date." I move my hands up her back, admiring the shape of her through her baggy clothes.

"What's an adventure date?"

"You've never had an adventure date?"

I grin down at her, and she responds with a curious smile.

"Can't say that I have."

"Well then, you're in for a treat."

21

ZOEY

TODAY, I officially summited a mountain. For the first time. How have I lived my entire life in Colorado and never done so before?

Probably because I spend most of my time bent over a computer rather than planning adventures.

"Watch your step. You might not think it, but going up is easier than coming down," Warner calls over his shoulder, navigating the rocky trail as easily as if he were strolling down a sidewalk on Main Street.

I keep my eyes on the ground, avoiding any obvious loose rocks. It's not long before the heavy steps start up an ache in the soles of my feet, and despite Grandma Minnie's boots being my size, they still rub blisters on my soles. The Band-Aids I put on a little while ago only help so much.

Still, I smile.

By the time we reach the trailhead, the sun is just sinking below the trees. The sweat on my skin makes me shiver, and I hurry to unlock my truck.

"You cold? I brought this." Warner sets his backpack on the bed of the truck and rummages in it until he pulls out a large black sweatshirt. It matches his outfit for the day—black baseball hat, black T-shirt, black athletic shorts, black socks. The only bits of him not noir are his brown hiking boots.

I wonder if the gothic color palette is his attempt to maintain his biker persona, even as he dresses for hiking.

What would it take to get him in a pink shirt?

He'd still probably look badass.

The sweatshirt is large on me, and I enjoy the soft warmth of it while ignoring the fact that I'm stinking it up with my sweaty body.

A shower is going to feel so good.

"Thank you."

I grin up at Warner, and he leans over to press a kiss at the corner of my jaw, his hot breath against my ear making me shiver for an entirely different reason. He's even kind enough to not wrinkle his nose at what I'm sure is a cloud of reek hovering around me.

Once we're on the road, me behind the wheel, Warner hands me a granola bar after hearing the grumbling complaint from my stomach.

"You had fun, right?" he asks between bites of his own snack.

I nod. "Are there more hikes like that around here?"

Around is a relative term, seeing as how we drove a good hour to reach the trailhead. But the views were worth it. Every time we broke through the trees, we could gaze for miles at the gorgeous, jagged tops of the Rocky Mountains. Living in Colorado my whole life, I had taken for granted the beautiful views from my apartment and car window. I never considered how much better they'd be if I got off my butt and climbed a little higher.

Warner chuckles, reaching over to give my knee an affectionate squeeze. "Plenty. We can climb as many mountains as you want. Especially if I get to hike behind you."

"Why's that?"

"Because I love the view." He draws his hand further up my thigh before giving another squeeze.

I snort and bat his hand away. "I'm driving! You're going to make us run off the road."

He leans back against his door, laughing.

Warner is tearing into his third granola bar when things go wrong.

The car sputters and shakes and stalls out. The engine goes quiet. Luckily, the brakes don't fail. I slow us down, coasting to the side of the road until I can bring us to a full stop.

"Did you run out of gas?" he asks, leaning over to study the dashboard.

"No! I still have half a tank."

I reach past the steering wheel to tap the display. Only the second I make contact, the gas needle quivers and drops to land on the E.

"Fuck." My forehead hits the steering wheel. "This truck keeps finding new ways to screw me over."

"It's okay, Zoey." A warm, comforting hand cradles the back of my neck. "We're maybe forty-five minutes from town. I'll just call ..."

His trailing off has me turning my head, and I catch Warner frowning at his phone.

"You don't have any service here, do you?"

His grimace is all the response I need.

I reach for my own phone, and my half hope is quickly dashed. No bars for me either.

"Okay. New plan," Warner says. "You chill out here, and I'll jog down the road till I get service or find a gas station. We passed at least one on our way out."

"See, I like that plan, except for the part where I'm required to sit in a truck alone on the side of the road with no cell service for who knows how long. Plus, look at you." I gesture at his body.

Warner glances down at himself, brow wrinkling in confusion.

I reach over to pluck at his dark shirt. "Walking on the side of the road, dressed like this, you're practically begging to get hit by a car. Meanwhile, I"—my hands wave at the colorful leggings I chose to wear on our hike—"could easily act as a traffic cone. We'll both go."

He sighs, but his lips curl into a reluctant smile. "Fine. We'll both go."

We're maybe five minutes into the walk when I remember why I was so happy to get back to the truck. My feet protest each step, demanding I elevate and ice them rather than continue using them to move myself forward. And then my muscles remind me that I spent half the day climbing a motherfucking mountain.

I know I'm slowing us down, but I try really hard to not wince every time my boot hits the asphalt.

"Zoey?"

"Mmhmm?"

"How ya doin'?"

"Great. Peachy. Top-notch."

"Liar." Warner stops me with a hand on my shoulder. "Your feet are killing you, aren't they?"

I try not to groan or sink to the ground. "They might be staging a slight protest."

"Here. Climb on my back." He crouches down, offering me a tempting ride. But I wave him away.

"No, no. I'm fine. See?" Picking my foot up high, I start a dramatic march. But the second my boot sole hits the ground, a variety of pains shoots through my foot, and I gasp at the shock.

"Yeah. Totally fine," Warner deadpans. "But maybe you could humor me?"

I'm tempted. I can feel myself giving in. But before latching myself to him, I announce my insecurity. "I smell."

A full day of hiking means I sweat through my clothes. And now, that sweat has dried into a crusty layer on the fabric and my skin. The only barrier between him and the stench is his sweatshirt, which I'm already mortified about dirtying up.

Warner straightens, steps into me, and ducks his head to bury his nose against my neck. His arms wrap around my waist, foiling any chance of escape. I'm forced to stand still as he breathes in my stink.

Then, shocking the hell out of me, I feel his tongue flick against my skin.

I groan, clutching at his shoulders, briefly forgetting all the different ways my body hurts. All I can concentrate on is the ache between my legs.

How long until I can convince him to soothe that?

"I like the way you smell," he whispers, hot lips brushing against my uneven pulse.

"Oh." It's all I can manage, and when he lets me go to offer his back again, I don't hesitate to climb on.

A few minutes pass in silence as Warner carries me down the dark road. His back is so warm; I melt against him. Copying his action, I find myself burrowing my nose into his neck to breathe in his smell. There's the salty tang of sweat, but that only seems to enhance his natural, delicious, manly scent.

He walks at a steady clip I never would have been able to maintain.

"How are you not tired?" I mutter.

A chuckle rumbles through his back and makes my nipples tighten. I wonder if he can feel them pressing into his skin.

"My job is manual labor. I'm used to going all day."

"That's some impressive stamina." I twirl one of his curls around my finger, enjoying another vibration of his deeper laughter.

"You have *no* idea." The heat in his voice makes me want to clench my thighs together. Only my legs are currently wrapped around Warner's trim waist, and all my muscles are slowly transitioning into jelly.

"Maybe I want to find out," I tease him, pressing a light kiss against his neck.

"In the middle of the woods? I never—" He stops mid-sentence and mid-stride, his whole body going tense.

The rapid shift takes away my happy, melty feeling. "What's wrong?"

Warner doesn't answer at first, turning his head slowly from side to side, as if searching for something. Then, he starts walking again. "Keep talking." His voice comes out gruff and only makes me more anxious.

"What should I talk about?" *Was it my flirting that upset him? Does he want me to talk about something less suggestive?*

"Anything. Just keep talking."

"Okay." I rack my brain for any topic, feeling put on the spot. So, I blurt out my first thought. "I want to make you something."

"What do you want to make me?" he asks.

"That's the problem. I want to make you something, but I don't know what. I make a lot of things, but I can't figure out what the right thing for is *you*. You're this sexy biker dude, so it's not like you're looking for me to crochet you something."

"You could crochet me something." Even though he's still scanning the dark woods surrounding us, I hear a smile in his voice.

"Really? You'd wear ... a scarf?"

"Sure, I would."

I grin, happiness glowing in my chest. *He'd wear a scarf I made him.*

"All right then. Do you have a preferred color, or do you trust me to pick for you?"

Warner doesn't answer. Instead, he stops, loosening his grip on my legs so I slide down his back to stand again. I'm proud that I only wobble a little bit, even as my feet pound with pain.

"Are you okay? Did you pull something in your back?" Despite his claims, I can't help thinking his rapid change in demeanor came on because of me.

"Do you have your bear spray?" Warner asks.

"Y-yes." I slide off my backpack, digging around until I find the bottle. "Is there a bear?"

Warner shakes his head. "Not a bear. Mountain lion. Female. Three cubs nearby."

Any other time, I might ask Warner how he picked up all those details. But my mind gets distracted when he tosses his baseball hat to the side and strips off his shirt.

"Do mountain lions not attack naked people? That can't be right." But I have to admit, I only read up on bear safety.

Warner doesn't address his choice to disrobe, even when he toes off his boots and shucks off his shorts. The guy stands in only his boxer briefs, and I'm not even able to admire the view because we're being stalked by a deadly animal.

"I thought she might leave us alone, but with her cubs nearby ..." Finally, he looks at me, his expression more serious than I've ever seen it. "When I say go, you need to run as fast as you can back to the truck."

Something about his phrasing throws me off. "You mean, *we'll* be running to the truck."

Another brief headshake. "Mountain lions are hardwired to give chase."

"You want to use me as bait?" I squeak.

"No. I'm going to distract it while you get away."

He steps away from me, as if giving me room to sprint. Even with my aching feet, I know I can still run, especially if my life depends on it.

But not if it means leaving Warner behind to deal with a wild animal on his own.

"I'm not doing that."

"Zoey"—his voice is so tense that I can almost imagine cracks running through it—"I know you're scared, but I promise I won't let it get to you."

"I *am* scared. But I'm not leaving you. Two against one is better odds." I flick off the safety on the bear spray, trying my best to make out any moving shapes in the darkness.

"I can take care of myself," he growls.

Now, I'm the one shaking my head. "I don't believe you."

"Zoey, I need you to go. Now." There's an edge of desperation to his command.

Since I can't find the animal in the shadows, I turn my attention and my glare to Warner. "I won't leave you."

Agitation radiates off him. As he steps toward me, I watch his amber eyes flit between my face and the surrounding woods. In the fading twilight, his irises look black.

When Warner grips my upper arms, I half expect him to give me a shove toward the truck. Instead, he backs me up against a thick tree trunk.

"They attack from behind. Stay here. Keep your spray out. And take this." Faster than I can blink, Warner crouches by his shorts to pull an item from his pocket and is back at my side. He presses a large pocketknife into my hand. When I flip the blade open, I find it's longer than any of my fingers and looks wickedly sharp.

Then, he steps away, backing into the road.

"What are you doing?" I ask. "Is this some weird making-yourself-bait thing?"

Warner drags his desperate gaze over me. "Don't be scared, Zoey. Please, trust me. You don't need to be scared."

"It's a mountain lion! I can't help it!"

But Warner isn't looking at me anymore. Instead, he stares upward, where the half-full moon peeks through the canopy of the trees.

Before I can ask another question, something in the night shifts. At first, I'm sure it's a breeze. Until I realize the darkness itself is moving, like the night has gained corporeal form.

The mass sticks to Warner.

He lets out a ragged breath. I hear a series of snaps, then my ears pop.

I blink. Once. Twice. Then rapidly, as if that'll fix whatever has gone wrong with my eyesight.

Because there is definitely something wrong.

Warner is gone, and in his place stands a large, fearsome gray wolf.

22

ZOEY

MY FIRST THOUGHT is that Warner was mistaken. It wasn't a mountain lion following us. It was a wolf.

But then an angry hiss sounds from the other side of the road a moment before a huge feline stalks out of the tree line.

Does the whole animal kingdom have a vendetta against me?

Before I can brainstorm how to fight both a wolf and a mountain lion, the cat leaps through the air. But not at me. The deadly claws swipe at the wolf, who bares its teeth and dodges away, only to circle back and snap at the lion's haunches. The two creatures trade a handful of near-miss attacks until they finally come together in a horrible collision.

Their sounds rip through the night air, loud enough to hear despite the crashing of my pulse in my eardrums. Even though I'm standing still, I find myself panting as I watch the terrifying display of claws and teeth gouging into fur and flesh.

Finally, after seconds or hours, the mountain lion breaks away. The animal limps slightly and gives one last defiant hiss before it slinks back into the shadowy night.

The fight was so distracting that I momentarily forgot the danger I was in, but it all floods my mind now as the wolf turns to face me.

The creature approaches slowly, stalking me even though I'm in the open. As it reaches the edge of the road, I remember the bear spray I'm clutching. When I raise the bottle, the wolf stops.

Then, shocking the hell out of me, it lowers its head and offers an almost-apologetic tail wag.

But if I thought I knew what surprise was, it is nothing compared to the terrified wonder as I once again watch shadows come to life. This time, the second time, the transformation is undeniable. The form of the wolf ripples, as if we'd sunk to the bottom of a pool and water shifted around us. Then come the rapid cracks, and my ears pop.

Warner crouches on the edge of the asphalt, butt naked, hands held up in surrender.

"Please don't spray me," he murmurs. "I'm just going to grab my clothes."

Carefully, he stands and walks to the pile he made a moment ago. Before the mountain lion came and fought the mysteriously appearing wolf. In the dim light of the moon, Warner's skin glows pale white, making the claw marks oozing blood even more pronounced.

My mind tilts and sways, and I try to clutch at some form of reality before I lose my balance and tumble into insanity.

But there's no sense to be made.

"Zoey?"

He's in front of me, dressed again, hands reaching. I flinch away, stumbling to the side.

"Did you put psychedelic mushrooms in my lunch?" My voice is a desperate rasp. "Am I tripping?"

Warner lets his arms drop and slowly shakes his head. "I know this is a lot. But we need to keep walking. I don't think the lion will come back, but I can't be sure."

Walking is such a normal thing.

Can I really do something so ordinary? With him?

Numbly, I nod, then push myself to take a few unsteady steps.

His hand stretches toward me again, but I move away, into the middle of the road.

"Y-you walk there." I gesture to the side of the road he's standing on with my hand that's holding the bear spray. Then, I shuffle across the middle line, claiming the opposite side before trudging forward.

"Zoey ..."

I ignore him, trying hard to concentrate, all the while too scared of what this new world is.

Men turning into wolves? That's fiction. Fantasy. Something from a strange dream.

A dream.

That must be it. I fell asleep at some point, and this is a twisted story my mind has made up.

In a dream, I don't need bear spray, so I let the canister drop from my slack fingers. I use my free hand to pull up a sleeve and pinch my arm.

I don't wake up.

No matter how much it stings.

Next, I try pinching the meaty part of my thigh, digging my nails in with a bruising grip.

But I don't blink and find myself in the bedroom of Grandma Minnie's cabin.

I'm still dragging sore feet through dead leaves on the shoulder of an empty back road with a wolf-man's eyes burning into the side of my head.

Everything about this dream seem so solid. So real. I'm fully entrenched in it.

My reeling mind reasons that a simple pinch won't wake me up. I need something as painfully real as this nightmare to shake me out of it. If I want this confusing world to disappear, I have to shock myself.

The handle of Warner's knife has grown warm in my palm. The blade shines as clear as a mirror as I raise it, setting the well-sharpened edge against the skin of my exposed forearm.

23

WARNER

The smell of blood hits my nose the same moment I hear her gasp.

Less than a second, and I'm at her side, staring in horror at the deep cut on the back of her forearm. My knife drips a delicate crimson stream, seeming to enjoy what it stole from her.

"What happened?" I press my bare hand against the wound, desperate to keep any more of her from leaking out.

Zoey stares up at me with wild, confused eyes. "Why can't I wake up?"

The desperate words are their own kind of blade stabbing deep into my chest.

"This isn't a dream, Zoey."

Moving slow, so as not to scare her, I ease the knife out of her grip. I toss it into the woods, not able to look at the weapon a moment longer. With careful hands, I extend her arm and examine the wound. The slash is long, but not as deep as I first thought. Quickly, I strip my shirt off again and wind the fabric tightly around the wound, hoping to staunch any further bleeding.

"You keep stripping," she mutters, gaze still distracted.

A tiny flare of hope streaks through my chest. Maybe she isn't completely terrified of me. Maybe I can save this.

But the second I'm done tying off my shirt, Zoey steps away from me, heading farther down the dark road. I follow.

Guilt tears at my insides. She cut herself because of me. I should've done more to prepare her for the change. Or done a better job of convincing her to leave me to deal with the mountain lion. Instead, I gave in to my secret desire to share every part of myself, and now, she won't look at me.

It's hard for me to fully comprehend how outlandish this is for her. The existence of werewolves has always been a truth in my life. The supernatural is my norm.

I glance over and clench my jaw at the sight of her walking with her arms wrapped around herself protectively, head bowed, a slight limp to her walk. What I wouldn't give to go back in time, reverse the clock fifteen minutes, when I had her body against mine, her laughter in my ear, her lips on my neck.

Zoey probably wants to reverse the clock for a whole different reason.

She just learned the world she'd thought she knew has more hidden bits to it. Dangerous, frightening secrets.

"You can ask me questions," I offer, "if you want."

Anything to get her talking again. But she seems uninterested in my olive branch as time and silence stretch between us. Just as I'm contemplating tearing out my hair by the roots, she speaks.

"How long have you ..." She waves a hand, taking in the whole of me while keeping her eyes resolutely on the ground.

"Born this way. Although I didn't turn for the first time until I was thirteen. A whole other level of puberty."

Instead of engaging, she moves on to the next question. "What do you eat?"

"Well, I'm not a vegetarian."

She doesn't laugh. Not even a twitch at the corner of her mouth.

I try not to sigh. "Nothing out of the ordinary. Although I do hunt small game when I'm in wolf form. And the pack will sometimes take down a deer or two."

"The pack?" Her voice ticks up a notch, and a new wave of bitter fear mixes with her scent.

I cringe. Probably shouldn't have revealed there's more than just one werewolf roaming Pine Falls.

If Roderick knew how easily I let that slip, I'd be in for a major beatdown. There are plenty of humans in town who are in on the secret, but those are locals. People who grew up knowing about us. Roderick is not a fan of *outsiders*, as he refers to them.

"We keep to our own," is one of his favorite mottos.

Zoey's breath hitches out faster than a moment before. She's panicking, and it's all because of me.

"I know this is freaky. But I swear you're not in a horror movie." I try out my most charming smile. "More like a paranormal romantic comedy."

Zoey's gaze flicks to the deep gashes on my chest, to the dark, ominous woods surrounding us, finally settling on my face with an incredulous stare.

I get her point.

When Zoey looks away again, we fall back into silence. She trudges forward, and I wince with every limping step she takes, fighting the urge to wrap a supportive arm around her waist.

"Who else?" she whispers.

Zoey never whispers.

Even still, I can't give her what she wants. "I can't name names."

Another few minutes of no talking, then, "The Dark Moon Riders."

I flinch. It wasn't a question though.

"Full moon?"

"We get a stronger urge to change those nights. The pack will head a few miles out of town and then go on a hunt."

"Silver bullets?"

"You looking to kill me?" I ask with an almost-hopeful laugh.

At this point, I might welcome her attack. Anything to bring back the vibrant, confident woman I know rather than this scared, confused shell of her.

"Are you looking to kill *me*?" She stares up at me now, her eyes so wide that they seem to take over her face.

And I lose all ability to joke about the situation.

"Fuck. No. Gods, no." I want to grab her arms, pull her into my chest, clutch her close until she understands how desperate I am about her.

But that would only scare her more.

Instead, I offer my vulnerabilities. Hoping to put us on more even ground. "Silver or lead. Gets us all the same. We're not immortal." I gesture at the cuts on my chest that throb with a constant sting. "Just more durable. And stronger."

"And warmer," she murmurs.

The comment came out so quiet that I doubt she meant for me to hear. But I did, and I hope.

As the minutes pass, I watch her from my peripheral vision, silently begging for more questions. But she's curled in on herself, and she doesn't pay any attention to me.

My body aches in a variety of ways. The bruises and cuts from my fight nag, but I know they'll be half healed by morning. It's the pain underneath my rib cage that's getting to me. The ache spreads, radiating out from the spot where Zoey has taken up residence.

If I don't find a way to earn her forgiveness, her acceptance …

I'm not sure when Zoey became such an important piece of my life. It could be as early as the moment she started crocheting while surrounded by bikers. All I know now is that the thought of her walking away makes me want to howl in denial.

I'll fix this. Somehow.

I've opened my mouth to say something, anything, when a set of headlights flashes up ahead.

The two of us freeze, and then I'm stepping up to the road, waving my arms frantically.

Soon, Zoey and I are sitting in the warmth of Mr. Morrison's pickup as he pulls back out onto the road.

"You kids are real lucky I decided to drive out tonight instead of waiting for the morning. Just think, you'd be walking another three miles before the gas station. And, shit, Warner, your chest is mangled. A mountain lion, you said? They normally don't go for you big fuckers. Gotta look out for kids and dogs, but not hulking fellows like you."

"Pretty sure it was a mama with her cubs nearby," I answer when the old man pauses to take a breath and a puff from his cigarette. The window is cracked for him to blow out his smoke, but the whole cab still reeks of it.

Not that I'm complaining. I'm just happy that Zoey's off her aching feet and safe from any other wild creatures roaming the woods at night.

Except for me, of course.

She sits wedged between the two of us on the truck's bench seat, doing her best to sink into the recesses of my sweatshirt. I'd find the sight adorable if it wasn't for the fact that she's so quiet and studiously avoiding making eye contact.

"Well, that'll do it. You'd better get those cuts seen to. Don't know what that cat had on its claws. Could get infected."

"We'll be stopping by the doctor first thing after we get Zoey's car up and running."

Mr. Morrison nods, flicking on his turn signal as the gas station comes into sight. Once we're parked, he climbs out, heading inside. I try to catch Zoey's eye, but she keeps staring at her lap.

"You okay to wait here while I grab us some gas?"

A nod.

"Do you want anything else? Food or a drink?"

She shakes her head, eyes firmly shut.

"Are you okay?"

No response.

I resist the urge to gather her in my arms, following Mr. Morrison instead. He stands with me in line as I purchase a canister and pay to fill it.

"Your girl okay? Seems shook up."

I clear my throat, thinking of what to say. As far as I know, Mr. Morrison isn't one of the townspeople who knows about the wolves. I give half an answer.

"The mountain lion was a lot for her to take in. She's from the city, you know?"

He nods and walks with me back out to the pump.

Not long before we're back out on the road.

Once we pull up alongside Zoey's old Toyota, she finally speaks, offering Mr. Morrison a quiet, "Thank you."

"No problem, Miss Gunner. I owed Warner here a favor anyway. He was the first one up on my roof when it sprang a leak. And in the middle of a rainstorm, no less! Glad I'm finally able to pay you back." He claps me on the shoulder as I wave him off.

The old man waits around while I fill the tank. Once Zoey starts the engine and it comes to life, no problem, he gives us a salute and continues on his way.

And we're alone again.

24

WARNER

"Which way is the doctor?" is the first sentence Zoey speaks to me since we got back in her truck a half hour ago. The entire drive to town was silent. No talking. No questions. She didn't even flip on the radio.

Ignoring my growing apprehension, I tried to let Zoey have her space. Her sense of safety.

Hearing her voice now is a soothing balm. At least I still exist a little bit to her. And she hasn't pulled the truck over and run away screaming.

"You'll want to head down Main Street until you get to the corner The Wild Rabbit is on, then make a right."

She nods, bringing the car to a stop at a red light. No other questions come, but I'm jittery with the need to fill the void, and my mouth moves on its own.

"I've met most of the nurses and doctors who work at the emergency clinic. They're all nice. They'll have you stitched up in no time."

Zoey blinks over at me, drops her gaze to the arm I clumsily wrapped for her earlier, then flicks her eyes to my chest. "I thought we were going for you."

The toneless way she speaks ramps up my anxiety, but I cover my worry with overenthusiasm, grinning wide as I reassure her, "Don't worry about me. This is nothing." I wave a dismissive hand at the claw marks. "They'll be healed up in a day or two."

The light changes, but we don't move forward. Zoey stares at my chest as if it's a puzzle she can't solve.

"Zoey, the light's green." I keep my voice gentle, afraid to startle her.

She shakes her head, but still wears a dazed expression as she accelerates.

We get halfway down Main Street before she parallel parks in front of Sawdust and Supplies.

"What are you doing?" I ask.

"You said you didn't need to go to the doctor," she mumbles, eyes on her hands.

"I don't. But you do. And I'm not sending you there on your own."

Her forehead drops, coming to rest on the steering wheel. The dejected curve of her body screams exhaustion, and I silently curse myself for not insisting on driving. I thought she'd prefer to have the control of being behind the wheel.

I climb out of the truck, close the door behind me, and circle around to the driver's side. Zoey barely turns her head when I pull her door open. She stares at me blankly as I unbuckle her seat belt.

"Scoot over."

She follows my order slowly, as if navigating through quicksand. Once she's situated on the passenger side, I take over driving the rest of the way.

Our time in the emergency room is surprisingly quick.

Without anything to hide my scratches, the nurse on duty insists on disinfecting and wrapping the wounds before handing over a T-shirt with their logo on it. I let her, especially because getting worked on means I stay close to Zoey as she has her arm stitched up. But with us being the only two at the clinic, we're treated fast, and it's not long before I'm driving us to the Gunners' cabin.

Only once I've parked do I realize Zoey has dozed off. I'd like to think she fell asleep because she's so comfortable in my presence. But this is pure exhaustion.

"Zoey?"

She doesn't twitch.

I walk around to her side of the car, popping open the door. Her head lolls to the side at an angle that'll give her major neck pain if she stays in that position much longer. Again, I try to rouse her.

"Zoey? We're home. You ready to go inside?" Gently, I smooth my hand down her arm.

She stirs, shifts, then settles again on the old leather seat.

Clearly, Zoey is already in bedtime mode.

My fingers smooth stray hairs away from her closed eyes. "Do you mind if I carry you inside? You can keep sleeping."

I'm not sure if I expect a response or not. I don't like the idea of hauling her around when she's likely to wake up, terrified that I'm touching her. But she needs to get inside somehow.

Just as I've braced myself to give her a firmer shake, she tilts her head up, eyes opening halfway to reveal blurry, unfocused pupils.

"Don't eat me," she mutters just before her hand reaches to clutch at my shirt.

I don't know whether to laugh or wince. Either way, when her fingers curl in the material at my chest, I take that as acceptance of my offer.

With my supernatural strength, Zoey's weight is easy to handle. I support her under her knees with one arm and pull the top half of her close to my chest with the other. The shape of her feels exactly right, and I suddenly want to walk away from the house rather than toward it. I could spend the entire night carrying her around, just to enjoy the feel of her luscious body against mine.

But I've pushed my luck way past the acceptable marker tonight. If I have any chance of winning her over, the best thing is to get her into bed, where she can sleep off the shock of everything that's happened.

As we approach the front door, I hear deep, warning barks. Not even Bruce's call is enough to wake Zoey. She's completely relaxed in my arms as I fumble with the keys in the lock. The minute the door is open, Bruce is there, sniffing my leg. Once assured I'm a welcome guest, he passes by, trotting into the front yard.

I leave the dog to take care of his business as I head toward the master bedroom, using my superior night vision to navigate without turning on any lights.

The old mattress squeaks as I lay Zoey down on top of the quilt. She turns into the soft surface, eyes never opening.

Maybe I should leave her now, walk out the front door.

But she's still dressed for hiking, smelling of sweat and blood. I don't particularly mind the scent, but I imagine Zoey won't be too comfortable spending the night in her boots, coated in grime.

With businesslike motions, I untie her shoestrings and tug off her boots, setting them on the floor beside the bed. Taking a trip to the bathroom, I soak a washcloth in warm water, then return to Zoey's side. After wiping her face, neck, and arms, I decide I've gone as far as I should, not wanting to cross more lines than I have. There's an extra quilt at the foot of the bed, which I unfold and drape over Zoey's prone form.

I'm just tucking in the edges when her eyes flutter open to land on my face.

"Was it a dream?" Her voice comes out in a whisper filled with cracks, and the answer I have to give is all the more painful for it.

"No, it wasn't."

She buries her head in the pillow, promptly sliding back into sleep.

And I leave her, heading back into the main room of the cabin. A scratch at the door has me letting Bruce in. I fill his food bowl and refresh his water. There's a notepad hanging magnetically on the front of the ancient fridge. I write Zoey a message, letting her know I took care of Bruce. My hand pauses before the next sentence. I want to write, *Call me when you wake up.*

But if she doesn't call, does that mean we're done?

I'm selfish, not wanting to give her such an easy out.

We can get through this. It's not the end.

I write, *Feel better.*

As I step out into the cool night air, I try not to panic at the memory of Zoey's vacant stare.

Will she ever see me the way she did before today?

Or am I just a monster now?

25

ZOEY

THE DARK RIVER pulls at me.

The current isn't as strong as it's been in the past, but the pressure is there, dragging me down. My limbs feel heavy as I crawl from my bed to open the back door and let Bruce out. I sit at the dining room table, and an hour passes without my fingers lifting to work on anything.

I stare a lot. I sleep a lot.

With no immediate deadlines, I don't bother going into town to work.

But I take my medication. A small floating log that helps keep my head above water.

And over and over, I remind myself of one thing.

I am *not* crazy.

Finally, one morning, as I stare at the teapot I haven't added water to, a thought creeps into my mind.

If I don't check in with my brothers soon, they'll think something is wrong. If they think something is wrong, they'll try to save me.

Do I need saving?

A spark of anger flares to life, inspiring me to light a burner on the stovetop and set water to boil.

I am not some damsel in distress. I do *not* need saving.

I just need to process this new world I live in.

Warner turned into a wolf. That has to be a fact or else it means that I'm experiencing a mental break.

Of course, if I tried to explain the events of that night to anyone, they'd most definitely suggest I talk to a doctor. Probably more like insist.

"I found out this town is full of werewolves, and then I stabbed myself to prove I wasn't in a dream," I mutter while spreading raspberry jam on toast. One of the many jars Warner identified for me.

How could the helpful construction worker also be a mythical monster? The two identities clash.

Maybe not so much when I add in the fact that he's a member of a biker gang.

A *werewolf* biker gang.

This shouldn't be real.

But as I wrap myself in a cardigan and take my breakfast out to the front porch, my mind feels clearer than it has in days. Like the cool mountain air is finally permeating my lungs, giving my brain enough oxygen to function.

Plus, the itchy stitches in my arm prove the incident with the knife happened. Then, there's the short note from Warner about feeding Bruce, which proves he was here that night.

I was not dreaming.

But werewolves? Seriously?

Bruce snuffles in the dewy grass, investigating scents only a dog can smell.

Or a wolf.

The warmth from my mug presses into my palms, driving away a stiffness in my joints. Slowly, conviction creeps through me, pushing at the dark doubt that threatened to pull me under the surface of that inner river.

It's time. Time to prove that the events of that night are exactly as I remember them.

The best way I can think to do that, other than storming into Warner's apartment and demand he transform again, is to call my mother.

No way could someone as curious and determined as Selena Gunner spend eighteen years of her life in this town and not know about the supernatural creatures living here.

Problem is, when I head inside and pick up the old rotary phone, there's no dial tone.

"You've got to be kidding me." I set it in the cradle harder than I meant to, then snatch it back up to hold it against my ear.

Nothing.

Growling and muttering about shitty, old cabins with questionable wiring, I pocket my cell phone and head out the back door. Bruce lumbers along at my heels. When I reach the tree house ladder, he plops down with a sigh, content to have found a new napping spot in the early morning sun.

I climb up, lifting myself through the hole in the floor.

After performing a quick sweep for spiders, I settle on the weatherworn boards and pull out my phone. There're two whole bars of service. Lucky me.

And of course, as soon as those little bars of service appear, my phone starts pinging like it's gone to a rave. Text after text after text. A whole array of phone calls and voice mails.

Quickly, I read and listen to them all, discovering I was right. Another day of radio silence, and I would've had a family reunion with the Gunner boys.

Briefly pausing my mission, I hop on the group text, assuring them that I am in fact alive and not in need of an intervention. Four immediate responses, like they don't have lives or jobs.

Guess I did worry them.

After a few more reassuring messages, I make the call I climbed into this tree for.

My mom picks up after the second ring.

"Sweetheart! I've missed your voice! And you're calling from your cell? You must be in town. How is it there? Found a good place to buy a cup of coffee? When I was a teenager—"

"Mom! Stop talking!" That comes out with more bite than I meant.

But after my discovery and this nagging worry about my mental health, I'm finding it hard to be happy-go-lucky. Besides, if I hadn't cut her off, she'd have gone on for another ten minutes with barely a break for breathing.

"What's wrong?"

At least she knows I wouldn't snap for no reason.

"Sorry. I didn't mean to yell. It's just ..." Different words play across my tongue, trying to fit themselves into the right question. I'm assuming that having grown up in Pine Falls, Mom would know about the wolves.

But wouldn't she have told me if she did?

And if she doesn't know, she'll probably think I'm losing it, down here alone in this cabin. Then, she'll tell my brothers, and there'd be no stopping them from migrating down here en masse.

Still, my need to solidify the truth overrides the experiment to distance myself from my family.

"When you lived here, did you ever notice anything ... strange?"

"You're being vague, sweetheart. It's making me worry."

A frustrated sigh gusts out of me, and I consider a different angle. "A few days ago, the truck broke down outside of town. When I was walking, a mountain lion attacked my friend and me."

A gasp filters through the phone. "Are you all right?"

"I'm fine. The mountain lion didn't touch me." I conveniently leave out the part where I decided to wound myself. "It didn't get a chance to."

"That's a relief. How did you get away?"

"A ..." I take a deep breath. "A wolf saved me."

The truth of that statement rings through the small tree-top enclosure. Up until this moment, I didn't allow myself to fully examine what had happened. The giant mythical-creatures-are-real blockade kept my mind from remembering that my life had been in danger and Warner saved me.

I might be dead if he hadn't transformed into his other shape.

Warner revealed a secret, terrifying part of himself to rescue me.

"Are you saying one of the werewolves fought off the mountain lion?"

My mom's question might as well be a defibrillator, shocking me back to the present moment.

Silent seconds sit between us as my lungs struggle to pull in air.

Then, I'm gasping.

"You knew!" If this tree house were any bigger, I'd stand up and pace, but all I can do is pound the floor with an angry fist as disbelief has my words coming out choked. "You knew there were werewolves!"

"Of course I did." She could be discussing the weather or a mildly interesting work story from the nonchalant tone she uses to flip the whole fucking world on its side.

"Of course? What do you mean, *of course*?!"

"Sweetheart, there's no need to worry about them."

I clutch my head, trying with all my might to keep my brain from exploding. "Werewolves are real. Supernatural creatures are living in Pine Falls. And you didn't think this was something you should *share* with me?" By the last sentence, I'm back to shouting because this is what my family does to me.

With the rest of the world, I can keep a cool, logical head. But put me in a room with another Gunner, and soon, I'll be hollering until my throat is hoarse.

"I did tell you."

"No, you sure as hell did not!"

"Of course I did. The werewolf stories were your favorites when you were younger."

Maybe I am in fact losing my tether to reality. Seems like that trait runs in the family.

"Mother"—I speak slowly to keep from yelling, but now, my voice comes out tighter than a guitar string—"parents tell their children *fairy tales*. Make-believe stories. Why would you think I, now twenty-seven-years old, would accept them as fact?"

She huffs on her side of the line, as if I'm the one being unreasonable. "It's not my fault you didn't want to believe that werewolves existed. I never told you they didn't. If you had asked me—"

"Why would I ask you that?!" I'm shouting again. "That is not a normal question!"

"Sweetheart, you know I'm all for dramatics, but I really think you're overreacting."

That's the final push. There is a precarious balance between horrified disbelief and manic hilarity. My mom has always been a master at upsetting my scales.

I laugh.

I laugh as if I were dying and this was my last chance to find something hysterical. I laugh to the point of tears and gasping. I laugh because I can't contain the unfathomably absurd love I have for my outrageous mother.

She's too ridiculous to stay mad at.

So, I laugh.

The phone slips out of my hand at some point, probably when I curl into the fetal position to keep my ab muscles from cramping. The device lies on the tree house's floor, a foot from my head, and I can hear my mother's voice calling out from the speaker.

"Zoey? Sweetheart, are you still there?"

I reach for the phone, pressing it to my ear. "Yeah, Mom. I'm here."

"And you swear you're not hurt?"

"Werewolf saved the day, like I said."

And now, I'm thinking about Warner coming to my rescue.

Right after he stripped down to his briefs. Guess that last bit of fabric tore off like Hulk's shirt when Warner shifted.

The replay of the fight flashes through my mind, and my humor fades at the memory of claws and teeth and blood.

I'm not hurt. Not really. But he was sporting some major lacerations.

And what about infection?

Can werewolves get sick? Can they catch rabies?

I open my mouth to ask my mom, but then slowly close it. For some reason, getting intel from her almost seems wrong.

If I want to learn about werewolves, I should go straight to the source.

That is, if he'll forgive me for treating him like a pariah after he saved my life.

"Well, you were lucky one of the pack was nearby. They tend to only hang around their own kind."

That spikes my curiosity, but I've already made my decision about who to bring my questions to. Maybe if Warner refuses to talk to me, I'll reconsider pumping my mom for info.

But right now, I have some groveling to do.

"I know. I was lucky. I'm sorry, but I have to let you go, Mom. I need to meet up with someone."

"Wait ..." She pauses for a stretch. "How are you feeling?" Mom clears her throat. "There, I mean. You're ... okay?"

Her hesitation speaks to how worried she is for my mental well-being.

I don't see a point in rehashing the last few days of my shocked zombie state, so I give her the current truth. "I'm fine. This is helpful, I think. Being on my own for a bit."

"Oh, okay. Well, I miss you."

"You already said that." I smile.

"I could say it ten more times, and it still wouldn't cover it. You've left me outnumbered. It's all men, all the time."

I chuckle. "Even if I were there, they'd still have the majority."

She rattles on a bit longer about my brothers and my father before we finally hang up.

As I climb down from the tree house, my brain is already strategizing.

Guilt sits like a heavy muck, coating my heart. The way I reacted, maybe it would be understandable to some, but I pride myself on how open-minded I can be.

That night, I treated Warner like a freak.

The need to apologize tugs me toward Pine Falls, but I resist the urge, instead returning to the cabin. Words aren't enough to make this right. He needs to know I'm not saying some empty platitude.

Plus, there's the whole thank-you-for-saving-my-life situation.

That werewolf had better brace himself for a Gunner apology.

26

ZOEY

I'M WEARING A DRESS. Which means I shaved my legs.

Do werewolves care about shaved legs?

When you're one second away from a pelt, does a little stubble really matter?

Still, I like the smooth feel of them rubbing together. After working out my apology, I decided to put effort into my appearance.

These past few weeks, a good day was when I showered and wore a clean pair of jeans. Most of the time, I'd just throw on some leggings and a T-shirt because I knew I'd get dirty.

But today, I'm not sorting through my grandmother's dusty belongings.

Today, I am apologizing to a werewolf.

Just as soon as I find him.

A little bell jingles as I walk into Sawdust and Supplies. There was no answer when I knocked on the side door that leads up to Warner's apartment, so I'm hoping to find him helping out behind the counter. But the only Jameson around is Rebecca, who's stocking light bulbs on a front shelf.

"Zoey. You need something?"

"Yes. I'm looking for your son."

She turns to me with a raised eyebrow. "Warner? Have you lost him?"

"In a way." I breathe through my guilt.

As more and more time passes and as I walk in the radiant sunshine of the day, the crippling fear from that night seems even more ridiculous.

Well, not the terror from being attacked by a mountain lion. That's completely reasonable. But the way I let myself become frightened of Warner.

The same guy who had given me a ride to my crochet club the first time I met him. The guy who had lent me some of his power tools so I could refurbish an old dining room table.

He'd hiked through torrential rain to find me in the woods.

He'd fought a mountain lion for me.

The man who's more likely to smile than scowl.

After the way he held me, the way he kissed me ...

And I treated him like a dangerous animal on the verge of an attack.

Somehow, I suppress my grimace of self-disgust and focus back on Rebecca. I wonder if I should explain exactly why I'm looking for him. If Warner was born a werewolf and my mom knows about them, no doubt Rebecca does too.

Last light bulb put in place, the shop owner gets down from her stepladder. But she doesn't take a few cautious steps down.

She jumps.

The distance can't be more than two feet, but there's something about the graceful way she lands, without even a wobble, that sets my mind wondering.

Is Rebecca a werewolf too?

The question almost slips out when I remember Warner's words. *"I can't name names."*

Would Warner get in trouble if the pack found out he'd revealed himself to me? And where do loyalties lie? Rebecca might not be the best person to tell the events of that night.

"I think I hurt his feelings, and I just wanted to apologize. Apology gift included." I gesture at my bag, which isn't the gift. I doubt Warner has any use for a tote that reads *Girls Just Wanna Purl.*

Rebecca shrugs, strolling toward the register. "I'm sure you're overreacting. Warner is the most easygoing person you'll ever meet. If you were talking about one of my other boys, maybe I'd believe you. But I doubt Warner is moping somewhere. No need to worry yourself."

Her words don't sit right with me. Is that how she sees Warner? Too laid-back to ever get hurt by anything?

Still, I wonder. *Am I blowing this out of proportion?*

I dismiss the thought.

No matter his reaction, I know how I acted toward him was wrong, and I need to tell him that.

"Either way, I'd like to apologize."

Rebecca watches me with an unreadable expression before answering, "Well, he's not here. Not sure where he's gone off to. You can leave your"—she eyes my bag with a baffled expression— "apology gift with me. I'll give it to him when I see him next."

I smile, even as I shake my head, thinking of how to explain my reason for turning her down. "That's kind of you. But the gift isn't exactly finished yet." At her raised eyebrow, I add, "Plus, there are the words. That I need to say. To make it a real apology."

Her second eyebrow joins the first, and I conclude that I'm not making much sense. Better escape before I lose Rebecca's goodwill. Getting on her bad side would make my many trips to the hardware store an adventure in discomfort.

Those are the worst kinds of adventures.

"Thanks anyway! I'm sure I'll be in soon. Almost out of stain." Waving over my shoulder, I head back out onto the street.

Fingers crossed, I try knocking on Warner's door again.

Still no answer.

I could text him. But selfish me doesn't want to give him a chance to avoid me if he's hurt or mad after how I treated him. This is an ambush apology.

He *will* know how sorry I am.

Then, after that, he can cut me out of his life if he still hates me.

A surprisingly large pit of despair roils in my stomach as I consider the idea.

When did Warner fuse himself so thoroughly with my happiness? He's basically a supportive ninja. Sneakily helping me until I come to rely on him.

Ninja biker werewolf. A force to be reckoned with.

The rumble of a bike pulls me out of my twirling thoughts. I stroll up to the curb, anticipation quickening my heart rate. Focusing on the far end of Main Street, I spot a black blur approaching. As the rider gets closer, for a minute, I think I've found my wolf. There's the familiar build on top of the dark bike.

But then I realize two things.

The biker has a shaved head.

And I can see this because he's not wearing a helmet.

Definitely not Warner. If it were, I'd have more to say to him than *sorry*.

As the rider passes by, I realize it's Warner's older brother, Roderick. We've never officially met, but Warner pointed him out to me. The brothers are shaped similarly with broad shoulders and lithe forms. Roderick has the advantage of a couple of inches, and his sheared hair, paired with a perpetually stern expression, sits him firmly in the *intimidating biker* category.

Good thing I've decided to never let men intimidate me.

Plus, there's something about the way he holds himself that's familiar. I realize he reminds me of someone I know. Someone I love.

And I don't mean Warner.

Roderick pulls into the gas station a block down. I head his way, certain he's my next best lead.

As I walk toward him, I consider my approach. If I'm right, then Roderick might share a similar personality with my oldest brother, Abram.

Stoic. Stern. Unerring sense of responsibility.
Best way to get them to do what you want is call on their honor.
Strategy solidified, I find myself smiling.
Time for an introduction.

27

RODERICK

THE WOMAN LIVING in the Gunner cabin smells like my brother.

Not enough to designate her as his mate. She only has a hint of him on her skin. As if they spent time together recently. Time where he touched her. Held her.

I find this curious and potentially disconcerting.

Warner enjoys the act of the playboy, but he's stopped following through these past few years. He smiles. He flirts. He goes home alone.

Until this woman. The one who keeps her eyes on me as she approaches. She smiles as if I were her friend. There is no fear or hesitation on her face, nor do I smell it on her. Even with the gasoline fumes rising from my tank, I should be able to discern the acrid scent of fright.

Nothing.

"Hello. I'm Zoey Gunner. You're Roderick Jameson." Even though she doesn't frame it as a question, the woman waits for me to acknowledge the statement. She stands just on the other side of my bike, watching me expectantly.

I nod, but only barely.

"Do you know where Warner is?"

After a moment, I offer another silent nod. Nothing more. And I wait, expecting her to get annoyed at my refusal to offer up the information.

Instead, her smile tilts in relief. "Good." Then, she steps closer and adopts an interrogative slant to her brow. "Roderick Jameson, do you love your brother?"

I pride myself on the ability to keep my thoughts from showing. As the leader of the pack, it is important that I act as the unmovable, reliable axle that everything else turns on.

But this unexpected question hits my blind spot, and I find myself jerking back in surprise.

She wants to know if I love Warner?

He is my blood. My pack.

He is also the one person in my life who I believe I could say anything to without fear of judgment. Not that I experiment with that. But the knowledge of the freedom provided by that connection still exists.

Do I love him?

Of course I do.

Intrigued despite myself, I nod.

"As you should." Her satisfied grin gives me the sense I would've gotten chastised if I had answered any other way. "Warner deserves your love. And he deserves to be treated with respect, doesn't he?"

For the first time in my life, I don't feel like a wolf.

Instead, I sympathize with a rabbit, slowly being led into a trap.

Still, I nod.

"Exactly. So, when this wonderful man, deserving of respect, who you love dearly"—her addition of words has me suppressing a reluctant smile—"is wronged by someone, he is unequivocally owed an apology. Wouldn't you agree?"

Something has me hooked, and I wonder what her conclusion to these questions will be. I'm already caught up in the snare, dangling helpless from a branch.

I nod.

"Good. To review, we've established that you love your brother. If he is wronged, you believe he deserves an apology. And that you know where he is at this very moment. Have I got that all right?"

The truth would be easy enough to give, but for some reason, I feel like this woman has tricked me into revealing valuable information.

Still, I don't lie if I can help it, and I can't imagine any way another nod would put me at a disadvantage. So, once again, I tilt my chin.

"Perfect. Now, I must admit, with a great deal of chagrin, that *I* have wronged Warner. And by our previously established logic, you would be betraying your morals and the love you have for your brother by not telling me where he is. Because if I don't know where he is, I cannot apologize. And Warner *deserves* an apology."

I was right. She is trickier than a fox.

Zoey Gunner hasn't even bothered to ask me to point her in the direction of my brother. She's simply explained why I am going to.

If she had asked, I could've said no. But now, that would only make me look like an ass.

Plus, I think I can see why Warner is fascinated with this woman.

He might have some competition if he doesn't put a more permanent version of his scent on her soon.

We stare at each other, the stalemate only breaking with the click of the gas pump to let me know my tank is full.

"Auto shop. Third Avenue." I give her the answer like it pains me when, really, I'm not all that reluctant.

Warner is a grown man. I don't need to protect him from intelligent women. He needs to learn to protect himself.

Zoey's face settles into a grateful smile. "Thank you. I'll let Warner know what a devoted brother he has."

"Don't do that," I respond too quickly, already hearing the relentless teasing Warner would subject me to if he found out the circles this woman talked around me.

She shakes her head with a smirk. "Brothers. All right. I'll keep your secret. But only because you were helpful."

I watch her peer around until her eyes alight on the street signs.

Zoey offers me a nod of her own, which I pick up a slight teasing edge to.

Guess I did nod at her a lot.

I'm just about to throw my leg over my bike when—

"Roderick"—she's on the curb now, staring at me with a stern expression—"you should be wearing a helmet."

Then, she turns and strolls off, thankfully focused on tormenting another Jameson.

28

WARNER

I'VE BEEN WORKING on this bike for two hours, the practice normally meditative. But I can't get Zoey out of my mind.

The events of a few nights ago play on a loop in my head, an old black-and-white monster movie, jerky and poorly constructed. Like my decision-making.

She's gone.

I fucked up my chance with the only woman who's ever made my wolf as restless as the full moon. For the first time in a long time, the beast and I are in complete agreement.

We want Zoey Gunner.

Then, an image stutters across my mind. The brave, enthusiastic woman of my dreams, staring at me with blank eyes. My teeth grind together at the memory of her complete shift in personality. Zoey shut down, as if she needed to protect herself.

From me.

She thinks I'm a monster.

She's not wrong. A portion of the town thinks the wolves are terrifying creatures to be placated so we don't fill the streets with blood.

Not that we ever would.

But we could.

Sometimes, I worry my wolf will wake and demand more control. That the animal in me will overwhelm the logic of my human half. That I'll do something to deserve fear.

A vibration fills my ears with a rumbling noise. It takes me a moment to realize I'm growling.

Just like a monster would.

I clear my throat, pushing the impulse down. Luckily, Harvey has the radio blaring hard core metal, so he didn't hear my slip. The guy knows about wolves, likes us even, but there still aren't many humans comfortable with being reminded.

I was naive to think Zoey would accept my truth as if I were merely showing her an ugly birthmark. A small blessing that she didn't run away, screaming her head off.

And if I'm being honest with myself, I could've kept it from her.

If I had been firmer about her leaving, she might've gone.

Or I could've stayed in my human form and fought the lion off that way. Would've taken longer and been bloodier, but I'm strong, and I heal fast. If I had gone that route, I might be with her now, getting nursed back to health. Zoey would probably be babying me this very moment. Maybe kissing my bruises to make them feel better while scolding me for being stupidly reckless.

Instead, I'm sitting here, alone, covered in grease, mourning the loss of her.

All because I wanted her to know. In that moment, the decision to reveal my secret seemed easy. Certain the connection I could almost see between us must mean something. That she wouldn't cringe from me, but accept what I was with open arms and her excited smile.

Sometimes, I can be completely dense.

Also, sometimes, I hallucinate. Because there's no way that Zoey Gunner just walked into Harvey's shop. Especially not looking like *that*.

The woman I know wears sweatpants, maybe jeans, and paint-stained T-shirts or possibly a soft sweater.

Zoey Gunner does not wear dresses. Definitely not white ones that hug her waist and have trails of copper buttons down the front. The material sways around her thighs, showing off a set of legs meant to make a man fall to his knees and crawl behind her in the hopes of catching an ounce of her attention.

And so I know, for certain, this cannot be her.

It's impossible she'd come into this shop with her honeyed hair down, curling softly around her shoulders. One small section is pulled away from her face with a glittery clip.

This can't be her.

Because that would just be cruel.

But the world is often cruel, which I know for a fact when, over the scent of motor oil, I finally pick up on that lovely tease of earthy maple-ness.

A loud clang reverberates around the shop, and I realize I dropped the wrench I was holding when my hands went slack.

The flesh and bone and temptation incarnate Zoey starts at the sound, her eyes finding mine.

"What the hell is wrong with you, boy?" Harvey rolls out from under the car whose oil he's been changing. "You throw my tools around, and I'm gonna kick your ass out of my shop."

"I'm sorry, sir." Zoey steps around the front end of the car, coming into Harvey's view. "That's my fault. I think I surprised him."

With a customer in the mix, the mechanic changes his scowl to a smile real fast.

"Well, hello there. I didn't hear you come in. How can I help you?" Harvey stands up, all six foot three of him. He's an intimidating figure, still sporting a good amount of muscle, even in his early sixties.

But Zoey doesn't step back. She just tilts her head and smiles up at him.

The sight reminds me of that first night, her sitting in The Rabbit Hole, surrounded by bikers, but not showing even the inclination toward fear. I'm just as fascinated with her now as I was then. If she came here to tell me to leave her alone, she's making the experience good and torturous.

Does she know I've been running the perimeter of her property each night?

I needed to know she was safe. And that she hadn't packed up to leave.

"The fuel gauge in my truck is broken. Would you mind taking a look?"

Of course. She's not here for me. Zoey was probably just as shocked to find me in this shop as I was to see her walk into it.

"Sure, ma'am. You parked out front?"

"Yes. Thank you." I expect her to lead him toward the door. Instead, she steps farther into the shop. Closer to me. "But the main reason I came to your garage was to talk to Warner. Would you mind if I took a moment to do so?"

Harvey's eyes go wide as he glances between the two of us. Luckily, he's not one to pry. "Sure. Give me your keys, and I'll see what I can find while you two ... talk."

"That would be perfect." Zoey rummages in the bag hanging on her shoulder until a clinking of metal sounds out. She hands the keys over, then strolls across the shop toward me.

Harvey gives me a final incredulous stare before heading outside.

Then, we're alone. And I experience one of the rare moments in my life where words don't come easy.

I should apologize.

But before I can figure out what words to say, Zoey takes over.

"How are the cuts?" Zoey waves her hand toward my chest.

Because I'm still reeling, my brain decides the best way to answer is to pull up my shirt to show the already completely healed gouges. Zoey leans in close, her eyes tracing over the pink scar tissue, where the mountain lion got in a few good hits.

"Fascinating," she murmurs.

My skin grows warm under her close gaze. Her scent seeps into my nose, so strong that I taste the sweetness on my tongue. My mind starts to drift into a dreamlike state, where I can float happily along and pretend she'll never walk away.

When Zoey straightens, she tilts her head to the side, staring down at me. The corner of her lip twitches, and I home in on the movement, the sparkle of her piercing hypnotizing.

"You like taking your shirt off around me, don't you?"

Is she flirting?

Hope heats my chest as I let my clothing settle back into place.

"Maybe I'm hoping you'll do something about it one of these days," I say.

Now, both of the corners of her mouth twitch, but she twists her lips until the movement disappears.

"Do you mind if I ..." Zoey glances around the shop, her eyes resting on a stool off to the side. One that's supporting a box of greasy, used rags. Seeing as how she's wearing a dress the same white as the tablecloth at a five-star restaurant, I expect her to dismiss the option as a seat, but she moves toward it.

"No, wait!" I jump up from my stool, making as if to grab her and keep her away from the mess, only to realize at the last second that my hands are covered in motor oil. I hold them up, skipping backward so I don't ruin the glorious image of Zoey in her pristine outfit. "Just ... here ..." Skirting around her, I reach for the box of rags myself.

But lifting it only reveals dark smears on the metal seat. That won't work.

"What's the matter?" Zoey's voice next to my shoulder has me jumping away again, clutching the container of dirty rags to my chest. "Is that stuff expensive?" She moves closer, her head bent to peer into the box.

"No. This stuff is garbage."

"Then, why are you hugging it?"

"I'm not."

Zoey smirks.

She's right; I am hugging them. I drop the box and kick it under a workbench.

"Can we sit now? Or do you have more garbage to embrace?" Her eyes twinkle, and one of her perfectly clean hands reaches for the stool.

"No, don't!" Again, I lunge in between the offensive seat and the perfect woman, using my body as a shield and trying to herd her back.

Zoey stops attempting to get at the stool. Instead, she stares resolutely up at me. The glitter is gone from her eyes, leaving behind sadness.

"I thought this might be how it went. And I understand. You don't want me here. I promise I'll go, just after—"

"Not want you here? Are you fucking with me, Zoey?"

She flinches back, and I regret how harsh my words came out. I'm flustered, my wolf is agitated, and the combination is turning me into an ass.

"Of course not," she says. "But you clearly don't want me to sit with you." Her wave takes in me and the stool I'm blocking.

"No. That's not ..." I trail off, a frustrated growl clawing at my chest. But letting the animalistic noise out would only make things worse.

"Just give me a minute to say my piece. I swear I'll leave you alone after I'm done. You'll never have to see me again." She crosses her heart with a finger, as if making a solemn vow.

Zoey leaving is the worst outcome I can think of. I'd rather have her in this room, shouting at me.

"I'm dirty." My oil-stained hands come to rest on my hips. "This whole shop is dirty. And you're walking in here, wearing white, like some kind of perfect fever dream. I'm just trying to keep you from ruining your dress."

Silence stretches between us as Zoey examines my face. She must pick up the sincerity because the upset fades from her gaze.

"Can I see?" she asks, reaching forward, her fingers wrapping around my wrists.

She raises them up, taking a close look at my filthy palms. The nails are crusted with grime, my skin appears dark and uneven under the coat of motor oil. Even now, I can see traces of the black rubbing off on her fingers.

Any second, Zoey will wrinkle her nose, loosen her grip, and ask where a sink with soap is.

At least, that's what most people would do.

It's my fault for forgetting that Zoey isn't most people.

Before I can stop her, she presses both of my palms against her boobs.

"What are you doing?" I choke, snatching my hands back, even as they beg to stay where she put them.

Zoey glances down at her dress, a smile creeping over her lips as she eyes the black prints now marring the pristine white fabric. A snort escapes, and then the next moment, she's doubled over in laughter.

The happy sound rings through the shop, bouncing off every surface.

I want to laugh with her. I want to moan at the loss of her perfect dress. I want to drag her into my arms and kiss her senseless.

Instead, I hold myself back because I'm still not sure where we stand. Clearly, Zoey isn't terrified of me, which I take as a good sign. But that doesn't tell me much. It's completely possible she convinced herself that night was a dream or a fear-induced hallucination. If that's the case, I'll have to decide if the best option is to just let her continue living a normal life, oblivious to what my truth is.

Zoey calms down, shaking her head at me as she walks back to the bike I was working on. I follow, a step behind.

"Sit," she instructs me, and I drop down on the low crate I was using as a seat.

I expect her to grab the greasy stool, but she ignores it to come stand in front of me. I have to look up at her from this angle, and my eyes are level with the destructive handprints.

"I can't believe ... your dress." I mourn the loss.

Laundry isn't one of my skill sets. I'm usually just proud of myself when I separate lights and darks, but I still know that grease and white clothing don't mix. It's a shame, no matter how good the shape of my hands look, clasping her chest.

"Don't worry about it. I got it from a thrift shop, and I think it shrank last time I washed it. Half the buttons are ready to pop off."

Now that she mentions it, I do notice how the material strains more where it covers her chest.

The sight makes me want to moan for a whole other reason.

"Warner?" A cool finger hooks under my chin, tilting my head up until I meet her warm brown eyes. "Werewolves?"

No selective amnesia then.

I clear my throat. "Yep. Werewolves."

She grins down at me, the expression sheepish and beautiful enough to make my heart hammer loud in my ears.

"I'm sorry I went robot on you."

"Robot?" I hesitantly return her grin.

"Yeah. I had some misguided autopilot setting to think stabbing myself was a good idea."

The reminder of Zoey holding that knife, covered in her own blood, has the happy emotions in my chest fizzling out. My eyes flick to her arm, where the stitches are visible. At least I'm not picking up any scent of infection.

Yeah, werewolves can smell that.

"You were scared."

"I short-circuited. A robot that lost its batteries. Completely shut down. *You* were scared, and I'm sorry."

Her fingers play with the hair that curls on my forehead. The movement is so soothing that I almost lose my train of thought. But I catch hold of it.

"*You're* apologizing to *me*?"

How could she think there's anything she needs to say sorry for? I'm the one who fucked up.

"Yes, and I brought you an apology gift."

"Zoey, stop. You don't ..."

But just like the night I met her, she ignores me as she rummages through her bag. And once again, she pulls out some kind of crochet creation.

"It's a scarf." She leans forward, laying the item around my neck.

As far as scarves go, it's not the best. The ends barely fall past my shoulders, and one side still has a crochet hook stuck in it.

Not that I care.

"I love it."

"Liar." She smiles and goes to take it back, but I lean away from her, wanting to keep the gift. Zoey slaps my chest lightly, laughing as she does. "Stop it. I'm not done with it. I just started this morning when I realized I needed to apologize, but I didn't think my crochet speed should dictate when I tell you I'm sorry."

I sit up straight again, letting her remove the half scarf.

"You keep saying you're sorry, but you don't need to. How you reacted ... that's reasonable. I should be happy you didn't try drowning me in holy water."

Zoey tucks the craft back into her bag before looking at me.

"You're right. I need to stop saying sorry." Her fingers land on my lips when I go to speak. "And I need to start saying thank you."

A gentle growl sneaks out before I can stop it, rumbling against her hand. Her mouth opens with a little gasp, but she swallows and pushes on.

"We were in danger that night, and you protected me." Zoey bends at the waist, bringing her face close to mine and threatening to overwhelm me with her intoxicating scent. "Thank you, Warner."

Fingers drop away, only to be replaced by her sweet lips. She brushes a gentle kiss against my mouth at first. A happy hum spills out of me, which seems to give her permission to lean forward and wrap her arms around my neck. To straddle my lap.

To drive me fucking wild.

29

ZOEY

Making out with Warner was not part of the plan.

But I think it's a fantastic addition.

I meant to just brush my lips against his. A quick thank-you.

But once I get a taste, I'm a ravenous shark, scenting blood.

Okay, not the sexiest metaphor. But seeing as how I want to consume Warner, I still think it's apt.

"Zoey." He groans my name against my mouth as I settle on his lap, my thighs spread and circling his hips so I can press closer. My dress rides up, leaving just the thin cotton of my underwear as a barrier between my center and his rough jeans.

My name on his lips is like hearing my favorite song on the radio. I want to hit replay, but I know I have no control over when I'll hear it again. So, I enjoy it while I can.

My fingers tangle in his soft hair. My tongue traces the seam of his mouth. My hips rock, pressing into his groin.

He gets hard beneath my onslaught.

And a stab of guilt rips through me at the realization, so quick and painful that I tear my lips away from his.

Warner flirts and charms, and he's given me a few kisses in the past, but that doesn't mean I have free range to maul him.

"I'm sorry. Hell, I'm attacking you." Bracing my hands on his shoulders, I try to rise from his lap, which turns out to be a much harder maneuver than getting there. Probably because I don't want to go.

An unhappy growl pairs with clasping hands on my ass, holding me in place. When I stop trying to get up, Warner buries his nose in my neck, and I can feel him breathing against me, his hot breath raising goose bumps all over my skin.

"You're not scared of me?" His whisper comes out hoarse, and arousal threatens to choke me at the feel of his mouth moving against my throat.

"No."

"And you"—his fingers flex, gaining better purchase on my butt— "want me?"

Want him?

My imagination takes hold, playing out the rest of this scenario. How he'd reach in between us to unzip his jeans. Then, after pulling my underwear to the side, he'd push into me. And I would get to ride him all the way to orgasm town.

The fantasy makes me lightheaded, and I almost forget to answer. But when he pulls his head back to meet my eyes, my abrupt, question-prone nature takes hold.

"I want to have sex with you. When do you get off work? And do you want to have sex? With me?" I'm not sure how I'll handle a rejection, but it's better to get a clear answer up front.

Warner blinks, and his hands relax. But they don't push me away. Instead, he trails his touch up and down my back.

As if to soothe me.

Oh no. Here comes that clear rejection.

"I'm not at work. Harvey lets me use his garage to store my projects." He nods over my shoulder at the gutted bike. "We can leave whenever you want."

So, that's a yes?

"Now. I want to go now."

Warner's mouth curls into a breathtaking smile, as if I just told him he won the lottery.

Not that I'm giving myself airs.

But just as fast as it appears, the joy on his face begins to dim.

"No! What's happening in your head?" My fingers press into his cheeks, as if I can force that glorious smile back on his face.

A chuckle sneaks out of his chest, but his eyes contain a wariness I want to make disappear.

"Zoey ... you wanting to sleep with me ... is that part of the apology?" He hesitates through his question.

"The scarf is your apology gift. Not my vagina." I cup his face. "I want to get you naked because you're handsome and funny and sexy and sweet." I start breathing heavier as I list his positive qualities. The image of him sprawled in a bed beneath me, all his clothes gone, has that ravenous shark feeling coming back full force. "Can I be on top? Do you mind? It's my favorite position. Or do we need to do it doggy style? I like that way, too, but only if we have a mirror so I can see you. Do werewolves have sex like humans?"

Realizing I've rattled off a whole list of questions, I bite my tongue and give Warner a moment to respond.

The guy stares at me with his mouth slightly agape, which just reminds me of how good he tasted. Not like any food. More like salt and heat.

And hell in a handbasket, I am hot. Feverish really.

When I left the cabin wearing a dress, I dealt with the chill of the fall day by blasting the heat in the truck and trying to stay in the sunnier spots when I was outside. But now that I've twined myself around the living furnace that is Warner, the combined heat of his body and raging force of my lust threatens to melt my brain.

Without warning, Warner stands, clutching me to him with his hands on my ass. Once he's upright, he loosens his hold so I slide down his body. My legs wobble as I gain my footing, and I learn that it's possible to get drunk on another human.

Or a supernatural creature.

Normally chatty, Warner is giving me nothing back, and his silence starts to pluck at my introverted anxiety.

This is one of the reasons I'm prone to turn into a hermit. No one can refuse to talk to you when you're alone. They can't hurt your feelings if you never try to be their friend. Or invite them into your bed.

My half-melted brain starts plummeting into the realm of self-doubt and formulates an escape plan. I'm so befuddled by Warner's nearness, the only get-out idea that I can think of is *run*.

Just as I take an unsteady step toward the exit, Warner's palm presses into my lower back, and he drops his head to whisper in my ear. "Yes, you can be on top. If I minded that, then I wouldn't deserve your time. We'll definitely do doggy style too. I'll buy a mirror if I have to. And werewolves have sex like humans, except that I have more stamina so you'll have to let me know when you need to take a Gatorade break."

Oh shit. I might have just come.

"I can fix it," a gruff voice announces, shocking me out of my lust inferno. The owner of the shop—Harvey, I think Warner called him —lets the door swing shut behind him as he reenters the garage.

Thank goodness I didn't succeed in fucking Warner here.

Still, an awkward silence descends over our group when Harvey's eyes land on me and his face gets a deer-in-the-headlights look. I glance down at myself, remembering the handprints on my boobs.

In the last few minutes, I have acquired a variety of stains on my dress. There are streaks on my waist and the skirt, where I pressed up against Warner, and I'm betting I have a few more clear handprints on my ass.

But who cares?

I'm about to fuck the guy. So what if the foreplay got a little dirty?

Harvey clears his throat, and a frown mars his whiskered face. "Your talk go well?"

"It's not—" Warner starts, but I cut him off.

"Just look at me." I twirl to show off the variety of oil stains on my once-pure-white dress. "Of course it did!" I end my display by letting all my excitement for what's about to happen infuse my grin. "Now, if you wouldn't mind letting me know the damage, we can get settled up. And then I can take Mr. Handsy home with me."

30

WARNER

WE END up at my place, mainly because it's closer.

And I *need* to be alone with Zoey as soon as possible.

Anticipation thrums between us, but we haven't kissed again since Harvey's sudden appearance broke us apart.

I'm biding my time.

"How long have you lived here?"

Zoey trails her fingers along the back of my sofa. I imagine those fingers giving my skin the same treatment.

I'm so frantic for her that I've situated myself on the opposite side of the room, trying to get enough distance that I can remind myself how to treat this gorgeous woman with respect rather than ravage her like a beast.

But, damn, her proximity brings out my animal.

"Three years," I can't suppress the needy growl in my voice.

A smile curves her mouth. "Any roommates?"

"No. Just me."

She meets my eyes, her stare wicked. "Good." Then, her fingers are at the edge of her skirt, pulling the material up and over her head until she's on display, dressed only in some peachy underwear that almost exactly matches her skin tone.

Zoey is all curves and soft edges. I can see her nipples through the lacy material of her bra. I want to suck on them, see how wild I can drive her with my tongue on those sensitive peaks. Then, I want to drag her panties off and tongue her core until she's screaming my name. I stalk across the room to where she leans back against the couch. I'm almost to her, hands reaching, when Zoey dodges my grip by dropping to her knees.

"What ..." My question trails off as she undoes my belt buckle and slides the leather free.

"Do you mind if I suck your dick? I imagined it once, and I haven't been able to stop thinking about it." Her fingers pause on my fly as she stares up at me. Waiting for my permission.

"Sure. Go for it." My attempt at sounding casual fails when the words come out on a choked breath.

Zoey makes quick work of my pants zipper, and her eager hands push the material down, along with my briefs. I'm half hard from the sight of her on her knees, and when she makes a happy noise and wraps her hand around the base of me, I grow to my full length.

"I'm STI-free," she informs me. "Tested three months ago and haven't been with anyone in a year. When was the last time you were checked? Do werewolves get STIs?"

Everything about her, even her curious questions about werewolf health, turns me on.

"As far as I know, we don't get them. But my doctor gave me the all clear a month ago." The words come out rushed; I'm happy to share the info, but I want to get to the promise in her eyes.

"And you haven't been with anyone since?"

I shake my head, losing my voice as she adjusts her grip on my hard length.

"Good." She gazes up at me as her hand slides up and down my cock, almost leisurely in the slow movement. "What do you like, Warner?"

When I hesitate, she leans forward, pressing a hot kiss to my stomach, making my ab muscles twitch in response. Her free hand wraps around the back of my thigh, gripping firmly, holding herself against me. And all the while, she strokes.

"What do you like?" she whispers again, breath warm against my skin. Then, her tongue sneaks out, teasing me with a lick, like an offering. Showing what I can ask for.

But all I manage is a confession, courtesy of my lust-soaked brain.

"I-I haven't ... done this."

Zoey doesn't back away in surprise. She simply nuzzles her nose against my hip bone. "You've never gotten a blow job?"

I shake my head, then answer, "No."

"Are you a virgin?"

That shocks a chuckle out of me, but then I'm suddenly groaning when her teeth pinch my skin. "No. Just never asked ... for this."

I'm having trouble remembering anything that's felt better than the rhythmic pumping Zoey refuses to let up on. My hips try to thrust in time with her movements.

"But you gave it?" She ends her question with another kiss on my stomach, and the image of my face buried between Zoey's legs has me growling.

"Yeah. Fuck. I want to lick your pussy."

Her grip tightens by a fraction, drawing out my panting and thrusting.

"In a minute."

Then, she places her lips against the crown of my cock and slowly drags me into the wet heat of her mouth.

And if I'd known this is what I could've asked for, I would have.

Zoey sucks me in deep, then hums a happy sound. The vibration massages my dick. My knees threaten to buckle.

She lets me slip back out, teasing the underside of my cock with her tongue as she does.

Curses tumble from my mouth.

Then, Zoey stands, letting me go, and I want to beg her to touch me again.

"Wait, Zoey, I'm sorry."

She raises one eyebrow. "Sorry for what?"

"I ..." I don't know exactly. "For whatever I did wrong."

Her curious brown eyes trace over me as satisfaction curves her mouth. "I was just going to suggest you sit down before your legs give out. I doubt I'm strong enough to catch you."

Zoey smiles at me, sweet and confident. She cares about me. About something as simple as my comfort during a blow job. The suggestion somehow ramps up the meaning of this encounter.

At least it does for me.

Instead of finding a place to sit, I snake my arm around Zoey's waist, tugging her into my chest. As I capture her mouth with mine, I spread my hands over her bare skin. She is soft against my hard grip. Wild, instinctual urges beg that I mark her. Not in a violent manner. I don't want to bruise her pillowy skin.

More like I want to tattoo my fingerprints on her.

Yes, my wolf whispers.

Be mine. I fight the desperate plea, worried I'll scare her away with the strength of my wanting.

In place of the words, I use my touch to worship her.

My tongue caresses hers, inciting happy gasps that I swallow down as gifts. Gently, I knead the flesh of her ass, rocking our hips together, hinting at the way I want to thrust into her.

Zoey cups my cheeks, only to keep my head still as she pulls away.

"You said I could go down on you." There's an accusing note to her voice.

I chuckle. "I thought girls saw giving head as a chore." That's the main reason I've never asked for it before. When I was only hooking up with someone, I didn't want to be selfish. Not when I wasn't giving them any more of myself.

"It's only a chore if you don't like doing it."

"And you like it?" My question is breathless as I stare down at Zoey's mouth, the sparkle of her piercing taunting me.

She uses her body, pushing her chest against mine, to back me up until my knees hit the armrest of the couch and I fall backward, bouncing on the plush cushions. Zoey stands tall above me, her dark honey hair curling over her shoulders, cocky smile plumping her cheeks.

With swift hands, Zoey tugs off my boots before fully stripping off my pants and briefs. Then, she climbs over me, straddling my hips, and settles the hot core of her against my rigid cock. A broken groan pushes out of my throat as my mind tries to deal with the delicious torture of being pinned down by lace-covered perfection. One thin strip of material separates us.

As I'm losing my mind, Zoey is still meticulously removing my clothing. She tugs my grease-stained T-shirt over my head, so I finally lie completely naked beneath her.

"This is my favorite position to finish in." She stares down at me, palms braced on my shoulders, waiting for an answer.

"Hell yes. I can't wait—" My grip is on her hips, lifting her up, trying to figure out how to tug off her panties when she has her legs straddling me.

"No." Slim fingers wrap around my wrists.

Zoey removes my hands, and I grumble in disappointment. Then, she pins my arms above my head, her face hovering just above mine, a sexy, scolding look in her eyes.

"You haven't been paying attention."

A disbelieving scoff bursts from my chest. I've done nothing *but* pay attention. My eyes haven't left Zoey since she sauntered into the mechanic's shop.

Zoey smirks, then leans down to bite my lower lip. Hard. She doesn't draw blood. But she does almost make me come.

"Warner, what do I want?" she murmurs against my mouth, her tongue coming out to soothe the spot where her teeth dug in.

I swallow multiple times before I can form words. "You want to ride me?"

This feels like a test. What will I get if I answer wrong? More importantly, what will I get if I answer correctly?

"Hmmm." She drops her head lower, and suddenly, I feel a hard bite on my neck. My hips jerk up in response, my body writhing in pleasure.

Zoey's human strength is no match for my supernatural abilities. If I wanted, I could easily break her hold, roll over with her pinned under me, and drive through her flimsy underwear.

But I don't want that.

Something in me craves Zoey's control. She's dominating me, and I've never had a more erotic experience in my life.

Nothing has ever felt so intimate.

"What do I want?"

Hell, I need to answer her. She demands it. I struggle to form thoughts and make them into words.

"My-my dick. You want to suck it."

At first, she doesn't respond. Her head only moves lower, and I brace myself for another tormenting bite. But then she places a soft kiss in the middle of my chest, and her grip on my wrists releases.

"That's a good werewolf," Zoey murmurs, her voice husky, her breath teasing the coarse hair on my chest.

I wonder if she minds that I'm not smooth, like some male model or the werewolves on a CW show.

The way her fingers flex in it, the way her nose traces through it, the way her lips press trails of kisses in it, make me think she doesn't mind my fuzz in the slightest.

Then, her mouth is level with my cock, and thinking becomes impossible.

I've seen calluses on Zoey's fingers—results from her DIY projects. But when she touches me, her skin is warm silk.

She slips off the couch, kneeling on the floor. Her breasts press into my thighs, tempting me. I want to cup them. The brief handful I got earlier in the shop was over too soon.

When she rides me, I promise myself.

Zoey grips the base of me so I stand erect.

Then, the erotic torment begins.

Her tongue drags up my entire length before flicking the tip. A bead of pre-cum seeps out, and I watch Zoey deliberately lick the drop.

It's possible that I'm bleeding—the nails of my fingers are digging so hard into my palms.

She then sets my dick on her full bottom lip and proceeds to work her way down. Zoey doesn't draw in every inch immediately. Instead, she pulls me in, bit by bit, every centimeter of my cock receiving an introduction to her mouth. She bathes me with her tongue, tightens her lips for a second of suction, then gives the gentlest of warnings with a light tease of teeth.

My breathing becomes frantic. Lust boils my brain. The couch groans as I grip the frame, needing something to hold on to. Something to keep me from tangling my hands in Zoey's hair and holding her to me so she has no choice but to finish blowing my mind.

Then, the wet heat of her mouth disappears, and I mutter a cursing protest.

"Warner?" The seductress aspect of her voice is muted, and she's back to curious. Honestly, I don't know which side of her I find more intoxicating.

"Yeah?" I try to keep the desperation from my response.

"What's your recovery time like? Is it faster because you're a were-wolf? Can I finish you in my mouth and still get to fuck you in a bit? Or should I bring you to the edge and then have you finish inside me?"

Zoey is lucky I don't shoot off just at the sound of those dirty, analytical questions dropping from her glistening lips. Especially when her hand circles my erection, continuing to work me over as she rattles them off.

"I, uh ..." Earlier, I bragged about my stamina. But the truth is, my other hookups never lasted more than one round. I clench my teeth and grip the couch harder as her thumb traces over my sensitive head in an almost-absent-minded manner. When I think I can talk, I try again. "In the past"—I gasp—"I've been one and done. But with you ..." The word morphs into a pleasurable growl. "I don't know, Zoey. Fuck if I know."

A satisfied smile curves her lips. "Guess we're taking you to the edge then."

31

ZOEY

THIS GUNNER APOLOGY is going better than I expected.

I love watching Warner writhe on the couch, tormented by the pleasure of my touch. Being in control in the bedroom—or in this case, the living room—has always made my blood run hotter. That someone so strong and powerful would give himself up to me is a heady sensation.

There's a tantalizing heat building in my lower belly as I run my mouth along his length. Warner tastes salty, especially when I flick my tongue over the slit of him.

He jerks in response, a low groan filling the entirety of his apartment.

I think we're nearing the edge.

Which means it's time for me to get mine.

I let him pop out of my mouth, and his erection bobs against his stomach, hard and wanting.

Warner's eyes meet mine. Hungry. Pleading.

I stand, moving beside his head to comb my fingers through his hair, all the while admiring the masterpiece of lustful male I've created.

"Zoey." He whispers my name as if his begging confuses him.

Warner knows I'm in charge, which means he has no idea what's coming next.

Or more likely who is coming next.

"Do you still want to lick me?"

"Yes." The word is ragged as his arms shoot out, strong hands gripping the back of my thighs to pull me closer.

I grin at his eagerness. "Take off my underwear."

His eyes get dark as he watches his own fingers pull down the lace, exposing me to him. Never have I had someone gaze at me with such intensity before. A girl could get high off this kind of attention.

When the fabric is on the floor, I fondle the silky strands of his hair again. "Do you want me to ride your face?"

Please say yes, I beg silently.

"More than anything," he growls. Now, his palms cup my ass, encouraging me.

Bracing my hands on either side of his head on the armrest, I straddle his shoulders, my knees sinking into the cushions. Warner slides lower, until his breath tickles the curls at the center of me.

"Fuck, Zoey." His lips brush my sensitive skin as he curses, and I clutch at the smooth leather of the couch to keep myself steady. "You're perfect."

My command of the situation slips. Like I stepped on the slick stones leading to dark water and the river snatches at my feet.

"I'm not."

Warner growls again, this time low and menacing. Then, I feel a long stroke against my folds. Hot and wet. His tongue tortures me, giving back the pleasure I plied him with only a moment ago.

"You're perfect for *me*."

Before I can respond, Warner's lips find my clit. After that, I'm too busy moaning and drowning in ecstasy to overthink his declaration. All my muscles tighten, my body wanting to curl in on itself, looking for protection from the intense sensation of a werewolf's mouth on my pussy.

At some point, my hands move from the couch to his head, my fingers tangling in his sweat-damp hair. I must look wanton, clutching him to me as my hips rock against his mouth.

But Warner doesn't tap out, begging for a break. Instead, he kneads my ass and presses me closer. He fucks me with his tongue in between bouts of worshipping my clit.

The noises that come out of my throat rival those of an animal. The response is a hum deep in his throat that sounds happy. Not a big surprise that a werewolf might like driving a woman wild.

"Warner," I gasp, "I'm close."

His assault becomes more frenzied, and when the brush of his teeth against my clit comes, I give in to the glorious pulsing of my orgasm. The tension in my muscles increases by tenfold, then snaps loose like a rubber band pulled past its limits. Some form of a whispered scream forces itself out of my throat.

Warner laps at me, clearly enjoying the taste of my wetness. I can barely keep upright and appreciate it when he slides my hips down over his chin and down his chest, until I can collapse on top of him without worrying about suffocating him with my thighs.

We both pant, and with the movement of his chest, I feel the brush of his hard length against my ass.

Which means I still have work to do. And, hell, am I looking forward to it.

"Do you have condoms?" My question is muffled because I've started nuzzling the hair on his chest. Who knew I'd like my man with some fuzz?

"I think so. In my bedside table."

"Sounds like we need to relocate."

That's all the instruction Warner requires. He stands, with me clutched against him, and strides toward a back room. After tossing me onto a wonderfully cushy bed, Warner flips on the light and stares down at me.

I rise up to my knees and open my arms, beckoning him closer.

He obeys, and for a few minutes, we let our heat and passion spill into a kiss. At some point, he unclasps the hooks of my bra, letting the material drop to the floor. Then, nothing is between us.

My nerve endings tingle as Warner's body presses flush against mine, and I want to rub myself all over him. More than that, I want to feel connected to him. Have him inside me.

"Condom," I command when I break off our kiss.

He leans over to open a drawer in his bedside table and pulls out one of those tiny three-packs found in any gas station. I pluck it out of his hand and check the expiration date hasn't passed before tearing the container open.

Once the latex is free, I shuffle back on the bed. "Lie down. I'm going to put this on you."

Warner reclines on the mattress, his moves as smooth as a predator's. His eyes stay trained on my hands, arm wrapping around my waist, as if to make sure I won't run on him.

I might enjoy him hunting me down.

The rubber isn't hard to slide on with him standing at attention. Once he's properly equipped, I mount his hips.

"Do you want to be inside me?" I ask, voice husky.

Warner's response is a tense nod and a tight grip on my hips. Still, he doesn't try to direct me. The werewolf follows my lead, and I reward him for it with another searing kiss.

Reaching between us, I wrap my hand around him, loving the heat that seeps through the latex. Warner will never let me be cold. It's impossible for him.

Still, I shiver as I sink onto him, but purely from pleasure.

"Zoey ..." Warner groans my name, and I watch with glee as the muscles in his neck strain. The werewolf stares at me with heavy-lidded eyes, his breaths escaping in short bursts.

This is what I crave, the sight I tried to picture at night when I touched myself. But nothing is as good as the real thing. My imagination couldn't conjure up the sturdy feel of his body between my legs or the rasp of his chest hair against my palms. My brain wasn't able to form the salt and musky scent of him or the exact pitch of his growls. Until a few days ago, I didn't even consider that he *would* growl.

And I never could have imagined the expression Warner would have when we finally joined together. The mixture of lust and need and worship rocks me.

In self-preservation, I close my eyes, focusing instead on the thick heat of him inside me.

Our moans mingle as I lift my hips and begin to rock. There will probably be bruises on my backside from the way Warner's fingers dig into me, urging me faster. Maybe it's crazy, but I love the idea.

In fact, I want his touch everywhere.

My hands sneak back, covering his and prying the grip away.

"Fuck. I'm sorry. Too hard?"

"Not at all. But try here." And just like in the mechanic's shop, I press his palms over my boobs.

Warner mutters a string of curses as he kneads my breasts, rubbing his thumbs over my nipples before pinching them. Encouragements spill from my lips, and I bear down harder. Suddenly, Warner sits up, capturing a tight peak in his mouth, giving it the same ravenous attention he offered my clit earlier.

Gasping his name, I lose control of my body and the situation. All I want is more. I need him to break apart because I feel myself cracking. His mouth is on my nipple, his one palm on my ass and his other on my back, holding me to him. The man surrounds me, fills me, and continues to give me everything I ask for.

My arm snakes behind my back, landing on his inner thigh. I trace upward until I find what I'm looking for. When my light grip cups his balls, Warner's head snaps back. His eyes meet mine, and I'm surprised to find them almost entirely black. I'm even more shocked to realize I like it.

"I'm close." His voice is rough, as if pleasure has torn at his throat. "Come. I want to feel it."

"Rub my clit." I lean back enough to give him access.

The second his finger presses against the nerves, I know I'm done for.

"Yes. Like that. Just keep—" Words fail as my muscles tense again.

I release him, only to immediately dig my nails into the flesh of his leg. Then, the snap comes, and I'm clenching and crying out his name.

"Zoey!"

He leaves off my clit, using both his hands to grasp at my hips, holding me to him, grinding into me. I'm almost too lost in my orgasm daze to hear his triumphant shout. Warner bucks, once. Twice. Then, he collapses back on the bed, dragging me with him.

Our postcoital recovery isn't relaxed. The two of us gasp and pant as if we didn't breathe the entire time we moved together. My fingers and toes continue to twitch with aftershocks. I flex them to ease the tension from my orgasm. In fact, I need to stretch every muscle in my body.

Intending to do so, I roll off Warner's chest, aiming for the space at his side. He catches me before I can get away, clutching my body to his.

"Where're you going?" he slurs.

I prop my chin up on his chest so I can meet his eyes. "Usually have to stretch after a workout like that."

Warner's body shakes with a chuckle. "Careful you don't fall."

Curious, I glance to the side and realize I was about to roll straight off the edge of the bed. Hitting the hardwood floor would've been a major mood dampener.

"Got it. Officially rolling in the other direction."

This time, Warner lets me go, and I bounce onto his cushy mattress.

Immediately, I extend my arms above my head, moaning in pleasure as my muscles welcome the movement.

"Fucking hell. Keep making that noise, and I'm going to be ready to go again before you know it."

"Promises," I murmur, settling into a comfortable sprawl.

Warner shifts onto his side, bending an elbow and propping his head in his hand to stare down at me. He reaches a hand out to my hair, and I hear a click. When he pulls back, I spy my hair clip in his fingers, glittering gold in the sunlight from his window.

The werewolf examines my little craft as if he finds it fascinating.

"Can I see you change?" I ask.

Warner raises a brow, setting my hair clip on the nightstand. "Into my wolf?"

I nod. "That's not offensive to ask, is it?"

As a smile stretches across his face, I get the sense I've done the complete opposite of offend him. He looks pleased, if slightly wary. The next second, he's off the bed and in the middle of the room.

Every inch of his glorious, naked body on display.

"This'll take longer than last time since it's not the full moon and there's no danger around. You sure you want to see?"

"Yes." I pull a sheet over me as I sit up, ready to watch magic in action.

"All right. Prepare to be amazed." Warner closes his eyes and stands completely still.

Almost a full minute passes without anything happening. Long enough that doubt shadows my excitement. Even after talking to my mother, I realize I'm not completely convinced I didn't imagine the whole incident. That my mind hasn't found another way to betray me.

Then, the space around Warner darkens, as if a black fog has risen in the air. The darkness clings to his skin, obscuring him, until I can't resist the urge to rub my eyes, trying to dispel the blur.

The distorted mass shifts, lowers, then dissipates.

And I'm alone in an apartment with a wolf.

A very large wolf.

"HOLY SHIT!" I push to my knees, leaning forward, then almost immediately flinch back, my ass hitting the mattress.

Silly me forgot to ask Warner just how wolfish he gets in this form.

Does his mind disappear? If I was in danger, he would've told me, right?

"Can you ... understand me?" I ask, silently wishing I had put some clothes on before this experiment. Wanting more than just a sheet between me and that impressive jaw full of sharp teeth.

The better to eat you with, my dear.

Then, the creature's shaggy head dips in a clear nod.

"So, you're still in there, Warner?"

Another nod, paired with a huff.

I think he's laughing at me.

Carefully, I climb off the bed, keeping the sheet wrapped tight.

My instincts scream at me, *Danger! Don't do this! Don't you like your organs inside your body?!*

But he trusted me with this universe-shattering secret. The least I can do is not make him feel like a pariah. And as I stuff the fear deep down in my chest, I realize something.

Warner is beautiful.

Apparently, werewolves aren't some grotesque, terrifying creatures of nightmares. He looks like a wolf. A very large wolf, but I've never interacted with a wolf before, so maybe this is normal-sized. His fur is a luscious, thick charcoal-gray that I want to bury my hands in.

I don't.

"Remind me to ask you more questions when you have the ability to speak," I murmur, settling cross-legged in front of him.

Wolf Warner stretches his head out, nose sniffing my hair. Then, a moment later, the air fogs again, and I lose sight of the animal. Soon, a naked man is crouched on the hardwood. Warner reaches out, wrapping his arms around me and gathering me to his chest.

"You're amazing," he whispers into my hair. "The day you came to town was the best fucking day."

It takes all my concentration not to stiffen at his words.

They sound so ... hopeful. Like this is the start of something.

Pine Falls was supposed to be an experiment. A chance to test my ability to live away from the safety cocoon my family wraps me in.

But I'm not sure I've proven I'm strong enough.

Still, I won't be done with the cabin for a few more weeks at least. I'm not about to disappear.

Yet.

32

ZOEY

"Careful!"

The word is shrieked at me the moment my butt brushes against a hard object. Freezing mid-sit, I glance to the side and find a familiar-looking woman steadying a plastic box that rests precariously close to the edge of the table.

"I'm sorry. Should I sit somewhere else?" I ask.

The Sip 'N' Stitch group has commandeered a large table toward the back of The Wild Rabbit again, and I went for the first free chair.

"No! Don't be ridiculous. I came here for you, Zoey Gunner. Just ... don't knock over this box unless you want to spend the next hour picking up sequins."

The glimpse of sparkle reminds me who I'm in a half crouch next to. As I settle in the chair, I examine the woman I glimpsed the first night I met Warner.

She's gorgeous with her strong features and dark eyes. The tan skin on her high cheekbones is colored rosy, like she spends plenty of time in the sun. Today, her black hair wraps around the top of her head in a braid crown, and I admire the little turquoise drops that dangle from her ears.

"You keep checking me out, I'm gonna tell Warner he has some competition." She gives me a saucy wink, making me smile wide.

"You're friends with Warner?"

"Best friends. Oh, the embarrassing childhood stories I could tell!" She sets down what I realize now is a cowboy boot and holds out her hand. "I'm Courtney Benally. Glad to finally meet you."

When I clasp her hand, rough calluses brush my palm. Apparently, vibrant footwear and out-of-season Daisy Dukes don't preclude a girl from working hard.

"Good to meet you too." Even as I pull my current project—the apology scarf I've almost finished—out of my bag, I study Courtney from the side of my eye.

My curiosity is fueled by one question: *Is she a werewolf?*

Courtney spends time at The Rabbit Hole, but she doesn't seem to be a member of The Dark Moon Riders. Does every wolf in town have to be a biker too? Could she be one of the townspeople who are in the know?

None of these questions are things I can just blurt out, so I search for a way to approach the topic innocently.

"You said you've known Warner since you were kids?"

Courtney nods, a big grin on her face. "Yeah. I hung out with him and Roderick when we were little tykes. Their mom's house is down the road from mine."

"He was as charming then as he is now. Quick to laugh," Amy Spencer offers, smiling across the table at us as her fingers wield a needle in a cross-stitch project.

Courtney leans close, muttering only to me, "Quick to tear up too. Sorry to tell you, Zoey, but you're shacking up with a notorious crybaby."

I snort, turning my head to whisper back, "Noted. I'll make sure to treat him gently."

Her eyes glitter as they meet mine, and I return to my original goal.

"So, I guess you know a lot about him. All his ... moods?"

Hell. I suck at this. I was not made for the life of a detective.

Still, Courtney's stare loses an ounce of humor, sharpening as her brows dip.

"I do in fact." Her shoulder bumps mine as she leans in closer. "Like how *animalistic* he can get."

She knows. And I never expected to feel such intense relief. But here she is. One more person who knows the truth about the guy I like. A potential friend that I could have an honest conversation with.

Keeping my voice low, I hold her eyes, trying to convey that I'm in the know too. "And you? Do you get ... *animalistic* sometimes?"

A wicked smirk curls her lips. "Hell. Yes."

She's a wolf.

"Hey, Zoey."

The sound of my name pulls me out of the delight of discovery. But when I turn to find Juliet hovering just behind my chair, more joy flowers in my chest.

"You made it!"

My friend smiles, but her lips pinch at the expression, and her eyes flicker around the busy restaurant. Something is stressing her, but I'm not sure what. Maybe she just has new-person-to-the-group jitters.

Well, as this is only my second Sip 'N' Stitch, we can be newbies together.

"Here, sit down. Did you bring something to work on?"

I climbed up to the tree house earlier today to text Juliet about tonight's meeting, and when I didn't receive a response, I grew bored and returned to the reception-less wasteland that was my grandmother's cabin. Unsure of Juliet's crafting interest, I brought some extra yarn and hooks.

"I did." The librarian settles in the chair to my left and reaches into her bag, coming out with a shoebox. There's a rustle when she sets it on the table and pulls off the lid.

"Paper?" Courtney asks, practically shoving her boobs into my shoulder to stare around me and get a better view of the colorful collection of card stock. "What are you making?"

"Greeting cards." Juliet holds up one that has a beautifully detailed mountain scene, rendered from carefully cut and layered paper. "I have more than I'll ever need." She blushes, as if admitting a failing.

"Lovely. You're so talented." This comes from a woman across the way from Courtney. "You just moved here not too long ago—do I have that right?"

"The end of May," Juliet murmurs, her focus on a set of scissors in her hands while her shoulders grow tense.

"That long ago? My goodness. Can't believe we haven't been introduced. I'm Karen Hanson."

The rest of the women around the table rattle off their names, but from the familiar tone a few use, I can guess they've run into Juliet at the library.

I get the sense that Juliet would rather not be the center of conversation, but Ms. Hanson doesn't seem happy with a simple hello.

"And I believe I heard you were unattached. Have you been out with any of Pine Falls' nice young men?"

I'm so surprised by her question that I drop my ball of yarn, then stifle a curse as I try collect it off the floor before it gets dirty and tangled. Juliet also flinches, tearing the delicate tissue paper she was cutting.

"I'm actively *not* dating right now," the librarian states, conviction adding an edge to her tone.

Ms. Hanson opens her mouth, but Courtney is faster.

"Actively *not* dating? What does that mean?" The wolf tries leaning around me again so she can meet Juliet's eyes. "Do you chuck books at people who approach you, carrying flowers?"

"Of course not," Juliet grumbles. Then, she gives the table a smirk. "I value books too much."

Some of the women chuckle, and most at least crack a smile. Mrs. Applewood, who's been throwing me disgruntled looks ever since I sat down, glares at the fabric in her hands.

Suddenly, the quilter's comments from the day Warner escorted me to lunch come rushing back.

"I don't associate with dogs."

At the time, I thought she meant my mastiff. Now, I'd bet all the softest flannel in Minnie's closet that she wasn't referring to Bruce.

Guess I found another townsperson in the know. Just not an ally.

"Well," Ms. Hanson says, bringing attention back to her, "maybe you just haven't met the right man. My son, for instance."

Juliet's lips flatten, and she doesn't respond.

Courtney swoops in with a wicked smirk. "I'm single! Why haven't you ever set *me* up with your son, Karen?"

The woman scowls at Courtney. "Because you already dated my son and broke his heart," she growls.

"Did I? Wait, who's your son?"

"Fredrick." Her face has turned the same bright red as Courtney's vodka cranberry.

"Fredrick?" The wolf seems to mull the name over, as if the memory of him is hard to recall. "Oh! Freddy!" She settles back in her seat. "Well, I wouldn't call what we did *dating*."

Juliet snorts up half her drink, and the poor Ms. Hanson gasps, reaching her hand toward her throat, as if expecting to find a string of pearls to clutch.

"Courtney ..." Amy, unofficial leader of the Sip 'N' Stitch gathering, uses a warning tone even though I swear I catch a quiver at the corner of her mouth. "Let's keep the discussion of other members' offspring PG-rated, okay?"

"Okay, Amy." But the werewolf immediately leans over to whisper in my ear, "Freddy is selfish in the sack. I spent a good fifteen minutes explaining the importance of quid pro quo as it relates to oral. Better off with a vibrator."

"Oh, Juliet. Dear, are you feeling all right?"

Some of the women at the table stare at the librarian with concern etching wrinkles in their brows.

My friend does seem distressed, her hands covering her face, shoulders shaking. A passerby might think she was quietly sobbing.

However, sitting next to her, I make out the muffled sound of unsuccessfully stifled giggles.

Courtney isn't the best at whispering.

"I'm fine," Juliet finally chokes out.

Ms. Hanson's knuckles are white on her knitting needles, and I consider if I need to escort Courtney home so she doesn't end up murdered in an alley with crafting supplies. "And you, Zoey?" The tightness in her voice makes the question sound like a threat.

"Me?"

Ms. Hanson nods. "Are you dating?"

"I ..." *Shit. Shit, shit, shit.*

Dating. One step away from a relationship. Then on the fast track to commitment.

This isn't a question I thought I'd have to answer.

But once again, Courtney comes to the rescue.

Kind of.

"She's fucking—"

"Courtney," Amy chides.

"Sorry. She's *holding hands* with Warner Jameson."

Okay, I guess I can deal with that description for now. Also, I think Juliet is going to pass out if she tries any harder to suppress her laughter.

I'm fine with being the butt of a joke if it makes my friend more comfortable.

"Well then ..." Ms. Hanson takes a long sip from her white wine before putting her full attention on her project.

Matchmaking is officially off the table.

After a minute or two of awkward silence passes, side conversations start back up, and Courtney seems content to bedazzle her boots.

Juliet is more relaxed now that the spotlight is off her and after the fits of hilarity Courtney put her through. Amy pulls the librarian out further by asking about the latest bestsellers.

After another sip of my drink, I relax back in my chair, estimating how many rows I have left.

"That's a fun pattern." Courtney reaches out to touch the scarf I'm finishing. Her finger traces the raised design repeated along the length of the scarf.

The symbol is simple—two triangles, each bisecting at a single corner. Almost like a bow tie. I realize I incorporated it without thought. Crocheting is often like that for me. An activity I can do instinctually as my mind relaxes or focuses on something else.

"Thanks. I hope Warner likes it too. This is for him."

"You made it. Which means he'll love it." Courtney smirks, and then her expression softens. "How are you adjusting?" Her quiet question has me meeting her gaze. There's a quick flash of black, and I realize she just gave me a glimpse of her wolf, clarifying the under-lying meaning of her question.

How are you adjusting to the whole mythical-creatures-are-real thing?

"Getting better. Not great at first." I hook my yarn and debate saying more. After a second, I admit, "Normally, I talk about life changes with my therapist." This time, I'm the one who tries to convey extra meaning with my gaze.

At her slight nod, I know she gets it. Normal therapists aren't equipped to deal with a werewolf discussion.

My eyes trace over the table, and I wonder how many of the women here know.

An idea forms.

"Are there any therapists in town?"

Courtney smiles and tilts her chin toward the leader of the club. "Amy has a practice."

"And she"—I keep my voice low—"serves all populations?"

After another subtle nod, the woman leans in close, and I discover Courtney does know how to whisper properly.

"Her partner is pack."

Something small and happy flares in my chest. A little glow. Something like hope.

33

ZOEY

I DON'T SPOT Warner when I first pull up to the construction site. Based off the men I *do* see, I can look forward to a sweaty version of the werewolf.

Nothing to complain about there.

I park next to a line of other trucks and check the time. I'm early.

Dust kicks up when I jump down from the cab of my truck. I debate waiting for Warner to come to me, but figure as long as I don't wander into the actual construction zone, there's no harm in me getting a peek.

Plus, I want to see where Warner works.

We've been *holding hands*, as Courtney so charmingly put it, for over a week now, and I'm curious about the other aspects of his life.

As I get closer to the skeleton of the house, there's the sound of power tools and people calling out to each other. A wall is raised from the ground with ropes and muscle. The whole process is fascinating.

I know how to make smaller things, and compared to a lot of people, I'd be considered quite handy. But putting together an entire house? Now, that's impressive.

This lunch date is starting off nicely, so of course, some asshole has to go and ruin it by letting out a wolf whistle. Briefly, I hope I misheard or that the sound came from Warner. But when I glance toward the perpetrator, I catch a stranger leering at me.

"Hey, sweetheart! Something you need me to help you with?"

A shudder slides down my spine. The guy assigning me a nickname would be annoying on its own, but there's an extra level of gross because *sweetheart* is what my mom calls me. I don't need some strange man yelling the endearment at me.

Trying to ignore the creep, I scan the different hard hat–wearing men, hating that one creep has ruined my joy at watching something being built.

And like all assholes, the guy chooses to double down.

"Gonna play hard to get? Don't worry. I like the hunt." The skeevy guy approaches me, wearing a smile with an air of menace lingering at the edges.

Werewolf.

I'm not sure how I know, but I do. There's something similar in the way the man moves to how I've seen Warner walk. Only Warner has never stalked me like prey before.

Fearful fingers clench my gut, encouraging me to retreat to my truck and lock the doors.

But then I *would* be prey.

The man is only a few feet away, his eyes slipping between blue and black, a triumphant grin curling Cheshire-like across his stubble-covered cheeks. Despite the facial hair, I can see now that he's young. Probably barely old enough to drink.

Not that it matters. If anything, young men are more dangerous.

"What is a pretty thing like you hanging around here for? Looking for some fun?"

He's about to step into my space, and my mind flips between fight or flight.

I won't be prey.

Before he can loom over me, I step forward, staring straight into his eyes.

"Do I know you?" I ask.

"What?" He stutter-steps with hesitation.

"You look really familiar." I put on my deep, thoughtful face, then snap my fingers as if I just remembered something. "I know! You're the guy who's bad in bed!"

He was not expecting *that*. Horrified shock slackens his face. Exactly what I was hoping for. I came here to meet Warner for lunch, not be accosted by a horny, power-tripping werewolf.

"Yeah. The sad sack in the sack. Mr. Pitiful Fuck. Everyone in town told me about you. Said you harass strangers because no one wants to give you a second go since you can't find a clit, even with a detailed map."

There's a little chunk of my brain that wonders if insulting a werewolf's sexual prowess is the safest route to take. But if a guy is going to harass me, supernatural or not, I figure it's better to let them know up front that I won't go down without tearing into them first.

"What the fu—"

"Ross." A man with thick brown hair, streaked through with gray, strides toward us. He's tall, wiry, and coated in authority. Not visibly, but it spills off him in waves as he approaches.

My aggressor turns to the man, red-faced. "Sir."

That's when I see, just behind the man's shoulder, is Warner. He stares at me with wide eyes and a bobbing mouth, as if he can't decide whether to grin or not.

Guess he heard my comments to his coworker.

"Is something going on here?" The older man glances between the two of us before his eyes come to rest on me. There's no accusation in them, just scrutiny.

"No." Ross is quick to assure the man, who I notice now has a vest with the label of *Foreman*.

"Correction"—I straighten my spine, glaring all three men down —"the thing that was *supposed* to be going on here was me picking up my friend for lunch." I gesture at Warner. "But instead, I have to deal with"—unable to find a descriptor to apply to Ross, I simply let my disgust infuse the next word—"*this*."

"You—" Ross begins.

"Yeah, *me*," I cut him off. "I had your pathetic number the second you walked my way. You ever try *hunting* me again, and I'll hit you with a face full of bear mace."

"*Bitch*." He bares his teeth, stepping forward.

There's a growl and a sudden powerful presence at my back, but this is *my* fight, and I can't back down. Growing up with four brothers made me tough. Or stupid. Jury is still out.

I pull my lips back from my own puny human teeth, getting up in his space yet again. "Try it, *wolf*. See what happens."

Ross freezes mid-threatening move, his eyes growing wary.

"Back off." The command cuts through the air between us, almost a wall. I've never heard Warner's voice so deep and menacing before. His warm arm encircles my shoulders.

For a second, I'm furious, thinking his command is directed at me. But when I glance up, his glare is all for the asshole.

Good. Glad to know he doesn't automatically side with his pack mates.

Ross opens his mouth, but a sharp throat clearing from the foreman has the young pup snapping his jaw shut.

"Back to work," the older man says, aiming the words at Ross.

I think the guy might argue with his boss, but after a pause, he shrugs and stalks away.

"You're Zoey Gunner."

I meet the man's intense gaze without flinching, giving him a brief nod.

"And you are ..."

"Mason Jameson."

My eyes flick to Warner, who offers a tight smile. "My uncle."

"You look like your mother," Mason offers.

The comment surprises me. In the past, I've only ever thought of how my complexion falls closer to my father's. My mom is blonde-haired, blue-eyed, while Dad and I are brunettes with brown eyes. But I guess the residents of Pine Falls have only ever met one of the people who made me.

"Did you know her?"

Warner's uncle shrugs, then walks away, his gait unhurried but still containing an air of authority.

The tension of the moment lingers.

Warner is the first to pierce it. "Did you tell Ross he's a bad fuck?"

I roll my eyes. "Yeah. If you and your uncle hadn't shown up, he probably would've pulled up a list of references."

The excitement of the construction site having worn off, I pivot and start back toward my truck. Even though most people would say I won that confrontation, I still feel gross. The leering weight of Ross's eyes left an invisible residue on my skin.

I need a shower.

"Zoey—" Warner starts, but I whirl on him, unwilling to be scolded for defending myself.

"He talked at me like I was a *thing*." My temper rises at the memory, and I glare at Warner, suddenly not feeling too warm and fuzzy toward men in general. "So, I gave him a taste of his own medicine. And I hope he chokes on the bitter taste. He deserved it."

We stare at each other for a moment before Warner nods. "You're right."

"You agree that he deserved it?"

"Yes." Warner scoops up one of my hands and presses a kiss to my palm before offering me a smirk with burning eyes. "But I was referring to the first night we met."

I try to remember what exactly he might be referencing. Warner doesn't let me struggle for long.

"You're way more than *kinda* intimidating."

34

WARNER

WHEN ZOEY DROPS me back off at work after lunch, I'm smiling. An hour of eating and getting her to laugh is a good way to spend my break.

But my happiness evaporates the second I see Ross's scowl across the worksite. It's aimed at Zoey's bumper.

If Ross were a human guy, he'd probably keep his anger to himself, maybe throw out some insulting comments the next time he crossed paths with Zoey.

But Ross isn't human. He's wolf. And what's more, he's an asshole.

From his angry expression, he's still smarting from Zoey's put-down.

That means the next time the two of them are in the same room, things could get a lot worse than some harsh words.

Werewolves hold grudges. I've seen it plenty of times over my life.

Most often, it's something small, like how Tanya never misses a chance to stick a mocking note on the back of Trent, the guy who harassed Isaac in middle school for being scrawny. To this day, half the time I cross paths with Trent in town, he's got a yellow sticky note on his back that says he's dense or he wears lacy panties.

Annoying, but harmless.

Moose, owner of The Rabbit Hole, heard one of the pack members complaining about the selection of beers he had on tap. It's been six months, and the bartender still won't serve the guy anything other than water.

Hilarious, but still harmless.

Courtney had a different experience. Twin brothers Jordan and Anthony remind me a lot of Ross. Young wolves that see their powers as proof that they're badass. One of them, maybe both, was interested in Courtney. I wasn't there when she turned them down, but whatever she said made it clear there was zero chance. Instead of accepting her decision and moving on, the brothers took the rejection as a personal offense.

For weeks, they bad-mouthed her to her face and behind her back. Never within earshot of Roderick though. He would've shut them up fast. One night, I almost went after them, but Courtney stopped me. She claimed they weren't worth it, laughing with her usual don't-give-a-fuck attitude.

That only seemed to piss them off more.

Then, one night, the pair followed Courtney out of the bar. A hunter herself, she sensed their intentions. She could've called for help, but she later told me that she was tired of their shit and ready to put an end to it. With a few years on the twins, Courtney could shift faster than either. She did, and in wolf form, my friend beat the shit out of the pair. When some of the pack finally picked up on the commotion and went to check on the noise, they found the men out cold and Courtney with a bloody muzzle.

No permanent damage was done, but now, Jordan and Anthony drop their eyes whenever she enters the room.

Because violence is the warning certain wolves need.

Maybe I should have told Zoey not to speak up like that against other werewolves. But I hate the idea of trying to stifle her fire. And I hate even more that one of my pack members made her uncomfortable. The woman who waltzed into a biker bar with a bag full of crafts is more badass than the piece of shit who hasn't learned what *no* means.

The memory of him stalking toward her, as if she were something to be hunted, has my wolf growling, and the sound spills out of my chest.

All the workers on the build site pause. Uncle Mason employs wolves only, so they're all pack members. Every one of them knows me.

And barely any have seen me get angry about anything. I'm sure the sound of my rage is a shock to all.

When they all freeze in their work, Ross finally looks at me. From the smirk on his face, I know he doesn't take me seriously.

Why should he?

Roderick is the pack leader, exuding strength and discipline. My mom is the second-strongest in the pack, our beta. Then, there's Uncle Mason, quiet and dangerous. But I'm the easygoing member of the family. The guy with a smile and a joke. I don't get into it with people.

Because I've never needed to.

But if Ross's actions go unchecked, Zoey will be in danger. He'll think he has a right to enact retribution.

I could get Roderick to lay down an edict. But *I* want to handle this. When it comes to Zoey's relationship to the pack, I'm her protector.

And Ross has threatened what's mine.

I approach him, my movements smooth and powerful, imbued as they are with the strength of my wolf that begs to be let free. All to put this piece of shit in his place.

"That bitch piss you off too, Jameson?" Ross throws out when I'm only a few steps away. "If you won't keep her on a leash, I will."

It's all I can do to stop myself from attacking him immediately. Instead, I let a snarl tear from my throat. When I speak, the word comes out deep, steeped in the magic of the pack.

"Challenge."

He steps back, shocked. "What?"

I don't need to repeat myself. Everyone here heard.

Uncle Mason steps up behind me, lending his authority to the situation. "You have been challenged. Name the time and place."

"This is ridiculous." Ross glances around at everyone nearby, as if searching for support. Someone to laugh with him. No one does. "She's just a human."

"*Challenge*," I growl.

"Fine." He throws his hands up, pretending exasperation when I can tell I've rattled him. "Tonight. In the woods behind The Rabbit Hole." With that, he stalks off to the other end of the worksite.

For the rest of my shift, I keep my distance. Not that it does anything to lessen my anger. I'm hefting double the load any human man could handle when a voice cuts through my angry haze.

"Maybe we should get you mad more often. Never seen you work so hard," my uncle says, appearing behind me without a sound.

He's good at that. Has the unexpectedly-creeping-up-on-people skill down perfect.

Luckily, I'm used to it, so I don't do more than flinch.

"If you think insulting Zoey is going to get you a better worker, you'll find yourself a man short in the future."

I know my ease at mingling with the human population in the town is not the norm for most members of the pack, but you'd think they could at least be civil.

"You like her. The Gunner girl."

I turn to give Mason my full attention. Something in his voice gave away that this might not be a casual conversation.

"Yeah, I do. She's ..." I trail off. But not because I don't have any words to describe her.

I have too many.

Strong, funny, sweet, creative, odd, beautiful, brave, sexy—

The list goes on, but I think my uncle would wander off after a certain amount of adjectives. Before I can figure out how to end the sentence, Mason is already nodding in a distracted way. He stares over my shoulder.

"I knew her mother, Selena. She was"—he waves his hand to indicate all the descriptors I didn't list, but acts as though he read them in my pause—"too."

It shouldn't surprise me that my family knew Zoey's. Pine Falls isn't big, and apparently, Selena Gunner spent eighteen years of her life here.

But from what Mason just said, I'm not sure *knew* is a strong enough word to describe whatever relationship they had.

"Did you two ... date?"

Hell, this is weird. My father died when I was young, so Mason took on that role. We don't really talk about women. Especially not the mother of the girl I'm falling for.

He offers me a smile that doesn't reach his eyes. "She left." He shrugs and walks away.

Fuck.

I think Selena Gunner broke my uncle's heart.

35

ZOEY

"Maybe a sexy demon lady ..." I murmur to myself, pencil poised over my sketch pad.

Sunlight spills in from the window above the kitchen sink, bathing the cabin in a warm afternoon glow. Good light for my current project.

Different ideas flip through my mind. I'm imagining a pinup girl from hell. Maybe lounging on a bed of fire. Just need to make sure it has a nice curved shape that'll sit evenly on the surface of a motor-cycle helmet.

I want my design to be perfect. Badass. Something the wearer will be proud to show off. Because the only way to put this art on display will be if the guy actually wears his helmet.

Some people might think I'm overly cautious, harping on this helmet thing. But I know I'm right.

Mom doesn't talk about her childhood much. She lost her dad at a pretty young age, so I guess there wasn't a lot she could tell me about my grandfather. But there is one thing I know.

How he died.

My grandfather went on a late-night ride on his motorcycle and got into an accident. She never said exactly what part of the crash caused his death, but I know that one of the few rules she insisted my dad follow was to always wear his helmet while riding. The same went for my brothers and me when we took out our bicycles or a set of roller skates.

She wasn't mean about it.

Mom would walk up to me, cup my face in her hands, and press a kiss to my forehead. Then, she'd whisper, "I love this head more than anything in the world. I don't want to see anything bad happen to it. Please, wear a helmet."

Who can say no to that? None of us ever did.

So, here I am, trying to jazz up a boring black helmet, crafting it into something Warner doesn't just feel obligated to put on.

Instead, I want him to be excited about it.

"Who am I kidding? He's not a demon-lady kind of guy." I tap my pencil on the paper.

Then, it hits me. So obvious that I laugh at myself.

I know what kind of guy Warner is.

He's a wolf.

An hour later, the design is sketched, and the outline is painted on a helmet I picked up from the motorcycle shop in town. I wasn't about to ask Warner for his and have him ride unprotected while I worked. Plus, this way, I can keep it as a surprise.

Just as I'm mixing paints to get the perfect shade of amber, Cyndi Lauper's voice fades away, and I can hear the click of the cassette tape coming to a stop. The poppy beat of "Girls Just Want to Have Fun" was apparently the last on this playlist. When a younger version of my mom introduced it, I wasn't surprised. I can only imagine how that song spoke to her—a girl homeschooled in a small Colorado town by a recluse of a mother.

I groan out a stretch before standing up to pick my next round of music. The tapes clack as I finger through them. There doesn't seem to be any particular order. I've listened to maybe a third, and I've heard everything from an adolescent version of my mother introducing '70s ballads, all the way to a late-teens Mom jamming out to the '80s glam rock. Her intros get better with time, but they're nowhere near the smooth delivery she has on her current morning show.

Since there's no point in looking, I close my eyes and pick a tape at random from the side of the box I haven't dipped into yet.

With the next round of music cued up, I move back to the kitchen table and my paints.

"Good morning, University of Denver. Well, good morning to those of you who aren't still asleep, hungover from last night's Sigma Tau Delta rager."

Smooth. Practiced. Engaging. This is more like the mom I know today. That, plus the mention of her alma mater, throws me off.

"Rumor has it that a few members of our illustrious football team were spotted streaking across campus around midnight. So, this one goes out to them ..."

Jermaine Stewart's classic "We Don't Have to Take Our Clothes Off" fills the cabin, but I'm still too befuddled to enjoy the humorous choice.

This is not the recording of a preteen girl holed up with her boom box in a tree house, playing at being a radio DJ. This is my mom in an actual studio. The one she had a part-time job at when she was in college.

But I know for a fact that the summer after high school, Selena Gunner packed up her truck, left Pine Falls, and never came back. And if what Mom told me is true, Grandma Minnie only came up to Denver on the days each of her grandchildren were born. She stayed long enough to give Mom a crocheted blanket before she turned right back around.

So, how did this recording end up in Minnie's cabin?

Could Mom have mailed it? Maybe as a strange kind of olive branch?

I stand to pace the main room of the cabin as I think.

No. Mom definitely said she didn't contact her mother until she was pregnant with Abram, and that was after she graduated.

An idea occurs, the possibility of it sending an uncomfortable shock of denial through me. But I have to know.

I pause the tape and flick the settings over to FM. Static. I scan through all the channels, and I get nothing. Same with AM.

But that's what I expected. I only hoped differently.

After carrying all my music around in a smartphone for so long, the boom box seems overly heavy as I lug it out the back door. Bruce lounges on the porch, soaking up the sun, and barely gives a twitch as I hurry past him.

The air smells like damp earth baking in the sun. A chill rides the breeze, raising the hair on my exposed arms.

I ignore the beautiful hints of autumn, focusing on my destination and what it might reveal.

Climbing into the tree house while clutching the boom box is awkward, but despite swaying a few times, I manage to get both it and myself through the entry in the floor without damage.

Luckily, I got tired of unplugging and plugging it back in and bought some batteries.

I sit cross-legged on the old wooden floor, hesitating with my fingers poised on the buttons. The stereo seems to gaze back at me, its speakers like wide bug eyes.

Tempting me.

Mocking me.

Shaming me.

I flip the on switch.

Static.

There's a tremor in my fingers as I press the button to scan for stations. A second goes by before, suddenly, a voice spills out.

"... the best deal in downtown Denver! Come get your new car—"

The stereo scans again, landing on a station playing Ariana Grande's latest hit. It scans again, finding a classical music station. It scans again. And again. At some point, a set of familiar numbers flashes on the little digital screen.

I attended the University of Denver too, transferring there for my sophomore year and on. Occasionally, I turned on the school's radio station to see what they were playing.

Today, whoever the jockey is has chosen some classic rock, but I don't bother to focus on the lyrics.

My heart cracks, little fissures in the organ spiking like splinters in my chest.

Because in this moment, I realize my theory is truth.

In the same way that I've been making this tedious climb to get service, so did my grandmother more than thirty years ago. A woman too proud to mend fences with her daughter crawled into a tree house just to hear that daughter's voice.

I press the Off button, needing silence to deal with my realization.

The stereo sits quietly, and I stare back at it.

This was all that Minnie Gunner had for family in the last years of her life. No one visiting her. No one calling her.

She only had the voice of her daughter, broadcasted from miles away.

The pain of this knowledge makes my muscles cramp and my head ache. I curl up on the floor of the tree house, folding under the weight of my sorrow and regret.

Whenever I thought of my grandmother in the past, I assumed she didn't want to know any of us. That she was fine on her own. That family didn't mean anything to her.

But I know different now. A woman who doesn't care does not keep recordings of her daughter's voice.

How many more tapes in that box are from a time after Mom left? How many times did Minnie crawl up into this tree house to listen to her estranged daughter's broadcasts?

"Oh God. I'm so sorry." I moan the words into my hands, feeling the tears coming, the sobs rising from deep in my chest.

What kept her away? But I think I know.

The river. I can imagine her drowning in it, just like I do. The darkness of the water a barrier between her and the person she loved most in the world.

What a horrible joke—for this woman to have been a stranger to me my whole life and only through her death am I getting to know her. The items in her house reveal glimpses of a strong, capable woman, who stored away love for her family the same way she jarred preserves. With dedication and so that only she knew what was contained within.

I'm not sure how long I let myself cry for her. It's more than the loss of a person that hurts me. It's the loss of the one person in my family who I see myself in.

Each piece of Minnie I discover holds a sense of familiarity, as if the same set of tools were used to create us both.

And I cry for the loss of love.

I could have loved her. I know it. If only I had gotten a chance to know her. If I had taken that chance.

But none of us took it.

Minnie didn't reach out to us, but we also didn't reach out to her.

Mom wasn't a gatekeeper. She never denied us access to our grandmother.

"Why didn't I know you?" I whisper to the boom box, like it will transport my message to whatever plane of existence my grand-mother floats in now. I've never been religious, but I can see the appeal. Wouldn't it be nice to know that I haven't lost my chance to know my grandma? To love her?

But all I have is this life, and Minnie is gone from it.

Loneliness creeps up on me like a jungle cat, slowly stalking me, then pouncing with a bone-crushing force that leaves me gasping for breath. My fingers scramble for my pocket, rooting around until I find my phone.

I dial each one of their numbers in turn, starting with the oldest.

Abram. No answer.

Byron. No answer.

Carver. No answer.

Panic has started to set in, and my thumb feels heavy as I try Donovan.

On the second ring, I finally connect.

"Zoey! Are you home?"

My brother's question has me tearing up all over again, but I try not to let on how weepy I am when I respond.

"Not yet. Still in Pine Falls. Suddenly found myself missing Denver though and thought I'd give you all a call. How's it been without me?"

"Hell. Seriously. Byron broke up with that girl he was seeing, the one who bartends at McConnell's. And now, we're all scared to get a drink after our set."

I let out a watery chuckle at the thought of my four brothers, too awkward to ask for a beer because the bartender is glaring at them. They're a talented crew, all taking after our dad, who works as a studio musician. The four of them have their own band, aptly called The Gunners. I refer to them as the Jonas Brothers, which annoys them to no end. So, I never plan to stop.

"Tell Byron to stop dating people at our favorite spots."

Byron is a serial monogamist. He gets invested super fast—grand gestures, romantic dates, weekend trips. Girls and guys all over Denver have fooled themselves into believing they're his forever. Unfortunately, the glitter of a new relationship wears off fast, and when Byron realizes they're not the one, he ends it.

I know for a fact that he's not trying to be insensitive. He really does want to find his forever person. I just don't think he knows what a forever person looks like.

"He never listens," Donovan groans. "We need you back to keep him in line. And to order our drinks for us."

"Good to know you miss your beer buffer," I joke.

"Come on. You know everyone falls to pieces without you." His words make my gut clench in a weird combination of happiness and misery. "Hold on a sec. I'll call them over."

"You're all together?"

"Yeah. Thursday is rugby night."

Of course. My brothers usually play a pickup rugby game on Thursday evenings. I glance at the time on my phone, realizing it's already after six.

Guess I cried for longer than I thought.

It's not long before a chorus of male voices spill through the speaker, all of them talking at once.

"When are you coming back?"

"What's Pine Falls like?"

"Why don't you call more?"

I let them shout out their questions, waiting for them to give me a moment to answer. When they finally quiet down, I take my turn at the conversation.

We spend the next few minutes catching up. Them telling me about all the shenanigans each other has gotten into. Me talking about some of my projects and assuring them that I'm not staying in Pine Falls forever.

Aware that I interrupted their game, I let them go even though all four of them try to insist I stay on the line.

When the phone call ends, I find myself so exhausted that I struggle to sit up. The combination of crying and wrangling my brothers over the phone drained every bit of energy from me.

So, I stay on the floor of the tree house, staring up at the patchy shingled roof.

Despite their exhausting chatter, there was one underlying message I couldn't help but pick up through that call.

They love me.

I'm not forgotten out here in this cabin.

At least not yet.

36

WARNER

OTHER THAN SOME BRIEFS, I'm bare to the chill autumn night. Not that the cold bothers me much. I run hot. We all do. Still, I'd rather be almost all the way naked in Zoey's cabin than out here behind The Rabbit Hole.

But she won't be safe until this is over.

Plus, I plan on heading to her place after this. I just need to make sure not to get too bloody or bruised. My goal is to keep this challenge in the pack. No reason for Zoey to know.

I think I can pull it off, especially because for this challenge, we're remaining in human form.

Fights in wolf form are usually fights to the death. Those are for serious crimes and would mainly be Roderick's responsibility.

But Ross's decision to fuck with Zoey is a different kind of crime.

And that's where wolves differ from humans.

If a human man approached Zoey the way Ross did, with the same outcome of no one being physically hurt, then the police wouldn't do shit about it. Human law doesn't seem to understand how minds work. How intimidation can take away someone's sense of safety. How insults can fester and turn into violence.

I won't let Ross retaliate against Zoey. If he wants violence, then I'll be the one to give it to him.

I bounce on the balls of my feet and shake out my arms, warming up my muscles. All the while, I watch Ross across the clearing.

He's laughing with a couple of the other young pack members.

He still isn't taking this seriously.

The challenge might have surprised him—they don't happen too often—but I can tell he thinks this is going to be like a normal weekend brawl between two wolves that've had too much to drink. A situation he finds himself in almost every other night.

Ross thinks because I like to smile and laugh that I'll be easy enough to beat.

And I realize how little my pack knows me.

I've grown up in Pine Falls, been around these people my whole life, and they still only see what I want them to.

Suddenly, Roderick is in front of me. "He's vain. Probably go for a roundhouse to show off. But I've seen him land it."

My brother's arms are crossed over his chest, and he stares down at me. He has maybe three inches on me, but the power pressing off him always seems to add an extra foot.

"You worried about me?" I give him a casual grin that covers the urge to scowl.

He snorts. "Try not to mess him up too bad. If Ross can't run tomorrow, he'll be hell to have around for the next month."

Roderick knows me.

He can see my fury under my joking veneer. He's also my regular sparring partner when both of our wolves are restless.

My brother knows how fast I am. How good I am at landing a punch.

But even he doesn't understand fully what Zoey means to me. What I'll do for her.

"We'll see," is all I say.

Roderick stares a moment longer before giving the barest hint of a nod and striding out into the middle of the clearing. All side conversations halt. The pack leader holds attention without effort.

When our father died, the pack was left without a head wolf. The next mantle could have gone to anyone in the pack. There's no inheritance rule. It's all tied up in a magical force. A lot of people expected our mom or Uncle Mason to be the next leader. But almost immediately, a change came over Roderick. Already six foot three, he seemed to grow taller, tower above everyone else. He was eighteen, barely an adult, but still had people turning to him.

The responsibility fell on his shoulders to care for the Pine Falls wolves, and I have never seen him falter.

But he also changed that day, and I couldn't help feeling like I somehow lost my brother. Or at least the slightly more carefree version I'd grown up with.

He belongs to more than just my family now.

"Challenge has been declared. Offense given and threats made toward a resident of Pine Falls." Roderick's eyes flick over to me, the only warning before he tacks on an extra bit to the charge. "And a potential future mate."

"What?" Ross shouts as I try to keep all shock off my face.

The pack leader basically just gave his blessing for me to officially pursue Zoey. I thought I was going to have to put up a hell of an argument to even get him to listen to me.

It's not unheard of for a werewolf to take a human mate—we'd probably die out if we didn't—but it's rare, and usually, the human has been around wolves for most of their lives. They aren't outsiders, like Zoey.

What could've changed my stubborn brother's mind?

"This is bullshit," Ross growls. There's wariness in his eyes. He thought this was a fight over him insulting my friend. Not my mate. Even the most easygoing wolf will tear out someone's throat when it comes to protecting their partner. "How was I supposed to know?"

"Maybe you should stop being a dick to all women. Just to be safe." This comment comes from a spectator.

I glance over to see Courtney has backed her pickup to the edge of the woods, dropped the tailgate, and unfolded a lawn chair in the bed of the truck.

She raises her beer. "Go get 'em, Warner! Rip off a limb!"

"Hey!" Ross glares at her.

She smirks right back before chanting, "Less hands, less ass grabbing! Fuck him up!"

There are snickers from some of those assembled. Mainly the females. Looks like Ross doesn't have many fans among the women of our pack.

Challenges are rare occurrences. Too many indicate instability in a pack. I can't help wondering how many women Ross has harassed enough to make them feel uncomfortable, but not enough for them to think it was worth a formal challenge.

I wonder how many here wish they could swap places with me.

Even more of a reason not to hold back.

Roderick raises an arm, regaining control of the crowd.

"Ignorance does not excuse your actions," he announces. "Let this be a warning. And be thankful you face a challenge rather than a trial."

My brother makes a slow circle, including all gathered in his cautioning. When his gaze sweeps over me, I realize his eyes have gone full black. Their depths seem unfathomable. Cosmic. Terrifying.

Note to self: remember to never piss off a pack leader.

"The challenge ends on a forfeit or a knockout. Shifting is prohibited. Commence." Roderick steps back, clearing the space between Ross and me.

In my day-to-day life, I tease people. Not in a malicious manner. My goal is always to make others smile. Get them to laugh. Most times, I'm playful, dancing around important topics, rarely speaking in a fully serious tone.

So, people don't tend to take me seriously.

Even with all the lead up to this challenge, I can tell from the unhurried way Ross raises his arms that he still doesn't believe I can be anything different from the joker he's always known.

I hit fast.

Wide eyes take in the fist heading for his face. Maybe if Ross had expected me to fight with ruthlessness, he'd have been prepared. He would have been ready to block. Despite having the same supernatural speed as I do, he's half a second late.

The bone of his eye socket makes an impression on my knuckles as a meaty thwack echoes through the clearing.

Thing is, werewolves are good at taking hits. While my punch would've laid out a human man, Ross only gives his head a quick shake before lunging at me.

He goes low, trying to knock me off my feet. Get me on the ground, on my back. But I dig in, bending forward and pushing back. And I use the position to pound on his ribs.

As we grapple, the surrounding pack members call out encouragements and jeers and advice.

"Keep your hold on him!"

"Go for the knees!"

"That's a mean punch!"

"Rip his balls off!" Courtney's cheer rises above the rest.

Without warning, Ross releases me, shoving my body away from his violently. The sudden shift has me briefly off-balance. Just enough time for him to land a blow to my gut first, then my jaw. I stumble back a step.

Roderick's warning flashes in my brain, and my arm shoots up in time to block the leaping roundhouse. If the blow had hit my skull, it would have been a knockout for sure. Instead, I'm able to grab hold of Ross's calf and use the man's momentum to fling him over my shoulder.

He hits the ground hard, but I don't let him have a moment to recover his breath. Every second counts.

"*Bitch.*"

That's what he called her. The word pounds in my furious mind as I leap onto my pack mate's chest and aim blows at his head. His arms protect his skull as best they can as frustrated snarls pour from his throat.

"Bitch."

"Bitch."

"Bitch."

"If you won't keep her on a leash, I will."

"You touch her"—I growl the words as I rain down on him with my fists—"I'll kill you. I swear it." The threat comes out on my adrenaline-fueled pants. My voice is low. Monstrous.

Unfortunately, speaking must've slowed me down for a split second because Ross is able to snatch my wrist and wrench it to the side. In that opening, he lunges up, delivering a brain-rattling head butt.

Black spots flicker in my vision, messing me up enough for Ross to heave my weight off him.

We both end up back on our feet, fists raised, eyes wary. The tang of iron fills the air. Blood seeps out of a gash on Ross's forehead and cheek. I can feel my own spilling from a cut on my brow, threatening to blind me.

As we circle each other, I catch sight of Roderick just over my opponent's shoulder.

He meets my eyes, his mouth forming two words. *Finish it.*

Of course, he knows.

I've only been playing with Ross.

Each one of my hits has been a few centimeters away from a point that could send the man into unconsciousness.

Because I didn't want him to black out.

I wanted him to hurt. To know that if he comes for Zoey, this is just a taste of what he'll get.

Still, Roderick is right. The fight needs to end.

If only so I can go be with her.

The grass is cool under my feet as I slide forward, feigning to the right. He leaps, trying for the high ground.

But I'm not afraid to go low. Dropping to the earth, I roll under his legs and rise up again behind him. Before Ross has time to land and turn, my body is already in motion.

Using his move against him, I swing my leg high, the force behind it as brutal as a hammer. He turns as if we choreographed the move together, placing his jaw exactly where I planned on it being. My foot hits the perfect spot, and his body crumples.

Ragged pants push and pull from my chest, the only sound in the woods with everyone else having gone quiet.

Roderick strides up to the fallen wolf, using the toe of his boot to flip the guy over.

We can all hear the air trickling in and out of his slack mouth.

"Knockout. Warner wins the challenge. If Ross commits the same offense again, he will stand trial."

Everyone gathered knows what that means. If I, not even the most powerful of the Jameson brothers, took the man down this quickly, no way would he stand a chance against Roderick. A trial would mean the wolf's death.

A few of Ross's friends come to collect him. Even though his face still pisses me off, I hope he'll take this loss with grace. Mainly because I want Zoey safe. But also because my brother shouldn't have to deal with idiots with death wishes.

But our pack hasn't had a trial in decades. Even Ross wouldn't be arrogant enough to stumble into one.

Not after I just handed him his ass.

37

ZOEY

BY THE TIME Warner cuts off his bike, I'm already half naked.

Living a mile away from the nearest neighbor has its perks. It means I can open the front door, wearing nothing but a bra and panties without scandalizing the gossipmongers in this small town.

I need this. Touch. Comfort. Connection.

Maybe combatting the darkness with sex isn't the healthiest method, but at least I'm not drinking myself into oblivion.

The front lawn is shadowed, but I can still make out Warner's form as he dismounts. And I can see the way he stumbles to a stop when he takes me in. Next thing I know, the werewolf is running toward me, a triumphant howl ringing from him. The sound has me shivering in anticipation.

Warner tackles me in the gentlest manner. He scoops me up in his arms and uses his momentum to carry us both into the house. My arms circle his neck, and my legs wrap around his waist, clinging as I laugh at his enthusiasm.

"Nothing is better than seeing you waiting for me like this." He rumbles the words with his face pressed into my hair and kicks the front door shut with the heel of his boot.

Disturbed from his nap, Bruce gives an exasperated huff before trotting back toward the guest bedroom he's claimed as his own.

"Really? You like me without clothes on? I never would've guessed." I can feel myself grinning as I move to meet Warner's eye.

Only I can't. He keeps his head turned away as he walks around the cabin with me in his arms. And for some reason, he seems bent on shutting off the lights.

"Don't bother with those." I didn't wear my cutest set of underwear, only to hook up with Warner in the dark. Plus, I made sure to use ice packs on my eyes to get rid of the puffiness from my earlier sob-fest.

"I'm setting the mood," he murmurs against my ear.

I shiver again.

Still, there's tension underlying his words. The same bit that has all the muscles in his neck tightening. My first assumption was that it was sexual.

But now, I'm not so sure.

When the only light in the cabin is the almost-full moon peeking through a slit in the curtains, Warner finally turns his head to kiss me.

His mouth is ravenous, his tongue eager. The werewolf stands in the middle of the main room, clutching me to him, devouring my mouth as if I'm the reason he can breathe.

When we finally break apart, he gasps out one question. "Couch or bed?"

"Couch," I declare.

For one, it's closer. But also, it works better with my plan.

Just because my mind begs to get lost in the passion of Warner's kiss doesn't mean I'll give in to the urge.

Something is wrong, and I'm going to find out what.

"I assume you want me on bottom," he says, his tone half humorous, half pleading.

"Glad that you're learning." My voice is all huskiness, and Warner responds to it eagerly.

He walks around to the front of the couch, settling us on the old cushions, him lying back while I straddle his waist.

I'm tempted to lean down and kiss the hell out of him.

But I can't.

Before he realizes my intention, I reach for the lamp on the table beside the armrest and flick on the light.

His body goes taut under me, and when I blink to adjust my eyes, I see why.

Warner's eyebrow has a nasty gash through it, and his face is bruised. He winces and avoids my eyes, but that doesn't stop me from wrenching up his shirt to find even more discoloration on his torso.

"Where did all of these bruises come from?" My words come out ragged with worry. He's riddled with injuries. "Did you have an accident at work?"

"It doesn't matter. They'll be healed in a few hours." Warner pries his shirt out of my hands, pulling it down to cover himself.

"It *does* matter. What happened? When did it happen? You weren't messed up like this when we went out to lunch!"

"Zoey." He groans my name, sitting up to bury his face in my neck and wrap his arms around my waist. The hold presses us tight together, which I would enjoy any other time, but now, I can't examine his injuries.

He starts kissing my skin, causing goose bumps to prickle all over my body.

The sneaky animal is looking to distract me.

I'm not having any of it.

My fingers comb into his hair, as if I'm giving him a normal gentle caress. Then, I fist my hands, grabbing hold of the roots and directing his head back until Warner meets my eyes. He pants, lust clear in his gaze.

He likes when I take charge. When I get a little rough.

"Warner." His name comes out of my throat in a sultry murmur, and his eyelids flicker at the sound. "What do I want?"

"You want to suck my dick?"

I almost smile at the hopeful note in his voice.

But I keep the humor off my face, instead giving his hair another tug before leaning down to bite his bottom lip. Hard.

He groans, deep in his throat, and his erection grows hard under my ass.

"What do I want?" My tone is more demanding as I repeat the question.

With his head pulled back, I can see the way he swallows. I can watch the tensing, then relaxing of his jaw. After a moment, he sighs in defeat.

"You want to know what happened to me."

My grip relaxes, and I use the pads of my fingers to massage his scalp and place a gentle kiss to his lip to soothe where I bit him.

"You don't have to tell me." I watch Warner's eyebrows rise in disbelief before I clarify. "But if you don't, I'm going to ask you to leave."

His embrace tightens again as wide eyes search my face.

Maybe it's unfair that I'd be fine with a friend like Juliet keeping her secrets from me while I demand that Warner share his or get out.

But Juliet wasn't covered in bruises.

And the rules of friends change when ...

When you're whatever Warner and I are.

"I got into a fight with another wolf," Warner admits.

"Werewolf or *wolf*, wolf?"

"Werewolf."

"Why were you two fighting?"

Warner grimaces before resting his head on my shoulder. "Because he would've hurt you if I hadn't."

Cold trails through my veins at his words, and I give an involuntary shiver.

"Could you elaborate on that?"

Warner loosens his hold, only to rub his hands up and down my back. The move is soothing, but I can't give up all the tension thrumming through me. My eyes flit to the dark window, wondering if I'll see the face of an animal on the other side of the glass.

"It was Ross. The asshole from my work. You insulted him, made him look stupid."

Some of my fear gives way to anger. "Good. That was the point."

Warner lifts his head to offer me a thin smile. His warm palms cup my cheeks, and he trails his thumb over my lips. "And I loved watching you talk circles around him." He sighs. "But my kind doesn't take insults lightly. And we hold grudges. When I got back, he made some more comments, and I knew things weren't over. Not in his mind." Warner's hold becomes firm, as if he's desperate to keep me in place. "I knew that if Ross ever came across you again, there was the real possibility he might hurt you."

"So, you fought him?"

Warner nods. "Werewolves are territorial. We'll get violent to protect what's ours. Especially if it's someone we care about."

Is that what I am? His?

I don't voice the question, not sure I want to hear the answer.

"But how does you two fighting solve anything? Did you ... kill him?" I hesitate because this is another answer I'm not sure I want.

"No! No, I swear." Warner presses a kiss to my forehead, so gentle that I have trouble imagining him getting violent with anyone. "Think of it like MMA. I just knocked him out. We weren't even in wolf form."

"Okay." I've never been a fan of the sport, but at least I have a mental image. "Still, what's to keep Ross from hurting me in the future?"

"It's a dominance thing. And a warning. He knows that if he hurts you, I'll come after him. Actually, if he comes after you, he'll face punishment from the pack." Warner grimaces, obviously realizing he's not explaining the situation well.

"I think you need to tell me more about werewolves. Do you all have different rules than humans? Do I have to follow those rules when we're together?"

Warner tilts his head as he ponders my questions. "We do. Have different rules, that is. And we monitor ourselves. The Pine Falls police force doesn't have jurisdiction over the pack, and they know it."

"That's disconcerting."

His lips pull tight before he shrugs. "In some towns, with other packs, yeah. It would be. But our pack leader is Roderick. You'll never meet a more honorable guy. And if anything, he holds us to a higher standard than any human laws would."

I think back on my brief interaction with the stoic werewolf. He was intimidating, but reminded me of my oldest brother Abram, one of the most honorable men I know. Maybe werewolf law isn't the worst thing in the world.

Problem is, it's hard to follow rules I haven't learned.

"And do I have to meet these standards too? Since we're hanging out."

Now, Warner stares at me with intensity. "Hanging out?"

"No changing the subject." *Especially to a topic I'm not ready to discuss.* "Am I going to get challenged to a cage fight?"

The werewolf relaxes back on the armrest, his gaze tracing over me, finally admiring my lingerie. "No. But if you piss off werewolves, I might have to fight a few more on your behalf."

Guilt and annoyance war in me.

"So, your injuries are my fault?"

His stare, which went heavy as he looked at my body, widens and jumps to my face. "No, Zoey. This is all Ross. He needed to be put in his place. Even if you hadn't set him down, I still would have called him out just for the way he came on to you."

Still, this seems to come back to me. And I don't like the circular way our conversation is going. Instead, I take advantage of Warner's willingness to share to ask another werewolf question.

"Do you live forever?"

His smile returns. He smiles so easily, and I enjoy the warm glow of his good humor.

"No. We heal faster, so we live longer. But not by much. Maybe add ten more years to our average life expectancy."

"Okay. And how are werewolves made?"

He smirks. "Lack of birth control."

That surprises a laugh out of me, but I clench my teeth down to stifle any more. Warner gives me his cheekiest grin as his callous palms drag up over my exposed stomach. When he reaches the lacy cups of my bra, his thumbs tease at the material, and I feel the heat of his touch through the fabric. My nipples tighten, and he gives a satisfied hum in the back of his throat.

Then, I notice two things. The first is an obvious hardening under my butt. The second is a blackness that seeps out from his pupils, erasing the lovely brandy color of his irises.

The change is fascinating. I find myself leaning forward, cupping his cheeks to hold him in place so I can watch it happen.

"Why do your eyes do that? Turn black?"

Warner blinks. "Emotion. If a wolf is enraged. Or aroused." He leans up to nip at my nose before dropping his head back to the armrest. "It shows our animalistic nature is coming out. It also happens right before a change."

I jerk back. "You're not going to change in the middle of sex, are you?"

The werewolf laughs at that, but stifles the amusement when he spots my frown.

"No. Don't worry. For one, as long as it's not the full moon, I have complete control over when I change. But also, when I'm in wolf form, I don't deal with sexual urges. That's all in my human form. All the wolf cares about is your safety."

"Good to know." I smirk down at him.

A sudden tug on my wrist pulls me forward until my face is flush with his. When my hair falls around us like a brown curtain, I feel safe from the world. Werewolf rules and human rules drift away. Warner gives another tug until I'm close enough for him to bury his head in the crook of my neck. I hear the deep inhale he makes, and the sound piques my curiosity.

"What's up with you always sniffing my neck? Are you planning on chomping down? That seems like vampire territory."

Warner chuckles and licks my quickening pulse. "It's one of your warm spots."

"Warm spots?"

His nose trails over the skin, teasing me until I can't help squirming in his hold.

"Mmhmm. Your scent is stronger here. Drives me crazy." His teeth pinch me, but so gently that all I can do is gasp.

"You said spots. Where else?" Hopefully, he's not about to shove his face in my armpit.

Warner unhooks my bra and slides it off my arms before pressing his nose between my breasts. "Here."

He licks my skin, and a shaking starts deep inside me.

Strong hands trail down my spine and over my thighs until his fingers press into the soft flesh at the back of my knees. "This is another."

"You want to sniff my knees?" Despite my rising arousal, I can't help snorting out a giggle. Against my chest, I can feel Warner smile.

But then his fingers reverse their journey until they find the center of me.

"This is probably my favorite though." And he starts to leisurely stroke me, which means I'm back to writhing against him.

Memories of our previous encounter flash through my mind. Half of me wants to repeat the experience move for move just to ensure the same mind-shattering result. But the other half of me wants to come up with new avenues to pleasure.

Suddenly, I realize my oversight. Last time, I treated Warner like a human man. I didn't even consider the possibilities that come along with his supernatural status.

"How strong are you?"

38

WARNER

I TILT MY HEAD UP, searching her gaze. If Zoey were a wolf, her eyes would be turning black. As it is, I watch her pupils expand with excitement.

With the odd tracks her mind sometimes takes, I can't fathom what her goal is. But I hope she has something dirty planned.

"Lifting this couch on my own wouldn't be a problem." Since I don't go to the gym, I can't offer my benching numbers.

"When you carry me ..." Her breath catches, and her pulse pounds so hard that I can watch it flutter under her skin.

"Light as a feather."

My human nods, her eyes tracking over me, and then she abruptly sits up, which pushes her ass into my straining erection. I groan, eager for the moment I can push inside her tight heat again.

"I've decided against the couch," Zoey announces.

"You want me to carry you to the bed?" *Please say yes.*

"No."

"Then—"

"How do you feel about fucking me up against a wall?"

My answer is to scoop her up in my arms, holding her close against my chest as I move to the middle of the room.

"Which wall?"

Zoey chuckles, smoothing her hands over my tight shoulders. Her touch is fire and torture, and I never want her to stop.

Instead of choosing, she leans into me and bites the lobe of my ear.

I grunt and stumble forward, finding the nearest space, an expanse of bare wood to press her up against. My hips and chest pin her in place, and she gasps when I rock against her.

But then she utters the one word sure to freeze all the heated lust coursing through me.

"Stop," Zoey commands.

And I listen, immediately stepping back and letting her feet settle on the floor. My eyes trace over her body, searching for where I went wrong. Nothing is obvious, but I yearn to know. To correct my mistake.

"Zoey, I—"

"Do you want to lick my pussy again?"

A shiver works a slow path through my body, and I can imagine blackness seeping into my eyes.

"Yes," I growl.

The thought of having Zoey's taste on my tongue brings my animalistic nature to the surface.

"Then, get on your knees."

I drop fast and press my face into her belly, breathing in her sweet, earthy scent. Zoey sighs a happy note as I nose through her curls, then lifts a thigh to give me better access. Her eyes flutter closed at the first swipe of my tongue. Hands in my hair, leg slung over my shoulder, bare breasts thrust forward. She is a goddess. Powerful. Taking what she wants from me without an ounce of embarrassment.

This is what I hungered for after that first night in the bar. I needed her, this woman who wouldn't be afraid of me or mine. Someone fierce and bold. Unafraid to dominate even the most terrifying of monsters.

Maybe Zoey Gunner isn't the type of person looking for control out in the world, but here, in our passion, she holds court. In our pack of two, she is the alpha, and I am her devoted beta.

A human who knows about my claws and fangs, yet still demands I drop to my knees and lick her cunt.

Her moans mix with gasps as her nails dig into my scalp. The sharp pricks go straight to my cock, and I fist myself, even as I circle my tongue around her clit.

"That's it," she groans, writhing against the wall, rocking into my face.

Arousal tastes sharp and tangy, not like food, but delicious in a forbidden way. I bury my face in her folds. Her warmest spot.

"Warner ..." Zoey pants my name, and I stare up at her through the valley of her breasts. Maple-brown eyes connect with mine. "Make me come," she demands.

My balls tighten, wanting to join her. But it's too soon. If I can last, I'll be inside her, surrounded by her tight warmth.

Sliding my lips back to her clit, I suck until she's gasping on screams. Her leg buckles, but I catch my goddess, slinging her other leg over my shoulder and pressing her to the wall as the orgasm ripples through her.

After a moment, I realize the painful, pleasurable grip on my hair has loosened, and instead, she's stroking my sweat-damp strands.

"Good werewolf."

I glance up to catch her little smirk, which has me chuckling. "Smart-ass," I mutter before pressing kisses to her soft belly.

Her scent surrounds me, thicker than syrup, and I'm still hard and throbbing.

A light touch strokes under my chin, tilting my head up.

"Stand up."

I slide her legs from my shoulders and rise up from my crouched position. Suddenly looming over her feels wrong. Zoey should have the higher ground. Wrapping my palms around her thighs, I boost her up until my new belt is her strong legs. We both groan as her damp center brushes against my erection.

But the delicious sensation somehow brings on a sliver of logic.

"Condom. Fuck. We need—I need—" *Do I have any with me?* My brain is barely working, but I cycle through the places guys normally keep condoms.

Wallets. But our health ed teacher told us that's a good way to end up with a damaged rubber.

Glove compartment. I drive a fucking motorcycle.

Bedside table. We're at Minnie Gunner's cabin. I doubt the woman kept a lot of contraceptives around.

"I don't have one." The confession burns my throat with regret, my forehead banging against the wall I have the most gorgeous, intoxicating woman pressed up against. But a small hope flares to life. "Do you?"

Leaning back, I find myself staring at a furiously blushing Zoey. Her fingers fiddle with the hair at the back of my neck, and her eyes dart around, as if trying to look anywhere but into mine.

Worry rattles through me.

"Zoey?"

"I was going to!" The words burst out of her, and her cheeks get even redder. "I was in the store, in the aisle, standing right in front of them, and then boom!"

"Boom? What's boom?"

"Your *mom* is boom." The sexual dominant from a second ago flees in the face of her embarrassment. "She walked down the aisle, and we made eye contact, so I panicked and grabbed tampons instead. This town is so fucking small."

Damn it, Mom. Way to be a cockblock.

"It's okay," I murmur. Her skin is scorching when I press a kiss to her neck, all that blood pooling just under the surface. "We can have sex another night."

The talon grip is back in my hair, pulling my head back until I meet molten chocolate eyes.

"Sex isn't only P in V, Warner. And I'm not going to be satisfied until I see you come."

Every muscle in my body clenches, twitching with anticipation.

Suddenly, the possibilities seem endless. One road is off-limits, but there are plenty of others that we can drive down. Will she stroke me with her strong grip? Or maybe she'll take me in her mouth again, not stopping at the edge, but instead pushing me all the way?

"Take me to the bed," Zoey commands.

Walking with a raging hard-on and a naked goddess wrapped around me isn't the easiest task in the world, but I manage. In the bedroom, I go to sit on the mattress, expecting my woman will want to take her place on top. But her next direction stops me.

"Lay me down."

The old springs squeak as her body bounces on her landing. The many soft spots on her jiggle, hypnotizing me, tempting me to sink down on my knees again. Her taste is already fading from my tongue, and I want it back.

My hand grabs her ankle, ready to pull apart her legs and expose that delicious core of her.

But Zoey shakes her head and scoots further back on the covers.

"Come here, Biker Boy. Kneel over me." And as she speaks, her hands cup her boobs, thumbs rubbing over her nipples. The pose is an offering.

I lose myself in the erotic nature of the idea. The temptation is so acute that my body has forgotten how to move.

"Don't you want to?" Zoey's question breaks through the shock, and I can see the uncertainty in the way she bites her lip.

"Fuck yes," I growl, crawling up her body, dragging my mouth over her bare skin as I go.

Every lick and nip has her gasping and chuckling. When my face reaches her chest, I tongue her stiff nipples in turn, a preemptive thank-you.

Zoey writhes under my ministrations. "I've never tried this. But— oh God—I want to watch you."

A growl of need rips from my throat. Despite the animalistic nature of the sound, my wolf isn't controlling my actions. I am all man at this moment, and my woman wants to watch as I use her body to find release.

With my knees pressing into the mattress beside her ribs, my erection bobs, the tip seeping liquid that drops onto her flushed chest.

Zoey presses her boobs together as her heavy-lidded eyes meet mine. She must be staring into pure blackness.

Bracing one hand above her head, I use the other to guide my dick to the cradle she's created. Soft. Warm. Erotic beyond belief.

My cock's head appears and disappears as I slowly thrust. Zoey hums a satisfied purr, her lips curving in a wicked smile as her fingers pluck at her nipples.

It's. Too. Much.

My speed increases, and the moisture that seeps from me makes each pass slicker. Soon, Zoey's skin glistens with my pre-cum, and I want to roar in triumph.

"Warner."

At the sound of my name, I realize I've been focused on watching myself thrust against her. I drag my eyes upward, meeting a fiercely commanding gaze.

"Zoey," I groan, her name a plea.

"Come for me." She's not begging. The statement commands my obedience.

Suddenly, I'm spilling. My cum covers her chest, marking her as I shout curses of pleasure, hands fisting in the pillow beside her head.

Zoey releases her chest, her palms cupping my ass as I jerk involuntarily with the force of my release. When I'm spent, I roll to the side, collapsing on the mattress. The ceiling shifts and blurs as the aftershocks of pleasure fog my mind.

The bedsprings squeak again, and I realize Zoey is leaving me.

"Where—"

She cuts me off, "Don't move. Be right back."

I watch her ass as she strolls out of the room. A minute later, she comes back, hands full.

"Careful with this. It might still be drying." She lays a motorcycle helmet on my bare chest. The protective wear has a fearsome wolf painted on the side.

"This is badass." I sit up, holding it with care. "Where did you get it?"

Zoey smiles, the expression a beautiful combination of shyness and pride. "I made it. Well, I painted it. For you. Do you like it? I can do a different design if that's not to your taste."

"You ..." My throat is suddenly tight with emotion, and I cough to clear it. "You're gods-damn amazing. I love it."

She grins wide, and I watch a beautiful red flush cover more than her cheeks. The tint traces down her neck and over her chest. That's when I notice the other item she's carrying. A damp towel, which she uses to clean herself. As the wet cloth wipes my cum away, I mourn the loss. My claim was temporary. Easily removed.

When will she let me mark her permanently?

What will I do if she never does?

39

ZOEY

MY MIND IS OCCUPIED by a debate over the font choice for a client's website when I pull up to the cabin. The mental back-and-forth has me so distracted that I don't realize I've parked next to another car until I remove the key from the ignition.

What the hell?

In the weeks I've been in Pine Falls, my only visitor has been Warner. But tonight is the full moon, so he's ridden off with his pack to go howl at the night sky and run around naked in the woods.

Or whatever they all do.

Tonight, I'm on my own. Or at least, I was supposed to be.

Any other day, I might have guessed that the visitor is Juliet. Only I just left the library, and she was halfway through a shift at the reference desk.

The mystery is solved the minute I climb out of my truck and get a glimpse of the SUV's bumper. More specifically, the bumper stickers pasted all over it.

Rugby—No helmet, no pads, just balls.

Happiness is a good ruck.

Support your local hooker. Play rugby!

And the last one, my favorite: *Be kind to animals. Kiss a rugby player.*

My brothers are here.

And if I had any last bit of doubt, it's blown to pieces by a shout from the front porch.

"Baby sister! You're alive!" Carver, the most enthusiastically affectionate of my four brothers, comes barreling down the stairs and across the yard toward me. Soon, I'm wrapped in a bear hug, being swung around like a well-loved rag doll.

"Don't break her," Abram, the oldest of us all, scolds.

When Carver sets me down, Abram gives me a gentle but firm hug, then passes me off to Byron for the same. Donovan is satisfied with ruffling my hair affectionately.

"What are you all doing here?" I stare around at their familiar grinning faces, not realizing until this moment just how much I missed them.

Carver drapes his arm over my shoulders and turns me toward the house. "You sounded lonely when you called. And we were tired of waiting for you to come back to Denver."

"We came to help you finish with the cabin," Abram explains.

"But you all have jobs. That, like, require you to be at them."

I'm the only one in the bunch who doesn't have the typical forty-hour workweek.

Abram is a district manager for a tractor supply company.

Byron works at a music shop, repairing instruments.

Carver is a physical therapist.

And Donovan works as a cyber security analyst.

Bunch of stand-up guys who shouldn't be playing hooky from their well-paying jobs.

"It's called vacation time. Ever heard of it?" Carver knocks on the front door, which sets Bruce to barking. "We've been waiting outside forever. Unlock the door."

I roll my eyes and fight a smile at his whining. "If I had known you were coming, I would've left you a key."

"But then we wouldn't have gotten to see your dumbass surprised look," Carver offers.

"I do not look like a dumbass ever! I always look like the smartest of asses!" I shove my brother through the now-open front door as he laughs.

"So, this is Grandma Minnie's place." Byron is the next in, and he moves to the center of the room, turning slowly to observe every angle.

I look at the cabin with new eyes, seeing it how my brothers see it. The space isn't hugely different from when I first arrived. All the furniture is pretty much the same, other than the upgrades I've made to them. I realize that despite my idea to potentially sell the pieces once they were refurbished, I haven't looked into any options for that task. I simply made everything look better, then arranged the furniture how I preferred.

As if this were my place.

The thought sends a spike of panic through me. I've been settling in. Getting comfortable here. Turning this cabin into an introvert's hideaway.

"What still needs getting done? Have you talked to the local realtor?" Abram starts flicking light switches, as if he thinks he's going to find a dud. Like I would let myself live in darkness.

Unfortunately, that isn't an unreasonable assumption based on how they last found me.

"No, I haven't. I guess I thought Mom would do that since she's technically the one who owns it."

Donovan silently wanders around the space, eyeing my handiwork.

"True. Then, we just need to make it ready for sale," Abram says.

We?

For the first time since I realized the car parked outside was Carver's, I resent my brothers' surprise visit.

I've spent weeks working on this cabin, and now, they're here to speed things along? Rush me through to the end?

This is *my* project. I wanted to go at my pace.

But that's life with the Gunner boys.

Say goodbye to my control.

40

WARNER

THERE ARE no clouds in the night sky, allowing the light from the full moon to spill down and bathe us in her cool glow. My wolf stretches under my skin, as if waking up from a long nap, and waits eagerly for me to take my animal form.

I'm eager too.

Once I'm wolf, my thoughts will be less focused. Instinct will take over, and I'll be able to melt into the rhythm of the pack.

Thoughts of Zoey will tuck into the back corner of my mind. Worry about leaving her will hopefully dim.

There's nothing to be anxious over. She'll be in Pine Falls, right where you left her, once this night is done.

A dark voice in the back of my mind brings out my doubt. *Will she though?*

Things between Zoey and me are good. But they're good in the same way that skydiving is good. All glorious rush and heady feelings, with the hope that once the rip cord is pulled, a parachute will deploy and keep me from smashing into a pile of blood, bone, and entrails when I hit the ground.

We're falling, and as long as I don't touch the rip cord, I can convince myself there *is* a parachute.

I can tell myself that falling for Zoey won't end in disaster.

"If you're separated, we meet back here at dawn. Head count is required before we head back to town." Roderick's normally steady voice is broken with a growling quality tonight. The change is gripping him as tightly as the rest of us.

A third of the pack is already in their wolf forms.

We've gathered in the field behind an abandoned barn. The land is owned by the pack, allowing us to park an entire fleet of bikes and cars here. Not everyone in the pack is a member of The Dark Moon Riders. Roderick said once that he thinks the pack instinct calls to some more than others, and those are the members who join the club. The ones who need that group around them for more than one night a month.

Prime example of someone who doesn't have any interest in joining: Courtney.

She sits on the bed of her truck, wearing only a T-shirt dress and probably nothing underneath it. I already have my shirt and pants off while a good deal of other people are stripping or completely naked. Modesty isn't a big thing among the pack.

"How's your lady doing?"

Of course my friend would feel the need to talk to me about the one topic I'm trying not to focus on. And at a moment when talking normally isn't encouraged. We're supposed to be connecting to our animal forms, not having a casual chat.

"Home. Safe." The growling is in my voice too.

Courtney's eyes haven't even turned black yet.

"Home? You think she's sticking around?"

Because I can't handle the panic that comes with any other answer, I give the one that will hopefully keep my wolf calm. "Yes."

Shadows caress my skin as a tension grows. Courtney grins while she watches.

"Glad to hear it. I'll have to make more of an effort."

I'm past the point where I can ask what she means. A series of painful snaps shudders through my body like dominoes falling.

Then, my whole view of the world changes.

Thoughts blur into a series of feelings and urges while my senses sharpen. I shake off the tingles of left-behind magic, then recognize the call of my pack leader, mixed with the tease of Mother Moon.

"Run."

The simple word infuses my limbs, guiding me to fall in and follow. Loose dirt shifts under the heavy weight of my paws as I pick up my pace.

We head away from the makeshift parking lot and let the forest envelop us. Scents flow into me with each of my deep breaths. I want to consume the night, and I can't help the joyful noises that push from my throat and receive responses from those flanking me.

Even as the thick branches block out the light of the moon, I can feel her glow on my back. She is glorious, giving off pure energy. My muscles surge with the touch of her magic.

My view of myself as an individual blurs until there are only thoughts of us. Thoughts of we. The pack moves as one massive, joyful procession through the night.

A scent drifts on the wind. Musky and warm. Hunger demands I follow, and I am not the only one. The animal flees from our pursuit, but it does not have the blessing of Mother Moon.

Soon, I feast on meat, blood dripping and pooling on the forest floor.

Zoey would hate this part. The thought is a light caress against my mind that drifts away like a breeze ruffling my coat.

My future mate is safe, and I will return to her when this celebration is done.

Belly full, I run again, soon mixing in with my pack.

We hunt and howl and fulfill a deep need in our souls.

The night passes, but I do not count the seconds. Time loses its meaning, and I give myself up to the wolf.

41

ZOEY

THE ROAR of a motorcycle rumbling down Grandma Minnie's drive has me smiling.

"Is Dad here?" Carver turns to the room, the plate he was half-done washing dripping water onto the floor.

"That can't be him. He has a gig in Boulder tonight." Byron moves to the front window, pulling the curtain open and peering out, Donovan at his shoulder.

"Looks like some pretty-boy biker guy," my youngest brother announces, and I try to stifle my snort as I start screwing the caps back on my paints.

Some of my humor fades when Abram stands from his chair, his looming rugby build taking up more than his fair share of the cabin's family room. He stares down at me, his face blank, but I know his protective instincts are firing to life, like a series of gears he always keeps well oiled.

"Who is he?"

"He's my ..." So many different words bombard me that I struggle to finish my sentence.

Friend? I don't tend to have wild sex with my friends.

Boyfriend? We haven't talked about commitment because that would mean I have to think about the future.

Biker werewolf protector? Well, I don't want to give my brothers any reason to think I'm hallucinating. Or that I need protection.

"Warner," I finish with a hopeless shrug.

"*Your* Warner?" My brother's jaw tenses. "Or does he think you're *his*?"

"What are you talking about?"

"We stopped in to see Mom before heading out here. She had some interesting things to say about the local biker gang." Abram takes a step toward the door.

Holy shit. Did she tell them about the werewolves?

"What interesting things?" I forget my paints, shoving my chair back to follow my brother.

Abram glares at me. The expression doesn't intimidate me, but it does make me worry about what is about to go down.

"She said these guys aren't like Dad's group. Not just casual riders. She said they make their own rules. That more than half this town is scared of them."

I grimace, not able to refute any of that.

Thanks a lot, Mom.

Abram clearly thinks The Dark Moon Riders are some outlaw motorcycle club that's smuggling guns and dealing drugs.

I want to tell him that they don't follow our rules because they *can't*. No lawmaker ever took supernatural creatures into account when they were drafting legislation. And, yeah, people are scared of them. But not because they terrorize the town. They're scared because the existence of werewolves is disconcerting.

If I was sure my mom had told my brothers about werewolves, then I'd make this argument.

But it seems like she left them in the dark on that important point.

And it's not my secret to share.

"Zoey?" Warner calls from the driveway.

I can imagine him staring at the SUV, wondering who my visitors are.

"Mom also said these guys get possessive when it comes to women. Like they think they own you."

What the hell?

"That's not—"

Heavy boots crunch on the gravel outside, and Abram turns away from me to pull open the door. I try to follow right after him, but Carver, Byron, and Donovan somehow get there before me. Their massive bodies clog the entryway. I'm not sure if they're keeping me inside intentionally or if they're just oblivious.

"Who are you?"

Even through the wall of Gunners, I can hear Warner's voice.

"Move, you oaf!" I shove at Byron's back, but he barely shifts his weight, waving me off as if I were distracting him from an entertaining show.

"You're the one who showed up here, unannounced."

Great. He's decided to be Abram the Asshole.

My oldest brother has a history of anger issues, but I thought he was dealing with them.

Apparently, therapy isn't working.

I growl and try to shove Donovan to the side with my shoulder. He smirks down at me before leaning to block even more of the doorway.

"Where's Zoey?" A deep warning note twists into Warner's question.

Trust my brothers to piss off the most easygoing werewolf in all of Pine Falls.

"Busy. Not that it's any of your business," Abram replies, voice cold.

This is quickly turning into an Occurrence.

And I've had enough.

"Stupid, overprotective, moronic, pigheaded brothers," I mutter to myself as I stomp over to a window.

The glass has grown wavy with time, and I still need to clean the panes to see out of it properly. But I'm not looking to wave from a window like a damsel in distress. This Rapunzel is getting out of her backwoods tower.

With an angry tug, I swing the window open, then throw my leg over the low sill.

"Stop trying to start a fight, Abram!"

All the men—scratch that, boys—whip their heads in my direction in time to see my toe catch on the windowsill, causing me to stumble onto the porch. I'm just able to keep from falling on my face, or my ass, and I make sure to come up glowering.

Warner seems relieved at the sight of me and even manages a tight smile before turning wary eyes back on my brother.

Abram stands on the top step, arms crossed, blockish face wearing a foreboding scowl that he still has turned on Warner. Most people would find the sight intimidating. My brother is huge in a Dwayne "The Rock" Johnson kind of way.

But Warner is a werewolf, so yeah. Game, set, and match.

Not that Abram knows he's got nothing on Warner.

"Get back inside, Zoey," mutters my brother.

"Get your head out of your ass, Abram!" I'm yelling. My family can always get me to yell. "This is an irrational response, and you three are enabling him." I throw my glare toward the Gunners lingering in the doorway.

"Zoey"—Warner speaks in a careful, almost-soft voice as he holds out his hand—"why don't you come on over here?"

And I realize that even while he talks to me, Warner keeps his eyes on Abram. As if he's waiting for my brother to make an aggressive move.

Against me.

"Werewolves are territorial. We'll get violent to protect what's ours. Especially if it's someone we care about."

Nerves course through me at the memory, and I rush to stand in front of Abram.

"This is my brother, Warner. They're all my brothers."

Warner gives me a tense nod, but doesn't lose any of the tension in his face or body. "They're trying to keep you locked up." He continues to use that overly calm voice. Someone might believe he wasn't upset.

But I can see his eyes.

The normal enchanting amber color bleeds into black.

Not good. Angry werewolf is not good.

Problem is, I can't think of a way to defuse the situation.

If I step toward Warner, I can guarantee Abram will approach too. He might even grab me. Warner wouldn't like that.

But if I move back toward my brothers, the wolf will think I don't have a choice. That they're trying to keep me contained.

And if I decide to say, *Screw you*, and sprint into the woods, leaving them all behind, who knows what kind of chaos would erupt?

It's while my mind cycles through all these impossible options that I notice Warner's eyes flicker to the side slightly, as if he hears something.

A moment later, the crunch of tires disrupts the tension.

A sunshine-yellow pickup truck appears, barreling down the driveway. When it comes to an abrupt stop, I swear I hear a squawk.

The driver's door flings open, revealing a grinning woman.

Courtney has arrived.

"Looks like I'm crashing a party! Sweet!"

Today, she has on a pair of torn jeans, a simple black sweater, and compared to the bejeweled footwear I've seen her sport, a relatively tame pair of purple cowboy boots. For the most part, she looks like a normal, beautiful woman.

That is, if I ignore the chicken she's cradling.

"What are you doing here?" Warner asks. He doesn't sound over-joyed at her appearance, but I'm relieved to hear resignation in his voice rather than the barely restrained anger.

"I came to give Zoey a housewarming present."

She holds up the chicken like we're in the opening scene of *The Lion King*. The bird writhes in indignation.

"She doesn't need a housewarming present." Abram's scowl is practically audible. "She's not staying."

Whatever distraction Courtney's sudden appearance provided evaporates. Warner's eyes seep into black again as he glares over my shoulder.

"Zoey doesn't need you making decisions for her," he growls.

This is a side of Warner I haven't seen before.

My domineering brother steps around me, practically flexing his muscles in an intimidation move. "And I'm supposed to let *you* do that?"

Warner scoffs. "As if I need you to *let* me do anything."

Courtney bounds up the steps to stand beside me, wearing a delighted smile. "If I'd known your place was so interesting, I would've come over weeks ago."

I don't have the mental capacity to respond, my brain too focused on how to defuse this situation. Things only get worse when Byron, Carver, and Donovan step forward, leaving behind their spectator roles in order to back Abram up.

Four against one. Warner will still win.

I care about all five of them. I don't want anyone getting hurt.

The thought pisses me off because they're all being so *immature.*

Abram steps up in Warner's space. "You'd better be happy I'm letting you leave here with your face intact."

They're so close, and it's as if the pin on a grenade has been pulled and we're just seconds away from a bloody explosion.

There is no doubt in my mind that there will be blood.

Since my brothers have abandoned the doorway, I'm clear to sprint inside. I search the cabin for some solution to the shitstorm brewing outside.

A mixing bowl full of soapy water and the sight of my crafting supplies give me inspiration. I grab the bowl, along with a container I set on the kitchen table earlier.

Back outside, the men are so wrapped up in making my life decisions for me that they haven't even notice I stepped away.

"Zoey's been doing fine, making her own choices these past few weeks without you looming over her," Warner snarls, nose to nose with Abram.

My brother lets out a hard laugh. "Like I'm supposed to believe you and your biker thug friends haven't tried anything?"

When he lifts his arms, ready to shove Warner, I lose my last twinge of hesitation.

I step up to the edge of the porch and fling the water from the bowl, taking half a second to admire my accuracy. The wave beautifully hits my target—their heads—soaking them both.

"Yeah! Hose 'em down, girl! I want to see some mud wrestling!" Courtney claps me on the back as the two men blink in surprise.

But I'm not done. Water is too easy to ignore in the heat of anger.

"Heads-up!" I call, and they're both dense enough to look my way.

They each get a face full of glitter.

The sparkles engulf them like a fairy princess bomb went off. Every shimmering bit sticks to their wet skin, clothes, and hair. They've gone from two irate, intimidating men to two disco balls. They belong in the middle of a pride parade.

Carver shoves a fist against his mouth, but it does nothing to suppress his delighted snicker. The noise seems to help Abram recover some of his mental faculties.

"Goddamn it, Zoey!" He brushes at his arms in disgust. "Do you have a lifetime supply of glitter?"

"You *know* I do!" I chuck the empty bowl and container at their feet, still furious despite the hilarious scene in front of me. "And I will happily plaster you both in it. Then, if you still feel like fighting, I'll grab my phone and record every ridiculous second, build a whole website to house that video, send the link to every person you've ever met, and make sure the entire cosmos knows that you two decided to become glitter gladiators!" By the time I'm done with my rant, I've reached a righteous volume that practically shakes the trees surrounding the property.

"Hell, that's some intricate revenge," Courtney whispers to no one in particular. She sounds delighted.

"Now," I snarl at the two of them, "are you going to get along?"

Abram glares at the ground, still trying to rub away the silver sparkles adhered to his upper half, but it's no use. Glitter is the herpes of the craft world.

The silence is broken by a choking snort. For a second, I think it's Carver again. But then I realize the noise came from Warner's throat. The werewolf stares at his hands, flipping them palms down, and then up again. Then, he throws his head back, laughing, as if he wasn't just seconds away from brawling.

He laughs so hard that he has to bend over, clutching his knees.

Seeing Warner lose it chips away at my fury, and I fight hard against a smile.

Then, faster than any of my brothers were likely expecting, Warner bounds up the steps, wrapping his arms around my thighs and lifting me into the air. He doesn't race away with me as his captive. Instead, he twirls us both around, chuckling as he buries his nose against my throat.

One of my warm spots. I can feel his breath there, the way he inhales deep.

For the moment, I'm able to forget all the worries over decisions I need to make. In Warner's arms, the world seems funnier. Not so full of impossible decisions.

I clasp his head, tilting his face until eyes of pure amber meet mine. Loving the sight, I press a gentle kiss to the middle of his forehead, sure my lips come away shimmering.

"Aw. You two are so cute; I could vomit." Courtney skips back down the steps and walks straight up to my oldest brother. "Here, you sexy, sparkly tower of a man. Hold my cock." She shoves the disgruntled chicken into Abram's arms, and he's too shocked to do anything other than accept it. A wild grin splits her face, and she gives him a hearty slap on the shoulder. "Just kidding! It's a hen. Now, where is that big dog I've heard about? I need to introduce him to Queen Omelet so he doesn't eat her."

42

ZOEY

I'M SUFFOCATING.

The glitter only mildly defused the tension between Warner and the Gunner boys, so I asked him to give me some time with them. But now, even asleep, my brothers fill the tiny cabin. Carver's snores sneak through the gap between the floor and my door. All four of them must give off a furnace's worth of heat because the air around me is heavy and warm. But not a comforting warmth. More like the warmth of a blanket being held over my face until I pass out.

The thought has me crawling out of my bed, feet quiet on the hardwood floor as I try to catch my breath.

Having my own room shouldn't feel this claustrophobic.

I need air. Fresh mountain air, not made stale by too many bodies exhaling in the same space. Bruce doesn't stir in his dog bed as I cross to the window, prying it open despite its old, warped frame. Every inch it rises pairs with the reluctant squeak of old wood against old wood. Still, I keep at the thing until it's close to fully open.

Cold air swirls around me, brushing against my exposed arms and making goose bumps prickle in its wake.

I pause to listen, both to the soothing sounds of the woods at night, but also to check if my efforts woke my brothers. If even one has stirred, he'll come to check on me. The Gunner boys can't help themselves. They treat me like I'm a baby bird, fallen from its nest. If left alone too long, I'll surely perish, too weak to deal with the cruel world.

Of course, my past has given them a reason to worry. I'm not entirely blameless.

But that doesn't mean I approve of how close they hover.

The thought makes me want to escape. For the past few weeks, this cabin has felt like a refuge. Now, it smells like a stale box, one that my brothers want to stick me in after cocooning me securely in bubble wrap.

One of my legs is over the low sill before I consider what I'm doing. Splinters catch at my flannel pajama pants, but I don't let that hold me back.

Jailbreak. I'm pulling a *Shawshank Redemption*.

Only, as I sneak into the chilly night, I admit my route is much more pleasant than crawling through sewers full of human waste.

Still, there's an element of danger.

The moon sits high in the star-speckled sky, having lost one sliver that would make it full. The light it casts is enough for me to see the vague outlines of trees and bushes. There are plenty of shadows.

Memories of a menacing growl creep from the recesses of my mind.

I push the thoughts away.

I'm only crossing the yard. Not running into the woods.

As I reach the bottom rung of the tree house ladder, I make the connection I can't believe I haven't before.

Could the animal that scared me have been a werewolf? Is that why Warner was asking what it looked like?

The idea brings on an uneasy chill that makes my fingers shake as I begin to climb.

If I was being stalked by a werewolf that day, then that means I didn't accidentally stumble into the wrong part of the woods. Someone wanted me scared. Someone might have been planning on hurting me.

And as I crawl through the entrance to the tree house, another realization pricks at me.

Climbing a tree might keep me safe from a wolf. But not a werewolf.

The minute I stand, I know something is wrong.

My bare foot on the old wood is accompanied by an ominous groan.

A loud crack sounds. My whole world shifts.

My terrified scream rends the calm night open.

43

WARNER

"Are you moping? I don't think I've ever seen you mope before." Courtney plops down on the stool next to me, bumping her shoulder into mine and jostling my beer. I clutch it close to keep the contents from spilling before taking another swig.

"I'm not moping. I'm brooding. It's a good look for me, right?" I try to offer her my normal charming smile, but from her grimace, I bet I didn't get anywhere close.

"What's wrong? No, wait, let me guess. Could it possibly be four cockblocks having a slumber party at Zoey's house?"

I snort. "Yeah. You could say that."

Zoey's brothers do have me feeling pissy. But it's more than that.

I'm angry at myself.

My first impression with her family was as a possessive asshole, practically begging to get into a fight. No one in this town, not even the people that know about the wolves and are scared of us, would use those words to describe me.

I didn't know I could get that way.

But the second I pulled up to her cabin and scented not just one

257

strange man, but four, my hackles were up. Zoey and I haven't talked about mating, but that doesn't change the fact that my wolf is pushing me to lay claim.

Then, when that Neanderthal Abram tried to keep her from me?

I'm not sure there's ever been a moment when I was angrier. Somehow, I kept from lunging forward and ripping his arms off.

But just barely.

Does Zoey know how close I came to doing something she'd never forgive me for?

A better man than me would take my overreaction as proof that I should leave her alone. Find someone of my own kind to be with.

But no matter how nice I am, how willing I am to help my neighbor, when it comes to Zoey, I'm selfish. I want her. I want all of her, and I'll do a lot more than snap my fangs at anyone who tries to keep us apart.

"Yeah, that older one is a real piece of work. Made me take Queen Omelet back home with me just because Zoey doesn't have a chicken coop. I mean, details, right?" Courtney waves for her own beer. "So, did she break up with you?"

"No!" Hell, I'd be in a lot worse shape if that happened. "She just asked me to give her some time alone with her brothers. Since everything was so tense. And she hasn't seen them in a few weeks." By the end of my explanation, I'm grumbling. Like a spoiled kid denied his favorite toy.

I can't help it. We were away on a moon run, and all I wanted to do was curl up with my woman tonight after pleasuring her in all the ways I could think of.

But no. I'm stuck at The Rabbit Hole, nursing my second beer as the clock ticks past midnight. I can't even get properly drunk because I have to drive myself home.

"Sounds like you need to get on their good sides."

"Me?" I growl. "What about them getting on *my* good side? You should've seen the way they were treating her before you got there. Wouldn't even let her out of the house. She had to climb out a fucking window!"

"Hmm," Courtney answers, not committing to my side. "So, they're dicks. But clearly, Zoey can handle them ... in her own way."

Courtney flicks at something on my shoulder, and I catch a glimmer of another glitter piece I must've missed in my shower. The memory of Zoey's method for shutting down a fight has me giving in to a reluctant smile.

But Courtney isn't done.

"Still, they're her brothers. Her family. What are you?"

My smile drops, and I can feel myself frowning. "I'm her ... mate."

"No, you're not. Not yet." Courtney, normally just as carefree as me, examines me with cool eyes. "Maybe not ever."

The bar door swings open behind us, letting in the cool night air that does nothing to soothe the panic caused by Courtney's words. As I'm trying to formulate a response, a heavy hand claps on my shoulder.

"Warner." Before I turn to look, I recognize Raider's voice. The shaggy, bearded man grimaces down at me, and I'm on edge. Raider isn't one to seek me out. Or anyone really for that matter. He's a seasoned member of the pack who keeps to himself. "Tell me, any reason your lady would be with a bunch of guys?"

Is that it?

Please let that be it.

"Zoey's brothers are in town. There're four of them. Big, blond guys for the most part."

Instead of giving me an understanding nod and walking away, my pack mate only looks more disturbed.

"Thought it was her, but them fuckers were crowded so close around her, didn't get a good look."

"What are you saying, Raider?" My wolf paces anxiously in my chest, setting my pulse pounding.

"We were riding through town and saw them take her into emergency care—"

"What?!" My stool topples over as I shoot to my feet and sprint. Zoey is hurt.

44

WARNER

I shove through the front glass doors to the emergency care, hating the sterile smell of the place and how it dampens Zoey's trail. The minute I pulled into the parking lot, I knew Raider was right.

Zoey is here.

And she's bleeding.

A young nurse sits at the front desk, and her eyes widen at my abrupt arrival. I don't stop to ask her directions. The place is small, and I know exactly which way to go.

"Not another one. Sir! It's already too—" The swinging doors that lead back to the treatment area cut her off.

The space full of medical devices sends me back to the night I revealed my true self to Zoey. A whisper of fear at the memory of the dead look in her eyes creeps through me. I thought I might have lost her then.

Please tell me I'm not going to lose her now.

Despite the place being empty of other patients, I can't see Zoey right away. There's a human wall between the two of us.

"Where is she?" Again, I'm coming at the Gunner brothers, all aggression, the words low and rumbling with a growl I can't keep contained.

Three of them whirl around, clearly shocked by my sudden appearance, but Abram keeps his gaze on his sister. And with their turning, I finally catch a glimpse of her.

She's sitting up on the bed. That's where the good news ends.

"Warner!"

At the sight of her pained smile, my frantic anger gets pushed aside by my helpless worry.

"Zoey." Before her family can decide if they want to keep acting like the human barrier, I'm stepping between them, reaching for her. Only my hands hover an inch away, as I'm worried about causing additional pain. "What happened?"

She's covered in scratches, most just tiny abrasions, but there's a thick one at the base of her neck, and there looks to be hastily tied bandages around spots on her arms and her legs. Bandages with growing red stains. The beginnings of bruises shadow her forehead, cheek, elbows, and knees. One ankle has started to swell, and she holds one arm to her chest, the angle of it off.

These aren't the signs of a small stumble. Whatever I missed looks to have gotten away with almost killing the woman I love.

I love.

I love her.

And here she is, broken and bloody from some mystery event. If I don't find out who or what hurt her soon, the violence boiling in my brain might find an unintended target.

"Here. Could you hold this one? It doesn't hurt as much." Zoey offers her left hand to me, and I accept it, cradling her palm as carefully as I would a baby chick.

"Did someone attack you?" A trembling starts in my chest, the product of barely contained rage. My wolf wants to break free and lay waste to the world.

She looks surprised and confused. "What? No. I fell."

"You *fell*?" I finally tear my eyes away from her for a moment, only to give Abram the most disgusted, hate-filled glare I can manage.

The excuse for her injures is the oldest in the book when it comes to abuse.

Brother or not, when I discover which one of these men hurt Zoey, he'll be lucky if I only kill him.

The blond man seems upset, returning my angry scowl with a tense jaw and helpless eyes. "She did fall."

"And who the fuck helped her?" I hiss.

Zoey snatches her hand back from mine, and I'm not surprised. I don't recognize myself in this moment. When I turn my head, planning to apologize for scaring her, a palm meets my face.

But not in a slap, like I deserve. Instead, Zoey smooths her hand over my cheek, petting me.

"Calm down. It's okay. I'm okay." Again, she gives me an attempt at a smile, but I can see her pain in the expression.

I huff out a humorless laugh. "Hell, Zoey. You look like you got into a brawl with a wild animal. You are *not* okay."

She trails her fingers over my face again, the tips of them tangling in my hair. "Well, I'll be okay. It's just some bruises. A cut or two."

"All right. We've clearly surpassed the acceptable amount of protectors." A doctor—whose name I can't remember—speaks with a loud, commanding tone as he maneuvers between two of Zoey's brothers, rolling a tray in front of him that contains some wicked-looking, curved needles.

How often did she get stitched up before coming to Pine Falls? Because here, it seems to be happening every other day.

"We have a very comfortable waiting room, and I'm sure Nurse Laura would be happy to brew some tea for you all while you wait." The doctor tilts his head toward the doors I recently burst through, and I spot the curly-haired nurse glaring daggers at me.

Funny, before I fell for Zoey, I was much better at getting people to like me.

"We're not going anywhere," Abram declares, and all the brothers nod in agreement.

The doctor, who I see now is wearing a name tag that declares him as Dr. Briggs, doesn't seem intimidated by the blond giant's glower.

"Yes, you are. This is my treatment area, and to give your sister proper care, I need you all out of my way." As Abram moves to argue, Dr. Briggs holds up a staying hand. "I'm not heartless. Miss Gunner can choose one of you to stay with her if she wants a companion."

"I'll stay." Her oldest brother says the words faster than I can think them.

Just as I'm about to step into his space, Zoey slides her hand back into mine.

"Abram," she says, gaining his attention immediately, "I appreciate the offer, but you're getting too intense. You're making me nervous. Warner is going to stay with me."

A prideful warmth fills my chest.

Of course, Abram doesn't simply accept that.

"*I'm* intense? That guy came in here, ready to murder." Abram points at me.

He's not wrong.

Zoey frowns at her brother, then turns back to me. "Warner, would you mind sitting in that chair?" She tilts her head toward a seat next to the bed. Since it's too far away from her for me to keep ahold of her hand, I press a kiss to her thankfully cut-free palm before doing as I was told. Zoey smiles at me, then gives her brother a more rueful version of the expression.

"I've asked all of you to chill out and sit down since we got here. Thank you for acting the hero, but right now, I just need to be the one in charge of me."

Abram stares between the two of us before releasing a frustrated but resigned sigh. "We'll be right outside those doors."

"I know you will."

The brothers file out, all of them throwing glances back at their sister. Each one looks equally concerned, which makes it impossible to tell who might have hurt her.

Once it's just the three of us left, the doctor proceeds to disinfect her cuts. Zoey's lips press tight, going white around the edges. She's in pain, and I don't want to add to her discomfort, but not knowing what really happened is making my wolf turn rabid. Helpless anger presses against the edges of my thoughts.

"Zoey?" I move to the edge of my seat, scooting it closer and offering my hand, which she takes with her uninjured one. "Can you please tell me what happened? Saying you fell doesn't explain all of this." I gesture to her skin, riddled with cuts, and her limbs that are possibly broken.

Dr. Briggs threads his needle. "You can talk, just try to keep still. This shouldn't hurt with the numbing agent."

Zoey gives a nod before refocusing on me. "When I said fell, I didn't mean I'd tripped."

The sight of the metal piercing the skin on her neck tries to distract me from her explanation. I remind my wolf that the needle is helping her, just like when she got her arm stitched up.

She continues, unaware of how close I am to losing it, "My brothers were making the cabin feel crowded, so I went out to the tree house. Every time I've been up there before, the thing has felt solid. But I guess it *is* a few decades old. Anyway, I climbed up, and the second I stepped onto the floor, my weight must've set it off-balance somehow. The whole thing fell and me along with it."

"Shit," I mutter.

That tree house is at least fifteen feet off the ground. Maybe twenty. I was right. She could have died.

With my thoughts threatening to descend into a panic spiral, I'm shocked to hear her light chuckle. When I glance up, Dr. Briggs meets my stare with a confused one of his own as he pauses his stitching.

"How does your head feel, Zoey?" the doctor asks. "Are you dizzy?"

"Oh, no. Sorry. I know this isn't a laughing moment. It's only ..." She glances at me, biting her lip. Another giggle slips out, and it's the sweetest sound I've ever heard. "Warner, you still have glitter in your hair."

That's when I know, without a doubt ...
Zoey Gunner is my future.

45

ZOEY

I ACHE EVERYWHERE.

But I'm alive, so there's that. Plus, I have Warner's warm body beside me as I hobble up the front steps.

Really, I'm not that broken. Just a bruised ankle and a broken wrist. All in all, I came out okay. I choose to forget the number of stitches the doctor said he put in me.

"Are you hungry?" Warner holds the door open for me while also keeping an arm outstretched in case I stumble.

Bruce wanders out of the guest bedroom and meanders up to me. I scratch behind his ears, always comforted by the big dog's presence.

"It's two a.m. I just need to sleep." I smile at Warner, softening my rejection of his offer.

"You heard her. Bedtime. We've got this." Abram comes in right behind me, sliding a hand under my elbow to lend his support.

Normally, I'd wave him off, but tonight, I don't mind having someone to lean on.

"I'll get you ice for your ankle." Carver heads to the refrigerator.

"Did you have enough blankets? I know we commandeered a bunch, but I don't need mine," Byron offers.

Donovan keeps quiet, but his eyes are locked on each one of my movements, as if he's ready to lunge forward if I tip over.

"Zoey?" Warner's voice has me glancing his way. "Do you want me to stay?"

Honestly, I'm surprised he'd even want to with the overbearing presence that is my brothers.

"She has us," Abram grumps.

"Stop it." I shush my older brother. "I want Warner here."

Just because Abram wants to take care of me doesn't give him the right to kick Warner out.

I take back my hand, maneuver around the mastiff, and shuffle toward the bedroom. The mattress creaks as I sit down on it, and my ankle thanks me for the relief.

Carver comes in, holding a towel filled with ice, and Byron approaches, holding his blanket.

"Don't you dare put that on my bed. No way will I be able to sleep, knowing you don't have any bedding." I wave a finger at him, but immediately regret how harsh the words came out when I see the lost look on my brother's face.

They all share it.

And for the first time tonight, I take a moment to imagine if it had been one of them who climbed up in the tree house instead of me.

How would I feel if I had found Abram or Donovan crumbled on the ground? What would it have been like to have to rush Byron or Carver to the emergency room?

My brothers are tough, strong men. Plenty of rugby games have ended with them bleeding from some random gouges.

But to see any of them truly hurt, my heart would break. I would physically ache for them. I would want to do anything in my power to take their pain away.

That's all they're doing now. Trying to ease my pain.

And I love them so much. I get the urge to cry, just like I'm back in the tree house, discovering the clues to my grandmother's loneliness.

I'm lucky to be so surrounded by love. Never having to doubt that there's someone who cares for me. Not when my brothers are near.

Despite the pain in my leg, I push back up to a standing position and hold my arms out to Byron. He moves forward with hopeful eyes, offering the blanket again. But I don't grab the material. Instead, I wrap him in a hug.

"I don't need another blanket, but could you make those pancakes I like tomorrow morning?"

"With chocolate chips?" His arms encircle me but stay loose enough to keep from irritating any of my injuries.

"Those are the ones."

When I step back, he looks more centered. He has a direction. A purpose. Even if it's something as simple as making me breakfast.

I hobble around the group, giving each of my brothers a hug before returning to the bed.

"Okay, time for some privacy. I need to change." My T-shirt is torn with splotches of blood all over it.

After final good nights, three of my brothers file out of the room, leaving only Abram, Warner, and me.

"She said privacy," the eldest Gunner repeats, hard eyes never leaving Warner, who hovers beside my bed.

"Abram."

The guy barely glances my way. Despite the swell of love I'm still feeling for my family, I am done with this caveman routine.

"Warner has seen me naked."

I feel more satisfaction than I should when my tough older brother flinches and blushes.

But I push on. "When I said I want Warner here, I meant with me. In my bed."

"You're injured, Zoey! You shouldn't be having ..." He trails off, and if I wasn't so exhausted, I'd find this whole exchange hilarious.

"Don't worry. Banging is not on the menu tonight."

Warner lets out a choked noise, and Abram's face gets a funny shade of red.

Normally, I would enjoy sparring with Abram, assured that I

could eventually get my way. But tonight, I'm too exhausted. I plop down on the bed with a groan. Then, I discover that sitting up is too much work. After collapsing back completely, I stare at the ceiling and try to figure out how to convince my brother to go.

"Warner is staying. Go away, Abram. I love you," is the best I can come up with.

There's a pause, and then I can practically hear my brother glaring.

"She needs to sleep. No trying anything." His heavy footfalls alert me that he's heading out.

I half expect my bedroom door to be slammed shut, but there's only a gentle click of the latch falling in place.

Warner's face appears above mine, a worried grimace on his mouth.

"Don't worry about him," I mutter. "He's just being overprotective."

"I'm not worried about him. I'm worried about you."

A delicious warmth caresses my face, and I realize Warner has laid his palm on my cheek.

"How are you doing?" he asks.

I take a mental rundown of my situation. "Sore. Some of the cuts sting. Tired." I try a shrug, but then I have to bite back a groan. Even though I stifled the sound, I can tell from Warner's furrowed brow that he picked up on the pain that just shot through me. Before he can go into overprotective mode, too, I add on a last important bit. "But I'm happy."

"Happy?" Now, his brows are up, and if I had more strength in my jelly arms, I'd reach up to trace them.

Instead, I nod. "It could've been worse, but I'll heal. Plus, my brothers are here. And you're here. So, yeah, I'm happy. Can you help me change?"

Warner's eyes rove over my face, and I wonder if he's searching for more injuries. He'll probably find some, seeing as how I'm pretty beat up. Then, he leans down and brushes a light kiss on the tip of my nose before disappearing out of my eyeline.

"You want the loose flannel ones?" There's a sound of drawers being pulled open.

"Sure. Anything to help you keep it in your pants."

He snorts, and then he's by my side again, helping me sit up so we can pull my tattered T-shirt off. And I can't stop a pout when he doesn't spare a glance at my bare chest.

"See? They're not even on, and you're already uninterested in half-naked me," I grumble.

Warner kneels in front of me, working his way up the buttons, but he pauses at my words. When I look down to meet his eyes, I find they are almost entirely black.

"Never think that I am uninterested in you, Zoey. Never."

A shiver sneaks through me that has nothing to do with the fact that my shirt is half open. I reach up to twirl a strand of his soft hair around my finger.

"How do you feel about putting banging back on the menu?"

That finally gets a grin out of him, but Warner shakes his head and finishes with the buttons. "You're evil," he informs me. "A wicked temptress."

"Sounds like the perfect partner for a werewolf." I keep my voice low even though there's a door in between my words and my brothers.

Warner chooses not to respond, and he slips off my torn pajama pants with efficient hands, then has me covered again seconds later.

"Under the covers, temptress." He pulls the blankets back for me.

"Are you staying?" I try to keep the vulnerability out of my voice as I crawl up the bed.

"Do you want me to?"

"Yes," I respond almost before he finishes his question.

Warner toes off his boots, hangs his jacket over a chair in the corner, then climbs onto the mattress beside me. Only he keeps his jeans on and lies on top of the covers. Before I can direct him to take his pants off and actually get in bed with me, he curves his body around mine, becoming the perfect big spoon.

"Can I ask you something?" His question brushes against my ear, bringing warmth and the smell of him.

"With all the questions I'm always throwing at you, I think you're due."

Warner chuckles, and I love the feel of the vibration against my back. "Abram, Byron, Carver, Donovan ... Zoey? Do you have twenty-one more siblings wandering around Denver?"

A goofy smile spreads across my face. "Mom liked the ABC idea, but after five kids, she said she was officially done. Skipping to the end of the alphabet was her way of making that point. And getting her tubes tied."

I expect Warner to snort or maybe start chuckling again. But he stays silent, and the quiet makes me curious enough to turn. When my eyes catch on Warner's face, I read a mixture of amusement, bafflement, and an eerie level of focus.

"I want to meet your mom."

"Really? You want to meet more of my family? Even after them?" My fingers flick toward the bedroom door.

Warner gazes at me, and again, he surprises me when he doesn't immediately offer up a joke. Instead, he murmurs a determined, "Yes."

The one word leaves me reeling, and I answer with the first thought that comes to my mind.

"I don't think she'll come to Pine Falls. She's never been back since she left."

His mouth struggles against a frown, and eventually, he leans in to press a gentle kiss against my forehead.

"We'll figure it out. Time for you to sleep. I'll ask more questions later."

46

WARNER

I WAIT until she's asleep before sliding away. Before I even leave the bedroom, I know that all of Zoey's brothers are still awake. Discovering their sister broken and bleeding had to be a shock. It takes time for that to wear off.

When I walk down the hall into the main room, four sets of eyes focus on me.

The Gunner boys are gathered around the kitchen table, each one clutching a hand of cards, and the two I think are Byron and Carver have beers beside them.

"How's she doing?" Abram throws out the question, sounding almost angry about having to ask it.

More like having to ask *me*.

"She's sleeping." I want to be back with her, lying close in that bed, making sure that each one of her precious breaths is still coming.

But I have questions.

I wish I didn't. The answers probably aren't going to help warm them to the idea of Zoey staying in Pine Falls.

"Has anyone been by the cabin? Other than Courtney and me?"

Every brother frowns, and Abram stands from his chair. "Why?"

I shake my head. "It's just a thought. Anyone have a flashlight?"

The youngest brother moves from his seat and pulls open a closet, coming up with a heavy-duty flashlight, and I head for the back door.

"Byron, Carver, stay here. Donovan with me." Abram hands out the orders like the brothers are their own military unit.

I get the sudden sense that Zoey's oldest brother would get along with mine. Or Roderick might murder him. It's a fine line when you have two personalities so similar.

The two Gunners follow me out into the yard. Damp ground gives slightly under my feet, and I silently curse the evening rains we've been getting. The water washes away helpful scents that might normally have clung.

When we come upon the wreckage of the tree house, I fight the urge to sprint back to the cabin to make sure Zoey is still breathing.

What was once a sturdy structure is now a crumpled mess. What's left of the frame lays on its side, but mainly, the ground is covered in broken pieces of wood. The little house exploded on impact. And Zoey was trapped inside.

Despite the rain, her scent lingers. But not the enticing sweetness of maple. What I pick up transports me back to that night on the back road, when she thought she was dreaming. I shine the light over the boards, settling on a section with red stains.

Her blood.

I can't fully stifle the growl crawling out of my throat, but I'm at least able to mute it to something more human-sounding.

"What are you looking for?" the youngest brother, Donovan, asks, coming up beside me, his eyes blank, even as his fists clench.

I suck in a few deep breaths, pulling on my sanity and moving the light in search of a few particular pieces of wood.

"A few weeks back, when Zoey told me she was climbing up in the tree house, I was worried it wasn't stable."

"Big fucking help, your worries," Abram scoffs.

I round on him, the growl coming again. He flinches, but doesn't back away, scowling at me.

"Seems I need to remind you this happened on *your* watch."

He bares his teeth and opens his mouth, but Donovan cuts him off.

"Why are we out here now? You thought it was unstable. It was. End of story."

"No. Not the end." I rein in my anger. "Because I was worried, I checked it over. The whole structure. Even climbed up in it and tested it myself. The beams were solid. Nothing should've knocked it down without a hell of an effort. Definitely not your sister just stepping in it."

The two men remain quiet, but I feel their eyes on me as I pick through the wreckage. Finally, I find what I'm looking for. One of the main support beams.

The wood is cracked near in half. If that happened just because of weight, there'd be splintering at the fracture.

But the break is clean.

"Someone cut this." I offer the wood for their examination.

"Fuck," Donovan mutters.

Even in the dim light, I can see the rigid set to Abram's entire face.

"You think someone tried to hurt Zoey on purpose?" he asks.

My hands clench on air, wanting to tear into something just at the thought. "I don't know. But I'm not seeing any other reason for someone to take a saw to the tree house."

The three of us search through the rest of the wood pieces, finding another with similar cuts. We bring them back to the house with us and relate the findings to the other Gunner boys.

"So, we talk to the cops, right?"

I nod. But the gesture is only meant to placate them. The cops in this town are either useless or they're wolves. If this was some trouble between humans, then the cops would have to handle it.

But Zoey is mine. That makes this wolf business.

Roderick is the one who needs to be informed. He's the one who will help me hunt down whoever is out to hurt the woman I love.

Let the Gunners go to the cops if it makes them feel better. The human police are good for handing out speeding tickets or breaking up a brawl at a bar. There's not a detective among them. The wolves on the force are smarter, but they'll soon know this is pack business and keep it off the books.

Whoever has been tormenting my mate will answer to a different set of laws.

Abram, who's planning his trip to the station the next morning, cuts off his words abruptly when the bedroom door creaks open.

Zoey wanders out, her eyes heavy with sleep, hair an adorable mess around her bruised face. She takes in our gathering, eyebrows curving up when she finds the five of us examining her.

The oldest Gunner is the first to speak. "What's wrong? Are you okay? Are you bleeding? What do you need?"

She twists her lips in a smirk before answering, "I need to pee. Do you all want to help me with that?"

Abram clears his throat, a red flush spreading over his cheeks. "Do you need help?"

Zoey leans against the wall, staring at her older brother. Then, suddenly, like the sunrise has come early, a smile splits across her face, threatening to blind us all.

"Don't ever change, Bam Bam." She turns toward the bathroom, calling over her shoulder, "Fair warning: anyone who tries to barge into the bathroom while I'm using it is getting a swirly." She shuts the door with a definitive click.

I'm the first one to chuckle, and then Carver breaks into loud, snorting laughter while Donovan covers a wide grin with his hand. Abram has taken on the color of a strawberry, but also seems to be fighting a smile while Byron rolls his eyes and deals another hand of cards.

"You want in, Biker Boy?" the guy asks as he pauses in the process of divvying them out.

The offer is tempting. Possibly an olive branch, a door cracked so I could pull it wider and find a place in the Gunner family.

For a second, I consider saying yes. I want Zoey's brothers to like me. To accept me.

But the sound of a toilet flushing and water running filters through the walls. In a moment, Zoey will be back in her bed, and there's nothing I want more than to be near her.

"Rain check. I'm going to stay with Zoey."

The four sets of eyes all come to me again, but it's only Abram who speaks.

"That's the right choice."

47

ZOEY

I PULL into a parking spot beside the picnic area, making sure to give Warner's bike a wide birth. Driving a stick shift with a broken wrist and a sore ankle is not the easiest thing in the world. Just as I turn off the engine, Warner is at my door, frowning at me through the window.

"Should you be driving?"

I tug on the handle, and he steps back enough to let the rusted door swing open before moving in close again.

"Not sure. Didn't break any traffic laws on the way here though. Wanna help me down?"

I extend my good hand, but Warner leans in to scoop me up in a damsel-in-distress carry. Arguing seems useless, but I do grab on to the armrest before he can walk us away.

"Wait! There're burritos!"

He chuckles, tilting me back into the cab of the truck so I can grab the paper bag.

"Good to go?" he asks.

"Yep!"

Warner uses his booted foot to kick the door closed, then walks with me toward a picnic table. Normally, I don't like being babied, but my ankle hurts, even after two days of icing and elevation. Plus, this way, I get to wrap my arm around Warner's shoulders and fiddle with the strands of hair that curl over his ears. They hang lower today, pressed flat, no doubt by the hard hat he's had on all morning. A light layer of dirt coats his skin, broken only by trails where sweat traced down his face and neck.

"You're dirty." I use my pointer finger to draw a twirl in the dust on his collarbone.

He swallows, his normally smiling mouth pulling into a grimace. That's when I remember how sensitive he was about his grime at the mechanic's shop.

I didn't mean to insult him. I was only making an observation.

Just as we reach the table, I stop him from putting me down by gripping his face in my hands and capturing his mouth with mine. He groans, deep in his chest, his lips parting enough to allow me entry. My affectionate assault continues for a good minute or so before I end with quick kisses to the corners of his mouth and the tip of his nose.

"Do you know what I think about when I see you covered in dirt?"

He shakes his head, brow dipped warily.

I let all the heat in my thoughts shine from my eyes. "I imagine what you'll look like later. When you get home. And step in the shower." The image is clear in my mind. The water cascading over his broad shoulders, coursing down his bare skin. "How I wouldn't mind an invite when it comes time to get you clean."

"Fuck, Zoey," Warner moans, sitting down on the bench with me in his lap. He buries his head in my neck, partially muffling his next words. "You can't be saying things like that when I have to go back to work. I'm going to be sporting a partial for the rest of the day."

Laughter bursts from my chest, and I pat his head as if he needs consoling. "Poor werewolf. I'm sorry. I promise to pretend like I don't want to soap you up."

He makes some adorable grumbling noises before giving me a gentle bite and pulling back.

"Besides, I'll make for a poor shower companion with my arm wrapped in plastic." I hold up my cast but regret the joke the moment I take in Warner's face.

Like my brothers, he seems to think my fall is somehow his fault. Which is ridiculous. I'm the one who kept climbing up in the decades-old tree house.

But I remind myself that if any of them were injured in a freak accident, I'd also be upset, knowing they were in pain. So, I forgive their hovering.

For now.

"Burrito time. And don't worry. Even though it broke my vegetarian heart, I got you one with beef."

He smiles with a playful curve to his lips, joy pouring from his eyes.

I guess Warner loves burritos.

Sliding off his lap, I place the bag on the table and start pulling out all the sides.

"You know ..." Warner trails off, hesitating.

"How will I be sure if I know unless you finish your sentence?" My shoulder bumps his, and he chuckles, nuzzling his nose into my hair in the animalistic way he has.

"What I was saying is, well ... this isn't the first time you've given me food."

"So?" I unwrap my burrito and take a bite, chewing for a moment as I consider his comment. Then, I balk in horror, swallowing dramatically. "You're not trying to give me those meat jars back, are you? Because that's a done deal."

Warner grins, and the sight eases a tight ball in my chest that formed when he hesitated.

"No. Those meat jars are mine. Don't worry." He bites into his burrito, chewing slowly and amping up my curiosity. Finally, he swallows. Not looking at me, he finishes his thought. "Exchanging food is part of the mating ceremony werewolves perform. So, gifting it indicates … that you want to mate."

"You mean have sex?" I'm confused. "Like, we wouldn't have done it if I hadn't given you the meat jars?"

"No!" Warner chokes on a laugh, but he calms down quickly, gazing down at me.

There's a hopeful glint in his eyes, and for some reason, the sight has me tensing up.

"A mate is a partner. Mating is like our version of marriage. But it's stronger. There's an element of magic to it. We're bound to our mate."

We stare at each other—him searching, me baffled.

Mating? Marriage?

"So"—I set down my food and clutch my head in my hands, trying to get my thoughts to stop their swirling—"the meat jars were like an engagement ring? Did I propose to you?"

"No, Zoey. No. It's not like that. Especially because you didn't know."

"Then, what are you saying?"

"I'm not—" he cuts himself off, then firms his mouth. "I am. I am saying something." Warner's focus on me intensifies. "I want you to be my mate. I want to be *your* mate."

Oh God. This is it.

Commitment. The future. Life choices.

"Pine Falls is supposed to be temporary."

Warner stares at me, face slack, as if I slapped him. Guilt rushes through me. That was the worst response that could have popped out of my mouth.

The worst, but also the truth.

He regains control over his expression, entreating me with his amber eyes. "That was before you came here, right? Before we met. Hell, Zoey. I'm gone for you. I can't be the only one feeling this way."

He fists his hand over his heart, and I know exactly what he means.

The affection I have for Warner is more than I've ever experienced toward someone outside of my family. It's hard to believe it came on so fast. That in just a few weeks, this man twined himself around my heart. He dug his claws into it, and I'm afraid of the pain that'll accompany prying that grip loose.

Hopefully, I won't have to.

"You're not the only one." I pick at a corner of foil on my forgotten burrito. A minute ago, I was half starved. Now, the idea of food makes me nauseous.

"Then, stay. You already have the cabin, and friends, and me. All you have to do is change your plans. Please, Zoey"—Warner cups my elbows and rests his forehead against mine—"don't end this."

From the strain of his voice, a bystander would think I have a knife in his ribs and that I'm twisting it.

The feel of him surrounding me is tempting. But I'm not one to lose my head, even if I have lost my heart.

And when I think of staying here, with the risk of that darkness crashing over me again while I'm out in the middle of the woods, alone without the safety net of my family ...

Alone like Minnie ...

I'll drown.

Panic chokes me.

I swallow. Then swallow again, trying my best to stifle the tears pressing against the backs of my eyes.

This was an experiment. Turns out, it was a failed one.

"Selling my grandma's cabin doesn't have to mean the end of us," I whisper hoarsely.

His fingers briefly dig into my skin, but they relax before he hurts me. "What are you saying?"

"Denver isn't a death sentence. Couples do long-distance all the time."

Warner physically flinches at that suggestion, leaning away from me and shoving up from the table. Then, he starts to pace, an anxious energy buzzing off him.

"No. My kind can't do long-distance. Going days, even weeks without seeing you ... without touching you?" His fingers tangle in his hair as a frustrated growl leaks from the back of his throat. "Being separated from my mate would be torture."

There's that word again. *Mate*. It's heavy, hanging between us. Something he expects from me. Something I don't even understand.

I probably never will.

Maybe this is why there's a separation between the humans and wolves of Pine Falls. We don't follow the same rules.

And with his dismissal of my compromise, the one bit of hope I had withers.

"I don't want to torture you." I know what mental turmoil is, and the idea I'd be the catalyst for Warner's brings on a wave of self-disgust. So, even as the words make my stomach churn and my throat tighten, they still find a way out. "Maybe ... you should mate someone else."

Warner stops pacing, staring at me like I'm the embodiment of a horror movie.

With the first sentence done, I hope the rest won't cut as much. "I'm not a local. I'm not a wolf. You're talking about forever, and I haven't even figured out what's happening in my life next week. You deserve better than me, Warner. Someone who knows where she belongs. Someone who will be a good mate."

Nope. That all still hurt.

"I don't want anyone else."

"Maybe not today." I pray that time really does heal all wounds because I am torn open and bleeding.

"Stop it!" He goes on his knees beside me, and I'm shocked to realize tendrils of black are overtaking the gold of his eyes. "Stop telling me how I'll feel. I don't need some wolf or a girl who grew up here. I need *you*."

I want to take back everything I just said. Tell him that I need him too.

Then, a vision of the empty cabin flashes through my mind. The rooms Minnie spent her final years in, with no company but that lonely stereo. Suddenly, I can see into forever.

My future, if I stay here, is just me, slowly collapsing into myself.

My brothers are overbearing, but they also keep me sane. They're who I need. Without their unswerving love, I'll fade away.

And Warner deserves more than a drowning ghost.

I stand up from the picnic table, trying not to wobble. He moves with me, hands going to my waist. I don't know if he's steadying me or restraining me.

"Don't go. Stay here. Choose me." Rough growls color his pleading.

I shake my head. "I can't. I never planned to stay."

"Plans can change."

"Just because they can doesn't mean they should."

Lunch is over. This was supposed to be a casual date. Me spending time with the guy I like.

So naive. I knew letting myself be around Warner would cause problems. He's too lovable for me not to have fallen for him.

And I have. Fallen, that is.

My heart will break. I can already feel the cracks splintering through me.

I have to trust that with the support of my family, I'll survive. Because I will have them. In Denver, I'll always have them. Not like here.

Stepping over the bench with a messed-up ankle makes a smooth exit difficult. My toe catches on the wood, and I stumble.

Warner catches me, of course.

More cracks spiderweb across the surface of my heart as I soak in the warmth of his hold.

This is the part in the movies where the couple has a final kiss. A farewell. But if I let myself taste him, I'll lose my nerve.

I'll stay.

And then I'll disappear.

So, I press my palms flat against his chest, applying enough pressure to make my intentions clear. He listens to the silent request, falling back a step, hands hovering, palms up, waiting for me to return to his embrace.

"Thank you for caring for me," I say, turning to my truck.

"I don't just *care* for you, Zoey."

Coward that I am, I keep my eyes forward, wishing I could run. But then my ankle would give out, and Warner would come after me, and I might do something horrifying, like cry in his arms and beg for forgiveness and promise that I'll stay.

So, I walk away at a normal pace.

But I don't look back.

48

ZOEY

CRUISING AROUND to clear my head is difficult when I'm driving a stick shift and my right wrist is broken and my left ankle is bruised. After stalling out for the third time at a Stop sign, I turn the headlights toward home.

Well, Grandma Minnie's cabin.

I don't feel like I have a home anymore.

Warner started to take on the qualities of a home. When I was lost, I wanted to be where he was. When anxiety made my shoulders tense and my back ache, he was my comfort. When I hesitantly thought about the rest of my life, he was there.

Not anymore though.

When I pull up the drive, the house is lit up, the porch lights revealing my four brothers lounging in the rockers I've restored. Each one of them has a different instrument. They don't seem to be playing —yet. When I shut off the engine and step out into the cool night, I catch a few experimental twangs.

Tuning up.

They're all focused on their instruments until I step into the pool

285

of porch light. Then, as if attached to the same puppet strings, each one tenses and leans forward.

"What's wrong, Zoey?" asks Donovan.

"You've been crying." Abram homes in on my face.

I brush fingers along the tops of my cheeks, finding that he's correct. Bet my eyes are a puffy red mess.

"Was it Warner? Glitter or no, we'll go fuck his shit up." Carver is already standing, setting his fiddle to the side.

"Knew we were going to give him a beatdown at some point," Byron says, as if compelled to add his voice to the barrage.

An uncomfortable wave of affection and resentment crashes over me.

I love my brothers. But sometimes, the only thing I need is for them to shut up.

"Just leave it alone," I mutter, heading for the front door.

"Not going to happen. Tell us where he is." Abram steps toward me, all menacing and tall. As if I would ever give in to his intimidation tactics.

Instead, my good hand slaps against his chest, attempting to shove him, but barely managing to make him rock.

"I don't need you to fight for me. I've done a good job of breaking him all on my own." I choke on the last bit and whirl toward the front door, hoping to make it to the bedroom before the inevitable flood of tears returns.

But my way is blocked.

"Mom?"

She stands there, tall and steady, blonde hair braided away from her face, a sad smile on her lips.

"Hi, sweetheart."

The next thing I know, I've got my arms wrapped around her waist, and she's hugging hard.

"I didn't think you'd ever come back here."

"For you, I'd walk naked through hell." Her hold loosens, but only so her hands can pat over me, as if checking that each one of my limbs is still intact.

Despite being cracked in certain places, I'm still physically whole.

She heaves a sigh and steps back, dropping her arms to clutch my hands. "Let's go inside and talk. You boys stay out here. I need time alone with your sister."

They listen to Mom's command without question. Twenty-seven years, and I still haven't figured out a way to get them to follow my orders like that.

In their minds, I'm still a helpless preteen.

Inside the cabin, Mom puts on a pot of water to boil while I pack up the crafting supplies that litter half the table.

As she carries our mugs over, I can't keep my mouth shut anymore.

"You came back."

She smiles wide, but her eyes tense, as if she's in pain. "Is that really so shocking?"

Even as she sets the tea down in front of me, I ignore it.

"It's been almost a year since Minnie died. Plus all the time since you left. Did you ever visit?"

My mother, normally the bright star glittering at the center of whatever room she's in, seems dim. She stares off to the side, eyes focused on nothing.

"No," she murmurs.

"Well then"—I wrap my hands around the mug—"what changed your mind?"

Now, she looks at me. "I came for you."

"Why? I mean, I know I got hurt, but it's not like I'm bedridden."

Mom studies me for a moment, and I shift in my seat. As if I have something to hide.

But I don't.

I *don't*.

"Abram called."

"To tell you about the accident." I already knew this.

"No. He called again, to talk about something else."

My teeth clench, grinding down hard, as I imagine what he must've gone running to our mom about.

"No, sweetheart. Don't be mad at him. He called because ..." She hesitates, gaze flicking around the room.

This version of my mother is strange. She's the most confident person I know. She never holds back. She lives life like it gave her lemons and she discovered that was her favorite fruit.

A quality I also admire in Warner.

Don't think about him.

"He called me to ask more about The Dark Moon Riders."

At the mention of Warner's club, I can't keep still anymore. What I said to him, what I did to us, is still too fresh. So, I stand. And I pace.

My ankle throbs with each step, but I deserve the pain.

"Did you tell him ..."

"No. That's not something your brothers need to know about."

"It is if they keep trying to fight them!" The old floorboards creak under my agitated feet. "So? What new insights did you hand out?" Turns out, I'm still smarting from her keeping me in the dark.

"I didn't." She watches me move, and I feel like an injured field mouse avoiding the attention of a hawk. "I asked him to tell me what *he'd* learned. He told me about Warner."

When she says his name, I try not to flinch. I fail.

"He talked about a biker who follows his baby sister around like a puppy. A man who looked ready to commit murder when he found out you'd been hurt. A man who makes you throw glitter and who you moon over like he's a block of cheese." A reluctant smile forms on my mouth at her description, but she's not done. "A guy who seems to expect you to stay in Pine Falls for longer than just the month or so it should take you to sell this place."

This time, I'm able to stifle my flinch, but just barely.

"Well, you don't need to worry about that. I just told him I can't stay."

"Why not?"

I almost trip, her words a slippery banana peel in my path.

"What do you mean, *why not*? You *want* me to move to Pine Falls?"

"I'd never claim to want that. But children move away from their families all the time. Across the country. Across the world. It's not like you'd be the first."

The idea sounds so reasonable when she says it.

Still, I shake my head.

"Maybe that works for some people. But you know how I get. How different I am from you all."

She scrunches her nose. "You all? What does that mean?"

"Come on, Mom. I'm the introverted black sheep in the family. You all seek each other out while I'm one step away from a hermit."

"So what?"

"So! You know how I am. I get lost. Cut myself off from the world."

"Zoey."

The amused exasperation in her tone frustrates me. She doesn't get it.

"You all drop everything to come save me. And I hate it. Mainly because I keep needing it."

"Sweetheart, no. We're not saving you. We're loving you."

"I ..." Words don't come easy as I try to explain something about myself I don't even fully grasp.

"We know how strong you are." My mom reaches out to clasp my hand. "And we also know that your mind lies to you sometimes. That it tells you that you don't deserve happiness. We're here to remind you that you do and that you're loved."

Mom tilts her head toward the front porch, and I hear the strains of Maren Morris's "The Bones." The same song I had on repeat the week leading up to my leaving for Pine Falls.

"To be honest, I think they needed to see you more than you needed them."

"They ... hell, Mom." My fingers curl into claws around their invisible collective neck. I'd never *really* strangle them. Only in my imagination. "They piss me off so much."

She chuckles but tries to restrain the reaction when I glare at her.

"It's disheartening. Having to choose to live with their constant smothering just so I don't drown."

Humor leaves her then, and she squeezes my palm. "You won't drown, sweetheart. I promise you."

"You don't *know*, Mom." I feel like there's only one person who does. And she's gone.

But maybe I can make my mother understand.

I pull free and hobble away, toward the back bedroom. The boom box sits beside the bed. I grab it and the precious wooden box full of decades-old tapes, returning to the kitchen.

"I found these. Do you recognize them?"

After gently placing the box in front of my mom, I set the stereo up on the counter, plugging it in.

"These ... they're not ..." When I turn, she has a tape in her hand, staring at it like she's cradling a ghost.

I limp over, choosing another from the collection at random and popping it into the player. After a moment, we hear a voice.

"Good morning, Colorado! It's your girl, Silly Selena, back with the best beats in town—"

Seeing the shimmer in my mom's eyes, I stop the tape.

"They're all you. Every one. Grandma Minnie listened to you. She loved you, but you never spoke." I sigh, collapsing into a chair across from my mom. "Living here, I can see myself drifting away. Just like she did."

My mom is quiet for some time, her fingers tracing over all the tapes.

"I understand, Zoey. Where you're coming from ... I understand. But it's not the same thing."

I huff, but she waves to keep me quiet.

"You know some of my childhood. That my father died in a motorcycle accident. That your grandmother kept me secluded. That I left when I was eighteen and never looked back." She sucks in a bracing breath, and I find myself reaching for my tea. "But that's just a rough outline. You deserve the whole story."

Selena Gunner settles into her chair, her voice taking on a quality that has thousands of people tuning in to her radio show every morning. My mom knows how to captivate an audience, and I'm not immune.

"Your grandfather was a friendly man. I'm sure if you ask anyone in town who knew him, they'd say the same. He was on the town council. He was a volunteer firefighter. He played with a band at the local bars. And some weekends, he would take his bike out of the garage and go on long rides with the local motorcycle club."

"Grandpa was a werewolf?" I clutch my chest, as if expecting to find a sudden growth of hair there, displaying my supernatural lineage.

Mom chuckles. "No, he wasn't. But back then, there wasn't as much of a separation between the wolves and the townspeople. Back then, everyone knew. They all got along just fine."

Strains of music drift in from the front porch, my brothers smoothly sliding into some bluegrass. The sound is naturally soothing and has my muscles relaxing without thought. But it does nothing to stifle my curiosity.

"What happened?"

Mom takes a sip of her drink before powering on. "The night before my sixth birthday, your grandfather went out on a ride. He didn't come back. Around midnight, Minnie got a call. Apparently, there was an accident with a tractor trailer. It ran multiple bikes off the road. Of course, all the other riders were werewolves. They were hurt but healed quickly. My father was the only one who died."

I try to imagine my mom as a girl, small and vulnerable. But she's so much larger than life that I struggle with the idea.

"By all accounts, it wasn't the club's fault. But your grandmother got it in her head that they were responsible. That the love of her life would still be alive if it wasn't for the pack."

"But it was the truck—"

Before I'm done speaking, she's already nodding.

"Yes. Still, when you lose someone you love, you don't always react rationally. Minnie went into overprotection mode. She had two people in her life she loved, and one was gone. So, she clutched me closer. She cut off contact with everyone who wasn't necessary. Home-schooled me. Forbade trips into town if she didn't accompany me. Her anger and distrust of the wolves affected some townspeople. And later, I learned the pack leader felt responsible. He also pulled his people back, not wanting to be the cause of any more civilian deaths."

The knowledge of this hits me hard. My family is the catalyst for the lines drawn through Pine Falls. The divide traces back to this event, the night my grandfather died on the wolves' watch.

"You see, sweetheart, your grandmother didn't drift away because she was introverted. She ripped herself away because she was grieving. And ..." She sighs a sad breath. "I do think she suffered from some mental issues. Ones she refused to talk about or seek treatment for. Sometimes, she'd mutter things about the wolves working with demons to collect souls. That they took my father's life in payment for mine." She digs her thumbnail into the woodgrain of the table. "It took me a while to understand my mother. Too long. By the time I started to work through what made her the way she was, I was already pregnant with Abram. I reached out to Minnie, and she came up for his birth. But she only stayed long enough to hear his name and to give me a blanket. Then, she said I'd made my choices and it'd be best if we kept to our separate ways."

"That's harsh." Sadness clutches at my chest. I can't imagine what I would do if my mom told me to keep away from her.

"It was. And I fell back into my resentment as easily as a pair of well-worn jeans. But I can't help thinking she didn't mean what she implied. That, secretly, my choosing to leave was something she approved of."

"I don't understand."

My mom's smile is sad. "After years of being kept secluded, I was adept at sneaking out. And I'm sure you know what's only a few miles down the road."

"The Rabbit Hole," I murmur.

She nods. "I met a young man there. A werewolf. He was kind and handsome and nothing like the monster Minnie had described. I was furious with her for painting a horrifying picture of the wolves. And I was looking for a way to rebel. So, I kept sneaking out to see him."

"You dated a werewolf?" *Like mother, like daughter.*

"For a little while. But then I turned eighteen, and I was accepted to college in Denver. I realized that dating him, riding on the back of his motorcycle, sneaking beers in the woods—that was all me searching for freedom from Minnie's fear. But I wouldn't really be free until I left."

"And the guy?"

"He wanted me to stay. To be his mate. But he wasn't the love of my life. For a little while, I worried that he might be. That I might have left a great love behind. But then I met your father a year later and realized what true love is." She reaches out to tuck a loose strand of hair behind my ear. "What I meant to say is, I think Minnie knew I was sneaking out. She was probably terrified that I was getting close to the wolves. So, when I left, even though I left her behind, I also left *them* behind. I think she would have rather given up the chance to see me than risk me associating with the pack."

The image my mother describes of my grandmother isn't exactly flattering, but it does give me another perspective to consider.

And yet the end result is still a rift that left the woman in Pine Falls lonely and cut off.

"I feel like staying here would be choosing to give you all up," I admit. "Maybe you're right. I'm not the same as Minnie. But I'm also not the same as you. You snuck out of windows for a chance at freedom. I wall myself up. Without my brothers' badgering, who's to say what happened in college won't happen again? I don't think I can do this alone."

Even thinking about that time in my past makes my chest tight.

What would Warner think of that version of me?

Logically, I know depression is a disease. That it's not my fault.

But I can't help the shame that cuts at my nerves when I imagine him witnessing me in my darkest place.

"Sweetheart, listen. Just for a minute. Sit here with me and listen."

"I *have* been—"

Mom puts her finger to my lips, cutting me off. I roll my eyes, but shut my mouth, bracing for her next argument, ready to rebut with more explanations of how different I am from my family.

We can't be viewed through the same lens. They're rib-crushing hugs while I'm tight smiles. They're permanent markers and I'm light pencil lines. They're vibrant life, and I keep to the shadows.

I have all these words ready to go, but with no chance to use them because my mother doesn't speak. She sits still and watches me. The only sound comes from the front porch, where my brothers harmonize their instruments, playing a folk song I recognize as one they commonly choose to warm up with. The music takes me to our backyard at family picnics and dingy bars, where I ferried beers to the stage.

"Don't you hear it?" Mom asks, her eyes boring into mine.

"The music?"

"The love." Her long fingers cup my cheek. "They're all here. Did you ask them to come?"

I shake my head, a thick lump in my throat hindering my ability to speak.

"And you'll never have to. Wherever you go, they'll find you. We'll all find you." Her face splits into a wide, teasing grin. "Our smothering is international. You think a couple hours' drive will stop them?"

Suddenly, I have to blink rapidly.

My mother leans forward in her chair, holding all of my attention. "If you love that man and you're leaving him because you're worried about losing us, don't. You could be in the middle of Denver, living in the house next door to mine, and still be oceans away. The thought of you breaking your own heart ... that's what scares me. I've seen what a broken heart does to women in our family. I think if you came back to Denver, we might lose you more than we would if you were far away."

And now that she says it, I can see that too. The idea of returning to my tiny apartment in Denver without the hope of seeing Warner again sets off more of those horrible cracks in my chest.

Never feeling his warm body against mine.

Never watching him smile while I ask my questions.

Never hearing his laugh again. Or his growl.

He's my wolf. Mine.

This pain, a deep ache in my chest, *this* is drowning.

I turned down everything he'd offered, for fear of becoming my grandmother. But I already am her.

She turned away from love, just like I'm doing.

The image of Warner's devastated face blares in my mind, threatening to crush me with panicked regret.

Have I destroyed my chance at happiness, just like she did?

"I told him to find someone else." The admission comes out on a whisper.

My mother covers my fisted hands with her own. "Sweetheart, compared to you, there is no one else."

49

WARNER

As I PACE around my apartment, I avoid looking in any mirrors. I don't want to see how black my eyes are.

Funny, I never thought falling in love with a person would bring out so many dark feelings. Love is supposed to be great. Lift you up. Make you feel like you're invincible. At least, that's what people tell you.

But I'm finding that love feels a whole lot like misery.

She's leaving.

The thought makes me want to howl. My wolf thrashes under my skin, demanding release. The urge to transform tempts me. To run through the woods until I forget what it's like to be human. Forget what it means to hurt.

But something keeps me here, in this stifling room.

I wrench open a window, just so I can breathe under the suffo-cating weight of losing her.

As I continue circling my apartment, an itch to tear the place apart grows. There's nothing obviously wrong with the space. I bought comfortable couches, mounted a decent-sized TV on the wall.

The kitchen is clean and well stocked.

But as I stare around, I can't help thinking of it as a black hole of emptiness. Because she's not here.

There are pieces of her. The scarf she crocheted for me hangs by the door alongside my new, decorated helmet. The sparkly barrette I unclipped from her hair the first time we slept together sits in the middle of the coffee table, reminding me to give it back.

I scowl, knowing I'm never giving that little bit of her up. Not if she's leaving me.

Each piece feels like a shout into an echoing cavern. A glaring reminder that my home, my life, doesn't have her in it any longer.

I try to imagine tomorrow, and the next day, and a week from now. Every time that I will come back here and there will be no Zoey. Just me and this empty apartment.

I can't.

The thought digs into me, and I'm brought back to the first night I saw her, sitting at the bar, drinking bourbon while she slipped her little hook through yarn. Just like I knew there was no possible future that involved her leaving The Rabbit Hole without me talking to her, I know now there can be no future where I live without her.

But she won't stay.

So ... that means I have to go with her.

Once the idea forms in my head, I know it's the right one.

Not necessarily the easiest, but it's *right*.

Here, I have my pack, but who am I to say my pack is more important than her family?

I was asking her to leave her loved ones behind without considering taking that route myself. Zoey even offered to try long-distance, and I threw that back in her face. Just dismissed the possibility. As if she wasn't worth the effort.

When, really, she's worth everything.

Zoey probably doubts that I ever cared for her.

My fingers tangle in my hair, tugging at the strands as a growl vibrates in my chest.

I never considered compromising. I asked her to give up her

family, plus a better situation for her job, and demanded she live in a town where I'm almost sure someone wants to hurt her.

Who would say yes to that?

What kind of man am I?

If only there was a way to go back in time and challenge my dense self. More growls spill from my throat, as if Warner from a few hours ago were standing in front of me.

But he's not. It's just me and my realization that I've made a mess of the best thing to come into my life. I need to fix this.

As I stalk to my bedroom, I pull my cell phone out and dial a familiar number. While it rings, I grab a duffel bag and start filling it.

"Warner," is my brother's only greeting.

"Roderick, can you come by the store? I've got something important I need to tell you."

50

WARNER

WHEN I STEP through the front door of the shop, I find more than just my older brother waiting for me. I'm not surprised at the sight of my mom behind the register. It is her store after all. My uncle lounging beside her isn't out of the ordinary either.

What has my steps slowing is the sight of my baby sister and brother relaxing on a display bench. Tanya and Isaac aren't the handiest of the Jamesons, and my sister has been avoiding working at the family business since Mom declared it was time she started earning a paycheck.

Apparently, this is now a family meeting.

On second thought, this should make everything easier. Tell everyone my decision at once instead of having to repeat myself or risk anything getting lost in translation.

Roderick is examining a new electric handsaw when I come in, but he immediately returns it to the shelf and gives me his full attention. He doesn't have to say anything for me to know I can spill my whole plan whenever I'm ready.

I open my mouth, but in her usual fashion, Tanya speaks first.

"Warner," she whines, "why are we all here? I've got stuff to do."

Her teenage dramatics make me grin. "I only asked to talk to Roderick."

"Yeah, but he was giving me a ride to the bowling alley. Meghan is going to go batshit if I'm late."

My little sister always knows how to wrench the spotlight out of someone else's hands in order to make sure it shines solely on her.

"Most seventeen-year-olds can drive themselves," I point out.

"Only the ones that haven't rear-ended cop cars," Isaac mutters, earning himself a flesh-melting glare from his twin.

"The varsity soccer team was running on the side of the road. *Shirtless*. That's worse driving conditions than a Category 5 hurricane. The cop is lucky all I did was rear-end his piece-of-shit cruiser."

A snort sounds from behind the counter, and I glance over to catch my uncle massaging away a smile with the tips of his fingers. Mom, meanwhile, ignores our bickering in favor of inventory. Or checking receipts. Or something else that involves staring intently at the paper in front of her rather than acting as mediator between her children.

"I'll drive you after I hear what Warner has to say." Roderick remains his unmovable, focused self, not bothered in the slightest by our sister's complaining.

"Fine!" She huffs, retrieving her cell phone from her back pocket and using the screen to ignore us.

Isaac leans his head back as if he's going to take a nap, but I know better. He's quiet, unassuming, lacking the intimidating factor that is a necessary piece of Roderick's makeup. But that only allows Isaac to hear and see more than the rest of us do. He passes around town unobtrusively. So, he knows things.

My guess is, he's wiser than most other seventeen-year-olds. Probably more than most people three times his age too.

I'll miss him when I'm gone. I'll miss all of them.

But not as much as I'd miss Zoey.

I love my family, but I don't need them the way I need her.

In only a few weeks, she's become the one for me. My partner. So much a part of me that the idea of losing her is on the same level as having one of my limbs ripped off.

But that's how it is for wolves. When we love, we do it deeply.

My only hope is that this knowledge will help my family understand my decision.

"I'm leaving Pine Falls."

No one was speaking before I made the declaration, but still, the shop suddenly seems a hell of a lot quieter.

Roderick is the first to respond. "She won't stay?"

My brother sounds regretful, but not as if he plans on challenging my choice.

"This isn't her place—"

"Of course it isn't!" my mom growls.

Her fierce input has me rocking back on my heels. I knew she wouldn't like the idea of me moving, but damn. Her voice came out so sharp that it stings.

"She doesn't know us. She doesn't know our ways," Mom continues with a snarl, abandoning her receipts and stalking out from behind the counter.

Tanya isn't staring at her phone anymore, and Isaac leans forward in his seat, eyes fixed on our mother. We all know she has a temper, but something about this reaction seems different.

More intense.

"Honestly, I don't care. She knows *me*," I say.

Does that sound like a line from a cheesy movie or what?

Mom scoffs. "Knows you? Come on, Warner. She's pretty—I'll give you that. And charming, I'm sure. But I can guarantee, if you let her, that girl will destroy you. She'll smash your heart. Probably won't even realize it. One day, she'll just decide she doesn't need you anymore. And then she'll walk out."

The surety in her voice throws me off. Mom talks like she's an expert on the subject. Like she knows everything there is to know about Zoey. Only the person she's describing sounds nothing like the woman I love.

"Where is this coming from? You've barely even talked to her." A growl rides my voice, an urge to defend my future mate seeping out from my wolf.

"She's a Gunner! That's what Gunner girls do. They *leave*."

"Rebecca ..." Uncle Mason looks distinctly uncomfortable, and I can't help remembering my guess about his and Zoey's mother's relationship.

But I'm not concerned with the past. Only the future.

"I'm not arguing that. But when she leaves, I'm going with her."

As my mother opens her mouth, eyes gaining fire, a loud knock rings out from the side of the building. Well, loud for werewolves. A human might not have picked up on it from this distance.

But I hear it without effort, along with the desperate words that follow.

"Warner! Your bike is parked in the alley, so I know you're here! You *are* here, right?"

Zoey.

51

ZOEY

My knocking sounds angry.

Is there a way to knock urgently that doesn't sound like you're pissed off?

Doesn't matter. Warner will find out I'm not angry when he gets the hell out of his apartment and comes to talk to me.

Okay, I might be a little angry. But not at my werewolf. I'm angry at myself.

How could I have walked away? What was I thinking, telling Warner to go find someone else? The idea of him dating another woman, kissing another woman, makes me want to break down this door. Not that I think he's upstairs with some sexy werewolf lady. Hopefully, he would need more than half a day to move on.

But there's no answer.

I step back, staring up at one of the windows of his apartment.

"Warner! Your bike is parked in the alley, so I know you're here!" Unless he walked somewhere? "You *are* here, right?"

Am I yelling at the side of a building for no reason?

Who gives a fuck?

My fist rises to pound again when a voice stops me.

"I'm here."

I turn, and there he is, stepping around the corner of the building, staring at me with wide eyes. His leather vest sits on top of a white T-shirt. My werewolf biker.

At least, I hope he's still mine.

"Did you come down the other stairs just to pull some sneaky shit on me?" I cross my arms and affect a glare.

His eyes trace over me. "No. I was in the shop."

"Hmph," I mumble as I stare at him.

He's so perfect. I mean, not perfect. One of his eyes opens a little wider than the other, there's a chip on his left canine, and his hair is disheveled in a way that was clearly not the product of styling gel. Plus, he tends to make jokes in serious situations, and he helps people to the point that he overextends himself, and he tried to push a lifetime commitment on me after only a handful of weeks.

So, he's not perfect.

He's just perfect for *me*.

"Are you knocking on my door for a reason?" Warner's smile comes hesitantly.

I hate it. Hate that he's holding himself back. That first night, the biker guy didn't know me, but he still walked right up to my side, multiple times, insinuating himself in my life when I was still trying to figure my life out.

I want that unwarranted confidence back. So badly that I decide to skip a few steps.

"I need to apologize, but can I kiss you first?"

Warner steps toward me, his eyes now hot. "You never have to ask."

I pounce on him. Or at least, I try to pounce. Unfortunately, my sore ankle has me stumbling face-first into his chest, and I gasp in pain as I try to use the hand with my broken wrist to grasp his shirt before I slide down to the pavement.

"Don't hurt yourself," Warner scolds, quick to grip me under my armpits in a not-very-romantic hold. He sets me on my good leg and wraps an arm around my waist to support some of my weight.

"That was supposed to be a much sexier move. I was envisioning jumping into your arms and wrapping my legs around you."

"That sounds appealing in every way possible. But let's put that on hold until you get some more healing under your belt." Warner grins down at me, smoothing stray hairs away from my face.

"I was wrong," I proclaim.

Before he can respond, I use my good hand to clutch the back of his neck and bring his face down to mine in a searing kiss.

At the taste of him, the feel of his sturdy body against mine, my proclamation is proven fact. How could I have thought for a second to give this up? To give him up?

I love my family, but they're a sure thing. I realize that now. I could move to China, and my brothers would come by plane or boat or teleportation machine to force their overbearing love on me.

Warner doesn't have to follow me. And I shouldn't ask him to. What Warner needs is for someone to fight for him. To choose him.

To love him.

I cup his face, pulling myself away more than I'm pushing him back. I could kiss him until the next apocalyptic event ravaged the earth. And then I'd only pause for a moment to check if there were any zombies nearby before returning to his tempting mouth.

But I hurt him, and he deserves another Gunner apology.

This seems to be a habit for me. One I plan on breaking by making this man as happy as possible.

"I'm sorry, Warner."

"Zoey—" He goes to interrupt me, but I cover his mouth with my hand, staring intently up at him.

"Let me say this?" After waiting for his nod, I continue, "You asked me to be your mate. To be with you forever. That's heavy, and it scared me. I don't think I was wrong to be nervous about that."

His eyes get sad, and I push on.

"I'm not always ... healthy."

Hell, I didn't think it would be this hard to say. There's an urge to use metaphors or skirt around the topic. But I want the word out there. It needs to be said. I need to say it.

"For the last few years"—tears are in my throat, but I swallow them down—"I've battled depression."

Warner's entire body tenses. Then, treating me as if I were formed from spun glass, my werewolf slowly gathers me into a hug that presses the entire length of my body against his. With my head tucked under his chin, a surge of comfort and confidence overcome me, and talking about it becomes easier.

"It hit me for the first time in college. I was away from my family, and I don't know if that triggered it or what, but things got bad. When my brothers didn't hear from me for a while, they got worried and made a surprise visit. I was practically comatose. They brought me back to Denver, convinced me to transfer schools and talk to a professional. That helped. So did medication." I draw in a deep, bracing breath. "But I'm not cured because there's no permanent fix. And I worry all the time that I'll have a bad episode like I did then and I won't be able to pull myself out of it."

"You want to be in Denver because of your brothers. Because they'd recognize it. They would know how to help you." Warner doesn't ask. He just realizes the truth.

I press my face against his chest. "I came to Pine Falls to test out living without my family around me all the time. Their love is a gift, but sometimes, I felt suffocated by it. I mean, you've met my brothers. You know what I'm saying, right?"

The brush of his chin against the top of my head tells me he's nodding.

"I didn't come here to add more love to my plate." Sucking in a deep breath, I pull back to meet Warner's eyes, making sure he's listening. "But you didn't care about my plans, did you? You infuriating werewolf." I'm growling through my smile. "You made me fall for you. Damn it, Warner. I love you."

Hope sparks in his gaze, but he holds still. He needs more, and I plan on giving it to him.

"Your love doesn't smother me because you listen to me. You're this wildly powerful supernatural creature, but I've never felt crushed by you." My thumb traces his bottom lip. "But when you said *mate*, I panicked. I'm scared. Scared that I'll make plans for the future and they'll come crashing down if I get sick again."

Pain creases the corners of Warner's eyes as he cups my face.

I stare up at him with determination. With love. "But I realized something." I wrap my fingers around his wrists, holding him to me. "I'm stronger now. And smarter. What happened in college was bad because I hadn't expected it. Couldn't plan for it. But now, I know how to take care of myself." My ankle smarts as I rise up on my tiptoes to brush a soft kiss against his lips. "And I know if I start drowning again, you'll be the one to see it. And I trust you to help me keep my head above water."

"Always, Zoey. Always." He growls the words, eyes fierce.

The sight warms every bit of me, even as it renews my guilt for how I treated him.

"I'm so sorry for doubting you. For rejecting your affection. For saying that I'd leave you—"

"You should've left. You'll do it anyway, so why not go now?"

The harsh comment makes me flinch, and I realize that Warner and I aren't alone.

We have an audience of wolves.

52

WARNER

OF COURSE MY family followed me.

Zoey is in my arms, saying all the things I've been dying to hear, but my mother's biting words demand my attention. I glare over my shoulder.

Rebecca Jameson stands at the mouth of the alley, my uncle laying a staying hand on her shoulder. With a jerk, she shrugs him off.

Roderick approaches with unhurried steps, his face not giving away any emotion. However, from the way his eyes flick between our mother and me, I'm betting he's considering whether the pack leader needs to intercede in this conflict.

Tanya and Isaac linger at a distance, hesitating to come closer. My sister bites her thumbnail in the way she always does when her anxiety rises, and my younger brother crosses his arms and wears a blank face. Isaac tends to be more like Roderick than me, facing conflict with a stony defense.

"This is between Zoey and me. We'd like a moment alone," I say as calmly as I can manage.

"So you can ride off to Denver together?"

"What?"

At Zoey's question, I turn back to her.

Tuning out my mom's unwanted comments, I try to have an actual conversation about our future. Zoey told me she loves me. All I want is a moment to savor the words.

"I shouldn't have asked you to stay here."

Zoey flinches back as if I struck her, but I keep my arms tight around her waist before she can stumble away.

"What I mean is, your life is back in Denver. Your family and friends. Your business opportunities. It was selfish of me to ask you to give all that up."

"Warner—"

"I'm coming with you." I speak over her, needing to get the words out. Needing her to know that I'll follow her anywhere.

"What about your pack?" Her eyes flick to my family and back to me.

"They aren't the only wolves in the world."

She's shaking her head, and I want to grip the sides of her face, keep the denial at bay. I want her nodding and smiling and telling me about the place we'll get together in the city.

"I don't want you to go to Denver."

Now, I'm the one flinching, and she's the one clutching me close.

"I want us to stay in Pine Falls," she says. "At least for now. I want us to stay here. Together."

Happiness balloons in my chest, and I'm just about to pull her in for another breath-stealing kiss when my mother's snarl shatters through my good mood. Again.

"Damn it, Roderick. You're the pack leader. She's an outsider. *Do* something."

Zoey's head jerks to the side as if my mother's words were a blow. My wolf bristles in defense, and I turn to examine my brother.

Will he try to step between us? Does he feel the same as our mother?

The man has his arms crossed, his eyes locked on Zoey and me. He's silent at first, and everyone waits for him to speak.

Then, Roderick shrugs. "She doesn't look like an outsider."

Mom's mouth hangs open before she snaps it shut and lets out another menacing growl.

Rebecca Jameson is not the bubbliest woman on a normal day, but this level of anger worries me. I get the sense that something deeper is going on that I'm not aware of.

"Mom, I know you want what's best for me, and you don't think this is it. But I'm telling you, Zoey is all I want. I'll only be happy if I'm where she is. If we're together."

My passionate words don't sway her.

She continues to glare at the woman in my arms. "Until she leaves you."

"Rebecca"—a new voice enters the fray, somehow both apologetic and commanding—"please stop putting my sins on my daughter's head. If you want to be mad at someone, be mad at me."

The gentle words come from the mouth of the alley, and we all turn in sync. Standing under the light of a streetlamp is a beautiful woman. Her hair hangs in a golden braid over her shoulder, and there's an impressiveness to her that's only amplified by her height. I'm guessing that she's close to six feet.

"Selena?" Uncle Mason whispers the name, and I realize who I'm looking at.

Zoey's mother.

The gorgeous woman smiles, but the expression is regretful. "Mason. Been a long time."

"Could've been longer and we all would've benefited," my mom snaps.

Selena Gunner looks back at my mother, taking in the defensiveness of her posture.

"I know you don't want me here. But this isn't about me. It's about our children. Believe me, I didn't expect something like this to happen. But it did. And I swear, Zoey is a more reliable person than I ever was."

"Am I missing something? I feel like I have half the story," Zoey asks as her gaze jumps around the group, taking in Mason's grimace, Roderick's scrutiny, Tanya's lost look, Isaac's confusion, Rebecca's disdain before finally landing back on me.

"Drama from another decade," I mutter, suddenly very annoyed that all of this is being bickered over when I'm trying to declare my love. "Not our problem."

"I mean, for what it's worth"—Zoey leans to the side, meeting my mother's glare head-on—"I love your son, and I want to be with him."

"You don't deserve him!" My mother's declaration tears from her, and I notice her eyes are half black with anger. "He fixes your car! He pulls you from trees! He nurses your wounds! And how do you pay him back? By threatening to leave town! Like mother, like daughter. But I won't let you play your games with my son."

She takes a menacing step toward us, as if she plans on ripping Zoey from my arms. Roderick and Mason tense, and I shift my body between my love and my mother.

Then, something in her words registers in my mind.

"How did you know Zoey was hiding in a tree?"

The color leaves my mom's cheeks, hinting that my instinct is correct. What felt like a slap to the face now feels like a hand around my throat.

The truth chokes me.

"You mentioned it." Mom waves my words away, keeping her glare trained on the woman I love. But now, it seems her glowering is an attempt to keep from meeting my eyes.

"No"—I speak slowly around the despair and anger that clogs my chest—"I didn't."

In fact, I haven't said much to my mom about Zoey at all. Every time I brought her up, I noticed the tight lines get deeper at the corner of my mom's eyes. A subtle hint that she was unhappy. So, I'd cut my stories short. Talked to Roderick or Courtney instead. But I thought she just didn't like the idea of me dating Zoey because human-werewolf relationships could be tricky.

But it was more than that.

"I'm sure you did. You just forgot." Her continued denial snuffs out my sadness and leaves behind rage.

"I did *not*. It was you. All of the shit that Zoey's been dealing with was you, wasn't it?"

Rebecca Jameson—who taught me everything I know about cars, who can turn into a wolf, who has unlimited supplies for cutting wood—crosses her arms over her chest defensively.

"You disconnected the truck's battery and messed with its gas gauge. You used your wolf to scare Zoey in the woods."

I want my mom to meet my eyes, but she won't. My mind is filled with the memory of Zoey soaking wet, shaking with cold, rambling about a large animal that had her climbing a tree for safety.

It's almost as bad as Zoey sitting in the emergency care unit, broken and bleeding. And no matter how much I might want to step into my mother's space and force her to acknowledge me, I'm more worried about keeping my arms around Zoey. Keeping her safe.

From my family.

"You sabotaged the tree house. Why? Were you trying to break her neck?" The words rasp and crack as I ask them, and I have to bury my nose in Zoey's hair, breathe a deep inhale of her scent to remind me that she's here. Not unmarked, but she's alive.

No thanks to Rebecca Jameson.

"That's not—"

"Are you fucking kidding me?"

For a moment, I'm sure a werewolf just spoke, the words menacing and infused with a growl. But then I realize the exclamation came from Selena Gunner, who stalks toward us, her eyes locked on my mom.

53

ZOEY

Earlier, I had the calm version of my mother. The one who smiles sweetly and hands out wisdom as if she had daily phone conversations with the Dalai Lama.

This is another one of her sides. The mama bear.

But this mama bear looks like someone shook a hornet's nest and shoved it up her ass. Rage of epic proportions I've never witnessed burn out of her eyes.

Mom lunges for Rebecca, stopped only by Warner's uncle, who steps forward just in time to wrap his arms around my mom's torso.

"You fucking self-serving asshole! You think you have the right to torment my daughter?"

"Mom—"

When her yelling cuts me off, I'm not too mad about it. I have no idea what I would have said. This exchange might have started with me, but it has the dark undertones of history weaving through it.

"Just because I hurt your feelings, you think that gives you the go-ahead to hurt her?"

"Without the tree house, she'd have no cell service. One more reason to leave. I wasn't trying to hurt her." Rebecca defends herself, even as she avoids meeting my mother's furious gaze.

"You could have *killed* her!" she shrieks. "You almost did! My girl —" She chokes—on rage or tears, I can't tell. "My baby girl could have died because you wolves can never let shit go!"

Rebecca turns her back, shoulders hunched, as if my mother's enraged comments are physical blows.

Taking a brief mental step back from the situation, I find it fascinating how, even though we're surrounded by mythical monsters, people who can literally turn into wild beasts, my mom is still the most frightening player in this game.

I also need to separate myself for a moment because the knowledge that Warner's *mom* has been secretly harassing me is almost too much to take in. It's not like I haven't interacted with the woman over the past few weeks. Her shop is one of my favorites, and every time I was a customer, she treated me with an efficient manner that never seemed out of the ordinary. Maybe it was naive, but I thought she might even like me a little bit.

Turns out, the opposite is true.

Rebecca Jameson hates me.

"Why?" The question comes out much louder than I planned, but probably as loud as necessary. When my mother is on the warpath, there's not a lot that can get her to pause, but she quiets momentarily at my ragged voice.

"Because your family doesn't get to hurt people without consequences." Rebecca regains some of her righteous rage as she shoots a glare my way. "You don't get to waltz back into this town as if your family didn't try to tear it apart! First, Minnie set humans against wolves, making our existence a struggle. Then, Selena pretended to love Mason—" Rebecca's voice cracks, and she lets out a growl, as if mad at her own sign of weakness before continuing, "She strung him along and then left without a word."

"That's not how it happened, Rebecca." Mason speaks in a deep, soothing tone, but Warner's mom doesn't let it calm her.

"Yes, it is! I was there the night you asked her to be your mate. I saw her run away. And I've watched that eat away at you since then." Rebecca widens her stance, ready to fight. "I've seen what Gunner women do to the men who try to love them, and I will not let my son be a casualty."

"You're insane!" my mom hisses. "You think my turning down your brother-in-law's proposal three decades ago gives you the right to attack my daughter? I can't believe I was trying to apologize to you!" My mom's brief hiatus from screeching has come to an end.

She struggles against Mason's restraining hold, and I pity the man. Sounds like he used to love her, and now, he only gets to hold her to keep her from hurting someone.

Not that I think he should get to hold my mom in a loving embrace. I'm one hundred percent Team Dad all the way. But that doesn't mean I don't feel for the brokenhearted werewolf.

"They were scare tactics. It's not like I was trying to hurt her." Rebecca meets my mother's eyes this time, defiance clear in her posture.

"You could have *killed* her! You almost did!" Mom is wild, to the point that I consider if we might have some wolf in our veins.

"She's alive—"

"It doesn't matter, you selfish bitch!" Shit. This is not a good indication of future Thanksgivings. "You almost killed my daughter!"

Mason Jameson is fully carrying my mother now as she tries to scale him to get at Warner's mom.

"I'm—"

"CHALLENGE!" The word roars so loud that I bet half of Pine Falls heard it.

And from the triumphant, slightly scary grin my mom wears, I think she somehow upped the stakes of this confrontation.

Every wolf, including the stoic Roderick, wears a wide-eyed expression. Tanya even lets out a strangled gasp and now clutches her twin's arm so tight that her knuckles stain white.

Clearly, I'm the only one who doesn't know what's coming next.

54

WARNER

ZOEY GLANCES UP AT ME, confusion twisting her brows. She has no idea that her mother just demanded to fight a werewolf.

Selena Gunner has no fear.

"Selena—" Uncle Mason starts, but the woman won't be censured.

"You know the rules." Zoey's mom jabs a finger toward mine. "Time and place. Name them."

"Do you see this idiocy?!" Mom stares at Roderick, even as she waves toward Selena. "This is what comes of wolves and humans associating. They think they know our ways. That they can be one of us."

"I couldn't give a *damn* about being one of you," Selena hisses. "But I sure as hell know I want to kick your ass. Especially"—the woman glares around at every single one of us, her eyes burning into mine last—"since no one else is willing to protect my daughter from Rebecca's ridiculous vendetta."

Shame spikes hard through me. Here I am, hoping to bring Zoey into my world, trying to convince her to be my mate, all while my own mother puts the woman I love in danger. Maybe her actions were born of some warped sense of protection, but that doesn't excuse them.

"No." Roderick's voice rings clear, cutting through the night. "You are not a wolf. You cannot give challenge."

A frustrated, strangled shriek comes out of Selena's throat.

This is not how I wanted my first interaction with Zoey's mom to go.

Suddenly, the woman stops struggling in Mason's hold. The switch in energy level is eerie, and I worry she hurt herself in some way. Selena stands still, and strangely, it almost looks as if Mason is embracing her rather than restraining.

I wonder if this is torture for him. To have the woman he loved in his arms, but to not really have her.

"Zoey," Selena says.

My woman turns to face her mother, clearly struggling to understand what she's missing.

Selena speaks in a steady voice, her gaze locked on her daughter's eyes. "If you stay here, Rebecca will hurt you."

I tighten my arms, realizing what's happening.

"Mom—"

Selena cuts her daughter off, "They have different rules than humans. She thinks I wronged the pack. She thinks she deserves retribution. And unless someone makes her back down, she'll keep taking her anger out on you." The steady cadence of her voice cracks on that last word.

My head shakes in denial as I pull Zoey into my chest. I'll never let anyone hurt her. She's mine to keep safe.

Then, I see my mother, standing rigid with her arms crossed, glaring at Zoey's mom. And I recognize the truth in the woman's words.

Without a challenge, without a punishment, she'll be free to continue tormenting Zoey. Maybe she was telling the truth when she said she never meant to hurt her. But she did. She hurt the woman I love. And she could easily do it again.

"Are you saying I should leave?" Zoey whispers the question, but everyone can hear it.

Selena shuts her eyes, as if pained, reacting to the devastation in her daughter's words. And across the way, my mother smirks, as if everything she said about the Gunner women was true.

A red rage clouds my vision, and I turn my body, shielding Zoey from the toxic resentment. Then, shocking everyone in the alley, I let my furious growl tear from my throat, aiming a disgusted glare at my mother.

The woman is so bent on driving away what she views as dangerous that she would crush my happiness in the process.

And she flinches from me, eyes wide in shock.

But Zoey doesn't cringe away. Instead, she turns in my hold, wrapping her arms tightly around my waist. Her gentle hands stroke my back as she mutters soothing noises. "Don't worry. I'm not leaving. I was just asking for clarification."

My heart clenches, but I keep my sight fixed on my mother, weighing my options. Every day Zoey stays in Pine Falls will be a day her safety is at risk. I can't be with her every second to fight off subtle attacks or tricks. Even if I could, Zoey would hate it. The last thing she wants is an overprotective male shadowing every step she makes.

The other option is, I could challenge my mother.

Yet, even with anger raging through me, I can't envision laying a hand on the woman who raised me. Who loves me. The idea makes me sick.

Needing guidance, I look at Roderick.

He stares back, likely reading the torment on my face. Then, he drags his eyes over the gathering, finally landing on our mother. "You do not accept Zoey?"

The woman who claims to love us beyond anything else stands taller under his gaze and nods. "I will never accept her. She does not belong in our pack. She does not deserve it."

Roderick doesn't betray a hint of emotion; he simply stares, as if waiting to see if she has anything left to add. But she only gazes back with a level of arrogance that enrages me to the point that I can't think of words. But I don't need to because Roderick always knows what to say.

"Your pride is more important than your son's happiness?" There's not a hint of emotion in his question, but she blanches, as if he spat in her face.

"That's not ... she won't make him happy!"

Roderick shakes his head, as if disappointed with her. So am I.

You always think your parents can do no wrong. But they aren't gods. They're humans.

Or werewolves, I guess.

"Warner has declared his intention to pursue Zoey as his mate. She is under the protection of the pack. Hurting her cannot go unpunished."

"Roderick, no!" Tanya steps forward.

My normally opinionated sister has been quiet up to this moment, hanging back in the shadows with Isaac as they watched the drama of my life unfold. Now, she's probably thinking that Roderick plans to challenge Mom himself. That she's about to witness a fight between her mother and her oldest brother.

"You don't have to punish her. Mom will apologize. She just ... she just didn't know Zoey was going to be pack. She didn't know Warner loved her. Right, Mom? Just tell them you're sorry."

My heart breaks for my little sister as she stares pleadingly at our mother.

But Rebecca Jameson is nothing if not stubborn. The muscle in her jaw stands rigid as she keeps quiet.

Roderick was right. Her pride is more important than my happiness. She can't separate Zoey from Selena.

And I have a choice to make.

I thought the solution to all my problems was having Zoey stay in Pine Falls with me. That my life would be complete. Everything would be perfect.

But that won't be the case with my mother here.

The obvious option is my original plan—moving to Denver. But that still leaves my mother unpunished. It means never returning to

LAUREN CONNOLLY

Pine Falls again because there is no way I would come back here without my mate.

Still, I know that no matter how furious I am with my mother, I cannot fathom the idea of fighting her.

My mind settles on the only option left. The idea of it eats away at me, makes me feel selfish.

In that moment, Zoey tightens her arms around my waist, and I glance down at her. There's a bruise on her forehead, scratches on her face, all from her fall. But despite how those must hurt, she still gazes up at me with trust. With love.

And I realize that I deserve to be selfish. My love for Zoey has never hurt anyone, which means we're in the right. I glance at my older brother, holding his eyes as a speak my choice.

"Exile."

55

ZOEY

WARNER'S BED is super comfortable, especially when lying face down on it. The comforter smells like him. Pine needles and fresh snow. I think if I were to be smothered to death, this is the best material to use to get the job done to send me away from this world peacefully.

Downstairs, the Jamesons are working out the details of exiling their mother.

All because of me.

The rational part of my brain reminds me that it's not technically my fault. I'm not the one who started this secret feud. It's not even like I demanded revenge when I found out Rebecca was behind my life's little miseries.

And I certainly didn't ask for her to be exiled.

But if I had never come to this town, there would be no reason for Rebecca to leave it.

I considered taking Warner up on his original offer of moving to Denver with me. Wouldn't that fix everything? We would be out of Pine Falls and therefore safe from Rebecca's revenge, and she wouldn't have to leave her home and her children.

But I don't want to go back to Denver. At least not anytime soon. Pine Falls has a hold on me. I'm feeling a connection not only to the town, but also to Minnie's cabin. It's almost starting to feel like my cabin. If I leave now, this whole trip would seem unfinished.

Plus, I can't help thinking that our relationship could use some time to develop with distance between us and my brothers.

So, add selfish onto my list of faults.

The apartment's front door opens. I should roll onto my back and ask Warner how things went. How he's doing.

But I can't force myself to meet his understanding, loving gaze just yet. Not when I don't deserve it.

"Wow. And people call me dramatic. You're on the express train to mope town, aren't you?" a feminine voice says, and I start in surprise.

The speaker isn't my mother. For one, I'd recognize her voice anywhere. And besides, she immediately calmed down once she was sure Rebecca would be punished for her treatment of me. Then, she helped me up to Warner's apartment and promised to stick around Minnie's cabin until Warner brought me back.

Curiosity has me flipping over.

Tanya leans against the doorframe, her sharp eyes taking me in.

She must despise me. Even though she's seventeen, on the cusp of adulthood, that doesn't mean she doesn't need her mother. I'm breaking apart her family. The guilt eats at me.

"Tanya, I'm sorry. Really. This isn't what I wanted to happen."

Warner's sister waves a hand, dismissing my words.

"I was there. I know." She pushes off from the wall and meanders around her brother's room, fiddling with his stuff, but never picking anything up. "Still, I'm pissed off." The girl raps her knuckles on the top of his dresser, the sound ringing so loud that I wonder if she's dented the wood.

That's when I realize I'm alone with a werewolf who now probably has a vendetta against me.

I should be scared. But she's Warner's little sister, no matter if she's ten times stronger than I am. I don't want to alienate his entire family in one night. So, I don't try to make a quick escape, deciding to wait for the berating she's about to deliver. Hopefully not served with a side of violence.

Her golden eyes, a few shades lighter than her brother's, examine me, and she smiles in a way that is both humorous and sad.

"I'm not pissed at *you*. I like you. You're the first girl to snag one of my brothers. And he is gone on you. It's great. I'm worried that one of them is going to date a total bitch, and I'm going to have to pretend to get along with her."

Tanya plops down on the bed, and I bounce as the mattress responds to her suddenly added weight.

"But I'm the reason your mom is getting exiled," I remind her.

Tanya stretches out beside me, and as we lie on the bed next to each other, I realize that despite her giant personality, I'm still a few inches taller than her.

For a moment, I think Warner's sister has decided to ignore me as she fiddles with her phone. Then, she holds the device high, tilting the screen so I can see. There's a photo pulled up, a selfie of Tanya as she presses a kiss to the cheek of a handsome boy who wears a rapturous expression.

"That's Carlos. My boyfriend. He's human." She lets her arm fall back to her side.

Tanya is dating a human. I wonder if anyone in her family knows.

As if hearing my question, she explains, "Isaac knows. We all go to school together. He likes Carlos. But I haven't told anyone else."

"Warner wouldn't mind." Then, I hesitate as I consider my words and decide to add on a caveat. "I mean, he wouldn't mind any more than a brother usually would. My brothers have always made my dating life a struggle."

That prom car ride pops back into my brain.

In my peripheral vision, I watch Tanya nod, and I wonder if she has her own list of Occurrences. Maybe we could share stories one day.

"Yeah, Warner will probably be the next one I tell. Maybe Uncle Mason. But Roderick and my mom worry me. Roderick's life is the pack, and he's said multiple times that werewolf-human relationships complicate things. And then Mom ... well, you saw."

I nod, trying not to cringe.

"I don't want her to be exiled. I mean, I'm not worried about Isaac and me. We can take care of ourselves. Plus, Roderick and Uncle Mason are pretty good surrogate dads. So, it's not like I'm freaking out about that."

I turn my head on Warner's pillow and catch the teenager biting her lip.

"My mom showing up today was a surprise. I'm getting by fine on my own, injuries and all, but it's still nice, having her around. I missed her." My offering is a quiet one.

Tanya blinks, her eyes extra shiny. But then she sits up abruptly. "I don't want her exiled, but she can't do what she did to you!" The girl leaps off the bed and starts pacing. "That was super messed up. Especially when you see the way Warner looks at you."

"What way?"

Tanya smirks. "Warner is friendly to everyone. This whole town, even the human half, loves him. You'd think he'd date more. Girls are always after Warner because he's the best kind of guy."

The thought of girls being after my werewolf makes me want to growl possessively. Some of my jealousy must show on my face because

Tanya points at me and gives a triumphant laugh. "Look at you! You're all about him. He deserves that. And he's all about you. And he never has been before. All the girls walked away with smiles on their faces, but moping on the inside because Warner never wanted anything from them. But you ... hell, he's ready to piss on your leg— he's so possessive." Her smile fades into an angry scowl that she directs at the window. "And Mom was going to ruin it all."

"I wouldn't have let her."

No matter what the wolf woman threw at me, I would've taken it. Because Warner is worth fighting for.

"But you shouldn't have to deal with her weirdness! And neither should Carlos! Or anyone I decide to date!" Tanya collapses back beside me. "You want to know why I'm not pissed at you? There it is. I want my brother to be happy, and *I* want to be happy. No matter who we choose to love, it's our choice. Not hers. I don't want her to be exiled," the girl repeats for the third time, "but I think she needs to be. At least until she understands what she did wrong. Until she agrees not to torment the people we date."

Tanya's logic chips away at the guilt I feel. As her declaration sinks in, I don't feel as horrible about the choices I've made. Our relationship has caused a rift in their family, but maybe with time, that gash will heal, and it might shape the Jamesons into something different. Something a little bit better.

"I'm glad you're not mad at me."

We lie side by side until the door to the apartment creaks again.

"Zoey?" Warner's voice carries back to me.

"We're in here!" I call out, sitting up, Tanya following my lead.

"We?" he asks, then appears a second later, eyes widening. "What are you doing here?"

Tanya's spine goes rigid, and she glares at him, as if preparing for a battle. "I'm dating a guy," she announces. "His name is Carlos, and he's a human. Zoey said you wouldn't mind, and as the alpha in your relationship, what she says goes."

Warner's eyes narrow, but I catch a twitch at the corner of his mouth. "Carlos, huh? What does Isaac think of Carlos?"

Tanya plants her fists on her hips, and even sitting, she gives off an air of defiance. "He thinks Carlos is too nice for me and that I'll steamroll him."

I hide a smile behind my hand, and Warner lets out a snort. "Well, there are worse things than all that."

"There are," she agrees. "Now, is someone going to drive me to the bowling alley? I'm a good hour late for my date."

"Oh, it's a date you've been clamoring to get too?"

"Just shut up and drive me!" Tanya punches the bed.

"That's not very nice. Maybe I'd rather stay here in bed with Zoey than drive my whiny sister to her date."

The way he says *in bed* sends a shiver down my spine.

Tanya also picks up on the underlying meaning, but she has a completely different reaction. With a gasp, she launches off the mattress.

"Ew! You've had sex in this bed, haven't you? Gross! Don't answer! Now, I have to go burn my skin off with acid!"

Warner grins wickedly, and I flip back over onto my stomach to hide the laughter threatening to burst out at her words.

"I'll give you a ride, just go wait by my bike for a minute."

I turn my head in time to see Tanya roll her eyes and stalk out of the room.

Then, I have the full attention of a golden-eyed werewolf.

Before he can open his mouth, I roll to my knees and open my arms wide. "How are you doing?"

Warner gathers me up against him, burying his nose in my neck before answering, "I'm ... I'm sorry. If I start talking, I'm not sure when I'll stop."

"And you need to take care of your sister." I cup his face in my hands, pulling back enough to meet his eyes. "Go. I'll be here."

His fingers dig into my back, clutching me close.

"Promise you're not leaving?" The vulnerability in his voice cuts at me.

"Here." I climb off the bed. "I'll give you some insurance."

With efficient movements, I strip off every last piece of clothing I'm wearing, only held up for a second when my shirt snags on my cast. I bundle them all together and hand them to an open-mouthed Warner.

"Can't leave if I'm naked, can I? Plus, this way, I know you'll hurry back."

When heat flares in his eyes, I quickly slide under the covers and wave him away.

"Go on."

A growl rumbles deep in his throat, and he leans over to plant a promising kiss to my mouth before storming out of the room, my bundle of clothes clutched tight to his chest like a lifeline.

56

WARNER

"But my hair!"

"Put the helmet on now, or you're walking to the bowling alley. I do not have time for this."

"You were a lot more easygoing before Zoey," Tanya mutters, delicately placing the spare helmet over her bouncy waves.

I ponder my sister's words as I rev my bike to life.

Was I more easygoing before Zoey moved to town and shook up my life?

Probably. Because before she got here, I had nothing to fight for. Nothing to hurry home to.

Not to mention, I had no reason to be on edge about my mom being exiled. I offered to help Roderick work out the details, but he flat-out refused.

Sometimes, being the pack leader is a shit job.

He did tell me she won't be barred from communicating with us over the phone. That is, if any of us wants to talk to her. I expect Tanya will and possibly Isaac, but despite Roderick's stoic expression,

I could tell how devastated he was that our mother pushed us to do this.

I, of course, am furious with her, and I know it'll be a long time before I'm in the right headspace to have any kind of conversation with her.

So, by tomorrow morning, Pine Falls will be down one wolf.

The bowling alley isn't far, but every hint of space that's put between me and Zoey has my wolf growing anxious.

Tonight was rough on my protective instincts.

Still, the knowledge that I have my woman's clothes bundled in my saddlebag gives me comfort. Assures me that she'll be waiting for me when I get back.

When we pull into the cracked parking lot of the aptly named 12 Lanes, I can hear the crack of heavy balls against pins, mixed with laughter, emanating from inside the building. Tanya dismounts and immediately rips off the helmet, as if the thing was burning her the entire ride. I expect her to toss the headwear at me, then race inside.

Instead, she clutches the helmet against her chest, ignoring my outstretched hand.

"Is Mom really getting exiled?" My take-no-shit sister looks suddenly vulnerable.

I fight a grimace and nod. "You understand why, right?"

"Yeah." The word comes out on a sigh. "I can't believe she won't let it go. I mean, I can hold a grudge, believe me. I still haven't gotten over the fact that Isaac cut the hair off all my Barbies when we were eight. But I'd get over it in a second if the other option meant giving up all of you."

"She's not giving up on you. Mom's just ... going away for a little while."

My sister snorts and finally lets the helmet go, handing it back to me before she turns toward the building.

I feel guilty and then angry because I shouldn't have to feel this way. But I can't help thinking I'm the reason we're losing our mom.

Then, an image of Zoey flashes in my mind. Her naked body as she crawled under my covers just a little bit ago. Her pale skin, covered in bruises and stitched cuts from her fall. And my heart hardens toward my mother.

"Text me," I call out to my retreating sister, and she turns back to glance at me. "When you're done and need a ride home, just let me know."

She waves away my offer. "One of my friends will give me a lift."

But before she can retreat again, I'm off my bike, crossing the worn blacktop and sweeping her up into a bear hug. "Nah, sis," I murmur against her thick brown hair. "You let me know when, and I'll be here for you."

"Pushy much?" The words are dismissive, but her tone is full of the same vulnerability from a moment ago.

Then, her arms wrap around my waist, and we stand still, hugging each other.

After a minute passes, Tanya shoves me away, straightening her spine. "Stop being so clingy. People are going to think I need baby-ing." She glares, but there's a glistening at the edge of her lashes.

I give her my goofiest smile in return. "You kidding? Everyone knows I'm the baby in the family."

She rolls her eyes, even as her lips fight to smile. "Get out of here. I'll text you when I need a ride home."

"Yes, Your Majesty."

"Begone, lowly jester!" She waves again before skipping toward the lit-up entrance of the bowling alley.

I watch her until she's out of sight, then climb back on my bike.

When I get back to my apartment, I take the stairs two at a time, anxious to see Zoey again. I wonder if she's fallen asleep in my bed. I won't wake her if she has, no matter how much I want to talk to her. To hear her say she loves me again.

But there's time for that. If she's asleep, I'll curl my body around hers and keep her warm.

When I enter my bedroom, I find Zoey propped up on my pillows, a crochet project in her lap. She has the blankets pulled up over her chest. Or at least, it looks like they started that way. At this moment, one edge sags enough that I catch a hint of her rosy nipple.

329

I get the urge to crawl on my knees to her, then bury my face in the valley of her breasts to breathe in her sweet, earthy scent and hear the delicate pounding of a heart she claims beats for me.

"Do you think your family will forgive me for what I've done to you all?"

Her question shocks me enough to leave off staring at the hint of her nakedness and search her eyes. "What *you've* done?"

"I tore open old wounds, and now, you're all suffering."

Apparently, my sister isn't the only one feeling vulnerable after this evening's confrontation. I cross the room, sit on the edge of the bed, just beside Zoey, and reach out to stroke her exposed shoulders.

"That's not on you. You didn't know about that drama. And it's not *our* drama."

Zoey goes to open her mouth, and I can tell she still plans on shouldering the blame. The thought pisses me off, and I give a definitive shake of my head.

"No. Don't play the martyr. You talk about opening wounds? It's been *decades*. A normal person would've let the old hurts heal. My mom is the one who's been tearing things open. She's at fault, and she's too stubborn to admit it. No one in my family will blame you. We know who hurt who. And we know who is innocent in all of this."

"If I had never come—"

"Please, Zoey." Now, my hands curl, clasping her, holding her in place. "Please don't ever think life would be better if you hadn't come here. You don't know what it was like before."

One of her eyebrows curves up. "You make it sound like you were living in hell."

"Not hell." I run my nose through her hair, filling my lungs with the scent that tells me she is meant to be mine. "More like purgatory. I was existing. Sitting in a waiting room. Lingering in a line. Restless, without a direction."

"I'm not that much, Warner. You can't think I mean that much." Her voice cracks.

"You do though. This might sound selfish, but I've always wanted someone. Someone who needed me and who I needed. I can live on my own, exist on my own, but I don't like it. You're my someone, Zoey. I need you."

She stares into my eyes, not shying away from the intensity in my gaze. "I came to Pine Falls because I felt smothered by my brothers' love."

I try not to wince, imagining my desperate declaration reminds her of their rabid displays of affection.

"Then, I came here and learned about my grandmother. After that, I worried that without their love, I'd curl into myself. That I'd fade into some kind of ghost person."

My mouth is open to deny it, but she shakes her head. I keep quiet, letting her finish.

"You don't smother me. Your love isn't a weight I have to fight off to keep from crushing me. Your love is like ..." She trails off, brow wrinkled in thought. "Your love is a strong hand on a ladder!" Zoey smiles, huge and bright, happy with the comparison.

"What's that mean exactly?" I ask, not without a trace of humor.

"You hold me steady, but you still let me climb to whatever height I'm trying to reach," she explains, as if it's the clearest thing in the world.

And once she says it, it is.

Emotions crash through me, threatening to drown my head and my heart. Needing a brief reprieve from the onslaught, I drop my hands between us and finger the craft in her lap.

"What are you working on?"

"I'm crocheting you an apology hat, to go with your scarf."

Damn, she won't let up.

In a fit of self-preservation, I grasp for a joke. "You seem hell-bent on me keeping my head covered. *Wear a helmet*, you say. *I'm making you a hat*, you say." I put on a high-pitched voice, making a complete mockery of her normal smooth, sultry tone.

Zoey laughs. "You caught me. I'm obsessed with keeping this head safe and warm." She sets her project to the side and cups my cheeks with her hands. The hard plaster of the cast is rough against my skin, just as the bare palm of her other hand is soft. She shifts, rising on her knees so she can press a kiss to the center of my forehead. "Mainly because I love the brain that's rattling around in it."

The words dig into my heart, ruthless, loving claws. With her movement, the blankets fall away, and I'm confronted with her bare chest and stomach and the teasing triangle of curls at the center of her. The sight has me groaning.

Even though I want to crush her to my chest, I'm wary of her battered body. Instead, I circle my arms around her in a gentle embrace, lowering her to the bed. She spreads out beneath me, muscles relaxed, and gifts me with a gorgeous smile.

I hunger for her mouth and take it with the passion I want to show the rest of her. For now though, I keep my fervor to the meeting of our lips.

Zoey gasps and moans, her fingers raking down the front of my shirt, fumbling with buttons until she has the fabric parted and can get at my skin. Her nails dig into me, as if she plans to scratch and tear until I'm covered in her marks.

"Do it. Be rough with me," I beg against her mouth.

She doesn't hesitate. Her hands dive under my shirt, her fingers clutch my back, and I groan at the delicious bite of her nails along my spine. My love doesn't break skin, but I long for a mirror so I can admire what must be a nice set of red marks scored into me.

Then, she has my belt in her grasp, undoing the buckle. Next thing I know, my pants are unzipped and being shoved down and that soft grasp is gripping my hard length.

I pry my lips from hers, rising up enough to tell her something like ...

We don't have to.

You're hurt.

But she's faster than I am.

"I love you." Zoey doesn't whisper or let the words out on a light gasp. She declares them with utter and complete confidence. "Do you love me?"

"More than anything," I growl in response.

She nods, a confident smile plumping her cheeks as her uninjured leg slings around my waist. A very demanding heel presses into one of my ass cheeks, urging me forward.

"Are you going to show me how much?"

The crown of me presses against her slickness, and my eyes threaten to roll back in my head. But that would mean I'd have to stop staring down at her, and I can't give up this view.

"You're perfect."

A red flush seeps into her cheeks, but she doesn't deny my words.

"For you."

Yes. Both my human half and wolf half are in complete agreement, howling together in triumph.

"For me."

57

ZOEY

"BUT WHO IS GOING to get us our beers?"

"Byron, I love you, but you need to grow some ovaries."

"The phrase is, grow some balls," Donovan points out.

"Ovaries are tough," I point out. "Balls are sensitive. If I aimed a kick between your legs, what would you do?"

Unconsciously, my brother guards his privates with both his hands, as if he thinks I'm going to enact the hypothetical situation.

Point proven.

"Exactly. Balls make you weak. Grow some ovaries, apologize to the girl, and stop dating people at your favorite hangout spots."

Byron grumbles while Donovan watches me with wary eyes, still trying to figure out if my question was rhetorical or not.

The four Gunner boys are gathered in the driveway, putting off their departure with an endless list of excuses. Some more valid than others.

"There's no cell signal here! No Wi-Fi!" Carver holds his phone up to the sky, as if an extra foot of height might change things.

"I'm going to fix that." Warner clomps down from the front porch, stepping over a napping Bruce on his way. My man looks delicious in his work boots and worn jeans. He's left his leathers off today, in work mode.

When I decided to stay in Pine Falls, my mom announced she was signing the cabin over to me. An early Christmas present. And birthday present. And next Christmas too.

She left the day after the confrontation with Rebecca, needing to get back to her job.

My brothers also have jobs, but they've dragged their feet an extra day, as if that's all that's needed to get me to return to Denver with them.

Their efforts are futile.

Since I'm officially staying, a few upgrades need to be made to Minnie's place.

My place.

And my werewolf is all too happy to help.

Despite their whining, Carver, Byron, and Donovan seemed to have warmed up to my boyfriend, reaching out to give him farewell back slaps and one-armed hugs.

Abram's arms stay crossed, and his face remains blank. That is, until we hear the crunch of tires on the driveway, and the hood of a familiar truck appears. The yellow vehicle has my oldest brother scowling.

"The building crew has arrived!" Courtney shouts from the driver's seat as Tanya leans out the shotgun window, gaping at my brothers.

"Oh my God! Is this what men look like in Denver?" Warner's sister asks at full volume.

Carver grins while Byron and Donovan shift in discomfort. Good. Maybe the besotted teenager will finally get them to go before they collectively lose their jobs.

"You need to get out in the world, girl." Courtney climbs out and saunters over to our little gathering. "Did I miss the glitter wrestling?"

If it's possible, Abram's frown gets deeper. He is not a Courtney fan. Too bad because she's one of my new best friends.

"Why are you here?" he asks, and I slap his arm for the rude tone he uses.

Courtney just smirks and flicks one of his bulging biceps before strolling to the bed of her truck and gesturing at an abundance of wood. "Building crew. Like I said."

"How much do you bench?" Tanya asks Donovan, staring up at my brother with sparkling eyes.

"Uh ..." He shifts uncomfortably, glancing my way for a rescue. "Around two fifty, I guess?"

"Really? That's it? Hell, I can do two fifty," she says, disappointment clear in her tone.

Carver coughs out a laugh as Donovan's face goes red. The teenage werewolf moves to join Courtney. The two women start unloading the wood on their own, my brothers watching with wide eyes. Warner moves to join them, leaving me alone with my family.

"Are they building a new tree house?" Donovan asks.

"The tree house." Abram points at me with an almost-accusing finger. "That still doesn't make sense."

"I told you"—I try keeping my voice casual—"it was all a misunderstanding. Warner's mom thought I wanted to take the thing down, and she thought she was helping me out by starting on it. She had no idea I still climbed up in the thing."

Lies. I hate lying to my brothers. But this thing between me and Warner is still new. If it doesn't work out, I can't guarantee they wouldn't use the knowledge of his family trouble to enact some intricate form of revenge.

Also, the amount of explaining necessary to get them to believe in the supernatural gives me a phantom headache.

"Did she at least apologize?" Abram glowers in the direction of town.

Out of the corner of my eye, I notice a stiffness in Warner's shoulders and a sad cast to Tanya's face. Apparently, werewolves have better-than-normal hearing.

"Of course." More lies. Need to get off this topic.

"We're not building a tree house!" Courtney shouts before disappearing around the side of the cabin. Leaving us all in suspense.

When she returns, it's to the full attention of her audience. Fists planted on her hips, she announces, "We're building a chicken coop. Queen Omelet has been wondering when she can come home."

"Oh God, you're actually going to raise chickens?" Byron stares at me in horror.

Instead, the idea gives me a wonderful sense of grounding.

"Yeah, I'm going to raise chickens." I catch Warner's eye as he hefts a load of wood onto his shoulder.

The happy grin he wears is like a hug straight to the heart.

Poor birds. They're going to have to deal with a wolf in their henhouse.

58

EPILOGUE

ZOEY

Six Months Later

I TROT down the steps of my front porch, heading toward Warner. He's got on his Dark Moon Riders vest and the helmet with a snarling wolf I painted for him all those months ago.

My man wears it with pride. In fact, a handful of other Dark Moon Riders have asked me to paint theirs.

My secret plot to keep all their heads safe is working.

"Hop on. It's time for us to ride off into the sunset. Leave all our worldly possessions behind and live life as true road warriors!" Warner holds my helmet out to me as he gifts me with a teasing grin.

"If you start calling me your old lady, I'm going to stab you in the leg," I inform him as I settle on the back of his bike. "With a crochet hook. Those things are blunt, which means it'll hurt more."

"I love it when you get violent," he growls through a grin and pulls me in for a hard kiss.

But we have somewhere to be, so once I'm panting, he lets me go with a wicked grin. Soon, we're out on the highway, roaring down the deserted stretch between Grandma Minnie's cabin and the bar.

Not Grandma Minnie's anymore. Mine.

Ours.

Warner moved in with me after a month. He had been spending the night every night at my place anyway, and living over his mother's shop was depressing him.

I've met some stubborn people in my life, but Rebecca Jameson puts every one of them to shame. Six months with no word from her.

Well, no word to the pack. Or to her older two children. Tanya lets us know that she's alive and checking in.

Thoughts of Rebecca leave my insides feeling twisted and confused. Part of me is grateful to her for raising such a wonderful man. Part of me is pissed at her for hurting him now with her silence. Part of me feels sorry for her for losing her pack. Part of me feels guilty about being the catalyst for her lashing out.

Maybe I should be furious with her for the danger she put me in. But I think I understand her fear of me. I did almost leave Warner and for no other reason than I was confused over what I wanted in life.

But my mind is clear now.

And I'm still here.

The bar comes into view up ahead, and my pulse quickens in anticipation.

Tonight, I will finally, officially mate my werewolf.

Ninety-nine percent of me is choosing to take this step because I love Warner and want to spend forever with him.

But there's that teeny-tiny one percent that is hoping word somehow reaches Rebecca.

I wait until the motor cuts off and the kickstand is down before dismounting.

"Do you have everything?" Warner asks as I rummage in his saddlebags.

"I think so. Not like I'd know if I'm missing something."

Roderick decreed that the mating ceremony ritual needed to be kept under wraps because we decided to wait a bit before going through with it. So, I'm in the dark.

"Did you bring the food?" Warner asks.

My hands pause. "You mean the snacks?"

"Not exactly. I mean the ceremonial food."

"What?" I clutch at the ziplock bag I packed. "I thought you meant something to eat afterward. While we're *drinking*. I did not bring *ceremonial* food!"

Dating a werewolf, I've gotten in the habit of carrying snacks because Warner is always hungry, and he gets over-the-top happy when I give him food. Or gift it to him, as he says.

When he asked me to bring food, I thought he just meant more of my usual.

Warner smiles as he asks, "What did you bring?"

"Nothing. I brought absolutely nothing, and we have to go back to the cabin so I can make something special. Something ceremony-worthy." I'm already re-strapping the helmet on my head.

But Warner steps in close, grabbing my hands. There's a mischievous tilt to his too-tempting lips.

"Nope. Then, we'll be late. Besides, I want to know what snack you brought for us to share."

I glare up at him when, really, I want to scowl at myself.

How could I be so oblivious? This is a mating ceremony. Of course it requires special things, like delicious dishes. This isn't a night out with the Sip 'N' Stitch gang or playing pool with the pack.

This is a werewolf wedding, and I brought ...

"No. I refuse. Mating you deserves a five-tiered cake."

Warner leans in, rubbing his nose over mine. "Tell me."

"I can't. You're a soufflé. Or a caramel apple pie."

"Those do sound good, but I want to know what you brought."

Feeling like the guilty party on a witness stand, I do my best to mutter my answer so low that even his wolf ears can't pick up on the word.

"Hmm, nope. Didn't catch that." His arms twine around my waist, and he leans down to nip at my neck. "Tell me. Tell your mate what you brought."

I groan, my forehead dropping to his shoulder. "Goldfish crackers."

Warner's body goes rigid for a moment, and I'm sure I've found a way to offend the most unoffendable man on earth.

Then, all the tension spills out of him with roaring laughter. He tilts his head back, letting the joyous sound fill the night air, and I'm caught between a scowl and a smile. Next thing I know, I'm in his arms, lifted high, and whirled about.

"Goldfish crackers. You are the perfect woman, Zoey Gunner." Warner shouts this out, and I'm betting everyone in the bar can hear him.

"And you're too forgiving," I scold him. "Please let me go make you something better."

My desperate fingers tangle in his silky hair, but he just lets out a happy growl as I tug at the roots.

"No. Our ceremony will have Goldfish crackers. It's settled. Besides"—he gently sets me down on my feet—"I can't wait another minute to be officially mated to you. I'll eat dirt if it means I can finally call you mine."

"Goldfish aren't dirt," I mutter.

Warner grins before pressing a kiss to my forehead and pulling me toward The Rabbit Hole.

Unlike the first time I stepped through the entrance of the were-wolf bar, this night, lively voices fill every inch of the place.

"They're here!" Courtney pushes through the crowd, wearing a glittery yellow top that sparkles like gold in the dim lighting.

All heads turn our way, and celebratory greetings get shouted as Warner waves a hello.

"To the woods!" Courtney shouts, marching toward a back door.

Roderick meets our stares across the room, and I pick up a grimace on his face in response to my friend's high-handed ways.

But Warner and I grin at each other and follow after her, melting into the group of wolves exiting the bar.

Even though winter has loosened its grip, the nights still get cold. Warner loops his arm around my shoulders, pulling me close to his warm body.

Perfect.

Soon, we're in a small clearing, the space lit by an almost-full moon. Two nights from now, the pack will go on a long ride and then a long run. I always miss Warner when he's away. I wonder how it will feel once this bond is solidified between us.

Will I ache less? Or more?

Doesn't matter. I still want to claim every inch of him.

A crowd forms a circle around us. The whole pack has gathered. There has to be close to a hundred, and knowing that they're all here to watch this mysterious mating ceremony between Warner and me has me wanting to hide behind my wolf. But that's the problem with circles. There's no behind when you're in the middle.

"Zoey"—Warner's soothing tone brings my attention to him—"we don't have to do this tonight. Not if you aren't ready."

He's misinterpreted my nerves.

"I want this. I just didn't realize we'd be stared at," I murmur even though the other wolves can probably still hear me fine.

He grimaces. "Sorry, but that's the deal. You're joining the pack, so the pack wants to see you. Just remember"—his warm hands cup my face, tilting me up so I can only see him—"they're all happy for us. For this. A pack gaining a new member is always celebrated."

"But I'm a human."

"You're mine," he growls. "And soon, you'll be theirs too." He nods his head toward the gathered wolves. "All of them will respect you. Protect you. Some will probably love you. I can't blame them."

I thought moving to Pine Falls meant leaving a big family behind. Apparently, I'm being adopted.

And this time, when I trace my eyes over the crowd, I notice the smiles and the encouraging nods. I see laughing conversations between different members and realize that I'm the only tense one in this group. Everyone else is here for a celebration.

After a long exhale, I give Warner a confident smile.

"All right. Let's make this official."

Roderick wades through the trees and wolves, joining us in the clearing. He raises his hand, and the murmuring crowd falls silent.

"Our brother wolf has brought a woman to us and wishes to mate." Roderick's voice sounds especially deep, as if he's calling to something. He stalks around the circle, and with each step, an electric sensation builds in the air.

Is this magic?

He halts beside us. "What do you offer?"

Shit, was I supposed to bring an offering too? I'm going to kick Warner's ass when this is done for not giving me a better outline.

As if hearing my thoughts, my wolf grins down at me. "He means the food. Courtney, did you bring it?"

"Of course I did." The raven-haired woman steps forward, pulling her purse off her shoulder. Only when she unzips it do I realize it's not a purse at all, but a small, fashionable lunch box. "This is a good batch."

Warner reaches out to accept a paper-wrapped item. When he peels the layers back, I see a soft white substance.

"Is that ..."

Warner nods, wearing a self-satisfied smile. "Goat cheese."

"My preferred cheese! You figured it out."

He steals a quick kiss. "We've lived together for months. Give me some credit."

"You get all the credit."

Warner straightens and takes on a tone as deep as his brother's. "I will nourish my mate. As she takes from me, I give to her willingly." He holds out his fingers, offering the soft cheese and nodding in encouragement until I understand I'm meant to eat it from his hand.

The tartness is delicious, especially as I lick it off his thumb. Black seeps into Warner's eyes as they lock on my mouth.

"What do you offer?" Roderick's heavy gaze redirects toward me.

I follow Warner's lead.

"I will nourish my mate. As he takes from me, I give to him willingly." A ridiculously hot blush covers every inch of me when I pull a ziplock bag from my jacket pocket and offer Warner a Goldfish.

His grin is delighted as he leans forward to snap the cheesy cracker from my hand, munching away happily.

"How will you live?" Another question from Roderick, who has turned back to his brother.

I listen for the words I'll need to repeat back, but instead of responding right away, Warner hooks his thumbs in his shirt and pulls the thing off, leaving him bare-chested.

"We're getting naked?" I mutter, clutching at the edge of my denim coat, wavering between feeling affronted or following suit.

Warner's smile is apologetic. "Just a little. Like, we're-going-to-the-beach-but-are-still-keeping-our-pants-on naked."

"You're lucky I love you," I mutter, letting my jacket slide off my shoulders and tossing it to the side. "Shirt and bra?"

He steps close, hands on my waist and pressing a fortifying kiss to my forehead.

"You only need to unbutton until I can see your skin here." His knuckle brushes the spot just over my heart, causing me to shiver.

I follow his direction, undoing buttons halfway down my front until my soft flannel falls open.

"We will live as one. Connected always. Her life, my life. Her blood, my blood," Warner announces, and then he leans down, pausing to whisper against my ear. "A small cut. Is that okay?"

He meets my eyes, and I nod.

I'm down for all of this. If mating Warner means fucking him in front of all these people, I wouldn't be happy about it. But I'd do it.

A cut is nothing.

His lips brush my exposed skin, just where the curve of my breast begins. A gasp escapes at the sting.

He bit me. As Warner straightens, I notice a small red drop on the bottom of his lip.

"I have to bite you?" I ask in shock, realizing it's my turn.

"Or scratch me. Whatever way you think you can draw blood. But it needs to be by your hand. Your own will."

"No wonder you didn't give me a rundown beforehand," I grumble.

Warner smiles, but I spy a flicker of worry in his golden eyes. His fingers circle my wrist, tugging me close and lifting my hand until it lays flat on his bare chest. Right over his heart.

"Imagine my love for you exists here. Right underneath my skin. You just need to get to it, and then it's yours. Forever." Warner is using his tempting tone, as if he needs to convince me to do this.

Because he's not sure I will.

The doubt spurs me on. I'll show him. I'll do whatever I need to do to convince Warner I want him forever.

"Which is better?"

"Sorry?"

"Nails or teeth?" I stare into his eyes, determined, undaunted. "Which is better?"

His expression goes slack with vulnerability, and then a fiery need scorches through his suddenly black gaze. He leans down, lips against my ear, breath hot as he whispers to me, "I want your mouth. Use your teeth."

I nod, wrapping my arms around his waist, pulling us flush, and pressing my mouth to the taut skin over his heart, kissing him just as he kissed me.

Then, with my puny human teeth, I bite him. The second I feel the skin give, I release my violent hold and swipe my hand over my mouth.

"That's not sanitary," I announce, holding on to my prim tone as Warner beams down at me.

He has my teeth marks in his skin, and he's clearly overjoyed by the fact.

Warner's hands cup my cheeks, thumbs tracing over the curves of my face. "Will you say the words?"

"Oh yeah. Sorry." I clear my throat and recall the few short sentences. "We will live as one. Connected always. His life, my life. His blood, my blood."

"It is so." With Roderick's words, a crack splits the air, and I gasp at the sensation of a hook catching under my rib cage.

The crowd cheers, and I swear I can feel their individual jubilation inside me. As if I am connected to them all.

Warner gathers me in his arms, holding me close. "You are pack. You belong to us now."

Family. Can't seem to escape it.

Not that I want to.

"I guess you were wrong."

Warner pulls back enough to stare down at me with his amber eyes. "About what?"

My fingers snake into his hair, letting the curls wrap around my fingers. "You said you didn't think I'd be up for the initiation process."

For a second, he looks baffled, and then his expression transforms into delighted humor, as he's no doubt remembering the first words he ever spoke to me all those months ago.

"And what do you think? Is this club better than Sip 'N' Sew?"

"Sip 'N' Stitch," I correct automatically. "And it has its perks."

Warner grins as his one hand reaches down to cup my ass. "And those perks are?"

Forgetting about the celebrating pack with their eyes on us, I hitch my legs around Warner's waist and pull his mouth to mine. Just before our lips touch, I speak a single word, filling it with all the love in my little human heart.

"You."

The End

~

Thank you so much for reading CLAWS & CROCHET. I hope you enjoyed Zoey & Warner's love story! You will soon be able to return to Pine Falls for more werewolf romance, and in the meantime you can spend time in the mythic-filled small town of Folk Haven! Check out the following books for more magical, small town, sexy romances.

SEDUCED BY A SELKIE
(Folk Haven Book 1)
Delta Novac hates Folk Haven, and as soon as she's done cleaning out her father's mess of a house, she's giving the town her taillights. But after she dives into the lake to save a drowning man that's not actually in danger, she finds herself with a sweet and sexy selkie shadow ready to do anything to get her to stay.

SUCKER FOR A SIREN
(Folk Haven Book 2)
Seamus MacNamara refuses to believe in the selkie mating myth: that his one true partner will rescue him from great danger. So, when the adorably beautiful barista he has a secret crush on gives him the Heimlich, Seamus ends up insulting her instead offering heartfelt thanks. Now he just wants a chance to redeem himself...and he's willing to go down on his knees to earn her forgiveness.

SWEARING AT A SEA MONSTER
(Folk Haven Book 3)
Moira MacNamara takes shit from no one, and that includes Levi Abadi, the enticing, infuriating monster who thinks he can dictate what she does with her own property. She makes a deal with him, sealed in blood. But now she can't help noticing how her veins thrum with heat every time he comes near...

VISIT FOLK HAVEN

Want more magical stories? Take a trip to Folk Haven, the small town full of mythical creatures and fated mates! Keep reading for a sneak peek of *Seduced by a Selkie*, book one in the Folk Haven series...

SEDUCED BY A SELKIE

DELTA

When my father died, he left me a lake house, and I hate him for it. As if losing him suddenly wasn't bad enough, now, I'm back in this middle-of-nowhere town in northern Georgia, forced to set his estate to rights.

Estate. Ha. That word makes his house sound impressive. Maybe from the outside. But step in the door, and everything turns into a death trap.

When I got the call from Folk Haven's police chief about my father's passing a few months back, I half-expected the cause of death to be something more gruesome than a heart attack. Not that I wanted my father to suffer. They told me his death was quick, and even if someone had been nearby, there would have been an infinitesimal chance he could have survived.

With Dimitri Novac's hermit lifestyle, that chance had turned into zero.

Which leaves me here, sitting alone on the end of his dock in the early morning, listening to the hollow lap of the water against wood, contemplating Lake Galen and mortality.

Maybe my morbid thoughts manifest a response because,

suddenly, I'm sure I'm staring straight at a lifeless body floating face-down in the water.

"Oh hell," I mutter, scrambling to my feet, unsteady on the floating dock.

The higher vantage point shows me the same image. Just past the mouth of the inlet, maybe a hundred feet away, a person is rocking in the waves like the leavings of a shipwreck.

Adrenaline and panic make my decision for me. I rip off my long-sleeved shirt and unzip my jeans, pushing the denim off my legs without the hindrance of shoes because I walked down here, barefoot. Pulling on my muscle memory from a long-ago summer swim team, I dive into the water and plow toward the prone figure, using a strong freestyle. The distance first appeared closer than it is, and as I continue to pump my arms, I try to remember how long a human can go without oxygen and still survive.

Is it long enough for me to reach them, drag them to shore, and start performing CPR?

Doesn't matter. I have to try.

When I lift my head, shaking water from my eyes, I spot the life-less form only a few strokes away. With a powerful kick of my feet, I cross the final distance. Despite my hope, the logical part of my brain informs me I am about to grab hold of a dead body.

Which is why I scream when the head pops up at my touch.

The man—because I see now that it is a man—jerks back at my holler, raising his hands above the water, as if surrendering.

"It's okay. I won't hurt you," he assures me in a rumble of a voice.

"You're not dead!" I shout, as if him being alive were an inconvenience.

His eyebrows creep up. "Would you prefer I was?"

"No." I suck in a deep breath, winded from my sprinting swim. "I ..." Words slip away from me as I glance behind him. At this new angle in the water, I spy a pontoon boat floating outside the mouth of the inlet.

Unnecessary adrenaline keeps my heart pounding hard and makes it difficult to organize all this new information.

"Hey." The deep voice recaptures my attention, and I meet the set of soft brown eyes in an otherwise blockish white face. "Hi." He greets me again, his smile easing the harder angles of his jaw. "You were swimming up to a dead body?"

"I wasn't *sure* you were dead," I correct.

That only has him smiling wider. "You're here to save me?"

As understanding of the new situation dawns, I struggle to keep afloat—literally and figuratively. My body tries to remind me it's been a few years since I trod water for any length of time.

"Do you need saving?" My breathlessness comes from a combination of the swimming and his focused gaze.

At some point, we must have drifted closer, pushed around by the subtle lake waves.

The swimmer's hand rises from the water, catching a strand of my hair on the ascent. The black threads spill like ink about my pale shoulders, my skin turning a ghostly shade from the chill of the lake. He stares at where the lock wraps around his finger in a tentacle-like grasp.

"People rarely admit to needing help." His gaze laughs as his grin goes lopsided. "Please, continue saving me. Likely as not, I need it."

If I had time, I'd put in the needed mental energy to identify the subtext of his words. But a movement over his shoulder distracts me.

The good news: I don't need to come up with a response to his oddly philosophical statement.

The bad news: our conversation pauses because I'm transfixed by the sight of a head breaching the lake surface behind my not-dead acquaintance.

The appearance is only the beginning. One to my left. One on the right. All around me, more heads appear, all equipped with goggles and breathing pieces, identifying this crew as a gathering of scuba divers. Seems I've shown up in the middle of a scuba lesson. Soon, we're floating in a crowd of heads.

And every single one is facing me.

That's when I remember my outfit. Without my shirt and pants, I'm left with the most basic coverings. A matching bra and underwear set I got on sale at a department store. Both scraps of fabric are blue and covered in pictures of cartoon bananas.

No doubt, that's why they were on sale.

This group got an unobstructed view of my bargain boy shorts as they surfaced.

I hate this fucking lake.

I keep my curses to myself. "Well, looks like you've got this under control."

The man lets my hair return to the water as I paddle backward. Once I'm clear of the group, I turn on my stomach and swim back to my father's dock, possibly moving faster than when I thought someone's life was at risk.

Embarrassment is powerful fuel.

When I reach the dock, I grab the metal ladder and place my feet on the slick, algae-covered steps sinking below the surface.

"Please don't let them be watching me," I mutter as I pull myself out of the lake, soaked underwear clinging to my backside and rigid nipples. *Note to self: swimming in April is cold, even in Georgia.*

When I'm standing tall—because I refuse to cower and hunch over in my half-naked state—a quick glance behind me shows my audience is still watching the show.

"Fucking peachy," I mutter.

Thoroughly done with this miserable morning, I offer the lot of them a salute, gather up my armful of clothes, and march toward the shore, reminding myself with each step that I will probably never see any of those people again, especially when I leave Folk Haven and Lake Galen for good.

So, what does it matter if they all have a permanent memory of soggy bananas decorating my ass?

Keep reading Seduced by a Selkie!

NEWSLETTER SIGN UP

Get another Folk Haven romance for FREE! Sign up for my newsletter to receive *A Selkie's Secret,* a novella that tells the story of Isla, a selkie, and Finn, the human she refuses to fall in love with...

ALSO BY LAUREN CONNOLLY

Find a list of all of Lauren's books on her website:

https://www.laurenconnollyromance.com/book-list

ABOUT THE AUTHOR

Lauren Connolly is an award-wining author of contemporary and magical romance stories. She has lived among mountains, next to lakes, and in imaginary worlds. Lauren can never seem to stay in one place for too long, but trust that wherever she's residing there is a dog who thinks he's a troll, twin cats hiding in the couch, and book-shelves bursting with the stories written by the authors she loves.

www.ingramcontent.com/pod-product-compliance
Lightning Source LLC
Chambersburg PA
CBHW021238190726
48289CB00005B/1377